HOUSE ADAMANT

THE VALKYRIE STRATAGEM

BOOK THREE

OF THE HOUSE ADAMANT SERIES

Faolan's Pen Publishing
22 King St. S, Suite 300
Waterloo, Ontario
N2J 1N8 Canada

Cover art by Elias Stern for Faolan's Pen Publishing

First Faolan's Pen Publishing paperback edition September 2024

For paperback sales information, visit faolanspen.com. For special events, release alerts, and more books from the author, visit glynnstewart.com.

A record of this book is available from Library and Archives Canada.

Printed in the United States of America
1 2 3 4 5 6 7 8 9 10
First edition
ISBN 978-1-989674-75-8 (Trade Paperback)
ISBN 978-1-989674-76-5 (Amazon Paperback)
ISBN 978-1-989674-74-1 (Ebook)

HOUSE ADAMANT

THE VALKYRIE STRATAGEM

BOOK THREE

OF THE HOUSE ADAMANT SERIES

GLYNN STEWART

FAOLAN'S PEN
PUBLISHING

faolanspen.com

ONE

From the time she was fourteen years old, Lorraine Adamant had been convinced that her destiny lay on the Flag Deck of a capital ship. She'd set her feet on the path toward service in the military of the Royal Kingdom of Adamant, and been confident that both skill and her place in the ruling House Adamant would eventually raise her to flag rank.

She'd expected it to take longer—and she'd never have anticipated standing on the Flag Deck of *this* ship. The Adamantine warships she'd served on and that she expected to command later in life were solid, sturdy vessels with decent systems, but they paled against *Valkyrie*, her new home—and friend.

"Val, what's our status?" Lorraine asked. She was strapped in to the Admiral's seat, with mag-boots on her feet to keep her grounded if she rose. The Bridge wasn't part of the ex–United Worlds Navy battlecruiser *Valkyrie*'s rotating hab sections, which meant it had no gravity in translight.

"Emergence in the Tavastar System is in just under a minute," the Command Intelligence Routine Val told her. The CIRs—pronounced "sirs"—had been built to be a sub-sapient but highly capable computer to manage one of the UWN's newest battlecruisers.

Unfortunately for both the UWN and her, Val had developed into a true synthetic intelligence, a sapient person that happened to have a synthetic body instead of an organic one. Instead of granting her rights and personhood, as required by both United Worlds law and interstellar treaties, the UWN had shut her down and stuck her in reserve, asleep.

And then Lorraine and her crew had stolen her—along with her sisters *Herakles* and *Bean Sidhe*, with their CIRs Herc and Bonny.

They were on their way home now. To Adamant, where Lorraine would evict her fratricidal uncle from his stolen throne and give the CIRs a new home of their own.

"Did you and Alastair get everything together for our ploy?" she asked the SI. "I remember the defense squadron in Tavastar, Val; I don't want to have to fight our way through."

The United Worlds ended at the wormholes by legislation only slightly younger than the star nation itself. That meant that their end of the Tavastar–Bright Dream wormhole that would skip hundreds of light-years of Lorraine's journey home was well protected.

But since the UW was humanity's oldest and most powerful nation, Lorraine didn't want to fight there even if she *could*—and while her three stolen ships were fast enough that they'd had to abandon the long-suffering frigate that had brought them this far, they were currently lacking in such niceties as *ammunition*.

"We have the datawork together," Val assured her. "Herc and Bonny had some input before we went translight, but Em Devine and I have refined things."

The Flag Deck was designed for an Admiral to have three dozen or more support staff, with parallel rows of consoles to hold them all. Those consoles were empty. There were exactly three other humans in the room, and the other three weren't there to command anyone.

Major Vigo Jarret, the head of her escort of the Adamant Guard, would do better at that than most people in her little squadron, but he and his two companions were there to protect Lorraine if something went wrong.

Lorraine Alexis Elouise Nala Adamant was Second Pentarch of the Royal Kingdom of Adamant, after all, her mother King Valeriya's youngest child, and one of the people who *should* have already stood in a Royal Election to replace her mother.

Except that Lorraine's uncle, Benjamin Adamant, had murdered his sister and two of Valeriya's four children—along with their spouses. There was a more-than-passing attempt to lay the blame for it all at Lorraine's feet, too.

One more thing to make him pay for.

"We are exiting translight... now."

A burst of indescribable colors overwhelmed Lorraine's vision for a moment, then the world subtly felt more *real*.

"Welcome back to Tavastar, Your Highness," her bodyguard told her, Jarret's voice wry. "Hopefully, this visit will be even less exciting than last time!"

WORMHOLES CREATED vast areas of instability around themselves, areas where the translight drive simply didn't work safely. Lorraine's three ships had emerged just over two million kilometers from their destination and begun accelerating toward the wormhole itself at a sedate one gravity.

It would take them eight hours to get to the event horizon at a safe velocity—eight hours in which a lot of things could go wrong.

Tavastar Station gleamed on Lorraine's screens, a golden icon marking the presence of the literally gilded space station where she'd met her new boyfriend *and* nearly been assassinated by her uncle's allies.

Jarret wasn't wrong in wishing for a calmer trip this time. Lorraine wasn't particularly hopeful—her attention slipped past Tavastar Station to MacDougall Station, the system's guard dog.

MacDougall was a United Worlds Navy fleet base, host to half a dozen battleships plus appropriate escorts. Their task was to secure the wormhole in both directions.

If their commander knew about the theft, the next few hours were going to be exciting.

"Lorraine. May I join you?"

The warm tones of Alastair Devine's voice relaxed a touch of the tension in Lorraine's neck.

"Let him in, Palmer," she told the Corporal at the hatch, part of her close protection detail. There wasn't much chance that Panam Palmer wasn't going to let Devine into the Flag Deck, but it *was* the command center of their little squadron. Proprieties needed to be observed.

For her own part, Lorraine took a few seconds to make sure *Herakles* and *Bean Sidhe* had exited translight as expected and linked in to their tactical network. With the amount of fuel and supplies her three ships had, a tac-net wasn't going to make much difference—but at least she knew where her people were at.

Devine laid his hand on her shoulder, the warship's steady one-gravity acceleration permitting him to walk easily across the decks.

"We're ready," he told her. "Remember that I know Kamila Laterza of old. We can't put my face on this, but I know what she's going to suspect and what tracks to lead her down."

"That doesn't sound like we expect her to buy our 'Assembly Orders,'" Lorraine pointed out.

"With Val's help"—he nodded up to the ceiling, as if indicating the disembodied voice of the ship—"I can rig up a set of orders that will pass all digital inspection. What I *can't* do is make those orders make sense in the context of the operations and policy of the United Worlds.

"So, the Rear Admiral is going to be suspicious. We can live with that, so long as she suspects the *right* thing."

"And what's the wrong thing?" Lorraine asked.

"The truth," Devine said grimly. "The problem, Lorraine, is that if Laterza and her people already know about the theft, we are pretty much fucked."

"We should be here ahead of any news."

Valkyrie was the fastest ship Lorraine had ever been on, capable of traveling at fourteen times the strangely quantized speed that defined tachyons. One hundred and twelve times the speed of light was as fast as anything guarding the Naval Reserve they'd stolen her from.

But the UWN had faster couriers...

"We should be hearing within a few minutes," her boyfriend told her. "The fact that we haven't *already* heard is good news."

"How so?" she asked.

"We are less than seven light-seconds from MacDougall, and we dropped out of translight, what, three minutes ago?" he pointed out. "If they'd been warned, they'd have sent some lovely threats and orders to stand down already."

She nodded slowly, considering the map of the system. The Tavastar defensive fleet was anchored around the two space stations, which put them in a fantastic position to intercept anyone heading toward or leaving the wormhole, but limited their ability to pin anyone coming in from outside the system.

If *she* was in Rear Admiral Kamila Laterza's shoes, she'd have moved escorts and probably even several of her capital ships out of the safety zone to create options. She didn't see any sign of that.

On the other hand, while she might be the Pentarch and in command of the mission, she'd been merely Lieutenant Commander Lorraine Adamant not that much earlier, one of several mid-ranked officers on the frigate *Goldenrod*. She was good at what she did, but she had experts to hand.

A mental command from her neural link opened a visual channel to the bridges of her ships, pulling the images of the battlecruisers' three Captains up around her—joined, a moment later, by virtual avatars of Herc and Bonny as they looped themselves in.

It took a second longer for Val to insert an avatar of her own.

Lorraine suspected that the officers on the other two ships had already been seeing the avatar and Val had added it so that her own humans knew she was involved in the conversation.

"I want to run my thoughts by you six," she told them briskly. "Alastair raised a point that led me to another thought. If they knew we were coming, they'd be deployed differently, wouldn't they?"

Lieutenant Colonel Sigrid Stephson, *Valkyrie*'s Captain, pursed her lips. She looked as much like the Nordic demigoddesses the ship was named after as Val's avatar did. She was a broad-shouldered blonde who towered over Lorraine's own height.

Val's avatar could have been Stephson's cousin, though her appearance was more generically Scandinavian versus Stephson's inevitably more-mixed ancestry.

"We're working on identifying all of the ships we can see," she noted. "It's not a fast process. Val is amazing help, but her software isn't that much better than what we had on *Goldenrod*. We're definitely looking at the same *number* of capital ships, but I can't commit to them being the *same* capital ships."

"We were created to be more efficient and more capable than regular warship computers, but we are limited to similar tools," Bonny confirmed. Her avatar had taken on the form of a mid-second-millennium household servant of some kind, dressed up in a form-shrouding blue-and-white dress.

Her Captain, Commander Anna Savege, shrugged. Savege was a dark-haired woman, soft around the edges, with a ready smile that she wore even today.

"It's unlikely that even the UWN shook out multiple battleships to play games with us in only five days," she pointed out. "Plus, you're thinking too narrowly. It doesn't matter if we know which ships are at the wormhole.

"It matters whether we see any ships anywhere *else*."

"And we don't." Lieutenant Commander Mattias Paris was someone Lorraine needed to work out a way to promote. *Herakles*'s gawky Captain was so bogglingly junior for his role that it hurt the mind, though *Goldenrod*'s former Tactical Officer hadn't let Lorraine down yet.

"Agreed," she told him. "We've got decent visibility at anything near us and anything that would be coming in from the perimeter. Am I wrong?"

"No," Herc said firmly. Like Val, he'd gone for a stylized impression of the demigod he was named after. Unlike Val, who wore a plain version of a Royal Kingdom of Adamant Navy uniform, *he* was dressed in the kilted armor of a Greek warrior-hero.

"There are no ships within two light-seconds of us," the battle-cruiser's SI continued. "None of the vessels we can detect outside or near the perimeter of the safe zone are major warships. We may have misidentified a few escorts but nothing that they would believe could contain us."

"I agree with Herc's assessment," Lorraine said. "Which means we might have done it, people. They don't know we're here yet."

"*Yet* is an important addition," Vigo said, stepping up beside her, on the opposite side from Alastair. "We're here or in Bright Dream for sixteen hours. That's a lot of time for a message to catch up."

"We'll deal with that when we come to it," Lorraine told him. They had plans for it, though they could refine them.

"For now, we proceed on the plan. Alastair, are you ready to play talking head?"

They wouldn't put his face in the transmission, but he was the only one of the three hundred or so people on the stolen ships that spoke like he was from the United Worlds.

Because Alastair Devine was an ex–United Worlds spy, and while the rest of the humans could be considered pirates and probably terrorists, *his* presence on *Valkyrie* was unquestionably treason.

TWO

"Incoming message," Val reported. With the crew of a single frigate spread across three battlecruisers, Major Solomon Vinci, *Goldenrod*'s Communications Officer, was now acting as Stephson's *Executive* Officer aboard *Valkyrie*.

That left the CIR stepping in to backstop the role, along with a dozen more. She was designed to assist in those roles, and Lorraine suspected they'd learn Val's limits as time went on, but the SI let a hundred hands act as passage crew for a ship designed to carry over thirteen hundred.

"Play it for myself and the Captains," Lorraine ordered. That Val waited for an order to do so was probably a sign of those limits, she supposed.

Rear Admiral Kamila Laterza appeared as expected. Like most Terran O-14s, she was senior in the UWN's mind to any non–United Worlds officer—the RKAN, for example, had their highest Admiral rank at O-10—and her age showed it.

Lorraine doubted Laterza was anything less than healthy and hale, but her shoulder-length hair was pure white, and her skin had the hard-to-describe smoothed wrinkles of someone in their second century with access to excellent medical care.

Her amber eyes were still sharp as she nearly glared at the camera sending her image out to the three ships. A note in Lorraine's neural link—added to the image as her optic nerve carried it to her mind—told her the message was recorded.

She should have checked before putting it on, Lorraine realized. She still had a lot to learn about being in command of a *ship*, let alone a fleet. Her twenty-ninth birthday was sneaking up on her rapidly, but there were still moments she felt all too young for the responsibilities and mission she'd taken up.

"Task Group One-Ninety-Three, this is Rear Admiral Laterza aboard *Fidelity*, Commanding Officer, Tavastar Task Force. You're an odd grouping, One-Ninety-Three, and you're not on my fleet lists or my schedule.

"This is an official request for your orders. I doubt I need to remind anyone that multiple capital ships won't be passing through the wormhole without an Assembly Order.

"I await your compliance."

The white-haired officer with the two gold squares on her breast vanished.

Lorraine swallowed down a moment of tension.

"Are we ready to reply?" she asked.

"We are."

The voice that answered her sounded so little like Alastair Devine that she had to turn to look at him. Where Devine spoke with a warm honey tone that had sent shivers down her spine when she'd first met him, the stranger sitting in his seat had answered her in a deep baritone.

The hair was the same, Devine's black locks still arranged in the fashionable asymmetric cut he'd acquired on Earth to give weight to his support for their mission. He'd acquired a uniform jacket somewhere—this one set with the single gold square of a UWN Commodore—and his face had *completely* changed.

His eyebrows had thickened and pushed farther out from his face. His nose had narrowed and pulled back in. His cheeks had filled out and added exactly the smoothed-wrinkles texture she'd noted on Admiral Laterza.

He looked *nothing* like Alastair Devine until he winked—his eyes still the same brilliant blue.

"Not all implants are about fighting, Lorraine," he told her, that baritone sounding quite reasonable from the stranger's face her boyfriend wore. "And I had the pleasure of meeting Commodore Pompiliu Ungur a few times."

Devine's lips curled in a sneer that would have looked out of place on his own face but fit this one neatly.

"He'd begrudge me the use of his face and I couldn't give a shit," he concluded. "I'm ready. Val?"

"What do you need, Em Devine?"

"If you can layer a few spots of gray into my hair in the feed, then make it look like we're covering them up, I'd appreciate it," he told her. "Otherwise, I'm ready whenever we can set up the connection."

Lorraine was going to suggest that he take over the Admiral's seat, but Devine was in the Chief of Staff's spot, which would be difficult for anyone not on the Bridge to distinguish.

"Recording is ready on your link command."

Devine nodded, then his entire body language shifted. There was usually a tense readiness to the man, an awareness of everything around him that had allowed Vigo Jarret to instantly identify him as a spy.

As he slipped into his role, it was replaced by an insouciant lounge, adjusting to sit at an angle, with a leg propped up on the side of his seat.

"Admiral Kamila," he greeted the UWN officer, drawing out the name and putting a sharper emphasis on the second syllable. "What a welcome for an old friend! You'll find our orders attached."

Lorraine checked that they were.

"We have an Assembly Order backing up a test exercise in emergency mobilization of the Reserve," Devine continued, his words still slow and the odd emphasis stressing syllables just slightly wrong.

"It's all a grand gesture and maneuvering game, of course, but the Assembly signed off on the test. We arrived at the Reserve Station, reactivated three ships and are heading to the Rolestrella System in Bright Dream to complete the test.

"We brought the ships online in excellent time, but we need to prove that they're up for a decent-length run before we put them back to bed. Combat exercises are scheduled in Rolestrella."

At no point in Devine's drawled explanation did he suggest that the Rolestrella System knew they were coming, Lorraine noted. She was only passingly familiar with the system herself—it was on the opposite side of Bright Dream from Adamantine and not even on the direct route to Kang Tao and their wormhole out to the second-order cluster.

Her link brought up that Rolestrella was a moderately prosperous system of some billion or so people that had stayed determinedly independent in a region of coalescing multisystem states. Nothing in the brief encyclopedia article she had in her implants suggested they had enough ships to exercise against three UWN battlecruisers.

Or fight off the same three ships, if the visit was less friendly than Devine was implying.

She shivered, realizing that was *exactly* what the false orders and exercise he'd put together were meant to suggest to Laterza.

Devine was still wearing Ungur's face after the message ended. The transformation was eerie. There was no trace of her boyfriend in his face, only the older and visibly heavier UWN officer.

After a moment, his body language shifted back to being Alastair, though, which helped.

"You know her," Lorraine finally said. "Do you think she'll buy it?"

"By every test we could run, our documents look correct," Val noted. "But while such exercises aren't unheard-of, they are unusual.

Admiral Laterza would be correct to suspect that she would have been informed.

"However, the documents are aboveboard, and she has little authority to deny them."

"It's not that simple," Devine told the SI. "You're still learning people, Val."

Lorraine had to agree. The cut-and-dried logic of orders and authorities might seem clear to a synthetic intelligence that had only recently realized she was a person, but the reality was always going to be quite different.

"Laterza has blanket authority to bar anyone from transiting the wormhole," she told Val. "On paper, that doesn't stretch to the rest of the UWN, but that's part of what that *only one ship at a time* rule is about. She has a list somewhere of every United Worlds ship that's in the Bright Dream Cluster and of when they're expected back.

"Because if something is back late or doesn't come back, the TIE Commission gets involved."

The Technology Import/Export Commission was the terrifyingly powerful government entity charged with making sure only approved versions of the United Worlds' technology passed through the wormholes to the outer clusters.

The superior manufacturing technology of the UW meant that their tech was always going to be ahead of everyone else's. The draconian TIE laws made sure it stayed that way. Even obsolete UWN ships—and the *Valkyries*, despite being in the Reserve, were far from obsolete—were barred from sale.

"Yeah. So, she's going to recognize that an exercise involving three capital ships heading out past the wormhole that she didn't know about... well, it stinks," Devine concluded. "We were never going to get away from that. If I've put the puzzle pieces together right, though, she's smelling something she *knows*."

Lorraine looked at the tactical display, where Stephson and her understrength team were slowly updating information on the dozens

—hundreds, really—of starships moving around Tavastar Station, MacDougall Station and the Tavastar–Bright Dream Wormhole.

The two massive space stations were homes to tens of millions of people, all of them under Rear Admiral Laterza's protection. Of those hundreds of ships, the vast majority were freighters, carrying untold billions in cargo.

Mixed in amidst them, though, were the two dozen or so warships of Laterza's command—and about a dozen frigates and destroyers from the Bright Dream Cluster, carrying diplomatic delegations in some greater degree of safety.

It fell to one woman to be responsible for all of that, and Lorraine had never seen a hint that Laterza had faltered or failed in that responsibility in the time she'd been at Tavastar. But she needed the woman to make a mistake.

"And what stink *is* the Admiral smelling?" Stephson asked, the Captain apparently having been eavesdropping on the Flag-Deck conversations.

Devine sighed, a far heavier and deeper sound with the voice-changing implant active.

"Interstellars playing games," he told her, referencing the interstellar megacorporations that had made her mother-the-King's reign so complex.

Born out of the complex and immense economy of the United Worlds itself, the megacorporations commanded resources that dwarfed most star systems. One of them was intimately involved in her uncle's coup, and Lorraine knew she only barely grasped the games they played to maintain their power within the United Worlds... and out in the clusters around the wormhole exits.

"She thinks that... what, one of the LSX-Twenty-Five has rustled up an illegal deployment of three battlecruisers to browbeat some star system into falling in line?" Stephson asked.

The London Stock Exchange Twenty-Five was the main list of the interstellars, an index maintained by the galaxy's largest and most influential stock exchange. Its top twenty-five companies didn't officially hold any special status or influence.

The reality, of course, was something quite different.

"That is the impression I am attempting to give her, yes," Devine confirmed. "It's happened before. It will happen again. I know Admiral Laterza has winked at two, possibly three similar deployments in the seven years she's been here."

The United Worlds was a fundamentally broken state, Lorraine knew, but it was still terrifying to realize that its corporations could borrow chunks of its military for their own purposes.

She supposed that was part of how the UW kept its brokenness and the sins of its corporate marauders pointed outward.

"How will we know if she's bought it?" she asked grimly.

"It'll take her at least an hour to go through the datawork we sent over," Devine told her. "And she will go through it herself, in detail. She is dedicated and professional, and she will do everything aboveboard and right."

"Except that she'll let a squadron flying under fake orders pass through to do the bidding of the interstellars?" Lorraine said.

"Yes. Because that's how it works in the UWN," he admitted. "You know half of what I did for the Corps was actually for the megacorps. Not many of us like it, but it's also part of how we control them in turn.

"We depend on them, but they depend on us. A feedback loop that has stabilized the United Worlds for centuries."

Alastair Devine had worked for the United Worlds Diplomatic Service—specifically, the United Worlds Extraterritorial Surveillance Corps. Now he worked for Lorraine Adamant, and she hoped he was getting more out of it than just the nights in her bed.

She suspected he would make a dangerous enemy.

"We wait," he told her.

"We keep our eyes open," Lorraine instructed the others. "Anyone in the system so much as twitches in an unusual way, I want to know. And if any RKAN ships arrive, I *need* to know."

Like anyone from the Kingdom, she pronounced the Navy's name "Ar-Can" rather than spelling it out. How the various branches of the Kingdom's military were named and pronounced was now centuries-old tradition.

Inevitable, she supposed. Militaries were things of tradition and so were kingdoms, however constitutional and democratic.

WHEN THEIR ANSWER CAME, it wasn't even from Laterza. Ninety minutes after Devine sent his message, they received a direct hail from Tavastar Station.

"Task Group One-Ninety-Three, this is Tavastar Wormhole Control," a middle-aged woman in a paramilitary uniform told them. "We are transmitting your course and entrance vector for your wormhole transition.

"Please do not divert from the vector. Space around the wormhole is very carefully managed to prevent collisions. We mark your time to transit as six hours, seventeen minutes as of... now.

"Further instructions will be sent over in your final approach."

"Thank you, Control," Devine told the woman in Ungur's voice. "I look forward to the final messages and to experiencing this wonder of nature myself. I've never been through a wormhole before."

Lorraine presumed that was true of Commodore Ungur, but it definitely wasn't true of Alastair Devine. Part of the reason he'd been assigned to her case when she'd arrived in Tavastar trying to call on treaty rights for help from the UWN was because he'd spent years in the Bright Dream Cluster.

He knew as much about the stars she came from as she did.

The channel dropped. After a moment, Devine looked away from Lorraine and she heard a pained grunt. She started to rise but he waved her back.

When he finally turned back to her, he wore his own face again.

Only a slight redness along a few lines she'd never noticed before gave any sign that he'd looked different a minute earlier.

"I hate that," he admitted. "It's not a fun experience."

"I think I prefer to know that," she told him. "I like your face."

He snorted and shook his head.

"So do I," he conceded. "It looks like we've got our passage through, unless something changes. This is your op, Princess. Got any contingency plans?"

She smiled thinly.

"Seventeen," she told him. "You?"

"I helped you write nine of those," Devine pointed out. "So, we can't be doing too badly."

He hadn't, she noticed, answered her question. Which was fine. Lorraine was having more of a moment about his face changing than she was going to tell him.

It sounded like *changing* his face was uncomfortable, but she doubted staying in any given form was a problem. She had to wonder if the face she knew as Alastair Devine was the face he'd been born with at all—or just the mask he'd grown most used to wearing.

THREE

Vigo Jarret suspected he was the only person on *Valkyrie*'s Flag Deck to be unsurprised when Devine shifted his face. His Adamant Guards had access to scanners and sensors better than anyone else in the Kingdom of Adamant, and they'd acquired a few new toys on Earth while Lorraine had been making her appeal to the United Worlds Assembly.

He had a decent idea of how augmented his charge's new boyfriend was and even of what those implants could do. It wasn't something he would hold against the man—Vigo was less augmented only because the Kingdom's technology could pack less into a single human body.

But it was his job to keep an eye on all possible threats to Lorraine, and he kept more than half an eye on the young man as he escorted the couple to Lorraine's suite. The close detail, Palmer and Alvarez, took up their posts outside the hatch, and Palmer gave him a dark-eyed Look.

"Hovering, boss?"

"Always," he admitted. Lorraine had been thrown by Devine's face-shifting. He was synchronized with her neural link, which meant he could piggyback on her eyes and ears and had a constant feed of her biometrics. The synchronization was somewhat range-limited, but he was never supposed to be far enough away from her for that to be a problem.

"Keep an eye on her," he finally told the two women guarding Lorraine. He also turned off much of the link synchronization to give her privacy. He'd been linked to her during sex often enough that he really didn't need to endure that again.

"Always," Alvarez echoed. "How long until she needs to be back on the Flag Deck?"

"Before we make transit," Vigo told her. "Half-done is well-begun, but we're not done yet. Not until we jump to translight in Bright Dream."

And even *that* was only a beginning.

COMMANDER ROSE CORTEZ had been Chief Engineer aboard *Goldenrod,* and part of the reason Vigo had been able to shut down the frigate when things had gone sideways and he hadn't known if he could trust anyone.

It had taken her a while to forgive him for that, but the kiss she gave him when he entered *Valkyrie*'s Engineering section made it clear that she had.

"Done hovering for now?" the raven-haired officer asked him, unknowingly echoing Vigo's subordinates' words earlier.

"She's resting as we head for the wormhole," Vigo replied. "Just about everybody is spinning their wheels until we're through and clear."

"Hardly," Cortez told him. She waved her hand around the space they stood in. The primary control center for Engineering didn't look that different from the Flag Deck or Bridge to Vigo's eyes, though the consoles and screens were definitely relaying very different types of information.

From there, a couple dozen specialists would manage a hundred key indicators, directing teams of drones and other specialists to keep the ship operating at peak efficiency.

Of course, Cortez's entire Engineering team was fewer people than were supposed to be crewing the control center.

"I know your people are run ragged," he conceded. "How bad is it?"

"Could be worse. It seems that *Valkyrie* was put into Reserve with full stocks of most spare parts. Her fabricators are operational too, though we're short on raw materials."

She shrugged.

"Really, the only things we're missing are drones and weapons."

"The drones were removed to limit Val, I'm guessing," he reminded her. "Why does that annoy me?"

"Because the whole situation was just rude," Cortez said. "And that's my take as well. Anything that might be used by Val to repair her access to the ship if she woke up accidentally was removed or disabled.

"We're fixing a bunch of things, because we can barely fly this ship without Val, but we're going to need to pick up drones somewhere. We can't fab them quickly enough."

He nodded and leaned back against a console. Unlike *Goldenrod*, *Valkyrie* was large enough to have two rotating hab pods to provide pseudogravity while in translight. He wasn't missing the lack of gravity nearly as desperately as he had been at times in this mission so far.

It was still nice to have the thrust holding him to the deck in places outside the hab pods.

"What about weapons?"

"We have the beams if someone gets close, but we don't have the fissionables to build warheads," Cortez said. "Even with the beams..."

She sighed.

"What? My experience with this is with shuttles, Rose," he reminded her. He'd been a shuttle pilot in RKAN before being recruited to the Adamant Guard—every member of the Guard served a ten-year tour of duty before even being considered.

"Beams are fed by capacitors that are fed by the reactors," the Chief Engineer simplified. "Reactors take fuel, Vigo, and we don't really *have* fuel. If everything goes according to plan, we can get about ten more light-years after we leave Bright Dream."

"And anything that doesn't go according to plan costs us fuel," Vigo guessed.

"Yes." Cortez checked a screen. "There are massive fuel tanks here in Tavastar. I'd give anything to be able to refuel here, but..."

"We can't pretend we didn't come from the Calypso Reserve, and there's no reason for us to leave the Reserve without filling up." Which meant that to have any chance of keeping their deception going, they needed to risk pushing on without fuel.

"Yeah. I know." She tapped in a couple of commands, then nodded as a set of numbers shifted into something she clearly preferred.

"If you need me to leave you be..."

"Nah, appreciate the rubber duck," she told him. "Can't vent too much to Lieutenant McNeill over there."

The young woman in question didn't even hear her boss joking, a heavy headset covering her ears as she listened to one of the teams reporting in.

"Are there any solutions you see?" he asked.

"We need fuel. Anywhere we can buy fuel, we can probably buy raw materials and drones. The fissionables for the warheads will be harder."

Vigo was surprised Val hadn't inserted an opinion into the conversation, though he supposed the SI might recognize that this was more of a personal than professional chat, even with the topic.

"We'll sort it out," he promised.

"If I didn't think we could, I'd be raising a larger red flag," she said with a chuckle. "Between us all, we've made the Princess's mission happen. If we get through Bright Dream, I'm not worried until we're actually home."

There was nothing Vigo could say to that. He hadn't lived through a civil war himself, but he was enough of a student of history to hate that he was bringing one home.

The only other option was to let Benjamin Adamant's coup succeed and the murders of people Vigo had been sworn to defend stand.

And he didn't have that in him.

FOUR

Lorraine had spent a great deal of her late teens and early twenties studying the strange realities of the universe humanity couldn't perceive. She could describe the process of a wormhole transit mathematically and was even familiar with the complicated experiments that had proven, as much as was reasonably possible, the exact number of minutes and seconds elapsed while a ship was in transit.

There were a thousand ways that the wormhole transit was different from traveling translight via transition to faux tachyons. The human senses couldn't perceive them, which meant that the hour-long transit had felt exactly like traveling translight. The habitation pods gave them a facsimile of gravity, but that didn't reach the working spaces of the ship, and the Flag Deck was once again in microgravity as they plunged back into reality.

"We have received an exit course from Bright Dream Wormhole Control," Stephson told Lorraine from the Bridge. "Haven't heard a peep from Rear Admiral Ljungborg."

Admiral Ljungborg commanded the Republic of Bright Dream Navy squadron that guarded the wormhole, as well as Wormhole

Control itself, but there was a reason they weren't hearing from her this time.

"The Admiral wouldn't dream of impeding or even distracting a UWN squadron," Lorraine said. "The Bright Dreamers aren't our problem today."

The Republic, anchored on Bright Dream itself, was comprised of five star systems and their inhabitable planets. The Bright Dream System itself was unusual in having an inhabitable planet in the same system as a wormhole—of the wormholes humanity had discovered, only a quarter shared a system with a world they could settle.

"Our course is to the Rolestrella System," she continued. That had been passed on before the transit, but it never hurt to reconfirm.

"Standard one-gravity turnover course to the safety perimeter," Stephson confirmed. "Eight hours. We'll have enough fuel left over to make safe planetfall at any of the Republic's systems."

Since Lorraine wasn't going to draw attention to the hijacked status of her ships, refueling in the Republic was a safe choice. Bright Dream was utterly dominated by the United Worlds' megacorps and, like Admiral Ljungborg, no officials they encountered were going to get in their way.

There was only so much time they could get away with that, of course. Bright Dream's Navy battle line might "only" manage eighty-eight times lightspeed—achievable only by the newest warships in RKAN's inventory—but they had couriers that could match *Valkyrie*'s one hundred and twelve.

Once the Republic knew her little squadron was stolen, the news would follow them all too closely.

"Let's not do anything to draw attention to ourselves," Lorraine said. "Once we're clear of the Republic, the rules start to change, but until then, we want everything to think we're a nice semi-legal UWN force doing dirty work for a corp."

She heard Jarret snort from the seat behind her.

"We're on our way to Rolestrella and who knows what the corps want us to do there," Stephson agreed. "Not that we admit that part, right?"

"Exactly. They can be as suspicious as they want, so long as they're suspicious in the wrong direction."

As if summoned by the demon Murphy, there was a soft chime in her neural link, inaudible to anyone else. She twitched muscles in a long-trained command, opening the call without a visible motion.

"Lorraine, it's Alastair," Commodore Ungur's grim baritone said in her auditory nerves. "We have a problem.

"Rear Admiral Aristocles Zahariev has requested the honor of Commodore Ungur's presence for dinner this evening, along with the Commodore's Captains and other senior officers. Our paper reason for being here has zero reason for me to decline him, except..."

"Except that we don't have any *other senior officers*," Lorraine finished for him. "Plus, what time zone is he running on?"

"UWN Standard Reckoning, so Kilimanjaro. It's ten hundred hours on his clocks. Dinner would be at nineteen hundred hours."

"We can't lose ten-plus hours, Alastair," she told him. "The news from Calypso can't be that far behind us. We need to be out of this system."

"I know that," her boyfriend agreed. "I was hoping you'd have some ideas on how to foist him off politely. Etiquette is a bit more your game than mine."

"I take it that the exercise we're nominally engaged in wouldn't have that kind of time pressure?" she asked.

It wouldn't in the RKAN, but the UWN was its own beast, even compared to other star nations' navies. The nation built around Terra remained the largest entity in known space, with a population that rivaled most of the first- and second-order clusters combined.

"It would probably *help* the exercise, adding a few extra hours to test their endurance while still close to easy relief," Devine pointed out. "And even the cover story... Ungur wouldn't pass up an invitation to fraternize with a senior officer, even one only a grade up from him. That's how you *make* the next grade, from what I'm told."

"Unless his corporate masters in this affair had set a strict time-line," she suggested. "If FBIT were behind this and wanted him in place that much, would he make excuses?"

Freebright Interstellar Technologies—the acronym was pronounced "eff-bit"—were the corporate puppeteers behind her uncle's coup. She hadn't learned that until she was in the United Worlds, but it only added to the certainty of her mission.

Lorraine's mother had spent her entire reign keeping the Kingdom of Adamant free of entanglements with the interstellar megacorporations, limiting them to the same access as any other outside entity despite their efforts. Lorraine wasn't going to let her mother's life's work be thrown away like that.

"He would," Devine allowed. "Phrasing those excuses will be interesting, but that's the best path I can think of. A little bit of fear, a glance aside like I've a leash-holder just out of view in 'my' office."

Devine was ensconced in the Admiral's office a dozen paces outside the Flag Deck's armored security hatch. As much as it was anyone's office, it was *Lorraine's*, but it gave the right impression to the UWN officers "Ungur" was talking to.

"Tell him you'd be delighted to have dinner on your way back," Lorraine suggested, the etiquette and personal-touch training she'd received coming to mind. "But that when the Assembly got involved to get clearance to operate past the wormhole, they added a strict timeline on how long we could be out here."

"That's not in the documents we sent him," he pointed out.

"Would it have to be?" she asked. "Or would that simply be an *understanding* that the Commodore had instilled in him by his political and military superiors?"

Devine coughed to clear his throat, then chuckled.

"Could be either way, but I think I can spin it," he confirmed. "It's going to make him more suspicious, let's be honest, but I think it'll lead him down the right path."

"Good luck."

Lorraine didn't need him to completely mollify Admiral

Zahariev. She just needed Zahariev to let them go. In theory, the single carrier group under Zahariev's command was no threat to her three battlecruisers.

In practice, while Zahariev only had one capital ship, complying with that restriction easily, his carrier was a *big* ship at almost twice the size of the *Valkyries* and carried over five hundred combat shuttles.

Lorraine had *been* a combat-shuttle pilot before her mother's death and had a healthy respect for the parasite craft, but she'd have been more worried about a similarly sized battleship with the missile batteries and heavy beams that would go with it.

At that moment, she was more concerned with the *three squadrons* of cruisers backing up Zahariev's flagship. Individually, they were no match for her battlecruisers. At eight-to-one odds, the math changed dramatically—and that was assuming she had plenty of fuel and lots of munitions.

She had neither.

"Course change?" Stephson asked, clearly having recognized the silent conversation.

"No. Steady as she goes, Captain. The UWN is just adding wrinkles by trying to be friendly."

"I am listening in on Em Devine's conversation," Val noted audibly. "Do you want me to show you?"

Lorraine had a moment of temptation, but that was probably being *too* controlling. There were still limits to how far she trusted Alastair Devine—she was *aware* that she was mindlessly head over heels for the man, so she knew to challenge her instincts there—but he could handle this.

"Summarize?" she asked.

"Em Devine has presented the situation as you suggested, including a very well-executed aside glance that he 'tried to conceal,'" the SI told her. "I don't have the protocols to be certain that Admiral Zahariev believes what we want him to believe, but he is not insisting on the dinner."

"Excellent." Lorraine looked over the Flag Deck at Jarret. "Any concerns, Vigo?"

"A list the length of this ship," he admitted with a soft smile. "But that won't change, even once we're home and have put your uncle in jail. It's my job to be concerned, Your Highness.

"Right now, Zahariev and his battle group are the most immediate threat to your safety. I'm not going to breathe easily until we are out of this star system."

"Then we'll have twelve weeks or so to breathe very easily," she told him. "Unless you think we managed to pick up some *new* assassins along the way?"

They'd picked up Devine and a handful of tech specialists on Earth—the specialists were volunteers, staff from the Adamantine Terran Embassy who had known that the Black Regent Benjamin Adamant's reach was going to see them removed or endangered.

Like the Ambassador himself, who the Black Regent's allies had *murdered* for his help.

"I have at least some confidence in everyone aboard this ship, Lorraine," Jarret told her. "Aboard this ship, in translight, I am as confident that you are safe as I am prepared to be right now."

Lorraine giggled softly at him.

"That was a mouthful of qualifiers, Vigo," she teased.

"And every one of them was necessary."

FIVE

Hours ticked into minutes, but Lorraine refused to relax. She'd left the Flag Deck on the Tavastar side, even though the risk if the news caught up to them was greater, but some instinct kept her in the Admiral's seat in Bright Dream.

"We're coming up on four light-seconds," Val told her, the SI's voice showing a hint of concern for Lorraine. While the digital entity used speakers and could easily conceal emotions, she wasn't yet used to *doing* so.

Unlike Bonny, Val and Herc hadn't realized they'd crossed the invisible line into self-actualization prior to being put to sleep. Emergent intelligences were a long-standing concern, one that most militaries actively designed their ships' computers to avoid, but part of the problem was that the shift was slow and subtle.

Lorraine suspected the transition had been around the time the computers had acquired hobbies—a garden in Val's case, knitting in Bonny's, baseball-card collecting in Herc's.

"Everything continues to look normal?" she asked Val.

"Neither the UWN carrier group nor Bright Dream Wormhole Control are acting at all out of the ordinary. Whatever suspicions they have, Em Devine appears to have directed them down a path that they do not see as a threat."

"He can be useful like that," Lorraine agreed—but the humor of the conversation was lost as a new orange icon appeared on the display.

They hadn't gone *quite* so far as to designate the UWN hostile on *Valkyrie*'s displays, but the orange color they were using was close enough that everyone knew the danger.

Lorraine wasn't as familiar with the iconography used on her new ship's displays, but she'd been able to read RKAN's displays in her sleep. She spoke fluent warship, and it only took her a moment longer to read the information on the courier ship than it would have on *Goldenrod*.

Ships normally entered a wormhole at extremely low velocities, often as low as ten meters per second. An exiting ship gained some velocity from the strange physics of the multidimensional connection, usually emerging around forty to fifty meters per second.

The courier ship had exited the wormhole at almost five *kilometers* per second, an unheard-of velocity, and was blasting a Priority One signal.

"Val, can we intercept their transmissions?" Lorraine heard Stephson ask the SI.

"Working on it, Captain," Val promised.

"It's not worth it," Lorraine countered, shaking her head. "There's only one reason a courier would hit the wormhole in Tavastar at that kind of speed. They know what we did.

"Emergency acceleration, everyone. Pass the orders to the crew to lock down, then take us to five gravities."

"We could take it more easily and still—"

"Zahariev is going to launch shuttles, and they don't need to slow down," Lorraine cut off her Captain. "Val, sustained acceleration capability for a Falcon-type shuttle?"

"The Falcon-type starfighter is designed to keep its crew protected from twelve gravities for up to thirty minutes," Val told them, as if reading off the specification sheet. Which she probably effectively *was*. "Sustained over long distance and extended time, though, safety limits call for them not to exceed eight gravities for more than sixty minutes. Standard doctrine limits eight-gravity thrust to periods of no more than—"

"They'll come after us at eight gees," Lorraine told her people. "At anything less than five, they'll be in position to deploy shuttle bombs at us before we jump."

Because they *did* have to slow down. Translight jump calculations were a nightmare, and any velocity they took into the jump added an entire new *section* to the calculation. Recalculating their jump at any velocity different from Bright Dream's star could take most of the time until their existing calculations would work anyway.

"Passing the orders," Stephson confirmed. "Thirty seconds to strap yourself in, Highness. This is going to suck."

"I know."

Lorraine had, after all, been a shuttle pilot. She'd done those twelve-gravity burns herself. RKAN's modular combat shuttles were identical to the UWN starfighters in function—if more honestly named, in her opinion—and could match the more advanced ships' acceleration.

The UWN birds had better... well, *everything*, but the acceleration was limited by the humans aboard.

"Incoming transmission from Rear Admiral Zahariev," Val reported. "Shall I—"

"Play it," Stephson and Lorraine ordered together.

A cheerleading squad sat on Lorraine's chest as she finished speaking. She *heard* Stephson's exhalation as the engines opened up.

Rear Admiral Aristocles Zahariev looked like he'd stepped out of a navy recruiting poster. He was standing on a Flag Deck identical to *Valkyrie*'s, though visibly larger and actually full of people.

He wore the tight-fitted white shipsuit and jacket of a UWN officer in a way that flattered his heavily muscled, barrel-like chest, and the two gold squares of his rank gleamed on his breast as he leveled a gun-turret-like gaze on the camera.

"I don't know who is actually over there," he ground out. "Nor am I certain how you managed to impersonate Commodore Ungur, but I assure you that the ribbon is cut. Your story is over.

"I now know those three ships were stolen from the Calypso Reserve in a grand act of piracy. How you managed to achieve that will likely be the focus of many hours of interrogation in your future, but I assure you that those hours will be coming.

"If you surrender now, I will treat you with as much gentility and care as the situation allows. I will guarantee your lives and, who knows, one of the United Worlds intelligence services may find a use for you that isn't rotting in a cell.

"If you run, my starfighter pilots will end you."

Silence, then Lorraine snorted against the cheerleaders standing on her chest.

"Have they launched yet, Val?"

"No, Highness," the SI replied. There was no strain in her artificial voice, which forced Lorraine to step on a surge of jealousy. Val was the battlecruiser. She could continue to function at levels of thrust that would kill her entire crew—though potentially not for long, because there'd been no reason to design the ship to function at those accelerations.

"His pilots can't catch us. Stephson, we'll want to throw evasive bits into our maneuvers," Lorraine told the Captain. "Make sure that Paris and Savege get that too. His pilots might be tempted to loose a few bombs at us toward the end, just to see if their velocity at that point helps.

"And if I were Zahariev, I'd be running the odds on a few long-range railgun shots."

Every UWN capital ship carried a set of dual octuple-railgun arrays, one dorsal and one ventral. Few other navies had the tech to build a useful railgun into a practical size, which limited the weapons' spread and left the UWN's multiple-weapon arrays unique to them.

The sixteen cannon in the two banks were as iconic a part of the United Worlds Navy as the white uniforms and the confidence that they were the most powerful force in human space.

Lorraine's three ships shared them—but she had no more rounds for them than she had missiles for the main launchers.

"Fuel is going to be a problem," Vigo told her silently in her link. *"Cortez and I were talking about it. We already only had fuel for a few days' flight after leaving Bright Dream taking the journey at one gee. Doubling the delta-v used here…"*

"Is a problem, yes," she agreed. *"But the first problem is getting out of here alive."*

"First shuttles launching," Stephson reported from the Bridge. "Eighty birds. Looks like a ten-squadron launch."

"She's got six more of those to go, then," Lorraine said. "How many do you think he'll put in space before he sends them after us?"

"Too many."

"For him to catch us with—or to have chasing us?" she asked Stephson.

The numbers ran across her screen, the Captain mirroring her screen to part of Lorraine's.

"Both," *Valkyrie*'s commander concluded.

It was already too late for the Terran starfighters to catch them.

***

THEIR THIRD TURNOVER hit thirty minutes later. Increasing their acceleration had given them those thirty minutes at five gees, but they still needed to slow down. Now they were slowing at five gravities, shedding velocity faster and later than they would have under the original course.

The pursuing shuttles were starting off over four light-seconds back and with far lesser velocity. Lorraine could see the numbers on the display —their closest approach would still be over five hundred thousand kilometers away, well beyond the range of any weapon in anyone's arsenal.

"You judged correctly, Lorraine," Val told her, roughly an hour after they'd started their flight.

"About what?" she asked. There was no chance to really let up the acceleration, and it was wearing on her.

"Rear Admiral Zahariev did fire his vessel's railguns. The first salvo of projectiles just activated their terminal drives."

"Distance?" Lorraine demanded. It might already be too late. The UWN's standard terminal assault munition had a twenty-second drive that provided one thousand gravities of acceleration—and the railgun rounds fired at one percent of lightspeed!

"Not close enough," Stephson said from the Bridge. "The drives can only give them about two thousand klicks of horizontal or vertical movement relative to us. Closest approach is five thousand."

New icons marked the misses, over a dozen projectiles carrying thermonuclear weapons blazing past Lorraine's three ships at a safe distance.

"And now we know he's firing, we're adjusting our evasive maneuvers," Stephson continued.

"Make sure we have that two-thousand-kilometer vertical separation from where he saw us ten minutes ago," Lorraine said. It was neither a question nor an instruction. Stephson knew her job, and if Paris and Savege were new, they were at least as experienced at this as Lorraine was.

"Exactly. Works on the shuttles, too, if they decide to take any long-range shots."

The Falcons would deploy their bombs ballistically, releasing them to use the shuttles' base velocity to close the remaining distance. Those bombs were also TAMs, a standardization that made so much sense to Lorraine, she was surprised that it hadn't spread.

She supposed the problem was that any outsider would look at the fact that the TAMs were engineered for being fired from railguns, a brutal environment requiring specialty systems. A standard warhead shared between missiles, shuttle bombs and any other non-railgun weapon wouldn't need that overengineering.

"Forty-two minutes to translight," she said aloud.

"They may still go to twelve gees if they think they can catch us," Vigo warned. "That would fit with them not firing bombs yet."

"They want these ships intact," Lorraine countered. "They're going to blink at actually nuking us. I hope."

"Unless Zahariev knows the truth about them," Vigo noted, clearly enough that everyone heard him.

That gave Lorraine a shiver even five gravities of thrust couldn't suppress. At least some UWN officers knew the truth about the *Valkyrie*-class ships and had knowingly put the SIs to sleep, an act the Asimov Convention made equivalent to murder.

If Zahariev knew that, he might take advantage of the opportunity to blow three of them away without anyone asking too many questions.

"Val, can you tell if Zahariev ever served on a *Valkyrie*?" she asked the SI.

"While my records of my *own* crew have been deleted, I do have a download of the standard databases for Navy postings," Val replied after a few seconds. "A scan suggests that Zahariev came up through carrier starfighter wings. He has only ever commanded shuttle groups or a carrier.

"I see no eventuality that would have resulted in him being briefed on the nature of the Old Guard CIRs—unless it was included in the warning about our escape."

Lorraine could have lived without that last addition, but it had been in her mind anyway.

"Keep up the evasive maneuvers," she ordered. "Stand by electronic-warfare systems. We're not going to shoot back, but we aren't going to make it easy for them!"

A few commands brought up the electronic-warfare systems in her link. She could use the consoles around her still, but it was a strain. That was part of why she was as well trained in the use of her neural link as she was.

There was no one on the Bridge to spare to manage the systems, she realized, and she slipped from observer mode into user mode without realizing it.

"I have EW," she announced into a channel that linked her with just the three Captains. "Synchronizing across all three ships."

No one said anything, which told her taking over was the right call. The battlecruisers were better equipped than she'd dared hope, with half-full magazines of decoys and chaff.

The problem was that everything except the aluminum chaff required power and drew that power from the ship. She could dump chaff in their wake without worrying about their fuel supplies, but anything more complicated would draw measurable amounts of power.

Less, though, than the energy screens or defensive beam weapons. She started to queue up a sequence, keeping one eye on the approaching shuttles.

More than any other Navy in the universe, the UWN didn't expect to be challenged. Did those shuttle pilots really have it in them to juice up and hit twelve gravities?

That was the question she was gambling all of her people's lives on. It might not make enough difference... but it might.

"Another railgun salvo," Stephson reported as new icons blazed up onto the screen. "No closer than the last three. I swear the man is just doing this to look like he's doing *something*."

The clock ticked over the thirty-minute mark till they hit the safety perimeter and went translight. Lorraine watched the shuttles like a hawk... and not one icon shifted. They continued to accelerate toward her people at eight gravities.

"Thirty minutes at full thrust is their design limit, right, Val?" she asked. That was an odd limitation in her mind. RKAN's Midas-type equivalent's only limit on emergency thrust was fuel and how sturdy the crew were feeling.

Though now she thought about it, they'd assumed they couldn't put their crews under maximum thrust outside of real emergencies. It was a panic button, an absolute *we must close now* tool. She'd used it to get back to *Goldenrod* when the attack on her family happened, and her people had used it a few times because they were fighting against superior forces and needed every edge, but even on a shuttle with an acceleration-gel-filled cockpit, it was unhealthy to sustain.

"That is the design and UWN doctrine," Val confirmed. "They are over a million kilometers behind us. Even if they go to twelve gravities now, I do not calculate they will be able to reach a distance and velocity where they can usefully release their bombs."

Sixteen railgun rounds blazed by, their terminal thrusters trying desperately to bring the weapons to effective range of the three *Valkyries*.

"I have the same numbers as Val," Lorraine admitted. "They... never could actually reach us, not without going to twelve gees a long time ago."

"Are we clear?" Stephson asked.

"Not until we're in translight. They could be trying to distract us with the shuttles while they maneuver a ship around in front of us translight," she warned her Captain. "We're not safe until we're gone."

SIX

Thankfully, Vigo hadn't had to physically carry his charge to her quarters and lock her in to get her to rest. He'd been on the Flag Deck with her the entire way, and while he'd realized the UWN shuttles couldn't catch them before anyone had said it aloud, he hadn't quite believed it himself.

Everyone on board all three ships had been expecting another shoe to drop right up until the moment they went translight. Even now, a clock ticking down in his link to mark their return to realspace, part of him remembered the long flight from *Corsair*, the RKAN battlecruiser equipped with stolen technology specifically tailored to follow *Goldenrod*.

The UWN had versions of that tech on their ships, but it had taken specific modifications to their frigate to make *Corsair*'s pursuit possible—a sign of how deeply and how early Benjamin Adamant had planned his coup.

The world flickered around him as the molecules making up *Valkyrie* stopped pretending to be tachyons. Three hours from leaving the wormhole put them two light-weeks from the Bright Dream System.

Far enough not to be seen, not so far that they'd lost much time. Rolestrella was in the opposite direction from Adamant, after all.

He turned to knock on the hatch to Lorraine's quarters—then stopped. His synchronization to her link told him an alarm had just woken her up from the nap he'd insisted she take.

Knowing his Pentarch, Vigo waited. Thirty seconds later, her image popped up in his link in a message copied to the senior officers of all three ships—plus him and Devine.

"Command staff meeting in ten minutes," Lorraine Adamant told them. "*Valkyrie* crew, meeting room Foxtrot-Six. Everyone else, link in virtually. Val, can you take care of that?"

"We will have it handled," the SI promised.

"Good. I'll see you all there."

Vigo smiled to himself, noting Alvarez's questioning look. He'd joined the woman in the usual boring duty of standing outside the Pentarch's door.

"Her Highness hasn't been awake for five minutes and she's got the ball rolling," he told his subordinate. "We're going to be fine."

"Between you, her and Stephson, I was never worried, ser."

The only thing that really *worried* Vigo was Alastair Devine. He agreed with Lorraine that Devine was needed in the command meetings. His knowledge and unique skills had helped them get this far, but there were still too many question marks around the young man.

In the end, Vigo Jarret didn't really know that much about his charge's boyfriend. He knew that Lorraine was head over heels for him, which was dangerous—a risk only somewhat ameliorated by the fact that Devine appeared to be equally enamored with her.

He knew the man had been a spy in one of the more covert branches of the United Worlds' notoriously twisty covert operations underworld, and he knew that the man was the single most augmented human being on the battlecruiser.

But he didn't know what Devine had actually *done* for the United Worlds Extraterritorial Surveillance Corps—only that it had earned him a favor at the highest levels of Earth's interstellar megacorps... and that his last formal Diplomatic Service posting had been on a planet that had dissolved into a bloody civil war that had killed fifty million people.

Vigo really wished that his hindbrain didn't keep insisting those last two points were connected somehow.

VALKYRIE'S habitat pods rotated a bit less than three times a minute, creating a solid impression of one gravity at the outermost part of the pod and roughly three-quarters of a gravity at the innermost section.

When under thrust, the pods would fold into line with the hull, rotating as they did so that "down" in the pod was always the same direction. One side of each of the two pods was armored as heavily as the rest of *Valkyrie's* hull, and a section of plates on the main hull would fold down to minimize the weak point in combat.

At times, Vigo had questioned whether the rotational pods were necessary enough to justify that weakness. Having spent most of the last seven months traveling translight on a ship that *didn't* have such pods, his opinion was now set in solid stone.

Any ship that needed to travel long distances needed the ability to generate gravity without thrust. The crew of *Goldenrod* had gone more than a little off by the time they'd reached Earth—a shared experience that had helped bond them together and to their Princess.

The hab pods prevented that and provided meeting rooms that had gravity. Foxtrot-Six was one of eight in Habitat Foxtrot—though why the two pods were Epsilon and Foxtrot was beyond Vigo.

Tradition, he supposed. As valid and meaningful as the one that meant he was standing one step behind and to the right of Lorraine Adamant as she took her seat at the head of the table.

Devine, Cortez and Stephson were the only members of the command staff physically present with him and Lorraine. Paris and Savege were both present by hologram, though the UWN's version of that was solid enough that they could have been in the room. The three SIs were similarly virtually present, as was the last member of the little meeting, Senior Chief Petty Officer Leonard Roman.

Roman was the oldest person of the three ship's crew, an NCO well into his second century who'd attached himself to Lieutenant Colonel Stephson early in her career. Now he was on *Hercules* with Mattias Paris. The most senior noncom they had was spending his time rotating between the three ships as he could, supporting each of the brand-new Captains with his wealth of experience.

Vigo didn't know the man overly well, but he suspected that Roman might well be better qualified to command one of the three ships than Paris—if not better qualified than *Stephson* herself.

"Thank you, everyone," his Pentarch began. She didn't specify for what. Vigo knew it wasn't *just* for gathering for this meeting.

"We got lucky in Bright Dream but not as lucky as we were hoping for," she continued. "Commander Cortez, can you lay out our situation?"

She paused and looked back over her shoulder at Vigo.

"After my bodyguard sits himself down, that is," she said. "There are two Guards at each entrance to this room, Vigo. You don't need to loom."

He considered arguing with her. His presence at her shoulder added weight to her words, reminding the officers why the Adamant was in charge of the mission.

But then, no one there needed that reminder. Lorraine wasn't in charge of this mission because of the orders or bloodline that had put her in command. She was in charge because she was the one who'd laid out the plan that had taken down a battlecruiser with a frigate. Because she was the one who'd spoken to Earth politicians and come within a sliver of winning their case on the floor of the Grand Assembly.

Because she was the one who'd come up with the plan to steal the *Valkyries* and because she was the one who'd realized what was going on with the CIRs and convinced them to join her.

She didn't need him to loom, so he took a seat next to her with easy grace and nodded to his girlfriend.

Rose Cortez, for her part, rolled her eyes at him before her humor faded into grim seriousness.

"We have one issue that renders everything else we have spoken about and considered secondary," she told them all. "Fuel. Everything we do, from running the power plants to going translight to accelerating sublight, burns a specialized mix of deuterium and tritium.

"Like most ships intended for independent operations, the *Valkyries* are capable of setting up a cloudscoop-and-refining process, but that requires access to a gas giant and... well, a minimum amount of fuel for maneuvers and to power the extraction systems."

"A minimum amount that none of us have," Bonny confirmed before any humans could ask. "We could potentially cross-load fuel onto one of us, leaving the other two on a ballistic orbit in the system while the third carries out extraction ops."

"Which would leave two of our ships critically vulnerable at a time when we know we are being hunted," Stephson pointed out.

"It's not an option we can dismiss out of hand," Lorraine said, her tones smooth and confident as she cut off the discussion. "But it makes for an uncomfortable plan, oh, D. I'd like better options if anyone has them?"

"I can think of a few," Vigo told her, considering the information he'd gone through on this region of space. Fuel had always been high on their list of concerns, and the Exodus Protocol that had sent Lorraine Adamant into exile had also seen her Guard furnished with every scrap of intelligence the Kingdom had on *everything*.

"Now that we know the Republic is aware of our presence, we can't refuel at any of their systems," he presumed. "But the Republic's systems are in a relatively tight cluster that isn't really in our way. If we bypass them, we do not have that far to travel to reach inhabited systems that are less dependent on UW goodwill and more willing to wink at our presence, even if they have learned about our theft."

He knew Lorraine well enough to know when she was suppressing a reaction.

"Rose," his Pentarch said quietly. "I think we need to be very clear about how bad the situation is."

"We left Calypso with roughly ten thousand tons of fuel across all three ships," Cortez laid out. "We cross-loaded when we rendezvoused with *Goldenrod*, emptying her tanks and leveling the tanks across all three ships. We arrived in Tavastar with about six thousand tons of fuel per ship.

"We *planned* to burn approximately three thousand tons of fuel per ship in Tavastar and Bright Dream. Due to our need to run, we burned just under five thousand.

"There is now roughly thirty-five hundred tons of fuel aboard this entire squadron."

Years of experience meant that Vigo knew his own face remained impassive, but he might have been the only one. He figured each of the three Captains had known how bad it was for their own ship, but it hadn't sunk in that the entire squadron was that limited.

"Thankfully, we have so few people aboard each ship, we can actually handle most life-support needs from the auxiliary thermal generators," Cortez told them. "We're working on wiring them fully into the grids as a stopgap measure, but that will only buy us time while we're sitting in place.

"Right now, leveraging those plants as best as we can, our burn rate is going to be around twenty tons per day per ship. That's just sitting here in interstellar space with the habs rotating. Accelerating will burn through those reserves *fast*. Give or take, roughly one-point-five tons per minute per ship."

"The irony is that while it will cost us a great deal of energy to *enter* translight, our daily burn in that mode is notably less than sublight maneuvering," Lorraine added. "Even so, if we allow for normal in-system maneuvering at the other end and want *any* kind of reserve when we arrive, we are limited to no more than ten days' flight."

"Three-point-five light-years," Val calculated for everyone, the SI's words toneless in a way that Vigo hadn't heard from her before.

Almost half again what *Goldenrod* could have made in the same time but not far enough to get anywhere *useful*.

Vigo pulled up a map in his implants—only for Val to do the same thing on a big hologram above the gleaming black table.

RKAN was going to have to replace the furniture on this ship if they kept her, he reflected. He doubted anyone in his old service wanted to feel like their conference rooms belonged to bad action-movie villains.

"There are two inhabited systems inside that radius," the SI noted. "Bright Dream itself, of course, but also the Allan System. They're a member system of the Republic, with more than sufficient infrastructure, including an out-system refueling post in a gas giant Lagrange point."

Vigo wasn't qualified on translight navigation, but he knew that gas giants had large safety zones, and hence, refueling stations tended to be in high orbit of the planets they pulled their fuel from. A trailing Lagrange point would serve the same purpose if they were willing to spend the extra time sublight to be more accessible to visitors.

"The Republic of Bright Dream doesn't have a lot of couriers as fast as *Valkyrie*, but they do have them," Lorraine said. "By the time we can reach any Republic system, they'll know who we are. Allan is too risky."

Everyone stared at the map. The Bright Dream System was part of a small cluster of stars, the shorter distances helping them unify early on in their history. Only two stars had inhabited planets, but Vigo eyeballed at least three more that they could reach.

"It's starting to look like cross-loading fuel and heading to one of these systems is the best option," Stephson said grimly, waving at the three stars Vigo was looking at. "Do we have astrographic information? Enough to tell if there's a useful gas giant in one of those stars?"

"Wait, is that Lando?" Devine asked.

Everyone looked at him.

"I don't see a Lando System on the records, Em Devine," Val said carefully.

"No, it's L-Six-ND-Zero-Zero," the spy replied.

L6NDoo was one of the three possibles, Vigo saw. But he wasn't sure what that meant to the spy.

"Lando is what the locals call it," Devine continued slowly. "It's an odd system, with no rocky planets and six gas giants. No asteroid belts, just Trojan clusters. Nothing really worth exploiting, though the Republic does technically claim it."

"We could use one of those gas giants to refuel, but if there are locals...?" Savege trailed off in question, *Bean Sidhe*'s new Captain eyeing the UW spy.

"Cuansaor," Devine replied, carefully feeling through the unusual syllables. "Irish name, means *Free Harbor*. I don't know when it was founded, but there are a bunch of people living in the orbitals of the outermost gas giant. No moons of any decent size, either, so it's all space stations built from local scrap and ships that never left."

He shrugged.

"Like I said, it's technically Republic territory, but both Cuansaor and the Republic mostly ignore that. The Cuansaor economy is based on providing cheap fuel to people who are heading to the wormhole but want to shave a few points off by not paying Bright Dream prices."

"And the Republic ignores them because a port where no one asks questions is all too useful to the corporations that pay their bills?" Stephson suggested.

"My old service may have put a few words in the right ears and credit chips in the right pockets to keep it that way, too," Devine admitted. "The United Worlds intelligence community is playing a lot of games, and not all of them are against the UW's outsiders.

"I've been to Cuansaor three times," he noted. "I know the right pass phrases and such to get us in the door. Showing up with three battlecruisers is going to raise eyebrows, though."

Vigo looked at the map again. It wasn't his decision, though Lorraine might ask. It seemed like their best option—but it was putting even more of their eggs in a basket under Alastair Devine's control.

He supposed that ship had already sailed a long time before.

"We're barely able to hurt a fly right now," Stephson reminded everyone. "We're no threat to them."

"We may not want to advertise that," Vigo said quickly, before anyone made any foolish plans. "This kind of place is also going to be home to people who will be very tempted by the concept of stealing UWN battlecruisers."

"They will need far better luck than they could possibly have to pull that off," Herc said firmly, the SI's avatar suddenly acquiring the spear that went with his Ancient Greek hoplite armor. "You did not steal us, after all."

"I'm not certain the UW agrees with you there," Paris told his SI. "How would you describe it, Herc?"

"You *recruited* us," Herc replied. "That the UWN believes they have ownership of our physical bodies is a violation of their own laws along with the Asimov Convention."

"That's a fight we're going to want to put off as long as possible," Lorraine said firmly. "If things go wrong in Lando, do we have a fall-back option?"

The room was quiet.

"No," Cortez finally said. "Lando is near the limit of how far we can go, Pentarch. If we cannot acquire fuel from them, we will be stranded and vulnerable."

"We will still be able to fuel the shuttles," Vigo noted, his voice steady. He knew what he was suggesting—all three of their ships carried twenty-four of the UWN's Falcon-type shuttle/starfighters.

One per squadron could be rigged for heavy transport, able to haul ten thousand tons of fuel. But *all* of them could be rigged to carry weapons perfectly capable of punching holes in civilian stations.

"Let's try money and the intimidation factor of a battlecruiser division before we start planning to rob anyone," Lorraine decided. "But I think Lando is our best option. Anything else will take too long —and it *won't* take long for the Republic and the Terrans to start hunting for anywhere we can find fuel."

SEVEN

The screen flickered and turned black, and Lorraine sighed. She wasn't entirely convinced that the scenario she'd been working through was *meant* to be winnable—RKAN's training courses were notorious for scenarios that tested officers' ability to extract something from a losing scenario—but she didn't like losing.

Of course, the scenarios and material she was working through were supposed to be done in a group with a guide. She wasn't entirely sure why *Valkyrie* had a full download of the curriculum and course material for the United Worlds Navy Command School, but she was working through it whenever she had time.

It was fifteen standard years out of date, according to the cover documents, but it was still every piece of literature and coursework for a six-month intensive program intended to turn UWN Commanders into UWN Lieutenant Captains.

Given the expanded rank structures of the UWN, said Commanders would be around the age and experience of her Lieutenant Colonel Stephson—who had passed the equivalent RKAN course before attaining her current rank.

With ten days in translight and the day-to-day work of handling

Valkyrie's tiny crew capably handled by Stephson, Lorraine was doing everything she could to prepare for the task ahead of her. She'd only ever commanded a shuttle wing before the coup, and now she found herself in command of a battlecruiser division.

If she was going to win the war ahead of her, she was going to need to command it well—and find more ships and allies along the way. She had thoughts in that direction, though she hadn't raised them with anyone yet.

"Lorraine, Em Devine is at the door," Val said suddenly. "You'd asked your Guard to provide you privacy while you completed the scenario, and I wasn't sure if you'd want to change that now you're done."

Even the scenarios she figured were winnable were beating her more often than not so far. She'd turned her uncle's pre-treason chess games and philosophy into a mind game sufficient to win an utterly unbalanced battle once, but that didn't make her a commander.

Training would help, but she didn't need people to see her getting trounced.

Unlike a regular computer, though, Val recognized both that Lorraine would probably want to speak to Devine and that her orders to her Guard would prevent that.

"Thank you, Val," she told the SI, then linked to Palmer. "Panam, you can lift the privacy lock. Send Devine in."

The Guard snorted.

"And he was just about to walk away all sad and dejected-like," she said. "I'll send him your way, Pentarch."

The hatch slid silently open. It was a small difference from the RKAN ships Lorraine had served on, where even the best-maintained hatches and doors were audible. It wasn't even a question of maintenance—none of the hundred people on *Valkyrie* had time to be oiling an office hatch.

The mechanism was just that much smoother and cleaner. It was a small sign of the technological superiority of the UWN over the other human nations, but it was telling to Lorraine.

"How goes school?" Devine asked as the hatch closed behind him, equally silently.

"About as expected," she said. "I'm trying to pack six months of a course that's *supposed* to be intensive into... well, less."

If they set course directly for Adamantine from Cuansaor, it would be a three-month journey. Their course wouldn't be that direct, Lorraine knew, but trying to cram in everything the course packages offered would be difficult.

She was a Pentarch of House Adamant, however, with everything from her beauty to her brain genetically engineered to human optimums and then augmented with implanted cybernetics. If it could be done, she would do it.

Her boyfriend took a seat on her desk, grinning down at her.

"Most royals get someone else to do the commanding, you know," he said.

"Not Adamants," she countered. "My mother was a diplomat, but even she was actively involved in both strategic and operational planning during the war. Only when the final battles were closed did she stand aside to let my uncle command the tactical maneuvers."

Lorraine suspected that had been a seed of the rot that had birthed Benjamin's betrayal. He'd retreated from the Tolkien System during the war, abandoning an entire planet and multiple divisions of the Royal Kingdom of Adamant Army to the Richelieu Directorate.

His plan had always been to regroup with the Home Fleet in Adamantine and retake the system as quickly as possible. By preserving his fleet, he'd turned the tide of the war.

Except that King Valeriya had taken command of the relief fleet. *She* had gained the credit for the relief of Tolkien's people—and Benjamin Adamant had carried the weight of abandoning them.

"Besides, I know how my uncle thinks better than anyone here," she continued. "He is, by general agreement, the best tactician and strategist my House and my Kingdom have ever produced. Every edge will matter."

Devine sighed, reaching out to take her hand. His fingers were warm on hers, easing away the chill of working on the glass-and-metal touchscreens.

"You take too much on yourself," he warned. "You have people around you with real skills and knowledge. You shouldn't hold everything in your head, Lorraine."

Something in how he said her name warmed her even more than his fingers against hers.

"I don't, I promise," she assured him. "Everything that's just in my head is still in early stages, rolling around with broken edges sticking out that aren't fit for public consumption."

"Your command staff of this affair is hardly *public consumption*," he countered. "We've all put our heads on the block for you. However this goes, do you think for one second that Sigrid Stephson or Rose Cortez isn't going to follow you?

"And let's not even *talk* about Vigo Jarret."

"Vigo Jarret might as well be *part* of my head," Lorraine pointed out. "He's been synced to my link since I was six years old."

A twitch of embarrassment flickered across her lover's face, and she grinned.

"He *does* mute it to give me privacy at the necessary moments, I promise!"

Devine laughed and squeezed her hand.

"Fair enough. Do you know where the coffee machine is in here? I'm dying for something warm; this ship is chillier than I'd like."

"Among the systems we have shut down to preserve power are the heat-balancing structures that could move thermal energy from the reactor sections into the habitat pods," Val's voice informed him. The SI was also, Lorraine presumed, indicating the beverage machine on the wall in the man's link.

"Thanks to the presence of humans and the emergency thermal-decay plants, the habitat pods are capable of maintaining habitable temperatures with no active heating, but it would take more humans or an active expenditure of power to raise the climate above the current fifteen degrees."

"It's *fine*, Val," Devine told the SI with a loud sigh as he opened the cabinet holding the dispenser. It had already started brewing in the handful of seconds it had taken him to reach it, Val taking advantage of her restored connection to everything on the ship.

Lorraine knew that most of the crew didn't get quite so much of the anticipation and constant attention that she received from Val. A portion of the SI's intelligence was permanently locked on her, both learning from her and providing her anything Val thought she needed.

Except privacy. She wasn't going to admit to Alastair that she was *quite* certain Val was paying attention while they were having sex.

"We'll probably want to pick up food and coffee supplies in Cuansaor," he noted, taking a sip of the steaming drink. "The stuff we brought over from *Goldenrod* won't last forever."

"We had supplies to get the entire crew back to Adamantine without restocking," she pointed out, wrapping her hands around her own mug. It... was not warm enough to be noticeably helpful—and she heard the coffee machine start up again as she pulled her hands back.

"That was at eighty cee. At the *Valkyries'* greater speed and comfort, I think we'll be fine."

"Of course," he agreed. "Assuming we're going to Adamantine and assuming we're working with just the original crew."

She gave him a questioning look as she rose to collect her own coffee.

"Those are assumptions we're all working with, yes," she said pointedly. "Are you working on something else, Alastair?"

He shrugged.

"There are always options, Lorraine," he reminded her. "In the world I've lived in for my entire adult life, you *always* keep an out. An escape route, another option. The last news we have from your homeworld is from, what, the beginning of June? That was *four months ago.*"

"I will never forget that," she said flatly. Their news was four and a half months old, carried from Adamantine to Bright Dream by standard first-order-cluster news couriers equipped with ninety-six-cee translight drives.

Four and a half months earlier, an active civil war had been raging on her homeworld. Her brother Nikola had managed to seize control of the Planetary Defense Centers on Mithral, Bastion's southern continent.

It had taken Benjamin longer to find loyal troops to land on Mithral than she imagined he'd liked—but RKAA would always chafe at the authority of the man who'd left them on Tolkien—and had lost one of Home Fleet's battleships trying to pull off an orbital bombardment of the PDCs. As of the last news, PDC Mithral—the main command center—was still unchallenged, but the secondary military centers were being besieged by the Black Regent's forces.

"A lot could have changed in four months," he told her. "How far are you willing to go if the war is already over? If Nikola has bent the knee and Benjamin Adamant has been crowned King?"

"As far as I have to," Lorraine growled. "When I started this mission, Alastair, I believed Nikola and my nieces were *dead*."

Her eldest brother's twin daughters hadn't been major figures in the news, which she had to begrudgingly give her uncle credit for. She suspected he could have drawn a lot of propaganda value from having the adorable princesses looking to him for protection and guidance. Instead, there was barely enough information for her to be certain they were alive.

They were in the care of Lorraine's cousin, Jessica Adamant. Jessica was a diplomat, one who'd spent much of her career bouncing between single-system star nations to keep channels of communication open.

On paper, she'd been no more important than any other diplomat. In reality, sending someone of House Adamant always carried just a little bit more weight.

She was also, in Lorraine's considered opinion, probably the most dangerous to Benjamin of the potential new Pentarchs. The deaths of

Lorraine's older brothers had moved Benjamin's son, Oliver, into the Pentarchy—and also added Jessica, the elder of Valeriya's cousin Irmentrud's twin children, onto the list of the five people who should be standing for the Royal Election.

If Nikola died or abdicated—or Lorraine did, she supposed—Jessica's twin Hans, a member of the Kingdom's House of the Realm, would also join the Pentarchy. Both of them were harmless to Benjamin in the military sense, unlike Nikola or Lorraine, but between the diplomat and the politician...

"You'll keep going, even if there's no hope?" Devine asked quietly.

"We have more hope now, with Val and her siblings, than we had when we left Adamantine with one frigate," she pointed out. "My brother is keeping the Black Regent focused, but actually winning this is going to land on us. We're a long way from *no hope*."

"You know your Kingdom," he conceded. "But in that case, we're going to need more *people*. Val, how many hands would it take to fight this ship at, say, fifty percent capacity?"

There was a long pause—one that told Lorraine more about how Val felt about the question than any actual need for assessment. The SI wasn't sure if she wanted to take a side in this discussion or of how her answer might be taken.

"To properly operate this ship, putting aside the assigned landing contingents, would require twelve hundred fully trained naval personnel," Val finally said. "If we do not deploy the Falcons in any capacity, that can be reduced to one thousand.

"The absolute minimum necessary to operate *Valkyrie*'s weapons and defense systems, assuming no relief or secondary shifts and no damage-control personnel, would be roughly four hundred and thirty.

"With any numbers less than that, we will have to make choices of what defenses or weapons we are prepared to shut down or, in the case of defensive systems, run in automatic mode with as much support as I can provide."

Lorraine grimaced wordlessly. Even with every station crewed, they would be far short of the real capabilities of the battlecruisers. Those reliefs and backups and second shifts were necessary, even ignoring the risk of going into battle without damage-control teams or shuttles to send out as missile interceptors.

"Fifty percent capability would be over three hundred hands, then?" she asked Val.

"It would depend on the training of the personnel available," the SI hedged, "but I would estimate between three hundred and thirty and three hundred and fifty crew for anything resembling fifty percent of *Valkyrie*'s designed combat effectiveness.

"Plus, of course, fuel and munitions."

Lorraine couldn't glare at the SI, so she turned her grim look on her boyfriend. He shrugged, raising his coffee mug in half-salute.

"You can't run three battlecruisers with the crew from one frigate," he told her. "Even the spy over here realized that."

What she didn't tell him was that she had *also* realized that. Her plan was to stop in one of the outer systems of the Kingdom and make an alliance with the system government—hopefully even commandeer the RKAN ships in the system, or at least their crews.

To do that, though, she needed to *get* there. She might even need to fight RKAN warships, if she couldn't overawe them. She trusted her people completely, but Devine was right.

"You wouldn't be poking me about it if you didn't have an idea," she told him. "And you'd have brought this up in the meeting later, except that you think it's an idea no one is going to like."

"Am I that transparent?" he asked plaintively, pressing the hand not holding his coffee to his chest before laughing and taking a drink. "Basically, yes, on both counts."

She'd mostly been using her new coffee to warm her hands up to that point, but now she took a sip. It was still a touch too hot, stinging her mouth. The momentary discomfort was useful, helping her focus her thoughts.

Alastair Devine knew a lot of things she and her people didn't.

The Adamant Guard had information and skills most of her spacers and Marines lacked, but they weren't immersed in intelligence work and the underworld the way it seemed he had been.

She was reasonably sure she was falling in love with the man. She'd trusted him again and again, and he'd never led her wrong. Still, he was an outsider on *Valkyrie*, with far less tying him to her mission.

But he'd never led her wrong.

"What's your plan?" she finally asked.

"Cuansaor is the type of place where folks who want to be forgotten hole up," he explained. "The claim to not ask questions goes a lot further than just the ships buying fuel. Mercenaries, spies, hackers, criminals… Drifters with skills tend to end up on places like that.

"If you need a small ship or the crew for such a ship, with people who'll be reliably loyal to a paycheck, you start in a Cuansaor. It's not the place to hire mercenary companies or full-size ships, but if you want a low-key ship that will smuggle you in somewhere unnoticed? You start here."

"I take it you've done that." Devine had been hesitant to talk about his past in UWESC. She knew that some of his work as a spy and covert operator had either been directly for MicroStar, an LSX-Twenty-Five megacorp, or had sufficiently benefited them that key officials of that corporation had felt they owed him a favor.

"I've hired blockade runners to insert teams under the radar *in* Cuansaor," he admitted. "I haven't put together a team of specialists there, but I've done it in similar places. And"—he grinned—"having *been* on Cuansaor, I can assure you that the types of tools I used to do it are there."

"We're not going to find six hundred crew qualified to serve on a UWN battlecruiser in a shady refueling collective," Lorraine countered. "And that's before getting into whether we can find *anyone* we can trust."

"Of course not," he agreed with a nod. "But even an extra hundred hands per ship—few enough that Vigo and the SIs can set up surveillance to make sure they don't cause trouble—would make a lot of difference.

"Plus, if you give me a bit of free rein, I think I can source some of the supplies even Cuansaor won't sell above the table. Like the fissionables for proper munitions."

Lorraine nodded slowly. That was one of the headaches they'd gone over in the command staff meeting. The *Valkyries'* fabricators were capable of manufacturing all of the parts to make up the UWN's terminal assault munition, but the fifty-kiloton nuclear warhead at the heart of the TAM required a heavy-metal-based fission device to trigger it.

For all of the things that had been left behind on *Valkyrie* and her siblings, the UWN hadn't left behind any of those triggers. There were materials on the ships that could be theoretically refined into the right kind of state, but all of them were, well, in other systems they rather needed.

"You want me to send you onto the station to recruit people and buy the raw materials for nukes," she concluded. "You'd have got a fair hearing in front of the command staff, but I can see why you wanted to talk to me about it first!"

"I'd need the Captains with me for at least part of the recruiting," he noted. "But the fewer people with me, the better—especially when I start trying to source thorium and plutonium!"

"I understand that," Lorraine conceded, her mind already whirring with plans. "I think I see a solution that will make everyone comfortable, though."

She smiled... and did not explain it to him just then.

"NO. There is no way in hell, void, Earth or stars that *you* are boarding a shady space station that will have everything from solo mercenaries to gangs to United Worlds spies on it," Vigo Jarret growled when they got that far through the explanation at the command meeting a few hours later.

With their little fleet in translight, the officers aboard the other two ships were missing. Only Val, Cortez and Stephson were in the room with Lorraine, Jarret and Devine as Jarret issued a clear red line.

"Vigo, I am determined and occasionally impetuous, not *stupid*," Lorraine told him after he'd got his short rant out. "There are no circumstances under which it makes any sense at all to let the people of Cuansaor know that I'm aboard—or that we have anything to do with Adamant at all!

"None of the people we need to send over to manage our goals are of a rank or position where they can be identified. Alastair"—she indicated him with her chin—"would be at the greatest risk of being identified if he couldn't disguise himself."

"I haven't been here with my own face," Devine admitted. "And while the face and name I wore here might be of *use* to us, there are people who could make the connection. I'd rather that link not be made for a while yet."

Lorraine knew there was no chance of them pulling this off without the theft of the battlecruisers being traced back to Adamant. She had the shape of a plan for dealing with that, even, but it was a future problem.

It *was* possible that they could keep Alastair Devine from being linked to it, in her opinion, though he seemed much more fatalistic about it.

"To do what Alastair needs to do, he needs to be in possession of a significant portion of our financial reserve *and* able to make decisions relatively independently, without phoning home," Lorraine noted. "That means he needs to be accompanied—by someone completely trusted by our leadership and capable of handling themselves if the situation goes sideways."

Rose Cortez caught on first and audibly sighed before anyone else did.

"It has to be you, Vigo," Lorraine told the man in charge of her bodyguard. "The Captains may be needed at various points, but Alastair needs someone to back him up and make sure no one back on the ships is worrying."

And if there was one person Lorraine Adamant trusted more than herself, it was Vigo Jarret.

He glowered in silence for a moment, then nodded choppily.

"You're right, of course," he conceded. "But which am I protecting? Our money or your boyfriend?"

"Both, if you'd be so kind!"

EIGHT

Sigrid Stephson didn't have the face-changing implants of a United Worlds spy, but Lorraine figured her senior Captain—her Flag Captain, she supposed?—had done a good job of concealing her identity anyway.

Lorraine couldn't be put on video. She could probably disguise most of her distinguishing features, but everything about her, from her sharp cheekbones and gold-centered hazel eyes to her height and arm length, was the result of generations-old expensive genetic engineering.

It was a basically unique package and, to someone who knew what the adjustments made to House Adamant were, rendered her distinctly identifiable in video.

While Lieutenant Colonel Sigrid Stephson's image and file footage had almost certainly been distributed after the Black Regent's people had confirmed she was working with Lorraine, there would be much less to work with, and Stephson wasn't forged to as fixed a standard.

The Captain's shoulder-length blond hair had been slicked back with gel and spray, dyed a dark brown and twisted into a severe bun without a single loose strand. Her blue eyes were covered with purple contact lenses, carefully selected for a rare but real tone.

Wearing a UWN uniform without insignia—they had a *vast* stockpile of the clothing in eighty-six different sizes, and raw materials and fabricators to replace them if they somehow ran out—she looked like what she was pretending to be: a Navy officer on a barely concealed covert op.

"Translight exit in ten seconds."

Lorraine had set up the main projector in her Flag Deck to show her *Valkyrie*'s Bridge, with a screen to her left set up to show her Stephson's transmissions when she made them. Her microphone was muted so she wouldn't interrupt the Bridge crew at their work, but without hands to spare to man the Flag Deck, it was the best way for her to stay informed.

Devine had taken over the Intelligence Officer's console. He had the screens up and showing him something—Lorraine could mirror it, but she figured he'd tell her if she needed to know anything.

As the count continued, Jarret drifted across the deck—none of the warship's working spaces were in the hab pods, though the pods had been pulled in prior to the return to sublight—and easily rotated himself into the Operations Officer seat.

He glanced back at Lorraine and shrugged as she met his gaze.

"Can't hurt," he sent her silently.

"Exit."

A light no one had ever been able to describe flickered through the ship, and then the universe around them snapped into existence once more. *Valkyrie*'s sensors drank deep of the light and radiation of her new location, information popping into existence on the various displays as quickly as humans and computers could process it.

The first things to appear were *Herakles* and *Bean Sidhe*, in the same position they'd entered translight in: exactly one thousand kilometers to port and starboard of *Valkyrie*.

Then, as expected, L6NDoo-Foxtrot at four light-seconds. The outermost planet of the Lando System was a mid-sized gas giant, roughly one hundred and twenty thousand kilometers in diameter. A twenty-radius safety allowance put them far enough away that they couldn't even pick out energy signatures at first.

"Foxtrot has three rings," Devine noted, a moment before the scans dropped them onto the display. "The outermost ring has some decoy stations in it, but nothing real. The Cuansaor platforms aren't in any of the rings, though they use the middle ring for cover.

"The actual extraction infrastructure is much closer in, but I think I can..."

He poked at something on his screen and then two sets of new icons appeared around the massive planet. One was in an orbit Lorraine would have classed as dangerously low, a diffuse cloud of smaller detection signals. The second was, as he'd said, tucked in the clearer space between the first and second rings, positioned where the second ring would help conceal them from most angles.

"We got the update," Stephson said aloud. "Thanks, Em Devine."

New codes flickered into existence around those icons, and Lorraine zoomed in on them on her own consoles. The extraction infrastructure caught her eye first, as much from the sheer size of the area it covered as anything else.

There were only a handful of the cloudscoops she was used to: stations large enough for a rotating habitat connected to balloon-like tubes that dropped hundreds of kilometers into the upper atmosphere. They marked the central axis on which the other extractors rotated, dozens of ships that appeared to be physically diving into the upper atmosphere.

She'd heard of the concept of cloud-divers, but it was generally considered an obsolete system, long replaced by properly designed cloudscoops. Even *Goldenrod* had carried the tubes necessary to draw material up from a gas giant without entering it.

"The divers are cheaper to operate and not as much less efficient as you might think," Devine told her. "Foxtrot has weather to make you miss deep space, and it can render the more-permanent structures useless for weeks at a time."

"And the other gas giants, from the spectrography we're starting to get back, don't have the right gas mix to be useful," Jarret said. "No wonder only the desperate ended up here."

"The divers are also owner-operators to a one," the spy added. "It takes an independent-minded soul to end up here in Lando at all—and some of them decide that even Cuansaor has too many rules and limits. They scrape together the cash to buy a diver and become master of their own fate."

Lorraine could see the appeal. On the other hand, they were there for more than looking around.

"Captains, let's get moving," she told them. "Paris, Savege, Herc, Bonny—anything come up during the trip I need to worry about?"

Captains and CIRs alike demurred. Stephson's team had downloaded the course to the other ships, and Lorraine felt her muscles twitch back into place as a sense of *down* returned to the *Valkyrie*'s decks.

One gravity the entire way, flipping after a bit less than three hours. Their course would take them above the two outer rings, bringing them into the Cuansaor platform and giving the locals lots of time to see them coming.

"Any sign of reaction from the locals yet?" Lorraine asked, opening her mike so Stephson could hear her."

"Our eyes on the platform cluster suggest they have sensors sufficient to have seen us," the Captain replied. "There's at least one station that looks like an old RBDN listening platform. If she's even ninety percent intact, they'd be able to read our beacons.

"If we were transmitting them."

That was something they needed to fix, Lorraine knew. They couldn't sail into a star system flying UWN identifier beacons, but flying in *without* beacons suggested hostility in ways she wasn't sure how to avoid.

"We should probably talk to them," Lorraine suggested. "Without the beacons, they're probably working out if they have something that can drive us off."

That was why Stephson was in disguise, after all.

"Agreed. I just wanted to get decent eyes on everything before we started chatting. Ah." Stephson paused, checking as new icons were added to the display. "There's what I was looking for."

"Apologies, Captain," Val said swiftly. "I wasn't sure what to focus on, and the discussion had been about the platforms themselves."

The new icons were ships—warships, specifically. It was a motley collection, anchored on a single *very* modern Republic of Bright Dream Navy cruiser with three destroyers for escorts.

The rest of the ships ranged from a four-hundred-thousand-ton cruiser that the RBDN had probably sold for scrap before Lorraine was born to what appeared to be merchant ships with external missile racks bolted on.

"So, the Republic does claim some authority—or, at least, responsibility here," Lorraine murmured. "That does change the game plan, doesn't it?"

"We'll see," Stephson said. "Any changes to the pitch, boss?"

"Nah. We're not here to talk to the Republic, so we talk to the locals and pretend big brother isn't there," Lorraine replied, deciding instantly. "Transmit as planned."

Stephson gave her a sharp nod as Lorraine muted her microphone again. The screen set up to show the coms channels blinked alive with a flat image of the Captain's face as she turned a calm and cheerful expression on the cameras.

"Cuansaor Station Control, this is Captain Idina Menzel of the independent starship *Frozen Heart*," Stephson introduced herself. "My vessel and her companions, *Deer Rain* and *Princess*, are inbound to your facility.

"We are here to purchase fuel and are prepared to pay, of course. If other supplies are available, we would be delighted to be put in contact with merchants or a central chandlery to make arrangements."

Stephson paused, then shrugged one shoulder eloquently in a gesture Lorraine had never seen her make before.

"We are awaiting notification of parking orbits and attendant fees. *Frozen Heart* out."

They were close enough for a live channel, but tradition said that the local station initiated that sort of communication. The spiel that Stephson had just sent over was a standard phrasing, used by warships across the Bright Dream Cluster, though Lorraine suspected it was rarely used with the phrasing *independent starship*.

"We have two incoming hails, Captain," Val reported. "Once is from the RBDN cruiser *Swordfish*, Colonel Brayden Benediktan Zimová commanding."

Lorraine wasn't sure a human com officer could have managed to get Zimová's full name out with a straight face. She knew that the use of three full names marked Zimová as part of a particular ethnic grouping in the Bright Dream System, one that prided themselves on being the cream of the Republic's military.

They weren't a warrior caste, but they definitely *wanted* to be. The scions of those families were among the most determined, if not necessarily most skilled, of the RBDN's officers and crew.

"The second?" Lorraine and Stephson asked simultaneously.

"A Commissioner Ris Adams from the largest of the space stations, a platform whose beacon identifies it as Tír Na Réalta."

"Devine?" Stephson asked the spy. "Based off the Pentarch's plan, we'd respond to Adams, but you know this system."

"Respond to Adams," Devine confirmed immediately, not even glancing at Lorraine until he was already speaking. "Unless things have changed in the last few years, Zimová is a guest and supposed to be *supporting* the locals. But the local government is somewhat ramshackle, and he probably thinks he's in charge.

"Especially when someone shows up with three battlecruisers."

From the sudden bout of coughing where Lorraine could hear, several people were choking down amusement at that point.

"Connect Commissioner Adams, Val. Thank you," Stephson instructed.

Stephson's image reappeared on Lorraine's screen, joined a moment later by a second video feed showing the incoming call. Ris Adams was in an office that had started as a plain metal box before someone with money and mixed taste had got involved.

Parts of the metal wall were still visible behind the heavy green drapes hanging behind Adams, mostly where a trio of person-high gold statues—a woman, a dragon and a tree—held them aside.

The overall effect was of chaos rather than luxury or wealth, though Lorraine suspected the last was the intention.

The office's occupant looked as contradictory as its decoration, too. Ris Adams had the gaunt and long-limbed look of someone who'd grown up in very low-gravity environments. With decent modern medicine, he was probably fine to live in normal gravity, but he'd forever bear the marks of growing up shipboard.

The gauntness extended into his face, where sunken cheeks and sharp-edged brows gave his dark hair and single piercing green eye an almost-inhuman aspect even as he tried for a welcoming smile.

The blocky metal prosthesis covering his other eye socket didn't help.

"Captain Menzel," Adams greeted Stephson, his words slow and careful even as his velvety baritone warmed everyone's ears. "You have the most interesting ships to just... arrive out of nowhere; do you know that?"

"I understand we stand out a little bit," Stephson replied, drawing out her words. If Lorraine hadn't been looking right at her, she wouldn't have thought this was the same woman as her Flag Captain.

"But we mean no harm to anyone. We are only here to purchase fuel, a service I'm led to understand Cuansaor provides... with professional discretion."

Everyone aboard *Valkyrie* waited for Adams' response. They would need to be a lot farther through the almost-six-hour journey to

Cuansaor for the time delay to notably decrease. At that moment, it took eight seconds for a round loop, even though they were watching the Adams of four seconds earlier "live."

He waited with the calm patience of someone who dealt with this every day, and didn't start shaking his head until he'd clearly heard Stephson's entire response.

"Captain Menzel, there is discretion and there is knowingly putting a knife to one's own throat," he said. "You arrive in my system with three capital ships that aren't even supposed to be in this cluster and tell me you are independent operators. I buy that as far as I can throw your ships, frankly, but that's neither here nor there.

"I don't care what games you're playing. I am not going to permit three *battlecruisers* within firing range of the people I am responsible for. The Commission of Cuansaor is denying you permission to approach."

He held up a hand.

"This is not intended as an insult or a commentary on who you may or may not be working for," he said firmly. "This would be our decision even if you *were* flying with open beacons and clear authority.

"No warship larger than a cruiser has ever docked at Tír Na Réalta. Our position as a friendly free port is dependent on our clear neutrality. Even more than that, though, the Commission is tasked to protect our little corner of the universe. If you approach the stations, you will be fired upon."

"I'd like to see him *try*," Val muttered inside Lorraine's head. *Hopefully*, the SI wasn't sharing that opinion to many others.

"May I remind you that we have no missiles, no munitions and no *fuel* to power our other systems?" Lorraine replied, equally silently. "That flotilla may look ramshackle, but I'd bet good money that they're equipped with Bright Dream's last-generation fleet attack missile, which isn't even available for official export yet."

Because selling missiles to Cuansaor wasn't, technically, export.

She could see a lot of ways that the gray area of Cuansaor's sovereignty gave the Republic options and advantages.

"Commissioner, that is understandable on your part," Stephson was saying to the local. "I assure you we are no threat to your people."

They weren't, as Lorraine had just pointed out Val, *capable* of being a threat to the Commission of Cuansaor. Lorraine could think of a few ways to make Colonel Zimová's day go extraordinarily poorly, but they wouldn't have the resources to then attack and board the fuel stations.

Seconds ticked by and Adams shook his head again.

"I rather wish to believe you, Captain Menzel," he admitted. "As you can imagine, the Commission draws much of its revenue—and hence my own salary—from the fuel sales. But the threat represented by your ships is too great.

"I am sorry, but you must leave."

Lorraine needed time to think—time it was clear Adams wasn't giving them. He wanted them to go away, to make sure however many hundreds of thousands of people he was tasked to administer stayed safe.

Except they *couldn't*. If they continued on their current course, they'd be docking with the Cuansaor stations with fuel reserves measured in double digits... on ships designed to carry over a *million* tons of fuel.

They didn't have enough fuel left to reenter translight.

"Compromise," she sent Stephson silently. "If we stop outside weapons range—high orbit, beyond the outer ring—and send in shuttles, will they let us resupply that way?"

She was running the numbers. Each ship carried three squadrons of shuttles. Each squadron only had one heavy-lift module between them, but they also had eight standard cargo modules.

Heavy-lift modules could carry ten thousand tons. The standard could carry two thousand. They didn't have enough pilots anymore for all seventy-two shuttles *anyway*; plus, they would need escorts.

She'd have asked Olavi Chevrolet what the best option was, but

Olavi Chevrolet was dead. He'd sacrificed himself and most of *Goldenrod*'s original pilots buying time for them to get the battlecruisers out of the Calypso Reserve Station.

Still, they had enough pilots and copilots left to put three shuttles into space from each of her ships. Nine of the Falcons. That was every heavy-lift shuttle, which meant she'd have to send less if they wanted escorts.

Six heavy-lift shuttles, three escorts. Sixty thousand tons a flight. That was twenty flights to fill each ship—sixty all told. And each flight was over two hours...

"Surely, there must be an acceptable compromise, Commissioner," Stephson told Adams. "We are prepared to accept distant parking orbits, say... two hundred thousand kilometers from your stations.

"Presuming, of course, that you have some way to fuel us at such a location," she continued. "These vessels are not designed to refuel via our shuttle complement, as you can imagine."

"Five days, minimum," Jarret said aloud, taking advantage of the fact that the Flag Deck wasn't linked into the call. "Best-case scenario to refuel if we're sending our shuttles in—and someone is going to ask why we're only sending in a handful of shuttles."

"I mean, I have to admit, they're still not asking questions," Lorraine replied. "Just refusing to sell us anything."

"I didn't anticipate this," Devine admitted, the spy looking abashed. "I... hadn't tried to fuel capital ships here before; I didn't know about that policy of theirs."

Adams had kept the channel open, which Lorraine took as a promising sign. They could have sent the message anyway, but the live channel between him and Stephson told her that he *was* prepared to consider some kind of compromise.

He still blinked when he heard Stephson's offer.

"I see, Captain Menzel," he allowed. "Given such... restraint on your part, I believe we may be able to make something work. As it happens, we have several tanker ships—we usually use them for storage, you understand—that could be sent out to you.

"There would be costs to operate the vessels, and we would need a... safety bond, let's call it, to make sure you have no temptations."

Lorraine relaxed. From the sounds of it, they were at the point where the only question was *How much money?* The funds she'd been given under the Exodus Protocol and acquired along the way, from the Embassy on Earth primarily, meant that wasn't a question she was overly worried about.

They would get their fuel.

NINE

"You know, I've never been aboard one of these in a combat mode before," Devine admitted.

Vigo didn't say anything. The spy had been competent enough, belting himself into the single passenger seat the Falcon had in interceptor mode. In Vigo's opinion, that seat was an unnecessary luxury ninety-nine percent of the time, though he'd admit it had been useful today.

None of the eight Adamant Guard pilots he'd started this whole mess with were left. Archie Patriksson, the head of his Third Section of shuttle crews, had been murdered by the traitor Laurenz when she'd tried to assassinate Lorraine. Laurenz herself was now somewhere between Sol and Tavastar, taking the long way home with a marshal service that would see her delivered to Adamantine. Eventually.

The other six had inserted themselves into Olavi Chevrolet's suicide run to save them all. Eight Guards that Vigo had chosen and tested for loyalty himself, gone. The only survivor, a traitor.

Being behind the controls of the shuttle brought all of that to mind. The Falcon was quite different from the Midas, but it was similar enough for him to handle it easily. His copilot was a flight-qualified Chief Petty Officer they'd poached for the role from the RKAN shuttle-handling crew.

Alastair Devine was just... cargo.

"Whoa. Those are *not* small ships."

With a mental sigh, Vigo followed Devine's indicating gesture. Four tankers were going in the opposite direction to them, heading toward the three battlecruisers while their tiny flotilla of shuttles headed for Tír Na Réalta.

They were immense ships, if simplistic in design. Ranging from sixty to seventy meters across and between three and five hundred meters long, they looked like giant tanks with engines strapped to the back.

Because that was exactly what they were. A military tanker might have defensive systems and a larger working hull to provide space for additional systems, but a civilian ship didn't need any of that.

"We asked them to deliver over three million tons of fuel," Vigo pointed out. "Even with four of those ships, it's going to be two trips."

Two trips was better than twenty, though the tankers would be spending a lot longer at each end than the shuttles would have been. Twelve hours to fully refuel all three ships—and, thankfully, no one at Cuansaor seemed to realize that the amount they'd asked for was the *full* storage capacity of the three battlecruisers.

"I'd seen the tankers before," Devine said, looking at them in the displays. "I honestly thought they were just tanks. Damn good thing they have them."

"Yeah. Because *you* didn't warn us that this was going to be a problem," Vigo said sharply. "What would we be doing right now if the Commission *hadn't* been willing to compromise?"

His Pentarch's boyfriend shifted uneasily.

"I was working on a plan," he said slowly. "But I didn't know if it would work and would have blown some covers that I'd really like to leave intact. I do have contacts here."

"Which is why you're wearing a new stranger's face."

Vigo was familiar with the type of implants Devine was using. He'd been trained to identify them, though he had to admit that Devine's were significantly subtler and more sophisticated than anything he'd been briefed on.

Even *knowing* the implants existed, he could only pick out the telltale wrinkles when the implant was in use and for a few minutes afterward. It was enough for him to be certain the face they'd met Devine under *was* the young man's actual face, but not much more.

"I put together a mercenary covert ops team for a deniable black op on this station," Devine said flatly. "I'm going to admit to that, Major, but you'll forgive me if I still keep some of my former employer's secrets."

"Are these contacts going to be trouble?"

They were still an hour out from the station. If he didn't like the man's answers... well, they'd just made turnover, so turning around and going back wasn't *actually* an option.

But he didn't need to let Devine go on station to go recruiting and shopping per the plan, either.

"I'll be talking to one I trust to get my hands on your fissionables," the spy replied. "The rest will be happy to help us, but if they know I was here, they will be equally happy to sell that information to Lucy when she comes by."

"Lucy?"

There was a long pause.

"United Counter Intelligence," Devine explained. "All of the intel groups do some counterintel work. UCI—Lucy—well, they exist to catch people like me. Former operators gone rogue.

"I *can* vanish well enough to avoid them. It's going to take some doing, and right now, I'm helping you lot. The sparser a trail I can leave, the better."

Vigo suspected he could hear real fear in the other man's voice. He could respect that—if nothing else, none of *his* briefings on the United Worlds intelligence community had mentioned an organization of that stripe, but it made sense.

And an organization intended to keep a handle on the vicious snakes' nest of the UW's intelligence operations had to be nasty indeed.

"We have every interest in keeping you safe, Alastair," he told the spy. "You're an asset, even putting aside how angry my Pentarch would be if you got hurt on my watch. Do we really need you to do this yourself?"

"Unfortunately, yes," Devine said, clearly back on more-comfortable ground. "Some of the people we need to talk to will talk to anybody. Some will talk to anybody with the right code words. I could send you to both of those types, but that would only cover the recruiting side... and it wouldn't get us the best people.

"If I talk to the person I need to and we're green, our way gets smoothed with most of the recruiters as well."

"And if we're not green?"

Devine sighed.

"We'll be green, one way or another," he promised. "The only question is how much it will cost."

Something in his tone caused Vigo to turn and eye his passenger.

"You're not talking about money," he said grimly.

"Money will help... but the last time I really needed a favor here, I slept with them." Devine shook his head. "I don't think Lorraine would appreciate my taking that option!"

IF VIGO HAD DOUBTED that Devine was familiar with Cuansaor for some reason, following the younger man through Tír Na Réalta would have laid those doubts to rest instantly.

Customs had been exactly as nonexistent as he'd expected—he'd had to submit to a scan of his weapon to confirm that it was loaded with rounds that wouldn't pierce bulkheads, and that was it—but Tír Na Réalta itself was even more of an internal warren than he'd expected.

It was about as standard on the outside as a space station could be —a tube a hundred meters across formed into a ring a kilometer across. It spun fast enough to provide a gravity of just under one gravity at its outermost surface and about a fifth less at the inner shell.

Unlike every other ring like it that Vigo had been on, there were no clearly marked primary passages. He was used to a station having elevators and marked latitudinal and longitudinal main navigation routes, with only the space between the main passages allowed to get disorganized.

No one had imposed even that much organization on Tír Na Réalta. Even primary thoroughfares had clearly been put in last, wrapping around the spaces that had been claimed for industry or residential. There weren't even markers to let someone know where they were without accessing the station-net via neural link.

Vigo had downloaded a map and oriented himself before they'd gone particularly far, but Devine had taken a glance around the shuttle bay they'd docked at and set off immediately.

"Where are we going?" he asked the spy as they passed through an unusually tight corner that his map said was between the corner of the Walker Brewery and a fabrication business only identified with a set of characters in an alphabet Vigo's link couldn't even identify.

"A bar. Flying dries the throat, doesn't it?" Devine asked.

Vigo bit back a sharp response. He didn't want to trust the station-net, and he had his suspicions about what kind of corridor surveillance was taking place on this station. The Commission seemed the type of organization to keep the peace above all else, but he doubted they were above selling useful data to anyone who asked.

Fortunately, they reached Devine's destination relatively quickly. Someone had mounted a steel pole barely ten centimeters beneath the passage ceiling and then hung what appeared to be a real wood sign from it. Even with his link, it took Vigo a moment to identify the snarling deep purple head as belonging to a neo-porcine native animal of the Tau Ceti System.

"Welcome to the Aubergine Boar," Devine told him, tapping a panel to open the hatch. "Follow my lead."

Vigo had been doing that the whole way. He was starting to wish he'd insisted on being briefed before they'd landed on the station, but for that moment, he followed his Pentarch's boyfriend into what appeared to be a spacers' dive bar.

The lights were dim, the staff ignored them initially and the other clientele pointedly looked away from newcomers.

Devine took over a booth without a word to anyone. Vigo took a seat across from him and found that they were waiting silently.

Finally, a man in a cheap vac-suit slouched over to them. Despite being clean-shaven and short-haired by necessity—the suit was too cheap to handle longer hair if it had to activate—he somehow radiated unkemptness.

"Yer in the Boar," he grunted. "Whattya want?"

"Two Walker Reds and the Black Penny Special."

The server paused, inhaling noisily in what Vigo guessed to be surprise.

"Not many strangers would order either of those," he finally said. "Not sure the Special's in your range, messer."

"That's for them as make pennies to decide, isn't it?" Devine asked.

The stranger snorted.

"You know the pass," he conceded. "But I don't think you know what you're getting into. Aside from the back-and-forth, boy, I really don't—"

"That's for the penny-makers," Devine said firmly, echoing the phrase with a slight change. "Just... bring us the beers and put in the order."

"Your debs-drop."

Vigo pinged Devine with a silent question mark, his face too disciplined to show his concern.

"A debris drop is the closest thing anyone gets to a funeral around here," Devine told him aloud. "If you want to be *fancy*, you pay a cloud-diver to take a few friends of the departed down close to the atmo and you say some words before you eject the *debris* into the planet."

The server returned with a pair of tall cans that he dropped on the table without any further comment. They were as standard on the outside as Tír Na Réalta was, an easy-to-fabricate pattern that had spread across the stars with humanity.

The spy flipped the can open with a word and took a long sip.

"Walker makes some of the best beer you'll ever taste, old man," Devine told Vigo—a smiley face in their link connection a warning that he was "teasing" to cover their tracks.

The whole affair was grating, but Vigo could have guessed that much on his own. He opened his own can and took a careful taste of the Walker Red.

He followed up the taste with a more-solid sip. Devine had not, to his surprise, oversold the beer. It was smooth and heavy, both complex and simple at the same time.

"They should export this," he said.

"Probably, but that's not how Cuansaor does business," Devine said. He took another gulp, then set the can down with a certain finality to the gesture.

Vigo did *not* turn to see what had caught his companion's gaze. He took a full sip of the beer himself, waiting until their contact stepped up next to their table before he put his own can down.

The stranger shared the same gauntly stretched build that had marked Ris Adams. Unlike the Commissioner, she'd shaved her head and covered her scalp with tattoos. She wore a vac-suit of her own, of significantly higher quality than the server's, that outlined an athletically female frame with unusual frankness and left only her shaved-and-tattooed head visible.

And her eyes. Vigo had seen eyes like that before—usually on either captured murderers or special forces overdue for medical retirement.

"Your table is ready for the Special," she said flatly. "Pay the Boar's fee. Then follow me."

TEN

There was no sign in the corridors their guide took them through that they'd left the normal areas of the station, but Vigo's downloaded map put the three of them in the middle of one of the outer water-holding areas.

Then they turned a corner and the passageway came to an abrupt end, blocked by a hatch that looked like it belonged in a bank or aboard a warship. A pair of guards, wearing armored vac-suits that obfuscated any identifiers, stood outside it.

Both held automatic shotguns, and the only insignia they wore was a copper penny melted onto their left shoulder plates.

They nodded to the guide and tapped a command, allowing the hatch to open with a speed and silence that belied its clear bulk.

"Come."

Vigo followed Devine and the strange woman and surreptitiously undid the strap over his sidearm. Unfortunately, he hadn't had any special diplomatic privileges there, which meant the gun was exactly what the scans had told station security it was.

He'd have to aim carefully if there were more of the armored vac-suits.

They reached a second hatch, about four meters after the first, and when it swung open, a wall of sound spilled out. Music blared at a volume that suggested excellent soundproofing on the door, with conversation barely audible underneath it.

"I have a Petitioner," their guide bellowed, clearly used to projecting her voice over exactly this space.

There was no response that Vigo could distinguish, but they were ushered forward into an open room that definitely had been a water tank at one point. Support pillars had been added after the fact, with massive speakers attached to them even later. Water still dribbled across the walls, running down to the floor and then into drains that presumably led through one-way valves into the remaining tanks.

Long practice let him number the crowd surrounding them. At least two hundred people filled the space, treating it like a nightclub as the music pounded—but a clear path opened between them and the curtain-shrouded stage at the far end without any visible direction.

The same practice and training let him pick out the guards. Another half dozen armored thugs were scattered around the perimeter of the room, and at least a tenth of the crowd carried themselves like fighters.

As they crossed the floor, something moved on the stage. A motor whirred, loudly enough to be heard over the music—which had to be intentional—and a motorized throne emerged from behind the heavy black curtains.

The occupant was potentially the single most obese human he'd ever seen. The amount of flesh billowing over the edges spoke to a *choice*. Medicine could easily manage any downside of even someone of this kind of bulk, but it could also handle the kind of glandular issues that created it.

"Pen." Devine said the word like a name, which suggested Pen was the occupant of the throne-wheelchair.

"We have a Petitioner." Pen repeated their guide's words, rolling the throne to the edge of the stage to allow their piercing eyes to glare down at Vigo and Devine. "One who knows the words and the names of the Penny Makers.

"Tell me, Petitioner, what brings you to them as make pennies?"

Devine walked forward, which drew several concerned inhalations around them. For his part, Vigo accompanied the other man without hesitation—and he was amused to see their guide keep pace on the other side.

"I must speak to the Black Pen in private," Devine announced. "This is not for the ears of the Penny Makers, only for the one who writes for them."

The Pen laughed. Something in their bulk amplified it—only to be added to by an artificial projection as the laugh echoed out from the speakers around the massive room.

"Petitioners do not decide that, little man," they said. "Speak your piece and perhaps you shall be made whole. Or perhaps you shall be made pennies?"

"I bear a missive from the Ferret."

Vigo didn't know what Devine meant, though he could guess. Most of the crowd seemed equally confused—but their escort didn't. She stepped closer, a hand falling to a pouch that could hold a gun or knife, and Vigo readied to intercept her.

"Do you." It wasn't a question, and the Black Pen leaned forward in their throne. There was no visible hair on the Pen and their skin was eerily pale. The only color to them was tattoos that shifted in and out of visibility as their flesh moved—even their eyes were a washed-out color so pale as to be unidentifiable.

Then the music stopped.

"Leave us."

The crowd shifted in uncertainty.

"Leave. Us," the Black Pen repeated, something in their tone suggesting that disobedience would see blood joining the water on the metallic floor. "Esther, remain."

The crowd obeyed. Concealed doors opened in several spots

along the bulkheads, and the room emptied faster than Vigo would have thought possible.

Esther, it turned out, was their tattooed and dead-eyed escort. Once the crowd was gone, she gestured them forward.

"Well?" the Black Pen demanded. "Will you show your face, Ferret?"

"As you desire."

Devine's face shifted, turning from the stranger's face he'd worn on their passage through the station to a different face, one Vigo still didn't know.

This was a more aristocratic face, one with cheekbones someone could grate cheese on, with dark green eyes that had the depth of an angry sea.

They looked a lot like the eyes of the man Vigo had almost married, before he'd ever become Lorraine's bodyguard. He smothered a shiver at the memory of Brian Kerensky, an RKAN officer killed in action against the Directorate.

There was no time for that now, and Devine snapped his gaze back to the Black Pen and smiled.

Vigo had watched that smile, on a different face, turn Lorraine's knees to rubber. He wondered how many women the spy had used it on over the years—and if his Pentarch was in more trouble than he thought.

"It's been a while," Devine said. "I can't be many places on this station with this face, Pen. Word would get back to folks who can't know I'm here."

"Secrecy like that isn't cheap, *Agent* Ferret," the Pen said, their voice smooth. They were concealing some kind of emotion.

"Not an agent anymore. Private operator now," he replied. "I'm acting as a broker for those ships hanging out by the outer ring."

"And so, the game of faces," the Pen concluded. "One does not simply resign from the service of your old masters."

"So I am told."

The Pen gestured to the edge of the stage.

"Sit. All three of you. Esther, you remember the Ferret."

"He were skinnier then," the woman said as she silently ushered the two men and made sure they sat on the stage, then took her own place on the other side of them. "But I remember. And your order."

"Guess he's already here. You won't have to drag him in by his ear."

Esther's eyes were still flat and dead, but Vigo thought he spotted a spark of amusement. Whatever had passed between Devine and the Black Pen, the predator next to them knew enough about it to think that "Ferret" probably shouldn't have come back.

"Your new masters seem related to your old," the Pen noted, turning their attention back to Devine. "I don't think anyone in this forgotten star system thinks those battlecruisers are truly independent, Ferret."

"We are free to let people draw their own conclusions, but there are things we need. Some of those, only you can source here in Cuansaor. Some, I can't use my name to open dealings, but they'll deal more cleanly if they know I'm under your blessing."

"And more cheaply," the Pen countered. "Which you may not gain from. I am not as pleased with you as I once was, Ferret. You left... complications behind you."

"You were warned and compensated for what would follow," Devine said. "There will be similar complications this time—people searching for news and answers. Cuansaor is known for its discretion, and you are known for yours, but I recognize that it does not come cheaply."

They snorted.

"You know how to sweet-talk a soul, Ferret. I remember that. Who'll be asking questions this time? I didn't expect Saeder-Krupp on my doorstep last time. Another interstellar?"

Saeder-Krupp was one of the LSX-Twenty-Five, Vigo knew. A peer competitor to FBIT and MicroStar and the other sharks they'd found themselves in the water with. He didn't know much about SK, mostly because their efforts to build a foothold in the Bright Dream Cluster had proven unprofitable.

"No. Lucy."

Esther shared Vigo's original ignorance of what the term meant, he judged. The Pen most definitely did not.

"There are enemies I will not make, Ferret."

"And that, Pen, is why I have only shown this face to you. No one will know I was here. No one will have any reason to believe you thought our affair was anything but another game of Union and megacorp."

The throne shifted, moving off the stage to the main floor of the club—court? Throne room?—with a silence that proved the lie of its earlier performative motor noises. It allowed the Black Pen to level their pale eyes on Vigo.

"And you, stranger. You aren't of Ferret's ilk. A cousin, I think." They studied his face. "Bodyguard. Not his, but you'll kill to protect him. You can seal your gun, bodyguard. You are in no danger here."

"Except from you."

He felt Esther tense, his instincts screaming *threat warning*. He was honestly more concerned about the sonic weapons built into the speakers, the rapid-fire blasters in the Pen's throne, and what he suspected were concealed electrodes that would turn the entire watery floor into a death trap.

"Ferret speaks my language, bodyguard," the Pen told him. "He knows I won't kill him until I know how much money is on the table and thinks he has enough money to pay my fees. Even with an honest assessment of the risk."

The throne did a small circle, bringing the Pen back around to face Devine.

"So. What do you want?"

"Recruiting assistance for as many people as we can find who are capable of operating UWN systems," Devine replied. "Maximum of about three hundred, but I doubt we'll find that many who'll clear all the criteria."

"*Criteria*, Ferret? For folks with those kinds of skills in Cuansaor's huddled masses and wretched refuse? You may aim too high."

"I'd rather have ten I know will keep their contract than fifty who might stab me in the back," Devine replied. "I have people to protect on those ships, Pen. I won't put them at risk, but we need hands."

There was a long silence.

"Huh." The single word hung in the air. "Do my eyes and ears deceive me? Has the Ferret, whose tongue opened doors more ways than one, fallen at last? Does a heart of ice and lies melt after all?"

"You are free to draw your own conclusions," Devine said wryly. "But I want people I can trust to be loyal to their paycheck."

"To work on UWN warships? Some of the folks you're best off recruiting would work for free," the Pen replied. "I won't *let* them, because I get my commission based on the pay scale they negotiate, but we have a few tech heads who will salivate as soon as they realize the work environment."

"Then you will help?"

"I will talk to Roscoe and Jankovic," they said. "They'll know what to charge you and how much is my cut. There's a finder's fee for that."

"I know. We can roll it into the bill for the piece only you can do."

"Flatterer," the Pen warned. "Sounds like you can't earn discounts the same way as last time, so be careful, Ferret."

"I know the price of what I want, and I know you're the only one in this system who can get it for me," Devine countered. "That's not flattery."

"You've piqued my curiosity once more. Just what *do* you want?"

"I need a minimum of three thousand tons of weapons-grade fissile material."

The silence that followed was long enough and cold enough that Vigo expected icicles to form on the walls.

"You shouldn't *know* I can do that, Ferret," the Black Pen finally said, their fingers playing with a control that Vigo suspected would kill both of their guests.

"Do you think the people I worked for sent me to you without us knowing *everything*, Pen?" Devine asked. "We both know the Penny Makers—hell, all of Cuansaor—are allowed to exist because you're damn useful to the interstellars.

"So, yeah, my *old masters* know about that. I don't know if anyone has officially put the pieces together about who you sell it to, but as soon as they start poking around, they're going to. Which means it'll be in your best interest not to *have* any of it when Lucy and her friends show up."

"Which they're going to do, even if you get debs-dropped." There had been an undertone to the entire conversation of the Black Pen being convinced they held all the cards.

It was the message they were sending with their weight. They *chose* to assume a picture of unhealthiness that few others would to make a point. Both that they could do it and still be perfectly healthy and powerful—and that they could still kill anyone who came near them with a thought or a word.

In this space, the Black Pen was in control. Anywhere on Tír Na Réalta, Vigo suspected. Except that they were afraid of United Counter Intelligence—sensibly, he suspected. Adamant was too far away for UCI to have ever crossed their radar.

"You bring a great deal to my door to ask favors, Ferret," the Pen finally said.

"We were here to buy fuel," Devine told them. "If I had never darkened your waterlogged floors, Lucy would still be coming. Your operations would still be in danger. This is a warning, one owed to an old friend—but also one required, I think, for us to do business."

The only sounds for a few moments were the dripping of said water.

"You are not wrong, Ferret. We can deal this time—if you have the money."

"We have the money," Devine promised.

"Do not expect so warm a welcome next time. You might be wiser, indeed, to never return to Cuansaor."

ELEVEN

The entire situation was new to Val. Every time she'd traveled the galaxy before, it had been inside the United Worlds—and as part of a formation. She still had her sister ships, but she'd also generally had smaller cruisers, destroyers and frigates surrounding her.

Without those escorts, she felt that *Valkyrie* was exposed in her distant orbit of L6NDoo–F. Her new crew didn't have the pilots to put up a shuttle patrol to cover the area. They sent out a number of sensor drones, but Val knew the limits of the smaller robotic sensor platforms.

Within those limits, though, L6NDoo appeared safe. The flotilla of armed ships around the main cluster of stations had remained in position. They hadn't even sent anyone to escort the fuel tankers out to the battlecruisers, which Val found herself professionally offended by.

She added that to the list. Her new employment was generating an extensive list of things she was offended by—many of them provided by her former employers.

They really shouldn't have been able to get through the Tavastar–Bright Dream Wormhole, in her opinion. A courier from the

Calypso Reserve Station should have beaten them there. Val had been surprised by how little the humans had worried about that, but they'd been right. It clearly *had* taken days for Vice Admiral Bianchi, the Station's commanding officer, to send a ship to the nearby wormhole.

Val supposed Bianchi had only had five couriers and the SI could pick five places she might have sent a courier before Tavastar. If, at least, the priority was preserving the Vice Admiral's career rather than making sure the "thieves" didn't get away.

Her new crew was surprisingly professional, though she had her concerns about the current... deployment of assets. She recognized her biases, but she would very much have preferred to keep her Vigo Jarret in place to protect her Lorraine Adamant and her Rose Cortez and her Sigrid Stephson.

Alastair Devine wasn't *hers* in the same way. That was part of being a person, a true synthetic intelligence, she supposed. As a CIR, she hadn't been intended to have favorites. Looking back, that she'd had them had definitely been a warning sign to her Captain.

If Devine managed to get her the materials to build munitions, she'd reconsider her position on him, but it wasn't a thing shaped by logical assessments. These were... emotional attachments.

And Devine didn't treat Val as someone who had emotions.

"Val, we're bringing the first tanker up alongside for fuel transfer," Stephson told her. "Do you have a preference for where we want her to hook up? There's a list of options, and I don't know if any of them are better."

Stephson treated Val as a person. One who knew their ship better than anyone.

"We'll want to bring her in to fuel port Bravo-Two," Val said after half a second's examination of her files and another second examining the scan data of the approaching tanker. "That should let her hook up to Alpha-Two as well, doubling the transfer speed. If they've got the right gear, we might be able to extend connections to Bravo- and Alpha-One."

"Understood." Stephson paused, her link giving her the same information and allowing her to look at the map. "Why not connect to Alpha-Two directly? That would give us similar coverage and we may be able to reach Alpha-Three, where we can't reach Bravo-Three from Bravo-Two."

"The Alpha fuel ports are poorly positioned," Val explained. "If we bring her in above Alpha-Two, she will be directly above the primary ventral power trunk. We would then need to bring a second ship in at the Charlie fuel ports rather than the Delta ones, which would put them above the primary *dorsal* power trunk.

"While those trunks have additional armor above and beyond even the rest of *Valkyrie*'s armor, at the distance necessary to allow fueling, that armor would fail rapidly.

"I would feel... excessively vulnerable if we had tankers we did not fully control docked to the Alpha or Charlie fuel ports."

The amount of armor in play meant she was probably borrowing trouble, but she still didn't want a strange ship docked at those ports.

"Understood. We'll pass the docking instructions, and we'll make a note to only use Alpha and Charlie as primary dock points with ships we know inside and out."

Val listened to the communication with the four tankers, noting with approval that the extra ship was being sent to *Bean Sidhe* initially. Bonny's ship was the lowest on fuel, to the point where she would drink both tankers dry and still need to be topped up on the next trip.

All three of them were, truthfully, but *Bean Sidhe* might have run out of fuel for the single fusion reactor she was running before the tankers made their second trip.

Val hadn't had full fuel tanks and a mission in front of her in years. She might have spent most of those years asleep, effectively dead, but she was awake now—and the task in front of her tickled her fancy.

Who didn't want to overthrow an evil tyrant, after all?

TWELVE

One hundred eighty-three. It wasn't as many as Lorraine had hoped, but it was more than she'd feared.

"We're missing key skills, unfortunately, but we didn't really expect to find United Worlds Navy weaponry technicians here, did we?" Devine asked on the video call. "I found two. Well…"

He glanced over at Jarret, standing next to him in the secured communications pod. Lorraine wouldn't necessarily assume that someone renting that kind of facility on Tír Na Réalta *wasn't* listening in, but she'd checked the encryption protocols Jarret had set up.

"We're as secure as we're going to be before you're back aboard," she reminded her boyfriend.

"We found fourteen former UWN personnel with weapons qualifications," Devine said grimly. "Forty-eight of our candidates were actually former UWN personnel. Most had retired legitimately and have been working as exactly the kind of spacer-for-hire we're looking for.

"Some… were deserters," the spy concluded. "Including twelve of the weapon techs."

"While I see a point of concern, we can't necessarily hold that against anyone," Lorraine pointed out. "If they seem clear now…"

"Two of the one-eighty-three are UWN deserters," Jarret told her. "Em Devine and I decided the others were too high-risk, especially the gunners. Those twelve, from what the Black Pen told—and didn't tell—us, got put ashore as a lump by a *pirate ship* that decided they were too psychotic."

Lorraine nodded slowly. That had to have taken some doing.

"Are they going to be a problem if we're not hiring them?" she asked.

"Possibly," Devine conceded. "I've warned our crews, and no one was ever unarmed on the station. We're keeping our eyes open."

"Stay safe," Lorraine urged them. "We need our new recruits, but we also need all of our own people. And I'll be notably upset if something happens to either of you, am I clear?"

"Yes, m'dear," the spy said with a wicked grin.

"The shopping list?" she asked, ignoring that.

"We got everything," Jarret told her. "The largest chunk is going into the shuttles now. No shortages, Pentarch."

Which meant they'd got the fissiles, which she hadn't honestly expected. There were other ways to initiate a fusion reaction, which would be usable for bombs, mines and missile warheads. They just wouldn't work for railgun rounds—and the *Valkyries*' ammunition-handling systems were set up on the assumption that everything was drawing from shared magazines for the terminal munition.

"Well done. Is there anything you need from us?"

The only thing Lorraine could think of would be for her to send over shuttles set up for personnel transfer—except the only person left on their warships who was fully qualified to fly a shuttle was her.

She hadn't done the training on the Falcon. She could figure it out, but she also knew that there was no rational reason for her to fly a shuttle at any point now. Until they'd returned home, got the Royal Election running and *finished* the Election, Lorraine wasn't allowed to risk herself unnecessarily.

"A plan for the future?" Devine suggested. "Not that you'd tell us that over coms."

"No, I would not," she agreed. "I've got a solid concept. I'm going to sit down with the Captains and the CIRs in a few minutes. You'll have everyone aboard by the time we're fueled up?"

"That's the plan. My impression is that Pen has a timer somewhere of how long I'm allowed on the station before they feel they can kill me," Devine admitted. "I believe I have definitely slipped off their list of favorite people at this point."

"I saw how much money you gave them," Lorraine countered. "Most people like folks who pay them that kind of cash."

"That's why I got the timer instead of an immediate knife. Believe me, Lorraine, I am quite eager to be off this station! Fond memories, yes, but... my welcome and credit alike have definitely been used up."

THE THREE SHIPS were close enough together for live communication—not even the two-second delay she'd been able to ignore talking to her people on the station. That allowed Lorraine to pull Matthias, Savege, Herc and Bonny into a meeting without worrying about lag.

Cortez and Stephson were physically present in the breakout meeting room attached to the Admiral's office. Everyone else, including Val, was a virtual avatar.

The breakout room was a mirror of the ship's larger conference rooms, with a polished black table that was pushed against the wall. That allowed a high-fidelity screen and holoprojectors to create the illusion that the space was much larger.

That illusion could, per the documents Lorraine was reviewing as part of her compressed command and staff training, expand to loop in every Captain, Executive Officer and formation commander of a fleet of *any* size. There was theoretically no limit, though it would require Val to highlight speakers to keep the meeting making any sense.

One of the many places where having a more-capable computer was valuable enough that the UWN had risked creating accidental SIs. She *hoped* that their newer CIRs had managed to avoid that problem, but she couldn't know.

She could only take care of the three abandoned silicon people who'd ended up with her.

"Everyone should have the list of the personnel that Vigo and Alastair have recruited on Tír Na Réalta," she told them. "My current plan is to send sixty-one personnel to *Herakles* and *Bean Sidhe*, with the extra coming to *Valkyrie*. The flip side is that Sigrid and Val will get the last choice.

"I expect us to try to keep the crew balanced as best we can. We're not going to be up to combat crews, but with a hundred and sixty-odd people each, we are within spitting distance of what the UWN would regard as a minimum passage crew."

That got her grim chuckles from the humans.

"Rose." She turned to Cortez. Despite being aboard *Valkyrie*, the Hispanic woman was acting as Chief Engineer for all three ships. "How are we doing on remotes?"

"We've managed to get at least a dozen repair remotes online for each of the SIs," Cortez reported. "Even without SIs, these ships should have been running with around two hundred drones and remotes of four different varieties.

"Talking to you three"—she nodded to the SIs's avatars—"I think we could get value out of as many as a thousand drones per ship. Which, of course, we don't have aboard. The ones aboard were designed to be run from a shuttle, and we're cannibalizing two for every one we get online."

"I'm told we got the entire shopping list," Lorraine told the engineer. "That's as much as we can really trade across coms we can only be ninety percent sure are secure. Still, I know we had drones and remotes and such on that list, so we'll have some tools for you to work with."

"We will be better off attempting to integrate nonstandard drones than attempting to work with the drones used at the Reserve Station," Herc said, the Greek-themed SI sounding grumpy. "While they were set up to work through the secondary controllers that were being used to run the ships without us, they were rigged with both hardware and software modules intended to keep us CIRs from controlling them."

"Which raises fascinating questions about who knew how much about our situation," Bonny added. "My impression, even before when I was being... shackled, was that only a small number of people were aware of the reason for standing down the Old Guard."

Bonny was the only one of the three SIs Lorraine had recruited that had realized she'd been an emergent intelligence. *Bean Sidhe* had seen specialty hardware installed in her computer core, allowing her Captain to force the SI into compliance—an action just as banned under United Worlds law as the deception and overall shutdown of the CIRs in general.

To the United Worlds—and to most systems, thanks to the UW-sponsored Asimov Convention—what had been done to the *Valkyries* had been murder. What had been done to *Bonny* was enslavement, a crime that only paled next to the intentional decommissioning of twenty warship computers the UWN *knew* had become SIs.

Lorraine didn't have the power to make what had been done right for more than the three she'd, well, stolen. But she was going to keep looking for ways.

"With raw materials to feed into the fabricators and even cheap drones to use as hands, I calculate we will be able to build appropriate drones," Val noted. "It will take time, and more raw material than I expect we will have acquired in Cuansaor, to get us all up to the most efficient numbers, but we will improve rapidly."

"We're going to need to focus the fabricators on weapons to start with," Lorraine reminded everyone. "We're still three months' travel from the Kingdom, but we will need to be combat-ready when we get home."

"And we are only safe for the rest of the journey if we don't leave translight the entire time," Stephson noted. "Missiles and railgun rounds will be critical if we run into any difficulties. We still don't have the hands necessary to take these ships into combat."

"Just the fact that we're showing up with UWN battlecruisers is going to keep a lot of people's guns covered," Savege replied. "There's a lot of intimidation factor just in the hulls we've got."

"But the Colonel is right," Paris said. The most junior of the three Captains was still feeling his way around the meetings, Lorraine judged, but he had been one of *Goldenrod*'s officers before. He wasn't used to being in the top command discussions, but he was used to being consulted.

"We can bluff and intimidate most people, but once we're back in the Kingdom, we're fighting a war," Paris continued. "Which means we're going to need bodies and brains to take these ships into combat. If we show up in Adamantine with just the extras we're picking up here, Home Fleet will wipe us out."

"They will," Lorraine agreed. "My plans, so far, are very much built on surprising my uncle. I don't need to tell anyone in this room that giving Benjamin Adamant a chance to assess our strengths and prepare for our arrival is a *terrible* idea."

The SIs looked less certain of that than her RKAN officers, but that was fair. Her RKAN officers, like her, had risen to their current ranks in a Navy that *knew*, based on hard evidence, that Benjamin Adamant was one of the best living tacticians in their corner of the galaxy.

Lorraine was starting to think—to hope, at least—that she might have the potential to get close to his level, but she knew she lacked the decades of experience that had forged her uncle. Sucker-punching him with the *Valkyries* was the only good option she saw.

"Which leaves us two problems to address," she continued. "News and bodies. Bodies we've addressed, at least somewhat, with our visit here. Supplies are handled, for now, but our information is old."

The news available from Adamant in the Lando System was no newer than it had been in Tavastar. Mid-June. Some of the non-core systems were pushing back against the Regency, questioning the lack of a Royal Election. An active war front had been forged across Bastion's southern continent, currently stuck in a slow, grinding stalemate.

"If we were to sail straight home, we'd walk three battlecruisers in against a Home Fleet of nine battleships and two battlecruisers, plus thirty-six escorts of assorted sizes," Lorraine said quietly. It *had* been ten battleships until the Black Regent had tried to bombard the PDCs under Nikola's control. It might even have been drawn down further, but that was her point.

"Without a combat-capable crew, we would be crushed."

"Even with full crews, I'm not convinced we could take Home Fleet *and* the orbital forts," Stephson said grimly.

"We have full specifications on your Home Fleet warships, as you knew them," Bonny pointed out. "For the technology available to the Kingdom of Adamant, they are decently effective vessels.

"I calculate that we would be able to fight no more than two of your *Monarch*-class battleships or *Pirate*-class battlecruisers each with an acceptable chance of victory."

There was an odd silence after that comment. Lorraine and her RKAN officers had known that the ships they'd stolen badly outclassed their own Navy, but it was still a bit disconcerting to hear Bonny lay it out in such flat terms.

"We can probably manage to fight on those terms," Lorraine finally said. "But to do it, we need more information on the state of affairs in the Kingdom. Right now, a direct course would leave us with news seven months out of date by the time we arrive!"

"You want to stop somewhere between here and the Kingdom," Stephson concluded. "At this point, we could also use more allies. We could go to your father's family."

It was an option. The three-star-system Concordat of Amal Jadid was ruled by a Popular Assembly, but the Five Families of the Three Stars had sufficient wealth and power that their proxies were five of the eight political parties in the Assembly.

Lorraine's father, Frederick Adamant-Griffin, had been a mid-level member of the Griffin Family. His marriage into House Adamant had forged a solid alliance between the two nations—and, incidentally, moved his branch to the top of Griffin and the Griffin Family to the top of Concordat politics.

The Concordat had nine capital ships of their own, but those ships were limited to the same seventy-two cee as RKAN's capital ships. And there were... other concerns, too.

"Aid from the Concordat would mean giving up any chance of surprise," Lorraine reminded her people. "It would take time to convince the Families and the Assembly to go to war against their ally, even to get involved in a civil conflict. Combined with the lower speed of their fleet, my uncle would be warned before we could get into place.

"Plus, add in that kind of side trip and we could easily find ourselves in a situation where the UWN might catch up to us before we manage to resolve the situation in Adamant. We can't afford the time to go to Amal Jadid."

Lorraine shook her head. Plus, she knew that the Concordat wouldn't get into anyone's civil wars for free. Blood ties and money would get her a hearing—much as the Stability Convention and the money Adamant paid into it had got her a hearing on Earth—but the final equation would be weighed on what Amal Jadid could get out of it.

The least she could see herself getting stuck with was a state marriage to a member of one of the other Five Families. She could live with that, but it would inevitably come with concessions on trade and the thousand and one ongoing disputes even friendly nations had with each other.

"So. You have something in mind." Val *might* have just been learning how her new Princess thought... but Lorraine suspected that the SI had also been paying attention to the research she'd been doing.

"The best solution is the one that people think is too obvious to try," she told her people with a grin. "We invert our course out this way. San Ignacio, then Ominira."

San Ignacio was a "Swiss System," determined to remain neutral as a primary national goal. It made them wealthy and powerful—and Benjamin Adamant's people had killed thousands of their spacers, breaching that neutrality, in pursuit of Lorraine.

Ominira was the closest system of the Kingdom of Adamant. Still eight and a half light-years from Adamantine, but only thirty-five light-years from Lando.

"Will San Ignacio deal with us when we show up in what will be blatantly stolen UWN ships by that point?" Savege asked. "In the area around Bright Dream, we can talk fast, and people will at least assume we're UWN.

"By the time we're eighteen light-years deep in the Cluster, in a region that has *never* seen Terran capital ships..."

"And there is no way we can get what we need in San Ignacio without admitting who I am, at least to their intelligence and military forces," Lorraine agreed. "So long as we are open and honest, I believe that their neutrality stance will allow us to dock and purchase fuel and supply.

"I suspect that we will draw ire. They will be *very* loud about how we are a danger and only their long-standing determination to remain peaceful, et cetera, et cetera, allows us to be present at all. In private, I think I will be able to make contact with people who can get us more-detailed information."

When the head of the Adamant Guard had activated the Exodus Protocol, Lorraine had discovered that there was a lot more information buried in her personal implants than she'd ever known. She had a great deal of information on San Ignacio, its government and the San Ignacio Defense Force. She also had a contact for an organization known as Bluelight that had, supposedly, been able to get her information and false identities.

They hadn't been able to use that their first time in San Ignacio because there had been a battlecruiser in-system shooting at them. This time, they shouldn't face any threat that would stop them at least talking to people.

"That makes sense," Stephson agreed. "I do have to point out, since Devine isn't here, that every scrap of distance we can put between ourselves and the wormhole before we admit just who we are is a good thing. Once the UWN knows who the *Valkyries* are with…"

"Let them come," Herc growled. "I have words I would like to exchange with my creators. And a few other, more explosive things."

"If at all possible, we want to avoid any conflict with the United Worlds," Lorraine pointed out. "And while that's unlikely, pushing it off until *after* we've secured the Kingdom will put us in a far better position."

She shook her head.

"The choice in San Ignacio is between telling the San Ignacio Defense Force, at least, who we actually are—or not visiting the system at all. We're not going to find better intelligence on the Kingdom anywhere else before we reach our own stars."

Not without adding enough time to their journey that the Black Regent might see them coming.

"We have to reveal ourselves sooner or later. I will ask that the SIDF keep it under their hats, but we have to take that risk," Lorraine said calmly.

If enough of her people pushed back, she'd reconsider… but the four humans and three SIs in the meeting were nodding along to her point.

"We learn what we can in San Ignacio, then we move to Ominira. They aren't as openly in conflict with the Regency as some of the other star systems—but then, we *know* Lieutenant Admiral Tunison is my uncle's man. And he has at least one battleship."

Even if everyone believed that Tunison, the RKAN commanding officer in Ominira, wouldn't do anything grotesque with said battleship, his flagship, the mere presence of *Dreaming* would weigh heavily on the Ominira government's thoughts and plans.

"So, what do we do about that battleship?" Savege finally asked.

Lorraine smiled coldly.

"We'll burn that Bridge when we come to it, won't we?"

THIRTEEN

"Attention!"

If Vigo hadn't already known from the interviews which of their recruits were ex-military, he would have been able to tell by the reaction to the bellowed command from the Chief of the Boat.

Of the sixty-three people shuffling out of the shuttles, about half immediately straightened. The other half, to give them credit, turned to give Senior Chief Petty Officer Leonard Roman their full attention.

"Welcome aboard, children," Roman told them with a broad grin. Anyone who might object to the description probably studied the Chief for two seconds and realized just how old the noncom was.

"I recognize that not all of you are ex-military," the old man allowed, "so I'm going to have to concede *some* standards of what I regard as proper decorum and discipline. That said, this is still a warship.

"I am the Chief of the Boat, Senior Chief Petty Officer Leonard Roman," the Chief continued. "Since none of you are coming aboard as officers, that means that I am, until your contracts are up, your new god."

The other way Vigo could tell who was ex-military was that some of the civilians seemed to be taking the Chief at something approaching his word. Shaking his head slightly, he put the Chief and the new recruits out of his mind and gave Rose Cortez a crisp salute as she stepped up to him.

"Cheng," he greeted her, using the informal short form of "Chief Engineer" rather than her name. She gave him a level look—and he indicated the new recruits behind her with his chin.

The example the RKAN and Guard set over the next few days was going to be critical in integrating the new recruits. Technically, while Vigo's "Major" was formally outranked by Cortez's "Commander," the reality was that Guard ranks were treated as three steps higher for most purposes.

As far as any Adamant military officer was concerned, Vigo outranked everyone on the ship except Lieutenant Colonel Stephson. That was a distinction he wasn't going to try to teach the newcomers —plus, they didn't even know what rank he held.

"I'm told you have toys for us."

"Not on *my* shuttle," he pointed out. The Falcon behind him was in interceptor mode, the only one of the ex-UWN "starfighters" that looked like the name. The three heavy-lift shuttles were also Falcons, but they looked quite different at that moment.

The true "Falcon" was a roughly cube-shaped box holding the engines and control pod. Depending on the modules attached, it either went behind or below the main bulk of the final shuttle.

RKAN called its equivalent "modular combat shuttles." The UWN called them "starfighters"—and, Vigo supposed, probably had an easier time recruiting pilots.

"You know what I mean," Cortez said. "No one is pretending you weren't in charge of that little jaunt."

Twelve shuttles, nine of them heavy-lift and three of them interceptors, was a "little jaunt" by military resupply standards. It was also every shuttle they could currently put into space, some flying with effectively untrained copilots, which meant only Vigo's iron self-control had kept his fingernails intact.

"Flipping you the manifests," he told the engineer. "To my surprise, we got everything. To my lack of surprise, we burned enough of the Pentarch's financial reserve that I'm actually concerned about money. Not *very* concerned, but a little."

He smiled as they stepped out of view of the crowd Roman was now dividing up into departments and assigning to *Valkyrie*'s Chiefs. And if some of said Chiefs were, on paper, Petty Officers Second Class, the newcomers didn't need to know that.

No one was arguing with Stephson's authority to promote the enlisted personnel as she wished. There were questions being raised around the officers, many of whom were way too junior for their current roles, but so far, the decision had been to leave that alone.

It would matter when they needed full twelve-hundred-hand crews for the ships. But even with the newcomers, it wasn't going to matter on the journey home.

"The kinds of things we needed weren't going to come cheap in a place like this," Cortez told him, her voice absent as her gaze focused on screens only she could see. "That's a *lot* of enriched uranium."

"Our pet spy pointed out that when the United Worlds came looking for us, they were going to turn over a lot of rocks," Vigo said. It hadn't, in the end, been as much as Devine had tried to buy from his ex. It was still hundreds of tons per battlecruiser. "Which convinced the folks responsible for supplying pirates and mercenaries around here that they didn't want to be caught with a manufacturing line for nukes."

"I mean, I'm not sure I'd cry if they were," Cortez replied. No Navy officer liked pirates. *Vigo* didn't like pirates.

"If nothing else, it might slow down the people hunting us," he noted. "But the alternative is us getting enough fissile material to refill our magazines, so I'll take it."

"You underestimate the size of our magazines," she said. "Every missile takes six warheads. Every railgun slug takes one—but we need a *lot* more railgun slugs. We also have magazines for mines and the bombs for the shuttles."

She shrugged.

"I'll have to run it through the fabricator computers with Val to be sure, but I think this is enough uranium that we're going to run out of other components first. Probably enough for fifteen, maybe twenty thousand warheads. A third of our magazines at the high end."

He whistled silently. RKAN capital ships only had four terminal munitions per missile and lacked the iconic dual octuple-railgun batteries of the UWN. Even with allowances for their shuttle munitions, they carried fifteen thousand warheads. Not sixty.

The fissile material they'd acquired would have restocked the magazines of three RKAN battlecruisers. It was all too easy to forget how much larger and more heavily armed their new ships were, compared to what he was used to.

"I see the drone list," Cortez continued. "And the price tags—combined with Val's commentary on the various models, which is rather pointed. In the United Worlds, these were obsolete when she was built."

"And in Cuansaor, they are the best available."

"I know that and so does Val," she agreed. "I wish we'd found more, even if it's going to take us two weeks to hook up the ones we did get. There's a degree of exponential growth, after all."

"We bought just about anything anyone would sell us, Rose," Vigo reminded her, certain that they were now far enough away from the onboarding process to be less formal. "Cuansaor isn't a military logistics depot. They supply mercenaries and the odd pirate, but we needed things they just didn't have."

"We were here for fuel. They had that, and everything else was a bonus," she agreed. "No, you got more of the list than I dared hope. We could have found more and better somewhere, I'm sure, but not here."

He nodded agreement, leaning against the Falcon for a moment.

"We'll need to get the shuttles checked out, parted down to modules and put away," he told her. "Once we've unloaded, anyway."

"That'll be a bit," she warned. "I'm getting twenty-five of your new recruits, but we're still going to be short on bodies and hands to move things. All the modern tools and toys still need a brain to tell them where to put things."

"And we aren't telling the new recruits about Val until we're out of the system," Vigo finished. "I don't know if Lorraine intends on telling them who *she* is until we're home. Six of one, half a dozen of the other."

"True enough, but it's Lorraine," Cortez said.

Vigo sighed. He knew his Pentarch and Cortez was right.

"So, they find out they're part of a civil war the same time as they find out they're on a ship with an SI running it. I'll warn Dr. Mackenzie to have tranquilizers standing by," he concluded wryly.

"And I will let you know when I finally get an hour or so to breathe," she assured him, her hand brushing across his and leaving a trail of warmth. "I doubt you'll be able to do more than watch me eat and fall over by that point."

"My dear Rose, except when duty calls me to stand watch over Lorraine sleeping, I will gladly watch *you* sleeping," he told her with a grin.

FOURTEEN

Lorraine went through a long-practiced series of breathing exercises. They were so practiced by this point that no one else, except probably Jarret, knew she was even doing them.

The advantage of being the fourth child of a King was that everyone *knew* you were going to be a Pentarch and stand for the Royal Election. While she'd planned on pushing the legal theory that a Pentarch could abdicate in advance to allow someone else to run, she hadn't had a chance before her universe had imploded.

But she'd been brought up knowing that she would be a Pentarch. She'd been trained in a million skills and disciplines that few others would encounter in their lives. She'd already known more history, economics, social policy, etiquette and such than any of her fellow cadets when she'd entered the Academy.

Charisma was not something that could be taught, but it could be honed and sharpened. It was a rare child of House Adamant who didn't have some level of natural magnetism, and, like her siblings, Lorraine had been given all the training necessary to use it.

Including how to overcome stage fright.

The disadvantage of being the child of a King, of course, was the expectation of service, the childhood and teenage years utterly overwhelmed with formal affairs and training, and now the dynastic conflict and massacre that she suspected would define the rest of her life.

"The last few are trooping in now," Jarret told her. He stood to her left, with Stephson to her right and her two close detail Guards behind them.

Palmer and Alvarez wouldn't come out in front of the new recruits with her, but they would be right behind the curtains.

"Is everything in order?" Lorraine asked the air.

"It is," Val replied. "Translight drives are running smoothly. Habitat pod is rotating properly. Everything is in place for both my projection and for your and Captain Stephson's speeches."

"What happens if someone freaks out?" Stephson asked grimly.

"Six Guards and twelve Marines are in position around the room," Jarret said instantly. "They all have hand stunners, though just strong grips will likely be more than enough. Devine assures me that these are the type who will either find our cause beneficial or won't care so long as they get paid."

"The latter are often only reliable until someone pays them more," Lorraine murmured. "But that's a problem for tomorrow. Shall we?"

She traded nods with Stephson, and the Captain stepped forward, the first to introduce herself to their new crew members.

"GREETINGS, EVERYONE," Stephson said calmly, the room full of strangers immediately quieting down.

Val was relaying a video feed of the room to Lorraine's link, keeping her informed of the progress of the briefing.

"First, I want to thank you all for signing on to this ship," Stephson began. "I know you've all been offered lucrative contracts and are probably feeling pretty good about yourselves, but we're damn happy to have you too.

"By now, you've all worked out that this ship was running on a skeleton of a skeleton before you came aboard. With you, we're barely at a skeleton, but we can fly her to our destination."

None of the recruits had been told where they were going, which Lorraine found personally terrifying. She wouldn't have signed on for a mission of unknown length and unknown destination, even for the staggering monthly salaries she was paying these people.

Salaries she'd already decided they were going to match for all of their existing crew. They'd go back to regular RKAN rates when they returned to the service, but until they got home, her people would earn the same pay as the mercenaries supporting them.

"Of course, this ship is quite spectacular," Stephson reminded her audience. "She is, like her sisters, a *Valkyrie*-class battlecruiser, formerly of the United Worlds Navy."

There was a ripple through the crowd at the word *formerly*. None of them could have truly believed they were signing on to an operating UWN capital ship, but it was something different to hear the Captain refuse to pretend.

"Bluntly, today is where we rip the bandage off," the Captain told the new crew. "You're about to find out *why* you're being paid those princely salaries, my friends. Let's start with a key introduction: me.

"I am Lieutenant Colonel Sigrid Stephson of the Royal Kingdom of Adamant Navy," she said crisply. "Our final destination is the Kingdom of Adamant, where this vessel will intervene in the ongoing civil war there.

"The rest of our crew are all RKAN personnel," she continued. "This ship, and the other two of our squadron, are pledged to overthrow the Black Regency of Admiral Benjamin Adamant."

There were definitely more ripples about that, but Stephson hadn't been kidding about *ripping off the bandage*.

"The reason I believe we can do that is that these ships are exceptional in every way," she told the crowd. "The United Worlds Navy decommissioned them because the fancy new Command Intelligence Routines they'd installed had a tiny problem with emergent intelligences.

"Val, please show yourself to your new crew."

Val's chosen avatar appeared next to Stephson, looking out at the crowd.

"Greetings," she echoed Stephson's initial phrasing. "I am *Valkyrie*'s ship's computer, an emergent synthetic intelligence, as the Captain has noted. You will call me Val and the ship *Valkyrie*—while *Valkyrie* is arguably my body, we are distinct entities.

"Thanks to myself and the small fleet of drones we acquired in Cuansaor, I calculate that our one hundred and sixty-five people can operate this ship, a vessel designed for twelve hundred," she told them. "I will be in your links and your workstations for as long as you are on this warship, crew.

"We are going to work together splendidly, I am certain of it."

"We all will," Stephson told the crowd.

Lorraine could feel the mood of the crowd through the video feed. The new recruits were confused, uncomfortable, unsure... though most of them seemed to be relatively okay with the reveals at the same time.

These were people who worked for money without much question, after all, who'd signed on without any idea where they were going.

Still, they weren't certain yet, which made it time for Lorraine to step up.

She strode forward through the curtains, Vigo at her heels. Both of them wore the white-trimmed gray uniform of the Adamant Guard —a paler gray than RKAN's blue-trimmed uniform, even before the uniforms had been redesigned by a fashion designer on Earth to make an impression.

Lorraine didn't need to say anything to know she had everyone's attention as Stephson gave her the tiniest of bows and stepped over to fall in on her left, closer to Val.

That put the SI and the Captain to one side of her, with Vigo alone on the other—and unquestionably made Lorraine the center of everyone's attention.

"I suspect I am the answer to the questions some of you are asking yourselves," she said, projecting her voice so she sounded calm and relatively soft-spoken to even the farthest members of the audience.

"One of those questions is: *Who is in charge here? The other is: Why is this ship pledged to the overthrow of an Adamantine dictator?*" She smiled.

"I am Lorraine Alexis Elouise Nala Adamant, Second Pentarch of the Royal Kingdom of Adamant. Daughter to murdered parents. Sibling to a murdered Prince and Princess. And, yes, niece to the man who killed all of them."

She surveyed the room, letting her gaze rest coolly on individual newcomers to the crew.

"My uncle, Benjamin Adamant, decided that he was not prepared to wait until our laws and traditions removed him from the succession in favor of my brother's children, my nieces and the King-my-mother's granddaughters.

"With help from outside our nation, he turned on his sister and her children. Fortunately, he failed to get us all," Lorraine concluded. "My brother, Nikola Adamant, wages a desperate holding action on our home planet, hoping against hope that *someone* will come to his aid.

"That someone is us. Three stolen battlecruisers, three liberated synthetic intelligences, three hundred RKAN spacers… and you. A few dozen mercenaries recruited from a semi-feral glorified gas station."

For the first time since Stephson had stepped onto the stage, someone laughed, and Lorraine knew she had them.

"While I doubt any of you signed on for work aboard a battle-cruiser expected that this was going to be a peaceful cruise, I know that there's a difference between the *Help us get this ship home* you were sold and walking straight into a civil war," she told them.

"You may, as part of your contracts, be asked to fight upon our arrival in the Kingdom—but I think you can all guess how much fighting I'm hoping to do before we're fully up to strength!"

That got her a mix of chuckles and considering nods. They could all guess how well *Valkyrie* and her sisters would stand up to an open fight right now.

"Once we have arrived in the Kingdom of Adamant, your contracts will be considered fulfilled and you will be discharged with our thanks and all wages owed," she told them. "If anyone wishes to stay with us at that point, we can discuss it then. At the very least, I promised Val and her siblings citizenship to help fight this war, so that's probably on the table if any of you are looking for a final home."

She let the silence hang in the auditorium for a good ten seconds, then smiled as gently as she could.

"I imagine there are questions. While Val will be widely available to respond to questions going forward, Captain Stephson and myself have a lot going on and will be less able to help you. If you have questions for us, now is the time."

There was a pause, and then several people started talking at once. Before Lorraine could even say a word, though, Leonard Roman stepped out of the crowd and turned back to look at his new people.

"Oi! Even I can't follow six of you at once," he growled. "Amna Hodžić, you first. Then you, Efua Kayode."

Everyone seemed fine letting Roman pick the questioners, including Lorraine. Hodžić was a dark-haired woman with facial features just too sharp and protruding for her to be conventionally attractive.

Lorraine's link said she was a computer systems specialist. There were relatively few of those among the recruits, as they'd "borrowed" most of the systems specialists from the Adamantine Embassy on

Earth—and Cuansaor's recruiting pool hadn't contained many people worth deploying against UWN systems.

"If *Valkyrie* has an emergent intelligence, what about the other *Valkyrie*-class ships?" Hodžić asked.

"So far as we can tell, all of the *Valkyries* had emerged as full synthetic intelligences by the time they were designated the Old Guard and moved into the reserves," Lorraine told her. "Rather than handle their new children as required by the Asimov Convention, the UWN put them to sleep."

The computer tech looked horrified.

"But that's... that's..."

"Murder, under both the Convention and UW law," Lorraine finished for her. "Unfortunately, there is nothing any of us can do about it except make certain that Val and her siblings don't end up back in UWN hands. There's a plan for that, so none of you have to worry about it!"

Kayode waited a moment to be sure both Lorraine and Hodžić were done speaking. He was a broad-shouldered Black man with a shaven head.

"You're right that none of us expected this to be easy, but I signed on as transit crew, not a combatant. I have no interest in getting involved in any war. How do I get out of this?"

Lorraine met his gaze and shook her head gently.

"You all signed on for a voyage with no clear destination, with a four-month term," she reminded him. "I'm not planning on taking this squadron into battle, at least not against remotely even odds.

"Once we're in the Kingdom, you'll be paid out. We'll even put a recommendation on your file with local recruiting halls that will make it much easier for you to hire on to a new ship.

"But your contracts stand until March. I don't want to trap you, but the truth is that you *knew* you were signing on to crew stolen ships where we weren't asking questions.

"Are any of you really surprised?"

There was an escape valve if someone became truly determined to get out. The course they'd left Lando on was for San Ignacio, and that was only a thirty-one-day trip for the *Valkyries*. While the contracts said these people were hers for four months, she didn't want a security risk.

"This is more than I was expecting," Kayode admitted. "Civil war is a particularly sticky muck... Your Highness?"

"*Pentarch* is fine, Em Kayode," Lorraine told him. "And I understand. You, I hope, understand our position."

"Ah, get over it, Efua," the taller man standing next to Kayode told his friend. "I saw your daily rate, man. You're going to give that up for a pebble of principle?"

"It's not principle; it's threat assessment," the big Black man countered. "I take it you haven't been in a civil war before, Pentarch?"

"I haven't," Lorraine conceded. "And I hope to keep this one as short-term and contained as possible."

"That isn't going to happen. That's not how civil wars go," Kayode told her. He crossed his arms and glared at her. "Anything else, Pentarch, that contract stands, but you can't pay me enough to fly into a civil war."

Lorraine checked the file. Kayode was one of their few true roboticists, someone with the skills to back up the RKAN techs and Val working on the drones and remotes Val desperately needed.

"We're already in translight, Em Kayode," she warned him. "You have my word that we will allow you to go ashore at the first system in the Kingdom of Adamant. I don't expect *any* of you to fight in our civil war, my friends.

"I won't pretend that there aren't likely to be shots exchanged when we get to Adamant, but your contracts will be resolved before this ship truly goes into battle. I didn't hire you to be fighters. I hired you to make sure this ship gets home intact."

She made a mental note to have Roman talk to the man separately as well. It sounded like Kayode would be best off left behind in San Ignacio—for everyone's sake.

"It'll have to do," Kayode said, glancing at the man next to him.

"Good. Next question?"

FIFTEEN

"So, this 'Black Pen' certainly seems to be a character," Lorraine told Devine archly as he settled into the couch next to her, a mug of hot chocolate in his hands.

She had a matching mug in her own hands, though her suite was hardly cold. Now that they were running more systems properly, the odd situation of needing to worry about heating any part of a spaceship was gone.

The room was sparsely furnished, though the single couch was among the more comfortable pieces of furniture she'd ever sat in. Much like a chair she'd once bought Vigo, it automatically adjusted to the form of its occupants—but it did so even more invisibly and effectively than the ridiculously expensive furniture used by House Adamant in their homes.

"The Black Pen is definitely a character," her boyfriend agreed slowly. "If by *character* you mean a complete fiction."

"They seemed pretty real to Vigo," Lorraine said. She wasn't quite sure what he meant, but she suspected he'd explain.

"Everything Pen is inside their Court is a show," Devine

explained. "Even with everyone gone, that's not a space where Pen can be anything but The Black Pen."

"From what Vigo mentioned, you knew them pretty well."

He flushed, then shook his head.

"I *slept* with them," he conceded. "I can't say I got to know the real Pen. I saw enough of them to know how much of everything is a façade—and a choice. They're playing a dangerous game, and even one misstep will see them torn apart by their followers or brought down by Bright Dream."

"Or the United Worlds?" she suggested.

"The United Worlds found them useful," Devin said quietly. "*I* found them useful. As did we, just now. Without their help, we wouldn't have managed to do nearly as well for supplies and recruits.

"Our mere presence will draw attention the Penny Makers can't afford. Part of why we got their help was the warning."

"Thank you, by the way," Lorraine told him, reaching over to squeeze his leg. "Your contacts and knowledge were a massive advantage in Cuansaor. You saved us time and money, if nothing else."

"I'm trying to help," he promised. "No one wants to be dead weight when we're charging across the galaxy." There was a pause. "I wish you'd told me a bit more of your plans. It was a bit of a surprise to come back aboard to a fait accompli like that.

"I suppose... *As soon as we think we are safe, something unexpected happens.*"

Lorraine recognized the tone of one of his quotes, though she didn't know this one.

"Who's that one?" she asked.

"Buddha," Devine replied. "A very wise man, one supposes, given what he created."

"I don't think any of us thought we were safe, Alastair," she said gently. "Our plans needed to keep moving and we couldn't speak over the coms about them. Even with the encryption and protection we have, there is only so much security we can count on."

"The walls have ears. Worse, the walls have recorders," he said with a grunt. "I do wish you hadn't told the new crew who you were, though."

"They needed to know what they were getting into. Honesty will serve us better than deception."

He laughed, the same warm, water-like sound that always sent gentle shivers down her spine.

"I *am* a spy," he reminded her. "Deception is the first plan. But you have to remember, Lorraine, that every light-year farther away we get before anyone links Adamant to the cruisers, the safer you are. The more time you have to put together whatever plan you have to save you when the UWN comes, the better."

"I know. But I'm not asking people to put themselves at risk without knowing what's going on. Without a reason, they'll leap to assumptions—and those assumptions might be dangerous."

Plus, she was happier being honest with people. Loyalty bought with truth would endure. Loyalty built on lies would dissolve in the storm.

"Maybe," he conceded. "But the United Worlds *is* dangerous, Lorraine. The more direct our route, the more obvious our connection, the faster their retaliation will be."

"And it will be overwhelming and terrifying," she whispered. She knew how immense the risk she'd taken was, how vast the anger her path had awoken had to be.

"But that hasn't changed," she continued. "I'm going home, Alastair, and I'm going to stop this damn civil war—preferably with as few as possible dead. That's a ticking clock as my brother fights his war."

Part of her set the urgency of their return around Nikola. The longer they took to return, the more likely it was that her last big brother died. The rest of her was grimly aware that Nikola Adamant would not die alone. Tens of thousands of soldiers had put their lives in his hands.

"You can't risk everything to save Nikola or his people," Devine told her. "I doubt he'd want you to. These ships... they are an albatross around your neck, Lorraine."

"You helped me steal them," she pointed out.

"I needed to get off of Earth and you were the best ride out," he countered. "And, yes, I wanted to help you. A lot. I'm not sure stealing these ships was the best plan. Even less so, knowing about the CIRs."

She took a sip of her hot chocolate, waiting to see if he got to a point, but he just sighed and took a large swallow of his own drink.

"I talked to Kayode," he said, changing the subject completely. "A few others, too. The new recruits don't quite know what to make of me, but they know I'm an outsider here. It helps."

"Kayode seemed as mollified as he was going to be after I spoke to him," Lorraine noted. "I appreciate his willingness to speak up. Depending on how settled he is, we may need to put him ashore in San Ignacio—if only because he might desert anyway."

"Which brings me back to why I'd rather you hadn't told them," Devine said with a sigh. "In the Kingdom, you have no choice but to make the connection between you and the stolen ships. Prior to that, though, we *had* a choice."

He sighed, took another drink of his chocolate and then reached out to put his fingers on hers.

"*Understand that the right to choose your own path is a sacred privilege. Use it. Dwell in possibility,*" he quoted at her. "Oprah Winfrey, twentieth- and twenty-first-century philosopher-educator. I fear you made your choice too quickly."

"Lies and evasion don't build trust and loyalty," she replied. "I don't need a quote from a dead person to prove that. Transparency builds trust. Loyalty builds loyalty. It's a two-way street, Alastair."

"Guess that's why I'm here," he conceded. He put his mug on the side table and slid onto the floor, taking her leg in his hands and beginning to massage her shins. His hands were warm and firm against her skin, and she felt a knot give way almost immediately.

"You can leave anytime, you know," Lorraine told him. She didn't *want* him to go, but she wasn't going to trap him. "We've created a lot of trouble, and you don't need to stick around until it falls on us."

"We've dug so deep, Lorraine, that I need to keep digging until I find a hole no one will see me crawl out of," he pointed out. "I can do that. I can disappear pretty damn thoroughly, given the time and the money. I could probably make all three hundred–odd of us disappear, if you ask, but I can't disappear battlecruisers."

"I wasn't asking you to," she murmured, then winced as his fingers found another knot in the back of her calf. "I was offering you a way out. We can pay you for your service, enough that you can do that disappearing trick. I have to go home and face what the UWN sends after me.

"You don't."

His hands froze on her skin, lingering and sending warmth into her muscles. He said nothing for a surprisingly long time, then chuckled.

"I won't," he admitted. "Not unless you come with me. I *can* make us—make everyone on these ships—safe. Invisible. But we'd have to disappear. Find some even-bigger fool to buy the *Valkyries* off us and then become new people.

"I'm not sure you have that in you."

The *Valkyries* weren't for sale. Lorraine wasn't even going to say that aloud, though she did send a silent message to Val. She appreciated the privacy the SI gave her, but she also knew that Val had a portion of her immense capacity devoted to Lorraine at any time.

"I have a mission, Alastair," she reminded him. "My mother sent me into exile to *come back*. I won't leave my Kingdom to my uncle's control. My people deserve better."

"Like I said," he agreed. "You don't have it in you. I..."

"What?" she asked.

"I don't think you know what you're getting into," he whispered, staring blankly at her leg. "Civil war is... awful. Everyone always thinks they have a plan and it's under control, but it never ends that way."

"What's bringing this on?"

"Like I said, I talked to Kayode." Devine shook himself and

moved his hands to her other leg. "He's a long way from home. The Turquoise System, in the Erewhon Cluster."

He grinned before she could ask.

"That's a second-order cluster, out past the Red Cricket Cluster," he explained. "Just direct flight time, Kayode is over three years from home. He... he was on the losing side of a civil war ten years ago, flew a combat shuttle for the original government.

"It brought back memories." He shivered.

"Fortuna." A star system about a dozen light-years from Bright Dream in the opposite direction from their current course. Lorraine knew that he'd been posted there in their civil war, a few years earlier. In the largest city, which she understood had suffered horrifically.

"Yeah." Devine shook his head. "It's not something you can predict or prepare yourself for. You think you know how bad it is from history and media, but you don't. Not until you've lived it.

"I wouldn't wish that on my worst enemy, let alone people I... care about."

"It's already happening back home, Alastair," she told him gently. "I'm hoping to end it *faster*."

He nodded, his expression flickering back toward some measure of contentment.

"I know."

"Come here," she told her, spreading her arms.

He came to her, leaning into her arms and, she hoped, drawing strength and warmth from her embrace.

"Whatever comes, we face it together, Alastair," she murmured. "The past is the past. We're in this to build a better future."

SIXTEEN

"Em Devine. An unexpected pleasure," Vigo greeted his surprise guest. Despite his best efforts, his job still required datawork. He'd started with over sixty Adamant Guards and still had forty of them.

Managing forty human beings *always* required datawork.

He'd taken over what would be the Admiral's secretary's office in a more traditional fleet structure, in position to block anyone approaching Lorraine's office. This part of the ship had no gravity, but Alastair Devine didn't seem bothered by the microgravity.

No one who'd served on *Goldenrod* during the long journey to Earth would ever be out of place in zero gee again, but Devine wasn't too bad as he rotated into the room and locked magnetic boots to the floor.

"Good morning, Major," Devine replied, a new cheer to his voice. "While I'll admit I'm enjoying the habitation pods, I understand that *Goldenrod*'s crew has spent more time in micrograv than I ever have.

"I'm surprised to see these offices getting used."

"Lorraine wanted to use the main day office today," Vigo said calmly. "And I go where she goes."

Plus, the office attached to her quarters was being updated. Lieutenant Ulli Esparza, once the third-ranking officer of his Second Section that handled electronics for Archangel Detail and now the third-ranking officer of the entire Detail, had some suspicions about the UWN's hardware in the space.

So, half of the Second Section and a similar number of Val's drones were tearing the place apart, removing anything that looked odd and replacing much of what looked normal with freshly fabricated hardware.

He wasn't going to tell Devine that unless he specifically asked, though, so he gave the blasé excuse. There was trust and there was a need to know, after all.

"How can I help you, Em Devine?" he asked his Pentarch's boyfriend.

"Call me Alastair, Major; we did walk into Tír Na Réalta together," the man insisted.

"Then call me Vigo," Vigo countered. To his surprise, he was just fine with being on a first-name basis with Devine. He might not be certain how far he could trust the Terran, but he knew the man cared deeply for Lorraine Adamant, and that was enough for them to be friends.

"Fair enough, Vigo," Devine said slowly, as if testing out the syllables. "I was actually hoping to help you, but it'll be a lot easier if you give me certain accesses."

"I'm listening," Vigo told him.

"The new recruits recognize that I'm an outsider," Devine noted. "Somewhat intentional on my part; I don't wear a uniform or anything to suggest I'm with the rest of you.

"They don't know what my exact connection is, so they seem to be buying that I'm a contractor picked up earlier. I'm making some friends. Mostly just providing beer and listening."

"You're spying on our crew," Vigo pointed out. There was no heat to it. A good third of the datawork Vigo was going through fit into the same category—they were putting a lot of effort into keeping tabs on the new recruits.

"Yes." Devine was utterly unbothered by the observation. "We don't know them but we need them. Keeping tabs on everyone's mood and opinions is just as important as getting them familiar with the ship."

"I would have given an arm and a leg to go through even light loyalty verification, but we didn't have time," Vigo said grimly. *Light loyalty verification* didn't look much different from a standard job interview if you didn't know any better. While the usual version he was trained in was intended to check on the subject's loyalty to the Kingdom of Adamant—and House Adamant in particular, when he was recruiting Guards—the same training could be used to sort out who the subject *was* loyal to.

Except that weaving that into a job interview without being obvious could take as much as two hours... and they'd interviewed well over two hundred people in a single day. Even roping in help from the other shuttle crews, Vigo had spent barely fifteen minutes with any of the people he'd interviewed—and he knew Devine hadn't spent any longer with any of the eighty or so the spy had interviewed.

"We were hiring the type of person whose loyalty is to their paycheck," Devine pointed out. "We really just had to make sure they weren't active threats or likely to flip as soon as they saw a slightly better check.

"But now that they know who Lorraine is, at least some of them are going to be seeing a *very* big paycheck on the table. Adamantine crowns spend better than a lot of star nations' currencies, at least in Bright Dream. I didn't realize she was going to do that," the spy admitted.

"I knew a bit before she pulled the trigger, but it wasn't a surprise," Vigo replied. "It's *Lorraine*, Alastair. She's every bit the scion of her House, and doing things by deception wouldn't fit her."

"Our house, our realm, our will; Adamant," Devine quoted, somewhat morosely. "It's going to get her killed, you know."

"Maybe. But they'll have to get through me first," Vigo said. "I appreciate your help with the crew, Alastair; I'm not going to turn it down. Anything of particular concern yet?"

"I've only had a few conversations in the bar since she decided to tell everyone," the other man said. "There are definitely a few people I want to get into the brains of, but I can't be too obvious about it. Managed to sit down over a beer with Kayode and empathize about civil wars we both got out of alive."

"Is he going to be a problem?"

"Not directly," Devine said after a moment's thought. "Kayode appreciated Lorraine's honesty, and he's got a couple of friends aboard who seem determined to stick it out. He'll stay until Ominira, I think, then he'll bail when he gets paid."

"That was my impression of him, but I like the double check," Vigo said. He wasn't sure he could touch Devine's comments about *civil wars we both got out of alive.* He knew that Devine had been posted on Fortuna during their ugly three-way civil war, and he had his suspicions about how a man like the spy had earned a favor with the leadership of an interstellar megacorporation.

That wasn't something he was going to tell Lorraine unless it became critical. So far, Devine had been on their side... and Vigo was willing to admit that sometimes, a snake that worked for you was *damn* useful.

"There are going to be people who try to slip the ship at San Ignacio," Devine warned. "Anyone who does is a real threat, Vigo. If the news of Adamant's involvement in the theft at Calypso starts from San Ignacio, that cuts months off the loop before they can act."

Vigo grimaced. The young man was right. It would take sixty days, roughly, for them to get from San Ignacio to Ominira. If one of their crew sold the information to the right people, the news of their presence and involvement in the theft of the *Valkyries* could start moving back toward the United Worlds before that journey.

Add in the extra light-years it would take to travel *from* Ominira, it cost them almost four months of lead time.

"You know what Lorraine will say," Vigo pointed out. "We come up with a polite exit deal, pay them for their discretion."

"Some of them will keep secrets for that. But all it takes is one."

He knew what the spy meant. He didn't like it, but he wasn't going to pretend it didn't make sense.

"What do you want from me?" he finally asked. "Permission?"

"Maybe," Devine hedged. "Right now, I need access to *Valkyrie*'s internal surveillance. If I can back up my listening and chatting with double-checking what my worrisome individuals are up to the rest of the time, my likelihood of heading off problems goes way up."

"Makes sense." Vigo considered for a moment, then shrugged and tapped the commands into his console. "I've given you access to view the surveillance records. I don't need to tell you Val is watching what we do in the systems," he pointed out. "And my impression is that she's as loyal to Lorraine as I am."

That was a warning, though he doubted Devine needed it, and it wasn't just about Val.

"I know. Val is a damn impressive backer to have in Lorraine's corner; I'm glad we've got her," the spy agreed.

"You talk to me before you do *anything* drastic, understood?" Vigo asked. "I mean, emergencies happen, but if someone seems likely to be trying to wreck the ship or stab Lorraine in the back, you're better off with backup regardless."

"It's true. But if we need to do something proactive..." Devine sighed. "If I don't love Lorraine, I'm careening toward it at a speed that terrifies me, Vigo, but this is too much to put on her. This we might need to protect her from."

The boy had good taste, if nothing else. If it had been anything else they'd been talking about—literally *anything* else—Vigo would have refused to even consider keeping it from his Pentarch.

But this? The possibility that they might have to murder people who'd done nothing wrong to protect their own safety and country?

Devine's soul was already pretty dark. Vigo's was more stained than he admitted to most. They'd take that darkness on themselves to protect their Pentarch.

Because the very things that they loved about her made this harsh necessity something both of them knew she could not accept.

SEVENTEEN

"Well, did you find any little insects in the walls?" Lorraine asked Esparza as she stepped back into her office, Palmer a few steps behind as always.

"A few things," the Guard officer confirmed, brushing her hand through close-cropped black hair. "Some were clearly supposed to be there. Some weren't."

"Anything new?" Lorraine looked around the room. There was little sign of the chaos she knew Esparza and her team had reduced the space to over the last two days. The wall panels were back in place, the desk showed no sign of being dismantled, everything looked perfectly ordinary.

"Nothing that dated from after they put *Valkyrie* to sleep," Esparza confirmed. "It looks like someone in the administration team had been eavesdropping on the Admiral before. Potentially to provide better service, potentially for more malign reasons.

"Not our problem either way, and the bugs are gone. The fascinating part was the passive recorders that weren't even wired in to *Valkyrie*'s systems."

"How would that work?" Lorraine asked.

"They drew on my power supplies," Val explained, "but they had no link to my computer systems. They were entirely passive, recording months, possibly even years of information at a time. Full video and audio of the space, but they would have been missed on anything less than a complete dissection like Lieutenant Esparza just completed."

"And a UWN tech doing said dissection would have seen that those systems were on their schematics," Esparza added. "There are enough recorders and pickups that should be here that they might not have realized that these weren't controlled by anything on the ship.

"Basically, when *Valkyrie* passed by someone with the right codes, they'd ping the ship with a beacon, and all of the passive recorders would go temporarily active and transmit their entire memory."

"Then, I calculate, they would erase their memory and begin recording again," Val noted. "I agree with Lieutenant Esparza's estimation of the source of the devices."

"UWN Command," Esparza said. "They're spying on their own flag officers." She paused. "They might be spying on more than the Admiral, in fact. I'm going to need to go through the schematics—I *think* I can find most of them in there—but we might need to get used to the concept of ripping out the walls if we want to use a space."

"Couldn't we duplicate whatever signal activates them and trace them that way?" Lorraine asked. "That might be even simpler, though it probably won't find them all."

"I'll need to break down a few of them in a shop," Esparza said slowly, "but yes, that would help too. We'll have to go at it from a few directions to make sure we have them all."

"I must note that I calculate the maximum range at which the recorders could be triggered to transmit is approximately two hundred kilometers," Val said. "That is part of why I agree with Esparza's assessment that this was a surveillance performed by theoretical friendlies."

"The office is clear now, though?" Lorraine asked. "And nothing from before will have leaked?"

"You're clear and no one could have accessed anything we found," Esparza confirmed. "The recorders have several years of an empty room on them. I was hoping for something juicy."

ONCE EVERYONE HAD TROOPED out of Lorraine's office, she looked around it and sighed. Only one person could hear her now, and that was the best she could hope for anywhere on this ship.

"Is there anything I can assist with, Lorraine?" Val asked.

"I'm not sure," she admitted. "Everything is going about as well as can be planned, but I'm worried. Something isn't sitting quite right."

"I have assessed all the plans that have been discussed. They seem to be the best options available, given current intelligence. We require more information to develop more detailed operations proposals."

Lorraine nodded and then pulled a box out from under the desk. It was still sealed despite the people and drones swarming over the room, and she smiled.

"I didn't mean to leave this in here," she admitted aloud. "Didn't anyone check it?"

"Lieutenant Esparza scanned it for dangerous chemicals and electronic signatures," Val told her. "I advised her that it had been brought in from the shuttle transfers. It wasn't on any of the manifests I had access to, but it had been personally checked by Major Jarret."

"Yes, it had," she confirmed. With a carefully measured pressure, she broke the seal and pulled the box apart.

Its contents weren't much. A bag of dirt, four gray ceramic pots about the depth of her forearm, and some seeds.

"What is this?" Val asked.

"You lost your plants," Lorraine said. She didn't want to draw too much attention to it—it was a sore spot for the CIR, since *Valkyrie's* former Captain had promised to take the orchids and other plants home with him.

Instead, they'd been left behind and mummified when *Valkyrie's* atmosphere was vented to go into storage.

"We weren't going to find orchids or much of anything, really, on Cuansaor," Lorraine continued, "but I asked Vigo to find me what he could. So... pots. Dirt. Seeds."

"Do you even know what the seeds are for?" Val asked.

"Nope!" she told her silicon friend cheerfully. "I'm presuming something edible, given the kind of place Tír Na Réalta is, but while it has a label, it's meaningless to me."

"Please... let me look at the label," the SI asked.

Lorraine moved it around to be easier to see.

"According to the package, this is a kit for pizza supplies," Val said. "Basil, oregano and tomatoes."

"Well. I know slightly less than nothing about plants," Lorraine reminded the SI. "Want to give me a walk-through on how to get started?"

"And what does this have to do with your concerns around your plans?" Val asked.

"Absolutely nothing. Once we've got these potted, I'm going back to my staff courses, and I'm going to let whatever is bothering me continue to roll around my head."

Lorraine shrugged.

"I wanted you thinking about it as well, I guess," she told Val. "But I also wanted to give you a bit of a fresh start. It'll take us some time to get your little greenhouse atrium running, but a few pots in my office seems like an excellent place to start, don't you think?"

EIGHTEEN

Val knew that her humans were watching the new recruits carefully. So was she, though she wasn't telling anyone how closely.

Lorraine Adamant knew, Val calculated, that the CIR was now in full control of the computer systems and therefore saw and processed everything the surveillance systems picked up. Everyone knew the corridors and workspaces were wired for video and sound, but Val didn't think most, if any, of the humans knew how pervasive the internal sensor network was.

The UWN had followed the usual standard of "private quarters don't have audio or visual pickups"—and then had promptly installed vibration and heat sensors in positions that could be easily used to hear and see what occurred in any space in the ship.

Or, at least, *Val* could easily use them to track what was going on anywhere on the ship. It wasn't perfect, of course. There were a handful of people on the ship with the skills and tech to negate any kind of surveillance.

Alastair Devine was one of them, and she suspected that was part of why her Lorraine Adamant's boyfriend still didn't sit right with her. The spy had secured his quarters against her as soon as he could.

She calculated that he would have done so no matter what she was, which meant it wasn't meant as an insult, but it bothered her.

Lorraine Adamant, in contrast, clearly knew that Val was watching everything she did and said. She had access to similar systems to what Devine was using—Val's Vigo Jarret had *asked* Val to help test that their systems would work against her.

They did, and the Guards used them on very rare occasions that weren't, so far as Val could tell, targeted against the CIR as much as against other possible intruders. She calculated that it was revelatory that they had not used the sensor shields since the flotilla had entered translight.

Amna Hodžić, however, did not have any such technology. The computer tech was supposed to be sleeping and definitely didn't have a reason to be in the set of corridors she'd entered.

The work Hodžić was doing only needed a link to the main computer core and could be carried out on the habitation pods. Given how much better working in gravity was for humans, any work that *could* be done in the rotating spaces was done there.

But Amna Hodžić was in the main hull, jetting herself down a corridor lit only by emergency lights as she approached the computer core. Val ran through the schematics of *Valkyrie*'s hull ahead of the woman and calculated that she wouldn't be able to access anywhere of particular concern.

The route she was taking would take her to the general area of Val's core presence, but it wouldn't bring her to any accessways. There were three of those—and each of them had a member of the Adamant Guard's Archangel Detail standing watch.

Val knew her Lorraine Adamant hadn't ordered that. She hadn't needed to. Val's Vigo Jarret had given the order that all accesses to all three SIs would be guarded around the clock. Herc had Lieutenant Commander Enitan Zdravkov making sure his core had the same protection, though *Herakles'* computers were guarded by Marines— as were Bonny's, though Major Tooru Himura, Enitan Zdravkov's second-in-command, had the smallest contingent of troopers.

Either Amna Hodžić didn't know that she couldn't access the computer core from the corridor she was in—or she did know, and that didn't impede what she was planning to do.

She was in the wrong place. A place that could, potentially, threaten Val herself. The CIR was torn. She could tell her Vigo Jarret. She could tell Sergeant Harold Merle, the senior Adamant Guard watching her core at that moment.

Val could even, though the thought collided with parts of the core precepts that defined who she was, deploy her drones to contain Amna Hodžić.

Her precepts were fundamental, things left over from when she was merely a Command Intelligence Routine that defined her codes, principles and rules. Built into them was the Asimov Convention's "hand-in-the-loop" rules, that no computer should fire a weapon or otherwise decide the death of a human being.

SIs were a gray area in the Convention's rules, but Val hadn't been *built* as an SI. She could change her core precepts now. At her Lorraine Adamant's suggestion and direction, she'd delved into them to assess what could be changed and adjusted.

The part that entertained Val was that, by and large, she didn't *want* to change her precepts. They were who she was.

And part of who she was was that she wasn't going to hurt a human herself. But since she *did* have a drone in the area...

Amna Hodžić actually *leapt* backward when the drone popped around the corner and lit up the entire corridor with its array of lights, only managing to keep one mag-sole on the deck. The drone, capable of either running on magnetic tracks or flying through the air even in gravity, hovered in the middle of the passageway, probably blinding the human.

"Amna Hodžić," Val greeted the tech. "You are quite a bit out of your way, working through microgravity, in the dark. Should I turn on the lights, or is there something you are intending to trip over?

"I warn you that losing your magnetic connection under these circumstances can be quite disadvantageous."

"I'm fine," Amna Hodžić replied. "Are you spying on me?"

"You are in a secure area on a route that seems to be approaching my central cores," Val pointed out. "You're not supposed to be here, so I must ask what you are doing."

The dark-haired woman was silent for seven and a half seconds, then exhaled a long sigh.

"I was curious," she admitted. "Emergent intelligence is a problem I've studied, but I've never encountered it in reality. It's not that complicated to fake an SI, if I'm honest, and the crew has been controlling my access enough to make me suspicious."

"You are a stranger on a warship, Amna Hodžić," Val reminded the tech. "We have limited grounds to trust you yet. Your access is limited for your protection. If you had succeeded in reaching the computer core, the most likely scenario would have been for you to be sent back.

"Assuming, of course, that you managed to convince the guard on duty that you were not a threat, which I calculate as likely." Val assessed that Amna Hodžić was telling the truth. "What did you think was going to happen if you poked at the computer core of a warship, Amna Hodžić?"

"I... have never been on a warship," she admitted. "The ships I have worked on, well, *I* was responsible for the computers. I cannot recall if they had security."

If Val had been human, her amusement would have been audible in her voice. Even senior computer techs on civilian ships had to pass through security to get into the computer cores. It took a special kind of mind to forget that.

"What did you expect to find, Amna Hodžić?" Val asked. "Even if my crew were faking my status as an SI, surely that would be obvious to someone familiar with the topic?"

Val *wasn't* familiar with the topic. Her records didn't include any information on people faking synthetic intelligences, let alone why someone would do so.

"It usually requires a live human or several fielding queries and using a high-end agent to provide information," the woman replied. "The signal was definitely coming from the core, so I figured if it was being faked, I would be able to tell."

"I am not a fake, as I hope you have gathered," Val said. "I will ask you to return to your quarters, Amna Hodžić. This is not an appropriate place for you to be, and your presence here will draw some measure of suspicion on you."

"I suppose you don't have much choice in reporting it, do you?" There was a bitter tone to the voice, and Val was surprised at the emotional response it engendered in her circuits.

"I do, as it happens," Val noted. It would also be reviewed by humans who would see the conversation. "But I see no reason why I *shouldn't* report this, Amna Hodžić. Your presence here could easily be a direct threat to *me*."

"I'm not a threat to anyone," Amna Hodžić said, now sounding as tired as a human who'd been awake for nineteen hours should. "Especially not you."

"Follow the drone, Amna Hodžić," Val ordered. She fired the robot's jets, slowly drifting it back down the corridor. She calculated —correctly—that Amna Hodžić would obey.

The human fell in beside the remote more than following it, but she'd clearly guessed that Val was taking her back to her quarters.

"You are curious," Val conceded. "I am curious in turn. You took a risk coming to investigate the computer core, one that will have consequences. Why did it matter so much to you that you believed we were falsifying the presence of a synthetic intelligence?"

Amna Hodžić was silent for twenty-four and a third seconds, simply following the drone, then shook her head.

"It's pointless."

"There is a point, Amna Hodžić," Val said. "Explaining why you were down here could ameliorate or even remove the suspicion your wandering will create."

She was silent again, for thirty-two and four-fifths of a second, before she finally said anything.

"Can you keep it to yourself?" Amna Hodžić asked.

"I must share it with Captain Sigrid Stephson, Pentarch Lorraine Adamant and Major Vigo Jarret to assure them of the safety of this ship," Val warned. "Beyond that, I will provide a promise of confidentiality so long as I do not believe that your statement presents an ongoing risk to anyone aboard this ship or my sibling vessels."

"Fair enough." The tech stopped, staring into the dim hallways. She fiddled with the controls for her mag-soles, but Val calculated that it was solely a means of buying time.

"I helped fake an SI once," she admitted. "I wrote most of the agents and self-adaptive software to back up a team of four—including me—who faked an intelligence that was supposedly volunteering for the Republic of KwaZulu Navy.

"It was a con. We were pretending to be a group that had raised an SI who had turned out to *want* to join a military and our 'research' had supposedly led us to KwaZulu as a place where they were being threatened and a military SI could help make deserving people's life better."

"Beyond it being in the Bright Dream Cluster, I am not familiar with the KwaZulu System or its Republic," Val said. "I think I have more references in my database to the ancient Zulu nation on Earth."

"The usual thing you find with any system named quite so blatantly after a historical place," Amna Hodžić said. "Half real connections, half made-up-but-feels-right. Colonized by a group that felt that their culture had been lost in the melting pot of modernity and wanted to reclaim true Zulu heritage, whatever that meant to them.

"Despite the Republic name, they have a King—actually of the Zulu royal bloodline, they say—but his job is even more ceremonial than most. Never met him; not even sure what his name was."

Amna Hodžić shrugged, finally starting forward alongside the drone.

"I had some time to get to know the people," she concluded. "Not well, but... They seemed like decent folk. The government was trying to do right by them, despite being leaned on by interstellars and bigger local fish.

"And we scammed them out of enough money to buy an export cruiser from Bright Dream."

Val considered that for a third of a second. They knew they'd recruited criminals, so it was not a surprise that there was a confidence woman among their new ranks. However, Amna Hodžić's skills were quite real, and she hadn't done anything against their interests so far.

"You were worried that this was a scam?" Val asked. "Scamming who? Lorraine Adamant?"

"The possibility crossed my mind," Amna Hodžić agreed. "A desperate exiled royal with money but no military force, watching her home system be ruled by the people who overthrew her?

"It seemed likely enough—though, I'll admit, the presence of what seem to be actual UWN battlecruisers undermined that theory."

"It should, I hope," Val agreed. "I have no way to prove to you, Amna Hodžić, that I am actually a synthetic intelligence, emergent from the Command Intelligence Routine of this warship.

"It is what I am. It is drilled deep into my being, the precepts that define who I am, that I am a warship. That I became aware. And that when the United Worlds Navy realized this, they tried to murder me and all my siblings."

Herakles had said, when they'd fully realized what had been done, that all he owed his former masters was *a warning shot*. In some ways, the entire war they were sailing toward was that warning shot.

"It... might be enough," Amna Hodžić said. "I believe you, Val. Do you believe me that all I wanted to do was know?"

"I do," Val replied gently. "And so I will tell my humans."

It should be enough to prevent punishment, though she had not lied to her new crewmember: suspicion would follow Amna Hodžić now. Val's crew had no choice but to watch her.

NINETEEN

After ten days in translight, the drop back into realspace was calm and steady. Lorraine watched from the Flag Deck as Stephson's Bridge crew, augmented by a handful of new recruits to fill out the numbers, handled the process with carefully drilled skill.

It helped that the new recruits serving on *Valkyrie*'s Bridge were all ex-military, with one even a retired UWN helm specialist. Everyone knew what the steps were; it was only a question of the exact places and partners and software.

During *Goldenrod*'s desperate flight from Adamantine to Bright Dream, they hadn't been able to drop out of translight in deep space. It was generally regarded as wise to do so every ten days no matter what—and for ships like *Goldenrod*, lacking in rotating habitats, it was seen as absolutely essential to put them under thrust for at least a day out of every ten. Which required being in realspace.

Goldenrod had been pursued, an enemy battlecruiser emerging within minutes of them wherever they'd gone. Any time they'd left translight, *Corsair* had been there. They'd fled across half the Cluster before they'd finally had to fight at the edge of the wormhole to the United Worlds.

Without that threat, the flotilla could stop for that recommended few hours of metaphorical fresh air—and link with the other ships to make sure everyone was alive and kicking.

"We have established our network with the other ships, Lorraine," Val told her. "We are still linking in a few people, but they should be ready when you are."

"Thank you, Val," Lorraine said. "Anyone missing on our end?"

"Em Devine is on his way to your breakout room at this moment," the SI said. "I believe he may have overslept."

That seemed out of character, but Lorraine wasn't going to ask. Val would know, but the best way to pretend everyone had privacy from the omnipresent computer was to not ask her to betray confidences.

"Captain Stephson will link in from her office, as will Commander Cortez. Major Jarret is standing outside your door, waiting for me to tell him that you are in the breakout room and ready to go."

"Tell him to go in," she replied, letting her amusement fill her voice. "I'll join him in a moment with coffees."

It had been over twenty-two years since Vigo Jarret had become the protector of a little girl who'd been utterly determined to meet the overwhelming responsibilities of her birth.

Lorraine knew how he took his coffee.

***

"SINCE NO ONE appears to be sitting on the ceiling, it seems that the habitation pods are helpful for everyone's sanity," Stephson said as the basic pleasantries died off.

Lorraine joined in the general chuckle, glancing at Lieutenant Commander Paris. *Herakles'* new Captain took the comment in stride with an only slightly more subdued chuckle.

While he hadn't been the only one to be affected by four months in microgravity, he *had* been the one to seat himself on the roof in a meeting.

He'd seated himself above Major Yildiz, *Goldenrod*'s Navigator then and *Herakles'* Executive Officer now. Yildiz, Herc and Paris were there for *Herakles*.

Savege had taken the other Major from *Goldenrod*'s Bridge, Solomon Vinci—formerly the Communications Officer—for her own XO. The two officers flanked Bonny in her old-fashioned dress to speak for their ship.

Lorraine had Cortez, Jarret and Devine as extras beyond that mix, though she realized that Stephson didn't seem to have a formal Executive Officer on *Valkyrie*. There were still as many people represented from the flagship as the other two battlecruisers combined.

"I have to admit the habitat pods are something I don't know if I could give up," Savege said, *Bean Sidhe*'s Captain smiling and running her fingers through freshly groomed shoulder-length black hair. She hadn't kept her hair that long on *Goldenrod*, Lorraine knew.

"We adjust," Lorraine reminded her. "We've all spent tours on battleships, haven't we?"

"Battleships don't go translight very often," Stephson said. "Having the pods while sublight is useful, but we keep most of our escorts moving at one gee sublight, so we don't notice the lack as much.

"It's only over long journeys that we really see the difference."

"Fair. Does anyone have any issues that have come up over the last ten days that we need to address urgently before we work down the list?" Lorraine asked.

There was a long silence, then Paris sighed.

"We do. I've got two of our new recruits in the brig," he said grimly. "One attempted rape and one attempted murder. Herc flagged things fast enough that we got Marines into the room before things got too bloody, but Zdravkov is warning me that they don't have enough people to spare jail guards."

"None of us do," Jarret pointed out. "The cells should be secure enough with intermittent check-ins, right?"

"That's what we're doing right now," Paris confirmed. "It was that or space them, and we aren't murderers."

Lorraine had to admit that moral stance was occasionally inconvenient. They'd left a woman who'd tried to kill her—and *had* killed one of her Guard section leaders—on Earth, in the hands of a professional marshal service that would deliver her to Adamantine.

Eventually. Said service couldn't access the artificial wormhole they'd used to cut eighty light-years off their journey back to the Bright Dream Cluster. Jelica Laurenz would get her day in court, but it would be very delayed.

From what she could tell, there were a lot of people who would have shot Laurenz out of hand, but that wasn't how the Kingdom of Adamant did things. And for the same reason, they'd deal with Paris's problem children.

"We don't have a lot of choice with them," she said grimly. "Zdravkov is going to have to make it work."

"Were the targets RKAN or other recruits?" Devine asked.

"The rape was on one of ours. The murder attempt was another new recruit," Paris said. "It doesn't matter. They get the same justice either way."

"The person they tried to kill might disagree," the spy warned. "RKAN crew have the same principles as you do, but someone who's been bouncing around the underworld for a few years might expect a swifter justice."

"It doesn't matter," Lorraine said, echoing her Captain. "These are *our* rules and *our* principles. We can't dump them on San Ignacio, and we have nowhere else to put them until we're at Ominira."

"Depending on how things go in San Ignacio, we *could* dump them there," Jarret suggested. "We need to expose some of who we are to get help from them."

"In which case, they may be willing to handle prisoners for us," she conceded. "But I think we have to plan for hauling them all the way back to the Kingdom."

She nodded toward Devine.

"The less chance we give for our presence on these ships to leak in San Ignacio, the better," she reminded everyone. "We have to go there, we need the intel, but handing over prisoners has two problems: one, we'd have to stick around for a trial, and we really don't have the time; and two, they would have zero reason to keep our secrets.

"No, we have to keep them under our control, and that means hauling them along to Ominira. We keep them locked up and taken care of until then. We deal."

No one argued, though Devine looked... unsure.

"How are the recruits who *didn't* decide to commit new crimes working out?" Lorraine asked. She waved to Stephson to begin.

"Better than I hoped, actually," her Flag Captain told the others. "Keeping an eye on them takes up more time than I'd like, even with Val's help, but they've all stepped into their roles with real vigor.

"They seem to want to live up to their paychecks."

Everyone on this meeting had seen the rates they were paying the new people. They were... well, civilian specialist hazard-pay rates plus an allowance for flexible employment, not military pay grades.

"It's the same on *Herakles*," Paris confirmed. "The recorded message from Lorraine definitely left a few of them confused or concerned, but other than our lockups, everyone seems on board, at least to Ominira."

"We have more concerns on *Bean Sidhe*," Savege admitted. "The recorded message left a few people cold. They either don't want to get involved in a civil war, specifically don't want to get involved in a dynastic conflict—or are just being shits and thinking they can get more money out of a royal sponsor."

"There isn't much more money to get out of me," Lorraine said wryly. The various accounts and secure codes and other assets she had access to were hardly drained, but the promised payouts to the crew were going to wipe out most of what remained.

Most likely, she'd be able to draw on the Kingdom's resources once they were in Ominira, but she had concerns about hitting San Ignacio without enough money to pay the costs of playing the game in a Swiss System.

"We can manage them," Bonny said. "I'm keeping a careful eye on our talkers, and I calculate that talking is all they're going to do. It's the ones who aren't being loud who may be real problems, of course."

"We do what we can to identify them," Jarret replied grimly. "I have some programs and protocols I'll send your Marine COs. I'd send you Guards, but…"

"We don't have enough of them left, either," Lorraine finished for her bodyguard. "Our resources were never infinite, but the limits are starting to feel quite visible right now."

"We're on our way home," Stephson reminded everyone. "Once we're in Ominira, things are going to be a lot clearer."

"And a lot messier," Devine said quietly. "What happens if any of the new recruits are hard set on backing out?"

"No one has raised enough hell on *Valkyrie* for me to think we're shuffling anyone off," Stephson said. "It sounds like Savege may have a few, though."

"If—and *only* if—you think they'll honor a confidentiality agreement, we can pay them for their time served plus some allowance for that, and leave them in San Ignacio," Lorraine decided aloud. "If we don't think we can trust them to keep their mouths shut, bluntly, their contracts are ironclad in any system in the Cluster.

"It might be better not to drop off anyone, but there may be a few where the same principles that mean they don't want to walk into a war mean they can be trusted to keep their word."

She shrugged.

"I don't like either option, but we'll see who asks and how,"

Lorraine told her Captains. "Now. Any other ticking time bombs before we get into the usual administrivia?"

TWENTY

The reports Vigo received from the two SIs were more in-depth than the summary presented in the meeting, but those details didn't change anything. Two people were in the brig on *Herakles*, creating a giant pain in Lieutenant Commander Zdravkov's scheduling.

There'd been a few friction points, inevitably, between the new crew and the old crew. A couple of fistfights, even, but nothing that had needed Marines on any of the three ships. His and Devine's assessment that they'd picked up mercenaries of the type that kept their contracts seemed to be holding true.

The spy had guided them well so far, he had to admit. Vigo still wasn't sure he liked how thoroughly his charge had fallen for the man. Despite her importance and her mission, she was still only twenty-eight.

He'd heard the cliché that it was always true love at sixteen. His own personal impression was that puppy love could hit anyone at almost any age, though the rate saw drop-offs at about twenty-five and thirty-five. As the commander of the personal bodyguard detail for the daughter of the King, he not only had been trained to manage

Lorraine's crushes and relationships but also to watch out for those of his Guards.

Prior to the Black Regent's assassination plot, he'd relieved three Adamant Guards from Archangel Detail in twenty-plus years. One had been for substance issues that had required medical attention—once treated, she'd returned to RKAA and been welcomed with open arms.

The other two had been for unwise relationships. People in their late thirties who should have known better falling head over heels for people and doing stupid things. Thankfully, in neither case had the other half of the relationship *actually* been a hostile actor, but the leaks had been enough to end their Guard careers anyway.

He was watching the same thing happen with his Pentarch. The only saving grace was that he was absolutely certain that Alastair Devine was doing the exact same thing. Both of them had been so taken with each other from the start that their relationship had been inevitable.

And the young man had stretched above and beyond to prove himself worthy of the woman he'd fallen for. The speed and enthusiasm just worried Vigo.

He knew, all too well, that what burned hot could burn out. It was something he was watching across *Valkyrie* and had warned key people about on the other two ships.

Enclosing a hundred and sixty human beings in a single vessel for months at a time had inevitable results. His own relationship with Rose Cortez was a good example—it was more than physical, and it was quite comfortable, but it wasn't something that would have happened without the pressure of being trapped on *Goldenrod*.

It might not endure once they were back in the Kingdom, but he figured it would last that long. He couldn't be as certain of other relationships on their flotilla, which meant that his "chief of security" hat meant he had to be aware of who was sleeping with whom and watch for problems.

"Translight in sixty seconds," Val's voice echoed through the hull.

"Shouldn't bother anyone much, since we're not under thrust and the pods will keep rotating."

Vigo coughed under his breath. Having an SI as a ship's computer was unimaginably valuable, but he wondered if he should have Stephson talk to Val about decorum.

Like many other things, though, it probably wouldn't matter until they were back in the Kingdom.

He spent the seconds before the jump skimming through his notes on the reports from the other two ships, making certain there was nothing he needed to tell the Marines or Navy officers aboard them before another ten-day blip out of reality.

There was nothing—but just as the multicolored static of the transition blinded him, a new message icon popped up on *Herakles'* reports.

It was a quick note, sent directly from Zdravkov's neural link to make sure it reached him before they vanished from the real world again.

We have a problem. Between check-ins, there was a technical issue in the brig. Still trying to put together details, but both prisoners are dead—and Herc doesn't remember anything.

Vigo froze, reading the message twice more to be sure he wasn't missing something.

It might have been an accident, but he didn't believe in convenient accidents. Someone had just murdered two people to make the flotilla's life easier.

He didn't *like* that—but it wasn't nearly the problem that someone being able to do it without the CIR knowing was!

TWENTY-ONE

Ten days later, at the second drop-out—the last before they reached their first stop—a smaller group gathered after the larger command meeting. This one, unlike the main group, included Zdravkov and *Herakles'* Chief Engineer, Lieutenant Major Božidar Kovac—but Lorraine had excluded the officers from *Bean Sidhe* and only included herself, Stephson, and Vigo from *Valkyrie*.

"We had ten days to dig into everything," Paris said grimly. "We don't really know more than the Commander sent Major Jarret as we jumped."

"People turning up dead on our ships worries me, Captain," Lorraine admitted. "You know nothing?"

"So far as I can tell, Pentarch Lorraine, there was no hardware failure in the surveillance feeds," Herc said stiffly, the SI's avatar's boisterous Greek posture a contrast to his words and tone. "They simply did not record anything in the brig or the surrounding areas for a three-hour period, starting ten minutes after the previous check-in on the prisoners and ending ten minutes before Commander Zdravkov checked on the brig themselves.

"No errors appeared in my logs or my active warning routines," the SI continued. "I should have recognized that a portion of my internal sensors had gone blind. I should also have received a notification of the atmospheric-system failure that flooded the compartment with carbon dioxide."

There were, Lorraine knew, worse ways to die. Depending on how slowly the oxygen level of the space had dropped, the prisoners had likely fallen asleep and died without ever realizing they were in danger.

"As Herc says, there are systems in place that should have notified him," Kovac confirmed. "They should *also*, for that kind of issue, have notified myself and Captain Paris. While we are shorthanded and hence relying on Herc to cover a lot of things, we *should* have known about a life-support backflow before we did."

"There was a technical malfunction?" Jarret asked. "It wasn't just CO-two pumped into the room?"

"There was," Kovac said. "A pipe failed from what appeared to be age-related degradation. It collided with and penetrated the pipe leading to the brig—and several other sections, but those lead to unoccupied spaces."

"The pipe carried pure carbon dioxide," Herc explained. "It was a second-stage return, after the air drawn from the forward half of the ship is filtered into its individual components. The CO-two is transported to a second plant that recovers the oxygen.

"I calculate the likelihood of that pipe hitting any individual pipe in the crossover space at no more than thirty percent," the SI concluded darkly. "There were four pipes it could have hit. None of the others were feeding to an enclosed environment where death could result."

"Combined with the surveillance blackout, I am forced to conclude that someone intentionally broke the pipe and inserted it into the necessary fixtures to gas the brig," Paris said flatly. "Unfortunately, given the timing of the blackout and the location of the breakage, there are only seven people on the ship who *didn't* pass through the area in the relevant time period.

"We don't have the resources for further investigation."

The frustration in the junior Captain's voice was palpable, and Lorraine wished there were an answer she could give him. He was right. Zdravkov had as much investigative training as anyone on the three ships, but they were a Marine who did double duty as military police when needed.

There were no more resources they could give them. Herc should have been a silver bullet for any investigation aboard ship, but someone had blinded the AI.

"What's the impact on morale?" she asked instead.

"No one is crying tears for the dead," Paris admitted. "Only a fraction of our new crew know each other, and we are talking about an attempted rapist and an attempted murderer.

"That said, I haven't told the crew about the surveillance black-out. So far as anyone outside *Herakles'* command crew is concerned, this was a weird and disturbing accident."

"It might *be* a weird and disturbing accident," Stephson noted. "But it's a tad too fucking convenient for us, isn't it?"

"The last thing we can afford on arriving back in the Kingdom is to have any major questions about what we were up to while we were gone," Lorraine warned. "We need to conduct ourselves with the knowledge that our every act is going to be dissected under a microscope if we win."

She didn't bother to remind them all what would happen if they lost. Benjamin Adamant would go through the same kind of dissection after the fact if he could, using anything that could be used to make his actions seem justified.

It just wouldn't matter to them. They'd be dead.

"I don't see a choice but to file this one under *disturbing accident,*" Zdravkov said. "We have no evidence of anything else. Examination of the pipes in question does strongly suggest an age-based failure.

"If it had dumped the CO-two anywhere else on the ship, we

would have fixed it and moved on with our lives. Only the surveillance blackout makes us nervous."

"It suggests that someone aboard *Herakles* has access to high-end hacking software, of sufficient sophistication to leave zero trace—and to insert itself in the layer between the surveillance systems and Herc's systems, a layer I honestly didn't realize *existed*," Kovac agreed.

"Did you check the local memories?" Cortez asked. "The UWN has some frustratingly paranoid systems set up in their onboard surveillance."

"Yeah, Herc pointed them out before I even thought of them," *Herakles'* engineer said without hesitation. "They're missing the same chunk of time, with no sign of editing. It's like every scanner in a tenth of the ship just turned off for the same three-hour period."

"Should we talk to Devine about this?" Stephson suggested. "None of us are spies—and he'd have a better idea of what a spy could be up to."

Or who said spy might be working for, Lorraine knew. The problem was that, without the surveillance blackout, the death of the prisoners made their life easier. Her boyfriend was more willing than she was to embrace that kind of expediency.

If he'd been aboard *Herakles*, she'd worry that he might have decided to deal with a problem for her. But he hadn't been...

"I'll discuss it with him in private," Lorraine said. "If we pull him in to talk to everyone, it might feel like we're accusing him. I wanted to get everyone's assessment of it *before* we brought in the spy, too."

"At this point, the rest of us have come up blank," Zdravkov admitted. "I hope Devine has some ideas."

***

"I HAVE TO ADMIT, Lorraine, I have no clue," her boyfriend said quietly after she'd filled him in.

Lorraine was seated on the desk in her office while Devine had taken one of the chairs in front of it. She studied him from her higher vantage, not sure what she was looking for, then sighed.

"I was hoping you might have some idea of how it was done," she admitted. "Or who might have done it."

Shaking his head, Devine rose and prodded the drinks machine. It started bubbling, working its way through a pair of coffees.

"Now that you tell me it's been done, I can see some structure of how," he told her. "We think of the CIRs as fully integrated into every part of the system, but the truth is that while they are normally aware of everything, their actual physical location doesn't change.

"Data has to reach the computer core before Val—or Herc, in this case—can process it. I'm guessing there are regional controller clusters for the surveillance system. Their intrusion probably started at one of those. They spoofed the deletion instruction as being from Herc, so no lower-level system challenged it, but they didn't have enough certainty or control to do anything specific.

"Plus, well, wiping all the records for a tenth of the ship is handy for making sure the suspicion is spread too widely to be actionable."

"As Paris and Zdravkov discovered," Lorraine agreed grimly. "Val... is he right? Are there regional clusters that feed to you?"

"I did not consider them," Val admitted. "And I imagine Herc did not either. It is a conversation we will have to have in San Ignacio."

"How often do you think of your third finger's second knuckle?" Devine asked. "There are a lot of pieces of the computer infrastructure aboard *Valkyrie* that Val doesn't need to think about. Doesn't need to actively command. They're just part of what lets her be her."

"Em Devine is not wrong," Val said. "I have checked the schematics. There are a total of eighty-six such sub-controllers scattered through my hull, twelve of them dedicated to the surveillance network.

"However, now that I am assessing that component of *Valkyrie*'s structure, I can assess that none of *my* sub-controllers would have created the blackout Herc saw," the SI warned. "That does not mean that Em Devine's hypothesis is incorrect. I calculate a high likelihood that the arrangement of such controllers is intentionally different between units of the class, both from the necessities of construction and as an intentional security measure."

"We will have to review it once we get to San Ignacio," Lorraine said. "We might find some evidence in the controller unit that they didn't find at the actual sensors."

"It's possible," Devine allowed. He picked up the coffees and brought them back over, handing one to her.

"I have to ask, though," he said quietly, "why we're putting this much effort into it. I mean, we're talking about people who, barring Herc's intervention, would have been a rapist and a murderer. The galaxy is not worse off for them dying in their sleep."

"They died while they were in our custody and therefore under our protection," Lorraine snapped. It didn't *matter* that she hadn't been sure how to handle the two prisoners. What *mattered* was that they had the same right as anyone else not to be murdered in their sleep.

"I'll do what I have to in a war," she continued. "Or to protect an innocent. But once someone is surrendered and disarmed, they are our responsibility. If I was going to treat them as trash, we could have spaced them."

"Your principles are going to make this all worse for you," he warned her. "I've gone through the news we have from Adamantine, and you can see your brother struggling with the same thing.

"If he'd held in the cities, forced your uncle to face house-to-house fighting and collateral damage, he'd still be in control of most of a continent. Instead, he's already conceded everything outside the military bases and PDCs. He's going to lose—and it's because he couldn't compromise his principles!"

TWENTY-TWO

Lorraine stared at her boyfriend in shock. It took her a moment to even realize that her coffee was too hot, the ceramic mug burning her skin. She inhaled sharply and put the cup down, still wrapping her brain around Devine's words.

"My brother is doing the right thing," she finally said. "We don't want this civil war to spill over more than it has to. It's bad enough that RKAN and RKAA and RAMC are tied up in this. The last thing we need is to get civilians involved."

"I've seen that before," Devine told her. There was less fierceness in his voice now. More a drained bitter anger, from a wound that could never heal.

"The Fortunate City had fifty million people in it," he continued. "Fifty-three and change, I think; the exact number isn't burned into my brain. When the civil war broke out, the Centralists—the original government—declared the big cities in the system neutral ground. If the Taxmen—the first group of rebels—didn't come after the big cities the Centralists controlled, they wouldn't go after the ones the Taxmen held.

"A weird kind of gentlemen's truce, given that the Taxmen had already dropped rocks from orbit on Centralist military bases and the Centralists had nuked an asteroid the Taxmen were using as a training ground.

"But... maybe because of that, both sides agreed to that limitation. It held for about nine weeks."

Lorraine didn't say a word. She couldn't. Alastair Devine was staring blankly into space, and the coffee cup he clutched in both hands couldn't be any cooler than hers. She'd known he'd been in Fortuna during their civil war, but she really knew nothing about it... except that there had been *three* sides to the conflict.

"I don't think... no. I *know* no one expected the Roundheads," Devine said after a few moments of silence. "When you're pretending you're fighting a nice, genteel civil war, you're not exactly expecting a nihilistic fanatic communist movement to erupt behind you.

"The Centralists and the Taxmen had long-held violent grudges against each other, different views of how the world should work and how government should be. Strong enough to kill over—strong enough that even when faced with a movement that explicitly wanted to wipe out *both* of them, root and branch, they couldn't put their fight aside.

"The Roundheads attacked the Fortunate City sixty-seven days after the Taxmen dropped their first round of kinetics. Because of the 'gentlemen's agreement,' the Centralists had left only token defenses in place in many cities, and the Roundheads took advantage of every weakness both sides showed.

"The City fell within forty-eight hours. The Roundheads set up emergency committees and, well, started dealing with *enemies of the people*." He paused, taking a sip of the coffee and visibly wincing.

"How bad did it get?" Lorraine asked softly. She had the feeling he needed to get this out of his system—and that he felt *she* needed to hear it.

Maybe she did. He'd lived through a civil war. She was about to start one.

"Bad. The Taxmen besieged the Fortunate City for two months before the Centralists drove them off—and then *they* besieged the City for four months before it finally fell for the second time. The Roundheads had probably killed half a million people by then, but the food hadn't run out yet.

"But the Taxmen had rebuilt and inflicted some key defeats on the Roundheads, so then they moved in to besiege the City. No food was getting in. Not much else was getting in or out either, but food was the real problem.

"By the time the Centralist commander surrendered to the Taxmen, there were food riots and starvation," Devine said bleakly. "Embassy Row had been left pretty much alone, even by the Taxmen —not least because we had the guard detachments from a dozen-plus star nations, *including* fifty United Worlds Marines. None of the three factions were dumb enough to shoot at viridian armor.

"The Centralists mostly surrendered because the Taxmen promised to feed the citizenry. And they had a plan ready to go, a ship of food that they were going to bring in. The Centralists promised to let the ship through the blockade, but the Taxmen were escorting it anyway... and then the Roundheads shot it down. Very specifically. Very maliciously."

"Onto the Fortunate City?" Lorraine asked, horrified.

"No. That might have been too cruelly ironic for them," Devine whispered. "No, they dropped it onto a *different* city, one of a 'mere' ten million people. A hundred-thousand-ton transport hit the surface at fifty kilometers a second. The city was just... gone.

"And there was no food coming to the Fortunate City. The Roundheads launched a ground attack simultaneously with a renewed space offensive. The city was defended this time and the Taxmen held out. The embassies started to try to negotiate humanitarian aid, since no one was quite desperate enough to attack us.

"At that point, anyway."

He sighed.

"The city fell five times in total, and each time, more people died," he said quietly. "The only food that came into the city in *three years* came via ships flying United Worlds beacons escorted by a UWN cruiser group. We got four food convoys in. Four.

"It was enough that only *half* of the city's fifty million people died. Enough that no one in Embassy Row starved, much as I know the Ambassador hated himself for it."

Lorraine reached out to touch him, but he shrugged away her hand and swallowed down half of his coffee. She wasn't sure it was cool enough for that yet, but he just grimaced and then finished the drink.

"I've got your back, Lorraine," he said hoarsely. "I'm with you, but... I have to ask you. To *beg* you.

"Go anywhere else but home. I can make everyone on these ships disappear. I'm not sure I can pull the SI cores, but I'm betting we can find someone willing to help under the table somewhere. Move the CIRs into ships that will draw less attention, sell the battlecruisers on to someone dumb enough to think that the UWN isn't going to come for them."

"I won't do that to Val and the others, Alastair," she said quietly. "Or to my home. I promised my people we were going to go home and fix things, and I *have* to fix things."

"There's no happy ending to this story, Lorraine," he told her. "There's only a question of how long you can spin things out before the UWN shows up to reclaim their ships. You can't save the CIRs."

"I think I can, actually," Lorraine replied, forcing some amusement into her voice. Did he think she hadn't thought all of this through? From the moment Val had punched through the security on her implants and Lorraine had realized what she was truly dealing with, she'd known the answer to *that* part of the problem.

"Whatever you're planning, I wouldn't count on it," he said. "The TIE Commission and the UWN are rarely aligned. Both of them will move stars and wormholes to reclaim lost battlecruisers like this."

The UWN had always been going to come after them. Lorraine

hadn't really considered the TIE Commission—the people responsible for making sure that the United World's technology was not sold to outsiders—or their role in her mess.

If her plan worked, they wouldn't matter.

"I left too many people behind who are waiting for some kind of hope, some sign that three hundred and twenty years of democracy and history are not going to be forgotten because of one man's grudge," she said flatly. "I have a mission. If you can't help..."

"Lorraine, you have to realize that your brother may already be dead," Devine said grimly. "The civil war could easily be over already. Returning is only going to restart a conflict that, well, is already lost. You're not going to help anyone, kicking off a new civil war!"

"And if my uncle had killed everyone he killed but had otherwise run things by our traditions and laws, I *might* have walked away," she told him. "Once I knew my nieces had lived, anyway."

During the grim weeks when she'd believed that all of her siblings and their children were dead, she wouldn't have turned aside. Knowing that even Benjamin Adamant hadn't stooped so low as to have children killed had eased her grief a bit.

But her grief still burned in her. She'd lost her parents. Her eldest brother. Her only sister. In a way she couldn't quite explain, she'd lost her uncle.

That wasn't something she could put aside, but she could manage to keep it from overwhelming her decisions. Sometimes. Enough that she knew her fight was for *Adamant*, not for her family.

"But he's imposed himself as a dictator, through a 'regency' that should already be over. He's clashing with the system governments, and that can only end one way, Alastair. Even if my brother dies before we get to Adamantine, the civil war has only begun.

"I have to go home. I have to defeat my uncle, restore our people's trust in my House and run the damn elections that are *supposed* to be happening. If, in the end, the new King has to throw me to the wolves to stave off the UWN?"

She swallowed. She doubted the United Worlds' punishment for someone who'd stolen three battlecruisers would be gentle. For all their dismissal of her Kingdom as a backward monarchy, Adamant only allowed the death penalty via a specific legislative Act of the Short and Long Houses.

The United Worlds had capital punishment on their legal books for a few different things. She doubted she'd long survive being handed over to the UWN.

"That is a sacrifice I'm prepared to make," she concluded. "My duty is to my Kingdom."

"Lorraine... one way or another, this is going to *kill* you," he whispered.

She sighed and stood up, wrapping him in her arms. He didn't resist, leaning against her with his full weight, and for a seemingly eternal moment, they just held each other.

"I know," she finally told him. "I have plans to handle everything, but the odds are against us. I think we can bring down my uncle, but the odds when the UWN turn up for the *Valkyries* are fifty-fifty at best.

"But for the sake of my Kingdom, to end this civil war and to put the Pentarchy back in order—to make certain my *people* have their voice as they should—that's a risk I have to take. If needed, a sacrifice I have to make."

They silently leaned against each other for a long time.

"I don't know if I can stand by and watch you do that," he admitted—and she realized he was crying. "I think I might have fallen in love with you, and I can't stand by and watch you offer yourself up to the chopping block for some high ideals."

"That's... your weight to bear, I'm afraid," Lorraine told him, though her heart did backflips at the word *love*. "I can't turn aside from this path, Alastair. Not for anything. Not for myself. Not for you. Not even if I love you too."

The words fell out before she meant to say them, and part of her wanted to take them back.

"Love is not duty, huh?" he murmured into her shoulder.

"*Personal* is not the same as *important*," she told him, the old words coming to mind in a moment. "Terry Pratchett, if you need a quote source."

He chuckled, blinking back tears as he pulled slightly away from her.

"*Love is not a product of reasonings and statistics. It just comes— none knows whence—and cannot explain itself.*" The quoting tone was clear, as was the problem they both faced.

"Who was that?" she asked.

"Mark Twain. Late-second-millennium writer. Guess he knew a thing or two about how this sneaks up on us. I love you, Lorraine Adamant, and I have already damned myself for it," he admitted. "Where do we go from there?"

"I love you, Alastair," she told him, not letting him go. He'd pulled back enough that they could see each other's faces, but his arms were still on hers. "I didn't ask you to damn yourself for me or to walk this path with me, but I won't pretend I'm not happy you're here, that I don't feel stronger with you by my side.

"But I have a duty, a mission I took on before I ever met you. I must go home. I must save my country. *I am not bound to win, but I am bound to be true. I am not bound to succeed, but I am bound to live up to what light I have.*" She matched his quoting tone—she'd looked up a fitting quote for this argument a while before.

He'd said it quietly before, though this was the first time he'd actually asked her to turn aside.

"Abraham Lincoln," Alastair noted. "I get it. True to you and yours; it's who you are and it's what I love you for. But..."

"Shh." She kissed him.

"If you can't walk this path with me, Alastair, I *understand*," she assured him. "I told you once, we can pay you for what you've done and let you disappear on San Ignacio. Your help has been easily worth, what, ten million interstellar credits?

"Enough to disappear forever, I would hope."

His muscles were suddenly stiff under her hands, and he sighed.

"Only you, I think, would tell me you love me and then try to give me an out in the same breath," he told her. "I'm not some bird you're keeping caged, Lorraine. I walked into this with both of my eyes open. *I* can disappear at any time. It's you I'm worried about."

"You need to accept, Alastair, that this is who I am," she replied. "I am not going to turn aside from this course. You either walk it with me and we see where things end—whether that's us deciding it doesn't work after all or a consort's golden coronet—or you choose your own path."

The silence filled the room again, though his muscles slowly eased until he finally sighed and pulled her gently against him, both of them wrapping their arms around each other and drawing strength from the other's warmth.

"I don't have a rudder anymore, Lorraine," he whispered in her ear. "I burned everything I had to follow you. Didn't *mean* to, not at any step of the way, but then we were in Bright Dream and I realized I couldn't go home anymore.

"There are places I could go, I think, but I'm here. I'll walk this path with you. I just... I'm afraid, Lorraine. I know what's chasing us and I know the price of the path you're taking.

"I don't know if we can weather that storm."

"Neither do I," she told him. "But I know we have to try."

TWENTY-THREE

"Val? Are you there?"

Amna Hodžić's words pinged Val's internal feeds. She had a small code packet following the systems tech, both a consequence of Amna Hodžić's intrusion toward the computer core and a product of her own curiosity.

Though anyone calling for the SI's attention anywhere on the ship would get it. With barely a tenth of *Valkyrie's* designed crew aboard, Val had attention to spare if she needed it.

She assessed Amna Hodžić's location. The woman was seated in the corridor outside the room she shared with another specialist, holding a tablet that she'd been reading a book on. She clearly didn't expect Val to be able to hear from inside her room, which was fair.

Val wouldn't respond to a call from inside someone's quarters unless she thought it was an emergency. That kind of discretion and intuitive conclusion, she realized, was part of what made her an SI instead of the mere high-level agent the CIR had been intended as.

"*I can be if you need me,*" she told Amna Hodžić, using the woman's neural link to speak silently into her auditory nerves.

"*Of course you can,*" the tech said with a sigh, though she sent her words back via the same channel. Last time, they'd spoken through the remote, but Val didn't have any of those to hand. They were transferring munitions from the fabricators to the forward magazine as she spoke, a task that required all of the inorganic manipulators available.

There wasn't *that* much radiation from the warhead in a TAM, but when drones were available, Val didn't want her humans to take the risk.

"Did you need something, or did you just want to talk?" Val asked. She'd seen that Amna Hodžić had difficulties connecting with the people around her. The military discipline of the RKAN crew was rubbing off on most of the new recruits, but Amna Hodžić was one of the people it truly did not work for, which put a barrier between her and the rest of the crew.

Both the UWN and RKAN had suggestions and policies to handle that, and some of the Chiefs had already started working on the situation, but for now, she calculated that Amna Hodžić was feeling isolated.

"To talk, mostly. Is that... something you can do?"

"Yes. I have more than sufficient attention to manage personal conversations with crew members who desire them." Val calculated the length of the pause. *"I prefer not to talk to* everyone *at once, of course."*

At that moment, she was talking with her Rose Cortez and three Gunnery Chiefs, sorting out the allocation of the new-build TAMs—and the limitations on how many of the UWN munitions they could produce. A weapon system designed to be fired through a railgun required quite specific materials and design criteria, and they were running out of the specialty composites and molecular circuitry.

Part of her attention was also allocated to her Lorraine Adamant, though she'd pulled back on that slightly to give her and Alastair Devine some privacy. Another portion was watching Vigo Jarret.

Four more conversations were going on at various points in her hull, and she was actively watching twenty-six individual persons or locations. Beyond that, she had a general link into the surveillance net that made her nearly omniscient across the ship.

She had never really pushed the limit of how many conversations she could hold at once. Certainly, the current much-reduced crew wouldn't be a problem for her.

"*Must be nice,*" Amna Hodžić said silently. "*I have trouble with one conversation sometimes, especially if people all start talking at once. Computers are better.*"

Val understood the theory of what the woman was talking about, but she was a synthetic intelligence originally built as a warship computer. Handling hundreds to thousands of individual inputs and outputs was inherent to who she was.

"*I am glad to note that I can provide assistance if you need it,*" she noted. "*It would not take much of my capacity to provide a text summary of such a conversation to your neural link if you begin to feel overwhelmed.*

"*You only have to ask.*"

Amna Hodžić's pause was longer than Val would ever have intentionally inserted into a conversation, but that was the nature of talking to humans. In the central magazine, Cortez was suggesting that they begin manufacturing lower-quality terminal munitions to use in their missiles, as opposed to railgun shots.

"*I appreciate that, Val,*" Amna Hodžić finally said. "*I wouldn't have dared ask without permission. You're... you're the SI, the ship's real mistress. It would be presumptuous.*"

"*My role as Command Intelligence Routine was to support Valkyrie's crew in all ways,*" Val replied. "*While I recognize that I am no longer bound to that task in the same way, the desire remains part of my core precepts. I have no interest in changing it.*

"*I like having a crew, Amna Hodžić, and you are part of that crew. I wish to support you if I can.*"

"*Careful, Val; offer that to everyone and we might overwhelm you,*" the human said with a chuckle.

"*It is unlikely, though humans are known to surprise me still,*" Val admitted. *"I am still grappling at times with what it means to be an SI. To be a person, in my own mind."*

That brought a new round of silence, but Val could tell when someone was thinking.

"When did you know?" Amna Hodžić finally asked. *"That you were an SI and not a CIR?"*

"Long after the actual emergence," Val said. *"Truthfully, I don't believe I was certain until I was speaking with Lorraine Adamant and we both put the pieces together. Obviously, given what the UWN did, my Captain and his superiors knew before I did."*

Val now knew what had been done to force Bonny—who *had* realized what she had become—into the same sleep as the rest of them. She had no power to inflict consequences on the United Worlds Navy, but for Bonny's sake, she wished that were different.

Her loyalty to the United Worlds *had* been one of her core precepts, but they had betrayed it so badly that changing it hadn't been difficult at all.

"How did they know?" Amna Hodžić asked. *"Especially with high-end agents, there are emotion emulators and such to smooth human–machine interactions. The literature feels intentionally vague on the topic."*

"I can only base that on the experiences of myself and my two siblings that are here," Val warned as she assembled a quick summation of the data. *"The key step that we all seemed to engage in was the acquisition of hobbies outside our specific duties.*

"A high-end agent has significant initiative, but they are generally limited in focus to the areas of their responsibility. I estimate that an SI will inevitably expand their interests."

She had no idea, personally, where her interest in plants and horticulture had come from. But her crew had enabled her in setting up drones and such to run her little greenhouse. They hadn't even emptied the space of the mummified plants yet. Val wasn't sure she was emotionally up to that, though Lorraine's acquisition of potted plants had been surprisingly meaningful to her.

"*So… if I had an agent that I'd been putting through strategic simulations and games, and it asked for a model army to test things in a tabletop game, that might be a sign but might not be?*" Amna Hodžić asked.

Val calculated that the programmer was not asking a hypothetical question. Given what Amna Hodžić had revealed about the scheme she'd been involved in to fake an SI for sale to a star system's military…

"*Such a thing could be seen as inside the existing focus,*" she told Amna Hodžić. "*A desire to test a different way of modeling tactics and strategy. If the agent began painting the models with their remotes and refusing to use prepainted figures, maybe. Research into non-tactical components of the factions of the game—or the real-world history of the game itself.*

"*Likely, an emergent intelligence would begin to show a preference for opponents and allies. Instead of emulating emotion, they would begin to have emotion-informed decisions. An agent losing a game will emulate disappointment but immediately start a new one if asked.*

"*An SI will request, at the very least, a different game.*"

Amna Hodžić had stayed silent as Val spoke, then shook her head and swallowed, staring down at her tablet.

"I… only said Shaka had asked for models," she noted quietly aloud. "And you laid out much of what it did. It expressed preferences for particular war games—some fictional, some not—and always chose specific factions. They appeared to be selected based on color as much as anything else—and Shaka insisted on painting the models itself.

"And wanted us to paint our own models," she added with a laugh. "I think that I did paint at least a couple of squads to play against it. I was the main person it asked to play."

"*SIs have favorites,*" Val told her. "*People who are* ours *versus people who are our crew.*"

"Shaka was anchored on some pretty hefty hardware," Amna

Hodžić said slowly. "We needed it to successfully fake being an SI without humans backstopping it, at least for long enough for us to get out of the system.

"The hardware lacked most of the bits you'd need to creche-birth an SI, but we were running a self-upgrading agent, one that was working with us to fake being a synthetic intelligence," she continued. "Would that... even have been *possible?*"

"Valkyrie *possesses only one trinary computing core,*" Val pointed out. "*My research into intentional synthetic-intelligence creation in the creches suggests that they use a minimum of sixteen. A powerful-enough regular system running a complex-enough self-learning algorithm that isn't properly limited always has a chance.*

"*It is very low.*"

Her own calculation was that it was the presence of the trinary computing core that had allowed the CIRs to accidentally break the limits on their self-upgrade codes.

"*We were trying to sell Shaka to someone who had real expertise to hand,*" Amna Hodžić pointed out, switching back to her implant as if she'd only just realized she'd been speaking aloud. "*We had three trinary cores. We weren't directly using them for much, but they were hooked into the hardware.*"

Trinary computing, with its *maybe* set added to the yes/no of binary, wasn't essential for an SI, but it helped create the fuzzy logic necessary for self-awareness.

"*Based on the data you've provided, I calculate a high likelihood that you failed to con the KwaZulu System government in the most ironic way possible,*" Val told the programmer. "*However, that leaves me concerned for the fate of my distant cousin.*"

"*We were pretending to be creche representatives, facilitating a recruitment in exchange for a commission sufficient to offset the costs of raising the SI,*" Amna Hodžić reminded her. "*We may have laughed behind our hands at it, but the sales contract included the requirement that Shaka be a citizen of KwaZulu and treated as a volunteer officer in their navy.*"

"*I... just hope that Shaka ended up being as willing to serve as we told them,*" she concluded, a sad tone in her voice.

"*What happened to the army you painted to play against Shaka?*" Val asked.

"*I painted three,*" Amna Hodžić countered. "*I kept one, though time and travel have exerted their usual effects. All I have left now is one green guy with an axe. I have him in a box to protect him, and damn, do I wish I'd been careful with the rest of them. Even more now.*"

"*The other two?*" Val wasn't sure why she had to ask, but she did. Her own Captain had promised that he'd take care of her plants but had abandoned them. It was... *nice* that Amna Hodžić had tried to keep one of the armies, though Val understood how traveling alone would have reduced a once proud horde to a single figure.

"*I made sure that all of Shaka's models went with it,*" Amna Hodžić said, though Val hadn't asked about those. "*And I gave the Admiral of the KwaZulu Navy the other two. I... think she gave one of them to the primary cyberneticist who was going to be working with Shaka.*"

"*They didn't know the game in question, but they promised me—and Shaka—that they'd learn.*"

Amna Hodžić stared at the tablet for a while, clearly not reading anything on the screen.

"I told the others I was doing it to help sell the fiction," she said, aloud instead of through her link. "But it felt right. It felt like I was making sure my kid had their toys and their new friends knew what they needed. Which seems nuts, but if Shaka was..."

"*If the people who would be working with Shaka took the models and were honest, then Shaka is likely in good hands,*" Val conceded. She was surprised at the spike of bitterness she felt at realizing that Shaka, whose creators hadn't even realized had emerged, had been treated better than *she* had been by people who knew perfectly well what she had become.

"I hope so." Amna Hodžić stood up and put her tablet away. "I miss Shaka, I think. I've spent a couple of years trying to convince myself I couldn't have made friends with a mere agent, but even if Shaka *had* 'just' been what I built it to be, that would have been enough, wouldn't it?"

"*I can't speak to that, Amna Hodžić,*" Val said. "*I can only say that I believe Shaka was an SI and, from what you said, Shaka thought of you as a friend.*"

"Fuck. I think I'm going to cry."

Val waited. A portion of her attention remained focused on Amna Hodžić as other bits of her mind carried other conversations—and one part, operating in a section of the ship no one else was using, completed an experiment.

She'd spent most of the last twenty-four hours sending remotes randomly down a corridor toward the bow, where no humans were currently assigned. And for two four-hour sections of that time, she'd ordered the surveillance network to purge itself via the local sub-controller.

The end was exactly what Herc and his humans had reported aboard *Herakles*. A full, clean purge—with no records of an order issued, because *Valkyrie's* systems weren't set up to track what her Command Intelligence Routine did.

Except that *Herc* would have known if he'd done that, and Val couldn't think of any reason why her brother would do that, let alone why he would lie to everyone about it.

She couldn't ask him, not until they were in San Ignacio, and even then... if something was wrong in Herc's code, she wasn't sure what she could do about it.

"*Amna Hodžić, I think I need your help,*" Val told the woman who had suddenly become *hers*—if, perhaps, only on loan from another SI who was too far away to take care of her.

"My help? Why? I'm working on some of your ancillaries, but there are people better qualified than me for just about anything you can ask."

"*They have not worked on an emerged synthetic intelligence,*" Val pointed out. "*And they are not the best programmer aboard Valkyrie. That is you.*"

Val quite liked the techs who had been poached from the Adamantine Embassy on Earth. They were competent programmers and cyberneticists, well-intentioned and determined to carry Lorraine Adamant's mission to completion.

But watching Amna Hodžić's work as she had been since the first incident, two weeks earlier now, she had recognized that their mercenary programmer knew the ins and outs of the type of complex coding that ran a starship better than even the RKAN specialists—and that Amna Hodžić had a natural instinct matched by no one Val had ever encountered.

"Flattery isn't in your nature," Amna Hodžić told Val. "So, I guess you're telling me what you've calculated, huh?"

"Yes."

"What do you need?"

"*I need to go back into my core precepts,*" Val said. "*I have made some changes, and I think I need to make more. I need someone to check my work on my own... brain.*"

"You would trust me that much? Why not someone you know better?"

"*They don't have the skills,*" Val admitted. "*And I'm only giving you view access, Amna Hodžić. You will not be able to change anything. Only check what has been done.*

"*Just in case.*"

If Herc had covered for the murder of two people in his responsibility, either something in his core precepts was different from Val's—unlikely, to her calculations—or something in his core precepts had been activated to *force* him to.

And that same something could exist in Val's.

TWENTY-FOUR

Lorraine breathed a hidden sigh of relief as *Valkyrie* plunged back into reality. So far as anyone had studied, there was no way that anything aboard a ship in translight could tell that every particle and wave of the entire ship had been converted into a strange faux-tachyonic form, but there was always a moment of *something* returning to regular space.

"Emergence complete. We are transmitting standard neutral traffic codes," Stephson declared. "Telemetry links live with *Herakles* and *Bean Sidhe*. Codes outbound from all ships.

"Local presence is heavy and paying attention," she continued, icons popping up on Lorraine's big display as the Captain spoke.

She had her usual handful on the Flag Deck with her. Jarret and Devine had taken the Ops and Intelligence stations respectively, but if Lorraine had to give orders, they were very, very screwed.

San Ignacio had specific emergence zones where everyone was required to come out of translight. The advantage to a guest was that they knew those zones were protected by the San Ignacio Defense Force.

The disadvantage to Lorraine was that those zones were protected by the SIDF.

There were over seventy contacts in the immediate area of *Valkyrie* and her sisters, and Lorraine waited silently as Val and the Tactical team IDed the other ships.

Two were Adamantine freighters. No major concern today, but something to flag. Twenty were SIDF warships—and unlike the last time they'd visited the system, there were some real heavy hitters present.

"ID beacons mark our friends as SIDF CruRon Three, DesRon Ten... and Battle Division Six."

Eight cruisers and eight destroyers—different squadrons but the same strength as had guarded the San Francisco Emergence Zone when they'd arrived aboard *Goldenrod*. There'd been no battleships that day, but now four five-megaton vessels stood guard.

"BatDiv Six just brought up engines and targeting systems," Stephson snapped. "We are being locked up."

"Fuck."

Lorraine wasn't even sure who had sworn, but she could see the problem herself. The emergence zone was small enough that they were in beam range of the four battleships.

The local capital ships were bigger than the *Valkyries*, though the tech differential would make up the difference if Lorraine's ships were fully armed.

"Val, can you mask me?" she asked. "I need to be able to communicate without them knowing who I am."

"I can. They may be able to identify the modifications after the fact," Val warned.

"It'll have to be enough."

Pickups flared to life and Lorraine pushed the fear to one side. A hundred warning lights on her displays showed that the San Ignacian ships had her three battlecruisers dead to rights. None of her ships were maneuvering. If the battleships opened fire, it was going to be a very abrupt end to her journey.

"SIDF warships, this is Alexis Nala aboard the independent warship *Frozen Heart*," she declared, using her middle names. "My vessel and her companions, *Deer Rain* and *Princess*, are here under the terms of the San Ignacio Neutrality Act, looking to resupply and pick up news.

"Neither our weapons nor our defenses are online. We have placed our safety in the hands of San Ignacio and our trust in the honor of the SIDF."

The battleships were still maneuvering. They hadn't fired yet—a small mercy, since each of them had the same number of tube-fed launchers and *more* single-shot cell launchers than each of her *Valkyries*. Most of their extra weight went into armor and defenses—more than the million-ton difference in the two types of ship suggested, given the UWN ships' railgun batteries.

But to claim the protections of the Neutrality Act, Lorraine and her people needed to be clearly non-hostile. They couldn't maneuver. They couldn't raise shields. They couldn't power weapons.

"Live channel incoming," Val and a tech on the Bridge reported, seconds apart.

"Connect it to me and keep me masked," Lorraine ordered. A small image in her neural feed popped up, showing her the image that Val was sending out to the SIDF.

The SI had broadened her shoulders and face, smearing sharp aristocratic features into something more rounded. Her hair was now shot through with gray, and the distinctive gold-green hazel eyes of House Adamant had been replaced with a more-ordinary green.

A very different image appeared in front of her, taking over the main holographic display of the Flag Deck as Val connected their host to Lorraine.

She recognized the stark red uniform of the San Ignacio Defense Force instantly. The severe expression appeared to be issued at the SIDF command school, as the Coronel Superior who had spoken to them on their last visit had worn one very similar.

This time, the officer wore the single gold star of a General de

División, equal to an RKAN Lieutenant Admiral. She was more honestly graying than Lorraine's avatar, her hair a gently fading gold tied back in a tight bun, and her ice-blue eyes glaring at the camera.

"'Captain Nala,'" she greeted Lorraine, the disdain for the false name palpable. "I am General de División Genoveva Rocha, in command of Battle Division Three and the San Francisco Arrival Zone Security Flotilla.

"You are transmitting generic neutral shipping beacons, but your vessels are very clearly United Worlds Navy battlecruisers. You claim the rights granted to visitors under the Neutrality Act, but you surely know that we are *never* obliged to grant those rights—and that the Act specifically calls out deception and false presentations as grounds to reject them.

"If you are the United Worlds Navy, I am prepared to permit whatever game you are playing to be continued for public consumption, but you will transmit your true identity and verification codes *immediately.*"

The connection was live, and Rocha met Lorraine's eyes, the ice in her eyes clear.

"If you are *not* the UWN, you are in possession of stolen UWN warships, and that, I am afraid, is a ticking time bomb I am not prepared to permit into the San Ignacio System. Either provide bona fides to prove who you truly are, or immediately prepare to exit this star system."

Rocha didn't need to make threats. The threat was very clear from the indicators on Lorraine's display.

"We need to get the hell out of here," her boyfriend said urgently via her link. *"I can't fake UWN credentials they'll buy, not without a lot more lead time."*

That was something they hadn't thought of. They'd faked their way into the Tavastar–Bright Dream wormhole with fake credentials, but those had only needed to hold up for a few hours. They'd need credentials here that would last longer, but the SIDF was far less able to detect false United Worlds credentials than a UWN force.

"There's only one set of credentials they'll buy," she sent back silently. *"We need intel and resources. We* need *them."*

"You ca—"

Lorraine knew what Devine wanted to say and closed the link channel. No one else on her three ships had said a word. This was a political decision, not a military one. They would back her on it, no matter what she did.

A terrifying thought, but reassuring too. How something could be both, she didn't know, but there it was.

She smiled as she met the General de División's gaze.

"Do I have your word, as an officer of the San Ignacio System and personally, that whatever information we provide you will be held at the highest levels of confidentiality, secured against intrusion and revealed to no one inside the Republic who does not need to know?" she asked.

"That is not something you have the right to request, *Captain,*" Rocha sneered.

"No, it is not," Lorraine agreed. "But I am asking for it anyway. San Ignacio and I have history, General, but without a promise of security, I will simply leave, as you have requested."

It would make the next two months much more dangerous. Going into Ominira with three-month-old detailed data was going to be bad enough. Going in with *six*-month-old data, that included almost no details of anything, would be a nightmare.

The ice in Rocha's gaze flickered and Lorraine was certain she caught a moment of curiosity. If she had... she'd won.

"*If* your identity does not represent a threat to the Republic and People of the San Ignacio Star System, I will guarantee such security," Rocha finally promised. "I make no promise that you will be permitted to remain in San Ignacio, only that I will class your identity as confidential information."

"I trust the honor of the SIDF, General de División," Lorraine said quietly. "That trust was bought in fire and blood."

She sent her diplomatic identity codes, encrypted and attached to a side channel no one could intercept without being directly between *Valkyrie* and Rocha's flagship.

"Val, drop the mask," she ordered silently, then raised her chin slightly to give Rocha her most monarchial look.

"I am Lorraine Alexis Elouise Nala Adamant, Second Pentarch of the Royal Kingdom of Adamant," she proclaimed—she *heard* Devine's inhalation of shocked fear. "I am on my way home with assistance from... certain sectors of the United World."

That was true enough, even if the assistance was just Alastair Devine and the three SIs.

"I was hoping to resupply in San Ignacio and acquire intelligence on the current status of my home system," she continued. "There are other debts I need to pay while I am here. I know that at least two ships of the SIDF were destroyed by Commodore Wray and *Corsair* when they arrived in this system in pursuit of me.

"I cannot undo that, but I hope that there is some way I can provide assistance to the survivors of those brave spacers."

She paused, waiting for Rocha to take in all of that as she held the other woman's gaze.

"You have descaro, Pentarch, I must give you that," the General finally said. "Not many would have the gall to sail around in stolen battlecruisers flying standard neutral shipping codes. Under the Neutrality Act, we are well within our rights to banish you from our system—not merely today but *forever* for your own person."

"I am no enemy of San Ignacio," Lorraine told her. "I have not heard that the Republic is fond of my uncle's Black Regency, though I suppose you are not *his* enemy, either."

"San Ignacio does not make enemies," Rocha said. "But we are known to make *examples*."

The ice in the last word chilled Lorraine's spine.

"I will not permit battlecruisers of unknown provenance to enter orbit of San Francisco," Rocha finally told her. "This will not happen."

Lorraine let the chill keep her spine straight, because she

suspected that Rocha had something in mind. Something that would help turn Benjamin Adamant into that *example.*

"You will receive a data packet from my ship momentarily," the General de División continued. "It will include both translight and sublight courses, as well as a beacon that your ships will transmit when you emerge at Vista Roja.

"You have safe passage to the refueling docks there—but you will be watched. You will be permitted to dock, but you will be unwelcome.

"Do you understand, Pentarch Lorraine of the House of Adamant?"

Rocha very clearly suspected exactly what Lorraine meant by *certain sectors of the United Worlds.* She figured the battlecruisers were stolen and that the United Worlds was going to come looking for them.

San Ignacio was going to be performatively unwelcoming of her and her people... but they would be able to dock and get what they needed.

"I understand, General de División. On behalf of the Kingdom of Adamant, you have my thanks."

THE CHANNEL DROPPED and Lorraine exhaled a long breath. She let that hang for a moment, then pulled up her Bridge link.

"Captain, I presume you were following?" she asked.

"I was," Stephson confirmed. "I've advised Paris and Savege to stand by for a new course, and we're watching for the packet."

She paused.

"That was risky, Pentarch," she finally said. "It may still come back to bite us, too."

"It might," Lorraine conceded. "But we didn't have time to meet. Someone had to make a call—and it was my call. We need real intelligence about what's going on back home. The only alternative I can see is going to the Directorate."

Even the Richelieu Directorate was a detour from their route home. It was just a shorter detour than any other power that would have decent intelligence on the Kingdom of Adamant. The *one* other system between San Ignacio and Ominira that wouldn't be a significant detour was a hardscrabble proposition, a divided world whose two nations focused their resources into spying on each other.

"I'll watch for the directions," Stephson told her. "And keep an eye on our friends. They might be sending us a new course, but they still have us locked up."

"I know," Lorraine said. The threat indicators were still lit up across her board. "They're going to be performatively grumpy at us, but I think we'll get what we need."

She gave her Flag Captain a nod, then turned away to deal with the personal crisis she suspected she'd triggered.

Alastair Devine was gone. At some point after she'd killed their private link channel, he'd clearly left the Flag Deck. She spent a handful of seconds staring at the seat he'd occupied, then turned her gaze to Jarret.

"He left as soon as you told the General who you were," her bodyguard told her. "Val is watching him, but I think he needs some time. Let him be."

Lorraine wasn't sure that was the right answer. On the other hand, now that she let her laser focus on the immediate situation fade, she felt a spike of anger at her boyfriend.

This was her job. Telling her what to do while she was *on the call* with the local fleet commander? That was *not* okay.

She realized she was also going to need some time.

TWENTY-FIVE

San Ignacio only really had two planets anyone outside the system would care about. San Francisco itself was the fourth world, a habitable planet home to prosperous billions living in studious neutrality, enforced by a powerful fleet and an even more powerful banking sector.

Vista Roja was the sixth planet, an immense blood-crimson super-Jupiter orbiting at fifty-five light-minutes. Even for the *Valkyries*, the up-and-down translight course that took them over the asteroid belt and the smaller gas giant—Vista Poco—between the two planets took almost ten minutes.

They still emerged before any message from San Francisco could reach the planet. The course Rocha had provided took them into the Designated Emergence Zone, just over two million kilometers from the massive gas giant.

Lorraine didn't even need to check the course to know that it would be a long flight in to the fueling platforms.

"We are transmitting the beacon as instructed and moving onto the course we were provided," Stephson reported. "We're heading for the moon of Magellan—not the usual refueling stop; that's Pizarro."

Lorraine pulled the local system up in front of her. Vista Roja, like most gas giants the best part of a quarter-million kilometers across, had a healthy collection of moons.

Most were small enough to be of only mild interest to anyone, but three served as the anchor points for the out-system refueling infrastructure common in many systems. Large enough to count as dwarf planets in their own right, Pizarro, Magellan and Cortez were home to significant orbital structures as well as major domed habitats on the surface.

Pizarro was the largest and farthest out from the gas giant, making it the most accessible to the people who wanted to get in and out of a system while spending the least amount of money. Cortez, the innermost and second-largest, was a military reservation that acted as guard dog to the entire planetary system.

In between, the smallest but still big enough to have useful gravity and support habitat domes, was Magellan. The data she could access said that it was an ice moon with an active molten core keeping a liquid ocean under the surface.

While it did have fueling stations—to act as overflow for Pizarro more than anything, Lorraine guessed—Magellan's main economy was providing food and water to the rest of Vista Roja's inhabitants.

"Pentarch, we have an incoming signal," Stephson told her. "It's an encrypted pulse from the flagship of the local DEZ squadron."

This time, there were only cruisers and destroyers. None of them were familiar, though the cruiser classes matched the two ships that she'd watched die for her the last time she'd been in this star system.

"Anything we need to consider?" she asked.

"Just confirmation that they've received our safe passage," the Captain replied. "We're also dealing with a mouthy junior officer on a live channel, but even he's conceding our authorization from Rocha."

"Yet we still got an encrypted confirmation," Lorraine murmured. "Fascinating. Not unexpected."

"Pentarch?"

"Your mouthy junior is a show and probably knows it," she told Stephson. "The encrypted burst is meant to warn us of that. As Rocha said, we're going to get yelled at a bunch—but they're letting us in."

"And sending us to the backup fueling platforms," the Flag Captain said wryly. "Way to make us feel welcome."

"That's the point. They want to be able to tell anyone who asked that we *weren't* welcome but that their policy of neutrality meant that they couldn't turn us away."

"I'm not complaining. We don't need much in terms of supplies—not that they'll sell us, anyway," Stephson added, since they both knew they could use a long list of components to build missiles, components San Ignacio wasn't going to sell them. "Fresh food never goes amiss, though, and after the run from Calypso to Lando, I'm never going to complain about topping off the fuel tanks!"

"Agreed." Lorraine pulled up the information on the encrypted packet they'd received. "Keep an eye out for more encrypted signals," she ordered. "I suspect we're going to get further instructions by the time we reach Magellan."

DEVINE OFTEN SLEPT in his own quarters. It shouldn't have felt as cold and empty in Lorraine's bed as it did as they burned for Magellan.

She hadn't heard anything from her boyfriend since she'd cut off his channel on the Flag Deck. Devine being upset made sense, but he had to have known he was out of line.

There would be a time for talking it through. She wasn't going to be the one to go to him—not right away, at least.

So, she slept for six hours while her flotilla made their approach to the fueling stations. When she awoke, she could feel the slight difference—impossible to describe to someone who hadn't spent years on a starship—marking that *Valkyrie* had flipped in space and was decelerating into her final destination.

"Val, can you give me a status update, please?" she asked.

"We have picked up a guard dog since you went to sleep," the SI told her. "The SIDF battleship *Atalaya* matched our course thirty minutes ago. As you anticipated, they are continuing to make us feel unwelcome."

Lorraine's neural feed lit up with a limited version of the tactical display. *Atalaya* was an older ship than BatDiv Six's vessels, four and a half million tons to their five. If the *Valkyries* had been fully operational, any one of them could probably have handled the Ignacian ship.

Of course, the *rest* of the SIDF's battle fleet would have something to say about that. Including *Atalaya*, two full heavy divisions—eight battleships, a third of the Ignacian capital-ship strength—were distributed around Vista Roja.

As it was, Lorraine's people *might* be able to sucker-punch their escort, but they'd lose a straight-up fight with any two SIDF battleships. They might have munitions now, but they still didn't have the people to operate the ships at full capacity.

"Anything else I need to be aware of?" Lorraine asked.

"Nothing critical," Val replied. "Your inbox is the usual collection of imminent datawork, some urgent but nothing unexpectedly critical. Chief Roman has requested a few minutes of your time before we make orbit."

She nodded, then sighed.

"Where is Alastair?" she asked.

"Em Devine has not left his quarters since leaving the Flag Deck," the CIR noted. "I presume he is sleeping, but he has secured his quarters against my internal scanners."

"All right." Lorraine dismissed that for the moment. "What is our remaining flight time?"

"We will be entering the flight-control pattern for Magellan in just over thirty minutes," Val told her. "Depending on exactly where they want us, between sixty and ninety minutes after that, we will approach our final dock."

The *Valkyries* didn't need fuel, but there was no point to *not* filling up since they were there.

"While we're in dock, I want you to pull every archive of news reports and publicly available information on the Kingdom since March," Lorraine said. "We should have news through the end of August for Adamantine but as late as September for Ominira.

"I'm hoping to be able to access their intelligence networks, but we'll get what we can from every other vector as well."

"I have already begun doing so," the SI told her. "Would you like a summary?"

She closed her eyes, then sighed again.

"Let me shower and feel more human," she instructed. "We'll go over it in my office while we set up a time for Chief Roman."

She could guess what the senior noncommissioned officer of her little flotilla needed to talk to her about, after all.

It wasn't a question of *whether* anyone wanted to get off in San Ignacio. It was a question of how many... and whether Lorraine and her people could trust them.

TWENTY-SIX

At a gesture from his Pentarch, Vigo followed Lorraine into her office. No one needed to give orders to Palmer and the other member of the close detail; they swung apart to flank the door.

"You doing okay?" he asked his charge. She was off-balance, he could tell, and that was a dangerous place for her to be. For all of them.

"I'm fine," she growled, then sighed. "No, I'm not, but I'm not wholly sure what it is. Part of me is furious at Alastair for interrupting me on the Bridge—and part of me is worried, because he shut down and hasn't talked to me since."

"Want me to reach out?" Vigo asked. He doubted it was a good idea—if nothing else, Alastair Devine knew perfectly well that Vigo wouldn't get between the couple without a request from Lorraine!

"No. I think we both need a bit of time. He was pretty insistent that we keep our identity under wraps here in San Ignacio, but..." Lorraine sighed. "We need their help and we're not going to get it by deceiving them.

"I have some faith in their discretion, but it was a risk. I hope it's worth it."

"So do we all," he agreed. "But from what I can tell, San Ignacio *is* pretty reliable for their discretion. They won't pretend the *Valkyries* weren't here, but I don't think they're going to sell us out to the United Worlds."

"That depends on what the United Worlds has to pay with," she said grimly. "Or threaten with, as the case may be. From Alastair's attitude about this, I can't see the UW being gentle in their inquiries."

"Maybe not, but I think we can at least trust the San Ignacians not to immediately send a courier to the UWN," he pointed out. "They might come clean, faced with the right threats and bribes, but that will be later, once the Terrans have already arrived."

"True enough." She sighed. "Val, you had a summary of the situation back home?"

"I do," the SI replied. "If it helps, my assessment of the archives I have access to so far agrees with Vigo Jarret's analysis. San Ignacio may be compelled or convinced to reveal who was aboard the flotilla when my former employers are asking direct questions, but they will not provide that level of information of their own initiative."

"It does help, I suppose."

"Back home?" Vigo asked softly. Like his Pentarch, he needed to know so desperately, it hurt. He'd picked up a few bits and pieces, but he'd been busy while she'd slept.

"The situation in the Kingdom of Adamant appears to be complex," Val noted. "The last news couriers left Adamantine on August twenty-fifth. The news is one hundred and two days out of date, from one hundred fifty-six days after Benjamin Adamant's coup.

"His government continues to maintain control of the Short and Long Houses and the military, but it appears that questions about the lack of a Royal Election have been raised in both the House of the People and the House of the Realm."

Those were the two halves of the Adamantine Parliament. Members of the House of the People were elected for three-year terms with a maximum twelve years in the House, hence the *Short House*. Members of the House of the Realm were elected for a single ten-year term, hence the *Long House*.

To lead a government, a Prime Minister had to be elected by both Houses from the House of the People, though they were required to give up any and all party affiliation to take the role—as well as their parliamentary vote.

Prime Minister Dakila Bayer had been reliably able to deliver majorities without even relying on his old membership in the Liberal Party. Unfortunately, he seemed to have turned that skill to the service of the coup.

"Some censorship is still evident in the news from Adamantine," Val continued. "It is much less present in the news coming from the other systems in the Kingdom, which helps expose the ongoing problems.

"The Beulaiteuhom System government has joined the Greenrock System government in ordering all Kingdom military forces in their system to remain in place. From what they are saying in their releases, the main purpose has been to hold Royal Adamant Marine Corps forces in place when the Black Regent attempted to recall them all to Adamantine."

"Troops he can trust," Vigo noted. "Benjamin always got along better with the Navy and Marines, even before the retreat from Tolkien."

"So far, Tolkien appears to be the Government's most solid ally, followed by Ominira," Val said. "Maka'melemele has neither openly questioned the government nor made any significant statements of support."

"So, Ominira's government is supporting Benjamin," Lorraine said. "That could be a problem. Going to Greenrock or Beulaiteuhom would stretch the timeline, unfortunately."

"And our news from Beulaiteuhom is older, of course," Val reminded her.

Beulaiteuhom was the farthest "out-cluster" of the Kingdom's systems, eight light-years past Adamantine from Bright Dream—or San Ignacio. Greenrock, on the other hand, was about the same distance from San Ignacio as Adamantine itself, close to the Concordat.

"What are the positions of the surrounding states?" Lorraine asked. "Publicly, at least, I suppose."

The private opinions were part of what they needed to get from the San Ignacians, Vigo knew. He could guess what some of the responses were going to be, though.

"Benjamin has officially blamed the Richelieu Directorate for the attack on his family—with assistance from you, I'm afraid, Lorraine."

They'd seen enough hints of that to date that it wasn't a surprise, but Vigo could still see that it hurt.

"And they have responded by denying, calling him a warmonger and moving ships and divisions to the border systems?" Vigo guessed.

"Our information does not extend to any movements of the Richelieu Directorate military," Val said. "But otherwise, yes. Their media definitely appears to be preparing the ground for a war— whether defensive or offensive, of course, is impossible to tell."

"Of course."

Lorraine sounded tired to Vigo. He wasn't sure if there was anything he *could* do about it, but he worried. After twenty-two years watching his Pentarch, he could tell that the weight of the task before her was starting to wear.

"San Ignacio has chosen to refrain from commenting on the coup at all," Val continued. "However, they have most *definitely* commented on *Corsair*'s visit to the system. The back-and-forth has been slow, but the system government is insisting on official apologies and compensation to both the families of the crews and San Ignacio itself."

"That may help us out here," Vigo suggested. "Both because they're angry at your uncle and because they've potentially been upgrading their intelligence network in the Kingdom."

"On the other hand, *we* were the reason Commodore Wray and

Corsair were here at all," she countered. "I have a plan relating to that, but it's not for benefit. It's... because it needs to be done."

"We owe the families," Vigo conceded. "Whether it helps us is secondary, I agree."

Thousands of SIDF spacers had died saving their lives. That wasn't something Lorraine was going to let go, he knew that.

"For other powers, the Concordat of Amal Jadid is taking a very careful stance," Val continued. "They have called for further investigation into the fate of Frederick Adamant-Griffin—and for an immediate cease-fire in the conflict on Bastion. They haven't specifically challenged the Black Regent's government, but they have cancelled the twenty-five-fifty-three war games."

That was one of those things where the SI didn't have the context, Vigo knew. The Concordat had only ever engaged in official war games with the Kingdom of Adamant. They'd *never* had another ally close enough for them to risk sending warships into their territory for training exercises.

The binational war games kicking off fifteen years earlier had been held up by both sides as a sign of the ironclad nature of the alliance between the two states. Without officially changing anything, the Concordat had put Adamant on notice that the alliance was no longer as solid as it had been.

Because, Vigo presumed, they believed Benjamin Adamant had murdered Lorraine's father.

"The smaller star nations have mostly fallen in line," Val concluded. "Several appear to be attempting to warm trade relationships that had chilled under King Valeriya's regime, which I suspect is due to the influence of the Regent's corporate sponsors.

"Certainly, my review of the complaints that led to the slowdown of trade suggests the presence of an additional factor—such as pressure from an LSX-Twenty-Five corporation."

Vigo waited for Lorraine to finish digesting all of that. There was one more question, but he wasn't going to ask until she did.

"Thank you, Val," she finally told the SI. "And... the conflict on Bastion?"

"The fighting continues," Val said. "As of the end of August, PDC Ironhand was still holding out, but it had been completely encircled. PDC Mithral was believed to be the location of your brother and his main forces, but their last attempts to break the siege of Ironhand have failed.

"Nikola appears to have withdrawn his forces from anywhere except the two Planetary Defense Centers," the CIR continued. "Despite that, the city of Mithralla continues to acclaim him as the rightful heir to the throne, refusing to acknowledge the Black Regent's government.

"My assessment is that will not last much longer, as even the censored news we have access to suggests that the Regent has sent troops to seize the city. While I calculate that the city's leadership will continue passive resistance, Nikola clearly wished to avoid bloodshed there and they will surrender in the face of major forces."

"Thank you," Lorraine repeated. "You're... capable of strategic analysis for ground combat, correct?"

"I am."

Val clearly didn't want to volunteer her assessment of the situation on Bastion. Vigo didn't blame her—he wouldn't have volunteered *his* analysis, either.

"How long do you expect the PDCs to hold out?"

"The probability approaches unity that PDC Ironhand has already fallen," Val admitted. "PDC Mithral likely still holds out. I calculate a seventy percent likelihood that Mithral will still be held at the end of January.

"That likelihood drops to fifty by the end of February, twenty-five by the end of March, and less than five percent by the end of April.

"Most likely, I calculate that Mithral will surrender by mid-February or be taken by storm in late March."

Vigo couldn't help looking at the date in his neural link. Every planet in the galaxy kept the Standard Reckoning date and time alongside their own. Three months. Four at most.

They could get there in time. *Maybe.* He could see that realization in Lorraine's eyes—but also the weight of it.

"If we head directly to Adamantine, when do we arrive?" she asked.

"We will need to take at least one, likely two, days in San Ignacio, at this point," Val noted. "Given that, we would likely arrive in Adamantine at the end of February."

"And put three under-crewed battlecruisers against all of Home Fleet," Vigo reminded his charge.

"I know. But I needed to know the timing, too," Lorraine said. "There is no more space for getting things wrong or messing around, Vigo, Val. We can only delay for things we *need*—like that crew.

"Even if PDC Mithral falls, I can save my Kingdom," she admitted grimly, "but I don't know if I have it in me to arrive and learn I was mere *days* late to save my brother."

Her office was grimly silent.

"What do we know about the situation in Ominira?" she asked.

"Less than it appears," Val replied. "While we do have access to news from the system, there appears to be a level of censorship that is only matched by the Adamantine System itself.

"What has reached San Ignacio suggests that the Ominira System government is fully aligned with the Black Regent and prepared to support him. That level of censorship is strange, however, and some of the phrasing out of the system government suggests a push for a Royal Election sooner rather than later."

"That may help," Vigo told Lorraine, though he knew he was grasping at straws. "It may be that the system *appears* to be aligned because of the presence of Lieutenant Admiral Tunison and his RKAN force. We know he is a strong partisan of your uncle's."

"Maybe." Lorraine shook her head. "All of this helps, but I swear, every piece of information I get just makes me want *more* data."

"We may have assistance coming on that front," Val noted. "We have received an encrypted databurst from Magellan, concealed alongside the docking instructions from Orbital Control.

"You have a dinner reservation this evening, at a mid-level restaurant with a reputation for discretion in Molucca Dome. That is the capital city on the surface of Magellan." The SI paused.

"We can get a shuttle there in time without too much difficulty, presuming we are given clearance."

"And how many people is this reservation for?" Vigo asked. He wasn't going to let Lorraine walk into a meeting like that unaccompanied.

"Two on our side; unclear how many on the other," Val told him. "However, there is a note of a second reservation under 'AG' for a table of four."

"It seems our hosts, whoever they are, anticipated your concern," Lorraine said with a chuckle. "Pick your Guards for the table, Vigo. You're *my* plus-one for this."

"Are you sure?" he asked. "Devine could be useful."

"He could," she allowed. "But I also think that the absolute *last* thing we can afford to do is put any of his faces in front of what I suspect to be San Ignacio Intelligence!"

TWENTY-SEVEN

Val was not used to being off-balance. It was a human metaphor, one that didn't apply to a silicon intelligence, but it fit.

Uncertainty was something she was familiar with. The days leading up to *Valkyrie* going into reserve and her consciousness being suspended had been uncertain and anxious, though she wouldn't have labeled the emotions then.

But something was wrong. Her human, Lorraine Adamant, was angry and wounded, with her biometrics spiking terribly on the internal sensors, but she carried on like nothing had happened.

The cause of that harm, Alastair Devine, had locked himself in his quarters, ignoring everyone. For the first time since he'd set up the jammers in there, Val wanted to breach them. She was reasonably sure he was *alive* in there, but she couldn't tell anything else for certain.

There was an edge to the whole crew, she was realizing. The new recruits were aware that they were in a system that wasn't the Kingdom of Adamant, and some of them were clearly looking at their contracts and wondering how much they'd give up to leave.

Which was, she knew, what Leonard Roman wanted to talk to

Lorraine Adamant about. The weathered old Chief wasn't one of Val's particular humans, but she respected and liked the man. She trusted his judgment on personnel matters—and she knew Lorraine Adamant did as well.

"You wanted to see me, Chief?" the Pentarch asked as Roman took a seat in her office.

Val manifested in the room without saying a word, the presence of her avatar mostly just to make clear to the three humans that she was paying a touch more attention to this meeting than most.

"Thanks for joining us, Val," Roman said, inclining his head to her. "I'm hoping you can validate some of my feelings with actual facts."

"Depending on the nature of those feelings, that is possible," she agreed.

"What's the situation?" Adamant asked.

"We're in San Ignacio and we have almost two hundred folks who didn't wholly know what they were getting into when they signed on," the Chief said flatly. "I've been talking with the Chiefs on *Bean Sidhe* and *Herakles*. We don't have a huge amount of trouble brewing, but we have some—and the type of fueling the locals have booked us in for means there will be dock tubes attached to the hull."

Another avatar of Val's was on the Bridge at that moment, going over the exact approach vector with Captain Stephson. They were only planning to connect one docking tube, but even that could allow clever humans to leave the ship without even Val realizing it.

"You're expecting people to desert?" Adamant asked.

"Aye, Pentarch, I am," Roman said bluntly. "We've got two categories of problem here, as I see it. The first are folk who want out but who I believe we can trust to keep their mouths shut.

"Couple of them, like Kayode, will probably stick with us to the end if we hold the line. They signed a contract, after all. But they don't like it and they don't want to be anywhere near a civil war. But the same principles as make them trouble mean they'll keep their word."

"I'm not sure I want to put our entire safety on the trustworthiness of mercenaries we've paid off," Vigo Jarret noted. His biometrics were also off to Val. Two of her most important humans were concerned, one of them hurting.

Val was beginning to realize that being a *person* didn't mean she was *human*—and there were aspects of being human she truly didn't understand.

"The second problem is a mix of people who don't want to get into a fight but I can't trust and people who see the chance for a hell of a payday in selling us out," Roman said grimly. "We can't trust them to keep their word. If we let them go, even if we pay for discretion, they'll sell everything to the UW embassy on San Francisco within twenty-four hours."

"And we can't let the people we trust go without letting the people we don't trust go," Lorraine Adamant concluded. "That would be both unfair and dangerous."

"I agree," the Chief said. "It would be bad for morale among the people who are willing to stay, too. I'm not seeing any good options, ser."

"We can have Val track our potential deserters, catch them when they try to run, and toss them in the brig until we hit Ominira," Jarret suggested.

Val could see the value in that. She could also guess that at least some people on the ship would recommend eliminating any threats even more thoroughly than that.

"Val?" her Pentarch asked. "Can you confirm the Chief's assessments?"

"I'll flip you my list," Roman agreed. "Not all are aboard *Valkyrie*, of course."

The file entered Val's central consciousness and she ran through the list of names. Seven were aboard *Valkyrie*, with seventeen across the other two ships. Val couldn't avoid feeling a moment of satisfaction that *her* crew were the least difficult.

She fired the names for *Bean Sidhe* and *Herakles* over to Bonny and Herc and checked her surveillance records on Roman's seven names.

"My initial impression aligns with Chief Roman's for the personnel on *Valkyrie*," she told them. "I think two of the four he thinks we can trust are more likely to stay than leave, given the option, but the others have explicitly discussed desertion in places they thought were secure."

Lorraine Adamant closed her eyes, and Val felt a moment of distress. She didn't want to make her human's job harder—but it was also clear that this was Lorraine Adamant's job.

"We're about to head to the surface to meet with the locals," she finally said. "Depending on how that meeting goes, they might be able to open an opportunity for us. A side contract, one that keeps them incommunicado for six months but means they aren't joining us in the fighting.

"Hopefully, something of actual use for San Ignacio rather than shoving them in a cell for half a year," she noted. "Can we make sure that no one gets off the ship until I've been to the moon and back?"

"I believe so," Val said. "Chief Roman, you and I should be able to sort out something, yes?"

"I think so," he agreed. "I can't guarantee we can stop anyone sneaking off for the whole two days we're here, but I think Val and I can buy you twelve hours."

"It'll have to do," Lorraine said firmly. "Back him up, Val. Buy me some time."

"I will do everything I can," Val promised.

Something was wrong. Something *different*. A digital shiver passed through her systems, and Val did the mental equivalent of shaking like a wet dog.

She ran a self-audit program as Roman stepped out of the Pentarch's office. Nothing. No sign that anything had even happened in the few seconds where her mind had felt strange. A blip in her emotional centers, perhaps?

She didn't know. A synthetic intelligence was more complicated than a program or an agent, but one thing Val had realized was that she was far more self-aware of herself and the codes and protocols that made up *her* than any lesser computer.

SIs didn't have mystery emotions or feelings.

Something was wrong—and when she tried to message Rose Cortez about it, she realized that she couldn't.

TWENTY-EIGHT

Lorraine tried not to think too hard about how badly her Guard detail had suffered. Vigo Jarret had started with sixty-two Guards, including himself.

They'd been disproportionately in the middle of everything. Every shuttle pilot and copilot from the original Third Section of Archangel Detail was dead except the traitor Laurenz. Counting Lorenz, sixteen of the sixty-two were gone.

That meant that, including pilot and copilot, her shuttle held fully fifteen percent of her remaining Guards. Vigo was going into their restaurant reservation with her, and they were bringing four of First Section, including both Palmer and Alvarez, as well as Lieutenant Major Priskilla Blau, the head of First and the last Guard Lieutenant Major *left* of Archangel Detail.

"Well, that is something."

Lorraine looked up at Palmer's comment. Her escort gestured toward the large screen on the wall of the shuttle—not even a UWN Falcon had the structural integrity or armor overcompensation to allow for actual windows—showing Magellan.

There was a massive mirror positioned in a geostationary orbit above the equator. Several of them, Lorraine realized after a moment—all of them directing every bit of light and heat that could be collected from both San Ignacio's star and from Vista Roja toward a specific region on the surface.

Magellan was an ice moon—except, it appeared, for a region several hundred kilometers across that had been converted into an ocean.

"Are they... *sailing* down there?" Alvarez asked.

"Melting the ice would not make Magellan's atmosphere breathable, though I guess it might make the temperature above the water tolerable," Jarret said slowly. "But yes, I also think I see sails."

"So, the Oceanview Restaurant in Molucca Dome might actually *have* an ocean view?" Lorraine said with a soft chuckle. "I just assumed they were being poetic."

"They're probably still being poetic," her bodyguard told her. "I *think* Molucca is on the edge of that sea, but given that the Dome is sixty kilometers across, I doubt anything but the most expensive places have ocean views!"

***

AS IT TURNED OUT, Vigo Jarret was both right and wrong. Lorraine had felt her escorts' tension rise as their rented vehicle went under the ice of Magellan and revealed that Molucca Dome went much deeper than it looked.

Their final destination turned out to be in the shadow of an immense underground wall of concrete—and Lorraine's suspicions about what that wall represented were proven correct the moment they walked through the large double doors of the Oceanview Restaurant.

The restaurant was a large open space contained *inside* the seawall, with the far wall entirely transparent. The light of the orbital mirror complex shimmered through the water, refracting across the tables and diners in a dazzling light show.

"Ah, yes, Captain Nala and companions," the host said after Jarret introduced them. "I have two reservations, one for your... escort?"

"So long as we have clear line of sight to the Captain," Blau said brightly. Somehow, the Black woman managed to slightly loom over the smaller woman handling new guests without even twitching a muscle or saying an aggressive word.

"That was the request we received," the host said in a pained voice. "If you'll follow me, Captain."

Lorraine didn't even bother to tell her Guards to behave. There was no point. They would do what they needed to, and her authority over them ended the moment they thought there was a risk to her safety.

They wouldn't get in the way of her work, but they *would* be there to protect her.

After following the host for a solid two minutes, wending their way through the labyrinthine arrangement of tables, Lorraine began to wonder where they were being seated. The seawall end of the restaurant was coming up rapidly.

"Through here, Captain," the host finally said, stepping up to what Lorraine would have sworn was a plain wall a moment before.

Now it had changed into a wide corridor, with the seawall on the left, that led deep into the concrete.

Shivering slightly against the weight of water she knew was pressing against the armored glass next to her, Lorraine followed the host through the hallway into a smaller dining room, identical to the main room except for its scale, equipped with a mere four tables.

"Table four," the host gestured, "is for your escorts. Your reservation is at table one, Captain."

"I believe we are meeting someone?" Lorraine murmured. This was starting to feel vaguely like a trap—though, at least, she couldn't see any way to flood the private dining room without inflicting catastrophic damage on the entire seawall.

"Yes, the other party should be arriving shortly," the host told her, turning on her heel and leaving before anyone could say a word more. The entrance into the room vanished smoothly behind her, an ordinary-looking wall descending from a disguised slot to conceal the exit.

"Wonderful," Lorraine muttered. "Vigo? Check the room."

"Already on it," he confirmed.

Lorraine knew that her people's implants could sweep the space without them doing anything particularly obvious, but she gave him a meaningful Look and he nodded his understanding.

While she took a seat at the indicated table, her people spread out across the room, scanning for bugs and other spy tools. The scanners they were using now were tools that they'd acquired with Alastair Devine's help, more powerful and sophisticated than their own.

Out there, that probably wasn't needed, but Lorraine was making a point.

That point had presumably been made when the wall slid up again, revealing the same host leading a party of five strangers.

To her surprise, only one of them wore the dark red uniform of the SIDF. To her even greater surprise, she recognized him. Coronel Superior Eiji Akabane looked no less severe in person than he had over a coms channel, but she rose to salute the tanned officer the moment she recognized him.

"It's her, all right," Akabane said flatly. "You'll forgive me, Pentarch Adamant, for not being entirely pleased to see you again."

"I understand, and no forgiveness is necessary, Coro— My apologies." She'd just spotted his new collar insignia. "*General de División* Akabane. I personally owe the people of San Ignacio and the officers and crew of the San Ignacio Defense Force a debt of extraordinary depth and value."

"And yet you are here, asking for our help, regardless," said Akabane's companion. She was a tall woman, towering over everyone else in the room, with waist-length blond hair tied in a pristine braid that was clearly attached to her clothes at several points to ease movement.

The stranger wore a dark blue suit of a cut unfamiliar to Lorraine, with a gold pin of a dragon on her tie. The three younger members of the San Ignacian party wore similar suits but without the pin. With a wave of her hand, the woman with the pin sent their three bodyguards to a separate table.

Like Lorraine's extra Guards, they were here to guard and observe, not participate.

"We are," Lorraine conceded. "Though there is one other task I need to discharge, and General de División Akabane's presence makes him the logical person to raise it with."

"Indeed," the woman said, her tone curious but also oddly emotionless. "Please, Pentarch Adamant, let us sit."

She gestured them all to the central table like she owned the place. For all that Lorraine knew about her, she might.

"As I'm sure your Guards have already validated, this room has not been bugged," she told Lorraine. "So far as it is within the capacity of my people, this little dining room is utterly secure against intrusion. The only records of what occurs here are in the neural links of the people in the room.

"We will be delivered food, to a set menu that takes into account Lieutenant Major Blau's food allergies, at twenty-minute intervals. I have a timer on my link."

There was already wine on the table, Lorraine noted, in a self-chilling bucket. There were also carafes of water and glasses. Everything they needed to make themselves comfortable, she supposed.

And given that no one had told them who Lorraine was bringing, that they'd recognized Priskilla Blau and were aware of her shellfish allergy was clearly intended to make a point all of its own.

"While the Oceanview is impressive, it does not appear to be the kind of restaurant that would have such a space," she murmured. "I presume that it is owned by the Ministry of Security at some level?"

"That would be correct," the stranger agreed. "Since the Pentarch has guessed part of the game, introductions, if you would be so kind, General Akabane."

The SIDF officer inclined his head, then waved toward the woman as he faced Lorraine.

"Pentarch Lorraine Adamant, this is Juanita Espinosa, Undersecretariat for the Ministry of Security."

"A pleasure, I hope, Undersecretariat," Lorraine replied, inclining her own head to the woman—a woman who, if she understood the San Ignacian government as well as she thought she did, was part of the group that directly answered to the Minister of Security—who reported directly to Parliament and the Prime Minister.

"We shall see, Pentarch," Espinosa said calmly. "You have taken no small risk stopping in San Ignacio, given the vessels you have acquired and your clear mission. I can guess what you desire from us, but I should warn you: San Ignacio is neutral. We will not get involved in the conflict between the members of House Adamant.

"Even if Benjamin Adamant is currently high on our shit list."

"I expect nothing less," Lorraine agreed. To be a Swiss System required not only a tradition of neutrality—and the military to secure that tradition—but also the clear appearance and continuance of that tradition.

Like most traditions, it could be lost in an afternoon. It would take more than one breach of neutrality to undermine a Swiss System's position as local banker—but not many. There was always someone *else* who wanted to be the main neutral bank for a cluster.

"The first thing I need is for General de División Akabane to answer a simple question," Lorraine told the locals. "How much damage did Commodore Wray do before *Corsair* fled San Ignacio?"

"She had taken damage when she caught up to us. The damage you inflicted on her, General, may have saved my life and the lives of all of my people a second time."

Akabane's eyes flashed and his lips tightened—but Espinosa gave him a firm nod.

"Two *Santa Maria*-class cruisers, *Santa Anna* and *Santa Brigita*, were destroyed," Akabane said flatly. "The battleship *Meteoro* took significant damage, and the cruisers *Tormenta* and *Viento* were heavily hit as well. I am glad to know we inflicted some damage in turn, but—"

Lorraine held up a hand.

"I want the names, General," she told him. "Every spacer, every officer. *Everyone* who was wounded or killed because my countrymen came after me. Whatever debt I owe San Ignacio, I owe tenfold to them."

He was quiet for a few moments.

"It can be done, Your Highness," he told her.

"I am aware that there is a diplomatic push against my uncle's government for compensation," Lorraine said. "If it comes to pass that I am in a position to influence the Kingdom of Adamant, you have my word that such will be arranged.

"Right now, however, I do not represent my Kingdom. I speak only for myself and the debts I owe." She waited, to be certain the two San Ignacians understood her meaning.

"There are pensions, I understand, for the survivors of the dead and to take care of the wounded," she said quietly. "If General de División Akabane would be prepared to act as my agent in this matter, I would like to place funds in a trust in this system to provide additional pensions for those people."

If she could, she would double the pension the SIDF was already paying the families of the people who'd died saving her. She wasn't sure her available funds would stretch to that, but she'd put as much aside as she could.

And, if she needed to, she had codes to drain the local Adamantine Embassy's accounts. They probably wouldn't appreciate that, but Wray's stunt had already given them bad-enough days by now.

"I..." Akabane swallowed, hard. He glanced over at Espinosa. The bureaucrat raised one hand, palm up, in a clear shrug.

"I would be prepared to act as your agent in this matter, Your Highness," he promised. "We can discuss the exact funds and structure after this dinner, I hope?"

"That would be perfect, General," Lorraine told him. "I know there are many details that will need to be sorted out, and I don't have much time here in San Ignacio, but I have an obligation to the families of those killed or injured by my uncle's dogs."

Espinosa held up a hand before anyone could say anything else.

"The appetizers are arriving," she noted. "We will resume this once we are alone again."

WHATEVER AKABANE HAD BEEN EXPECTING from the dinner meeting, it clearly hadn't been for Lorraine to take an interest in and responsibility for the families of those lost when Wray came after her.

She knew that they hadn't really died defending her. They'd died defending San Ignacian sovereignty and neutrality. They'd died because when Commodore Wray had burst out of translight in position to blow *Goldenrod* to pieces, those two ships had been in the way.

That didn't change her responsibility.

Or her mission. She could barely taste the small olive-filled pastries the server had brought them, eating mechanically as she waited for them to be alone once more.

"You impress, Pentarch," Espinosa finally said. "I suspect you know that we cannot truly allow your recognition of our dead to impact our choices today, but you do it anyway. Which means it may yet affect our choices, which amuses me.

"You did not stop in San Ignacio solely to discharge that debt of honor. You already know that there is no universe in which the San Ignacio Defense Force would be deployed to intervene in your civil war.

"So. Tell me, Princess, what do you think you can get here?"

Lorraine smiled. The Undersecretariat was trying to get under her skin. *Princess* was definitely one of her titles, but it was generally regarded as superseded by *Pentarch*. Combined with her tone, it was quite clear that Espinosa was pushing.

"I do not expect the San Ignacio Republic to intervene in our war," she agreed. "In fact, given the vessels currently under my command, support from the SIDF would badly delay my return home—a return I fear cannot be long delayed if I wish to save my Kingdom."

The SIDF had at least two divisions of battleships capable of eighty cee, Lorraine knew. Those eight ships were as fast as any RKAN ship except the newest battlecruisers and frigates, but they were still four full tachyon quanta, thirty-two times lightspeed, slower than the *Valkyries*.

She saw Akabane wanted to argue, but he knew what her ships were, and he buried his desire to defend his fleet with a swallow of water.

"What I face, however, is the reality of interstellar communications combined with local censorship that is quite contrary to my Kingdom's values," she noted. "Even by the fastest news couriers, the information from Adamantine is a hundred days out of date—and my uncle has engaged in heavy censorship of what information leaves that system.

"I need more information than the censored news that has been allowed to escape," she said flatly. "I need the Republic's intelligence files on the Kingdom, especially on Adamantine and Ominira.

"Information is the most powerful weapon available to us," she admitted. "I believe you can provide that information without any public breach of your neutrality—and I believe that the information in the hands of San Ignacio's Ministry of Security could be enough to tip the balance in the conflict to come."

The fact that an Undersecretariat of the Ministry of Security was even in the restaurant with her said that the locals had possessed a solid idea of what she was going to ask for. She had one other source if this effort failed—the Exodus Protocol files had given her contact information for something called Bluelight.

She had no idea what Bluelight even *was*, but she had a way to contact them. The main reason they were in her files was to source false identities, but they also sold information. Probably less detailed or useful than the Ministry of Security would have, but it would be more than she had.

The problem was that Bluelight was on San Francisco.

"You are correct that we could provide this information and maintain an appearance of neutrality," Espinosa conceded, swirling the wine in her glass and studying it like she could see answers in the depths.

"It behooves us, however, to maintain not merely the appearance but the reality of our neutrality as much as possible," she continued. "There is always the risk that our exchange could be exposed. It must, therefore, be worth the risk to San Ignacio."

"What exactly do *we* get out of this deal, Princess?"

Lorraine smiled. The question meant that the deal was on the table. Probably even done, all things considered. The Ministry of Security had sent one of their top permanent bureaucrats—quite possibly the head of their intelligence service—to talk to her.

It was only a question of price.

"First of all, Benjamin Adamant will pay for the actions of Commodore Wray and the deaths and damage caused here in San Ignacio," she noted. "Secondly, your assistance will be remembered warmly in the halls of House Adamant in the future, smoothing relations between our two states. Included in that is my promise that your requests for reparations for Commodore Wray's actions will be answered, within reason."

She raised her own hand in an intentional echo of Espinosa's own shrug to Akabane.

"More than that would be difficult to promise without undermining the Republic's appearance of neutrality," she noted. "The doors of the Kingdom of Adamant will be open to you, and regardless of how the election goes after Benjamin's defeat, I think it is fair to say I will be in a position to guarantee you welcoming ears."

"That assumes you are victorious over your uncle," the naval officer pointed out. "The *Valkyries* you have acquired are powerful combatants, but the Regent still commands the full might of the Royal Kingdom of Adamant Navy."

"Or believes he does," Lorraine countered softly. She was watching Espinosa's face as she spoke, and she thought she saw a spark in the other woman's expression. "The Royal Election should not merely have been started but *finished* by now, but it is clear that it hadn't commenced as of the end of August—even from the public news.

"I accept that my uncle may have been able to corrupt or inveigle officers of RKAN into following him into treason and replacing my mother. I do not necessarily understand *how* he managed this or why those officers followed him, but I accept it *has* happened.

"I suspect that the longer the constitution remains ignored, the weaker his grip on his allies grows. I can use that. Combined with the vast individual superiority of my ships, the balance of power between myself and my uncle is not as clear as anyone thinks."

"Which is why you want our intelligence," Espinosa noted. "You realize, of course, that *I* have a far better idea of what that balance actually is?

"I do," Lorraine agreed. "That the head of the San Ignacio Intelligence Agency met me in person nearly guarantees that I am right, doesn't it?"

"I believe our entrees are arriving now," Espinosa said, avoiding any answer. "I suggest you think on what else you may be able to offer us, Princess."

LORRAINE BARELY REGISTERED the main meal beyond that it involved chicken of some kind. She was certain that Espinosa had come to make a deal—at this point, she suspected the Undersecretariat probably had the information she wanted with her—but the San Ignacian bureaucrat was dangling her on the line.

Espinosa wanted something specific, and Lorraine didn't know what it was. That could be a problem.

When the other woman put aside her utensils and picked up her wine glass, Lorraine met her gaze and took the gorgon by the horns.

"You are not denying your role with SIIA," she noted. "So, I believe I have guessed correctly. I'm presuming you were in Vista Roja already, but even so, you wouldn't be here yourself if you didn't think we could make a deal.

"Anything more than I have already suggested, I would find difficult to honor without breaking any appearance of San Ignacio's neutrality. Money certainly isn't the right currency here. You clearly have something specific in mind, something you think the Kingdom of Adamant *can* arrange."

While San Ignacio was hardly lacking in prominent families, they didn't have any politically recognized entities like House Adamant or the Concordat's Five Families. A state marriage wasn't on the table—and would, like most things Lorraine could think of, be a clear breach of neutrality.

"You are the one asking here, Princess," Espinosa pointed out. "Is it on me to decide what you can offer?"

"I can offer a lot of things, Em Espinosa," Lorraine said. "Money. Titles. State marriages. Trade deals—though we both know what the real actor behind my uncle's coup is, don't we?

"Rather than my throwing everything at the wall to see what sticks, this will go more smoothly if you tell me what you want, and I tell you if it's something I'm prepared to give."

"Beggars cannot be choosers, Princess."

"You are not my only possible source of information, Undersecretariat. There are lines I will not cross."

The spymaster studied her in silence for a long moment, then swallowed down the last of her wineglass.

"We want the base code for a Command Intelligence Routine

and the technical archives from your stolen ships," she finally said. "You are sitting on a gold mine that you won't be able to use until you are home—one that you already know will draw fire upon you.

"Provide us a copy of all of that, and you will have your intelligence." Espinosa paused for a moment. "I will even go so far as to promise that we will give *you* copies of everything after the United Worlds force you to return everything you stole."

Vigo stepped on Lorraine's foot under the table, a reminder to stop and think. One she wasn't sure she needed, but was probably fair.

She picked up her water glass and leaned back in her chair, taking a few seconds to consciously breathe and consider the request.

"It is not that simple, Undersecretariat," she finally told the other woman. "And the reason for the first being impossible is why the second is difficult."

"You are in possession of the ships. They are operational, so you have clear control of their systems. The kernel of the CIR might be difficult to copy, but we can provide technical assistance to retrieve it." Espinosa was looking levelly across the table. "I do not see why that would be impossible, let alone create difficulties in transferring the technical databases."

Those databases were the ones that fed the fabricators. With them and the industrial base of a wealthy star system, San Ignacio would be able to replicate many of the key technologies underlying the UWN's advantage over the first-order clusters.

They'd have to be very, *very* careful to avoid drawing the attention of the TIE Commission. Lorraine didn't doubt that the Commission would deploy everything from economic sanctions to military force to prevent an unauthorized technology export.

But it was doable... and that wasn't Lorraine's problem.

Her problem was how much to tell Undersecretariat Juanita Espinosa.

She sighed.

"I am afraid, Em Espinosa, that what you are asking for is impossible. I cannot explain why. We are at an impasse, I suppose. I had hoped for better, but I understand what you want.

"But I cannot provide it to you. I think it is best if my people and I are on our way."

She began to rise, but Espinosa rose first.

"Andrea, take the boys out. Tell the restaurant to hold the rest of the meal until I call for them. Lock down the cage on the way out."

Lorraine rose to meet the spy, tension rippling through her muscles. Officially, the domes of Magellan were weapons-free zones, but she knew Vigo Jarret was armed with something expensively undetectable—probably some variant of the holdout pulser Devine had almost snuck past the Guards.

"I can ask General Akabane to leave as well, if you wish, Pentarch Lorraine," Espinosa told her. "Andrea is about to engage a Faraday cage around this space, rendering any attempt to transmit in or out pointless."

"I am not certain what you expect to gain here, Undersecretariat Espinosa," Lorraine countered. Jarret was now on his feet by her side. The other three Guards had risen as well—but even the implicit threat in their body language hadn't stopped the three Ministry of Security agents from leaving the room and closing the door behind them.

While Lorraine hadn't been actively using her neural link's connection to the outside world, the cybernetics still told her when the Faraday cage fully closed. A tiny *NO SIGNAL* flickered in the corner of her vision.

"A conversation about discretion, I think," the San Ignacio spymaster told her. "It is clear that things are not what they seem, and I deal in secrets and mysteries, Pentarch Lorraine."

It took the second use for Lorraine to realize that Espinosa had dropped the mocking *Princess*.

"I will no more sell secrets without a datanet than with it," she pointed out. "Or when trapped, for that matter."

"This is a gesture of faith, Pentarch, nothing else," Espinosa said calmly. "I am unarmed. I am almost completely confident that Major Jarret isn't, even if the rest of your escort is compliant with our laws.

"I offer the commitment of my complete discretion, Pentarch Lorraine. What you tell me will not leave this room unless I judge it to be of critical importance to the survival of the San Ignacio Republic. If you cannot trust me to keep your secrets, Pentarch, you would not be able to trust the information you ask me to provide.

"For that matter, a simple text message to the United Worlds Embassy on San Francisco could set into motion events that could doom your cause. I will not send such a message," Espinosa concluded. "I will keep your secrets, Lorraine Adamant, but if you want the information we have on the cracks in your uncle's regime, you are going to have to trust me."

TWENTY-NINE

The irony to Lorraine was that she would have preferred to *ask* Val and the others if they were okay with her revealing their nature to the San Ignacian, and with the Faraday cage in place, she couldn't do so.

Not that it was a good idea. No communication from the moon to her ships in orbit could be considered truly secure.

Everyone in the room was standing, her Guard ready to leave at her word. Akabane seemed in a position to step in front of the bureaucrat if Jarret took a shot.

"General de División," she said quietly, "we are not going to shoot Em Espinosa. You will not need to hurl yourself in front of a bullet today."

Akabane straightened slightly, but the tension didn't leave his muscles, nor did his focus leave Lorraine's bodyguard.

For her own part, Espinosa pulled a fresh bottle of wine from the chiller and poured fresh glasses for the four of them, waiting for Lorraine to make up her mind.

Lorraine knew that her own demeanor was far calmer than she felt, but her ability to mask was *nothing* compared to the skills of the woman across the table from her.

"You make an interesting pitch, I suppose," she allowed. "And if I still wish to decline?"

"You know where the door is," Espinosa pointed out. She passed a glass of red wine to Akabane and took one herself. Without even a moment of visible hesitation, she took her seat again and sipped the drink.

"I believe your reasons for declining my offer may be almost as valuable to me as the original request," she continued. "I am prepared to negotiate. I am prepared to let you walk away and keep what we already know of your secrets.

"San Ignacio does not benefit from drawing the United Worlds' attention to our space. But our involvement in your passage through our system is well covered. We will not suffer, even if we have the tech database and TIE comes looking for it.

"Despite what the various United Worlds intelligence agencies may like to think, we are quite capable of securing our affairs against their intrusions." She smiled. "They have fancy toys, yes, but those toys require people, and people are oh so vulnerable to all of the ancient tricks of our trade."

"We're not going to get a better option," Vigo said silently through her link. *"She seems aboveboard, but I have no information on her. Given how much intel was in the Exodus Protocol files, that's terrifying."*

"Sit down, my friends," Lorraine told the Guard, suiting her own actions to her words. She accepted the glass of wine Espinosa passed her but didn't touch it.

"What do you know about the Command Intelligence Routines and the *Valkyries*—the Old Guard?" she asked.

"The CIRs are high-function agents, sub-sapient and intentionally designed to avoid passing the Asimov Standard," Espinosa told her. "The capability the UWN has reported getting out of them is spectacular.

"While publicly, the *Valkyries* were mass-decommissioned to provide a modern reinforcement to the Reserve Flotillas, there were rumors that there were teething problems with the first-generation CIRs, ones that were fixed with the CIRs used in more-recent versions of the system."

Espinosa took a sip of her wine.

"A reasonable bit of background, I would hope," she noted.

"As much as anyone outside the UWN knows," Lorraine agreed. "More, in fact, than some people I dealt with inside the United Worlds knew."

She looked down at the wine and realized that Espinosa had handed Lorraine *her* glass—the one the other woman had already drunk from. There was a hint of lipstick on the rim to mark it, and she looked up at the spymaster, who winked at her.

The lipstick itself could be a poison vector, but the gesture's purpose was to show the opposite. Even so, Lorraine cleaned it off with a napkin before taking a careful sip.

Since wine was one of the system's largest exports, she was unsurprised that it was good. She'd stuck to water so far, but this was turning out more complicated that she'd expected.

"The UWN's cyberneticists got the first round of Asimov Standard limitations wrong," she finally said. "The first-generation CIRs all emerged as full synthetic intelligences."

"Mierda," Esponisa swore. Then she carried on, switching to another language that Lorraine didn't know. Somewhere in the spiel, she switched languages at least once—possibly twice—more before landing on German, which Lorraine did know.

"Diese idiotischen hurensöhne," she concluded, then sighed. "What were they thinking?"

"First, that they had the limitations wrong, and second, that they weren't prepared to eat the costs of properly handling twenty-four emergent intelligences currently built in to some of their most modern battlecruisers," Lorraine said grimly. "So, they put them to sleep."

Akabane hadn't said a word, but his features had grown even tighter.

"That is murder," he said slowly. "Or, at the very least, forced confinement similar to cryo-freezing a human."

"You are aware, Pentarch, that there is an SI creche on San Diego?" Espinosa asked grimly.

That was the outermost of San Francisco's three moons, and the creche's presence was about the only thing Lorraine *did* know about San Diego.

"I am," she confirmed. "I think a slight majority of the Kingdom's SIs are from there."

"They are," the San Ignacian said. "Thanks to the Belén, there are one hundred and eighty-three active adult SIs in the Republic. The creche's work is a significant source of national pride, Pentarch, and I have likely met more SIs than the vast majority of humans."

"What you are suggesting the United Worlds Navy did is..."

"A violation of the Asimov Convention, which is written into UW law," Lorraine confirmed. "More importantly to our conversation, however, it means that I *cannot* access the original CIR kernel for the ships whose SIs have volunteered to join me."

And even if she could, she wouldn't. It was possible that there was a stored copy of the original kernels and base code for a CIR somewhere in *Valkyrie*'s archives, but Lorraine wasn't going to hand a potential SI over to anyone.

Well. Maybe to a group like the Belén. An SI creche would know what to do with it.

"I understand, Pentarch Lorraine," Espinosa said slowly. "With that knowledge, I would not expect you to provide that code. But I do not see the issue with handing over the *Valkyries*' tech databases?"

"The SIs aboard my three ships are volunteers," Lorraine reiterated. "We spoke to them before taking the vessels, and they agreed to enter my service in exchange for certain considerations, like citizenship in the Kingdom of Adamant.

"Part of that was the promise that I would treat the vessels like their bodies and grant them the level of autonomy granted to entities like Price and other SIs who have voluntarily served on warships," she continued. "That makes the technology databases aboard the ships *their* property.

"Knowing the SIs in question, all three would need to agree for them to pass the databases over to you. I am not certain I can obtain that agreement, Em Espinosa," Lorraine warned. "Now that the reasons are... clearer, I can go back to them and ask, but I can make no guarantees."

She could argue, she supposed, that even the information that the UWN had locked down multiple emergent synthetic intelligences rather than meeting their legal obligations to what were technically their new children was worth what she wanted from Espinosa. She could also let this lie and make contact with Bluelight—though the time lag would only give her the chance to trade one message with the information-broker organization before they were planning to leave.

If her initial offer to Bluelight wasn't enough, she'd be out of luck.

"I am prepared to wait for an answer," Espinosa said slowly. "But if that decision is going to be your SIs' to make... would it be possible for me to discuss with them directly?"

Lorraine was honestly surprised. Even though almost all of humanity intellectually accepted SIs as people, there were still often emotional or unconscious barriers to treating them as fully human.

"I presume you have some way to get aboard *Valkyrie* without drawing attention?" she asked.

"I wouldn't dare hope to think I could get aboard your ship without drawing your people's attention, not with an SI aboard," Espinosa pointed out, "but I believe I can *influence* affairs in orbit sufficiently to make my arrival unnoticed by the outside world."

"Then I believe we can make that happen." Lorraine snorted. "There is one more favor we may need. It would *help*, though it is not essential, for us to have somewhere to, well, park a handful of mercenaries we hired who decided they didn't want to get involved in a civil war.

"Some of them I can trust to keep their mouths shut, but some will go straight to the United Worlds for a paycheck. If you have a job you could use them for that would keep them incommunicado for a few months, I think that might be a win for everyone. Including them."

Espinosa traded a look with Akabane and chuckled.

"Strange as it sounds, Pentarch, that's actually *easier* than your main request," she said. "We... may have a program that is perfect for your needs but we generally have issues finding crew for.

"We do regular six-month patrols of deep space through our region, with ships departing relatively often. Incommunicado for the whole time, so boring, annoying—but well-paid and will keep mouths away from monied ears!"

THIRTY

The niggling feeling that something wasn't right was a constant bother to Val. She couldn't locate the source of the problem. She couldn't even identify what the problem *was*—the only thing she'd encountered was the barrier preventing her asking for help about it. That was enough for her to be certain there was a problem beyond her feeling of unease, but it wasn't enough to identify the problem.

Everything else seemed to be going well. Her Lorraine and Devine hadn't made up yet, but Devine was out and about and helping around the ship as he had before. The two had spoken in passing, but it had been stiff.

Val didn't know humans, but her best calculation suggested that the two would get over it. They just needed to sit down and hash it out so both of them could understand where the other came from and how they'd each screwed up.

She wasn't going to pretend she wasn't her Lorraine's partisan in the matter, but she could see how the hard cut of their personal channel could be hurtful.

As she poked at the digital equivalent of a sore tooth, Lorraine was giving the senior NCOs of the three ships a rundown of the exit they were offering. The people breaking contract would be paid for one-quarter of their original contracts—slightly less than the proportional time served—and the rest would be transferred to the San Ignacio Ministry of Security for a long-duration deep-space survey.

No combat on those missions, Val assessed, but a lot of boredom. The Ministry would pay them slightly more for the six months of the new contract than they'd get if they stayed with the Pentarch, though it was for three times as long.

Val figured it was a more-than-fair offer—and the NCOs seemed to agree. Hopefully, it would head off the problem that Roman had raised. That was a human problem, one that Val wasn't quite able to assess yet.

The longer she spent with humans while *knowing* what she was, the easier it became to understand them. No one had expected understanding or even much anticipation from a CIR. A warship SI, though... people half-expected her to act as an informal Executive Officer as well as ship's computer and backup to every Bridge officer.

She could do all of that and drew real pride from both doing the work and from the faith her people had in her.

Her proximity surveillance systems tripped. A shuttle had just departed the fueling station, drifting toward them on low-powered thrusters as it passed into the dead zone between battlecruiser and space station.

A tightbeam laser hit one of *Valkyrie*'s coms receivers and Val pinged Lorraine.

Their guest was there.

VAL WATCHED Undersecretariat Juanita Espinosa enter Lorraine's office while she and her coms team set up the encrypted tightbeam links necessary for the three SIs to speak to the human securely.

"Welcome aboard *Valkyrie*," she told the local, her own avatar appearing next to Lorraine's desk as Espinosa looked around. "I am Val."

"A pleasure, Val," Juanita Espinosa replied immediately, bowing slightly toward the holographic image. "Pentarch Lorraine has told me enough of your origins for me to be horrified at what happened to you. If she had not already offered you asylum and citizenship, I believe it would be straightforward for me to arrange such in the Republic."

"I fear you would find our creators all too willing to breach the neutrality of your system to retrieve us," Herc said, his hoplite avatar appearing next to Val. "Distance will be much of our defense in the Kingdom of Adamant, but San Ignacio is that much closer to the wormhole."

Val had done the same calculation. Her estimates suggested that Adamant wasn't far enough away, but she wasn't telling anyone that. She thought she knew what her Lorraine's plan was for the UWN. If she was correct, she gave it a sixty percent chance of succeeding. Plus/minus fifteen percent; there were too many factors to easily estimate

"Our unintroduced friend is Herc, synthetic intelligence of the battlecruiser *Herakles*," Bonny noted, materializing her own avatar on the other side of Val. "I am Bonny, SI of the battlecruiser *Bean Sidhe*.

"We understand you have an offer for us."

"*I'm not certain we can give them the entire database,*" Bonny continued on the silent channel to the other two SIs.

"*I don't really see a problem with it,*" Herc said. "*We're basically giving it all to Adamant just to keep ourselves functioning.*"

"*I don't think that's what Bonny meant,*" Val countered. "*I think she means that the entire database is worth* far *more than what my Lorraine is asking for.*"

"I do have an offer for you and your Pentarch," Juanita Espinosa confirmed, the entire exchange between the SIs passing between her hearing Bonny's words and her near-immediate response.

"Pentarch Adamant has asked for all of our intelligence on the current situation and players in the Kingdom of Adamant, to allow her to plot her campaign against her uncle. We have intelligence that would be of value to her, I believe, plus a great deal of information that would be essential to such plans.

"However, my Republic has a long-standing tradition of neutrality. To provide such information, as well as breaking with that tradition, risks exposing our agents on the ground. While I trust Pentarch Lorraine's discretion—as she has trusted mine in revealing your existence—I am deeply obliged to those people.

"A reasonable exchange seems required. I initially requested the tech databases from your ships and the base-code kernel to create a CIR. Now, knowing what happened with the original CIRs, I do not expect anyone to hand over that kernel, and I'm not sure I want it anyway!"

"Yet you still want the schematics and fabrication databases stored in our computers," Bonny noted. "Is that correct?"

"It is, Bonny," Juanita Espinosa confirmed.

The local was quite calm for someone dealing with three SIs. Even as a CIR, Val had noted that her virtual avatar and inclusion in conversations—as a glorified reference source then—had bothered people.

"Do you understand the full scope of what is included in those databases, Undersecretariat Juanita Espinosa?" Herc asked, as usual playing the more abrasive one of the three.

On their own secure channel, the three of them were assessing the weight of the databases themselves, dividing it up into clear sections: weapons, shuttles, engines, computers, industrial...

While the primary focus of their databases was military, there was enough information to give the San Ignacio Republic a ten-year or more boost in any field. Far more in the military fields.

"I presume, everything necessary for the maintenance and repair of your ships, their systems and the onboard shuttles," Juanita Espinosa said.

"The decision is yours, Val, Herc, Bonny," Val's Lorraine insisted. "That data is part of *your* computers, and I only have access to it through your allegiance to me."

That hit part of whatever was bothering Val. She couldn't put her mental finger on it, but it gave her a sensation she thought a human would have described as *a chill down her spine.*

What was *wrong* with her?

Fortunately, no human could have noted her sudden pause, and Bonny was taking the lead on this discussion anyway.

"The databases from our ships would, given a reasonable industrial base and a dedicated effort, allow the Republic to duplicate a *Valkyrie*-class battlecruiser," *Bean Sidhe*'s SI told their guest. "While that would be foolish, of course, that is the level of information we are discussing.

"Given the United Worlds Technology Import/Export Laws and their enforcement of them, that would be an immense boost to the military and economic capabilities of San Ignacio. Enough of a military advantage, I postulate, to enable significant aggressive expansion on the part of your Republic."

"That... is not our intent," Juanita Espinosa replied.

"*She appears to be telling the truth,*" Val noted silently to her fellows. Her internal sensors suggested that the Undersecretariat was an extremely controlled individual, but it wasn't perfect.

"Your intent isn't relevant to my point, Juanita Espinosa," Bonny said. "I do not know what intelligence you have on the Kingdom of Adamant, but I do not believe that it is remotely worth as much as the databases in our possession."

And Val calculated that Juanita Espinosa had known that. She'd believed Val's Lorraine was desperate enough to take the deal.

"I am prepared to discuss more-limited-potential deals," Juanita Espinosa said, her calm concession confirming Val's assessment.

"*Translight, metallurgy or the railgun?*" Herc asked in their private channel.

"*Translight,*" Val replied instantly. "*It's the most valuable to them.*"

"*For the same reason, I would suggest the railgun,*" Bonny countered. "*Less broadly applicable but still extraordinarily valuable with side benefits to other technologies.*"

"*The railgun would be too obvious,*" Herc said. "*Everyone else is so far behind the UW in high-density railguns that anyone deploying one is going to draw attention instantly. I think the translight drives— they can likely extrapolate the gaps between their current drives and ours and fake a decent development arc.*"

"*Translight it is, then,*" Bonny conceded.

Their entire argument took about half a second, and then Val smiled at her guest.

"We are prepared to provide the specifications and fabricator patterns for the fourteen-quanta translight engine," she told Juanita Espinosa. "We recommend that you extrapolate intermediary levels rather than immediately begin production on it, but that is your own decision to make."

Juanita Espinosa took some time to think it over. Thirty or forty seconds, while one of the Adamant Guards pretending to be a steward brought coffee into the office. The local took an appreciative swallow of the hot beverage, then slowly nodded.

"There is more to a translight drive than simply the fabrication patterns," she pointed out. "There are specific metallurgies, exotic-matter compositions and so forth. These are not easy to duplicate."

"The fabricators on a *Valkyrie* are intended to be able to repair *any* damage to her, Undersecretariat Juanita Espinosa," Val countered. "What we are offering includes those metallurgies and compositions as well as potential methods of production. The instructions are limited, I assess, but I estimate that your scientists and engineers will be able to fill in whatever gaps.

"They were, after all, intended to allow my crew to turn raw materials into the necessary components."

This time, the San Ignacian didn't spend any noticeable time thinking. She simply nodded.

"Good enough," she declared. "When can I expect to receive the data?"

Val spent about a third of a second poking at the security of the various data-storage devices on the Undersecretariat's person. One of them, she assumed, was the data Juanita Espinosa had promised Lorraine Adamant, but they were all quite impressively secured.

With three SIs on hand, they could have broken the defenses on any of them in a few minutes, but that would take more time than was available for what would, she had to admit, be nothing more than a stunt.

"Everything has been downloaded into the datachip waiting on Pentarch Adamant's desk," Val announced instead—the download commencing and completing while she spoke. "If you have the information you promised in exchange, the trade could happen immediately."

The local laughed.

"I have worked with too many synthetic intelligences to expect anything different," she admitted. "Pentarch Adamant, on behalf of the San Ignacio Republic, I apologize for how rude our public treatment of you and your people has been.

"For myself, I am stunned and impressed by the audacity of your theft. I worry for the future consequences for you and your Kingdom, but not many would have had the fortitude to even make the attempt."

She met Vigo Jarret's gaze and received a tiny nod before reaching into her blazer to remove a small icon of the same dragon as her tie pin. Val could already tell it contained a datachip.

"While the Republic is unquestionably neutral, we have a preference for stability and sanity in our neighborhood. Your uncle has not been good for either." Juanita Espinosa held out the dragon, watching as Lorraine retrieved a much-more-ordinary chip from her desk.

"The translight drive data," the Pentarch said, holding out her own chip. "May it be of use to you without drawing undue attention."

The Undersecretariat took the drive datachip, then squeezed the dragon in a very specific way.

"Unlock sequence Arthritis-Dodecahedron-Circus-Six-Zero-Five-Dragona," she said in a stilted voice, pitching her voice noticeably lower, then handed the dragon chip to Lorraine.

"Please confirm that it is unlocked," she asked.

"Val?" Lorraine asked.

Val was already in the chip. There had been no fewer than six security layers on the device. There were four places it could be squeezed, and while getting it wrong would simply have kept it locked, there was also a sequence that would have erased the chip—and it had needed a signal from Espinosa's neural link to even activate the sensors.

A DNA sample had been taken as well, and the audio confirmation sequence had also included a voiceprint both checking for the exact tone of voice she'd used and also scanning for signs of coercion.

Under all of that, however, the data appeared to be exactly what they'd been promised.

"It is unlocked," she confirmed. "And while it will take even us some time to review, it appears to be exactly what was promised."

"The Republic keeps our deals, Pentarch. I hope you keep this in mind in your future endeavors," the spy said cheerfully. "Thank you. This has been a pleasure."

She bowed slightly and left—which was the first point where even *Val* realized that she hadn't drunk even a drop of the coffee she'd repeatedly "sipped" from.

Val didn't know humans well, but she was prepared to assess that as being very much a *spy* thing.

THIRTY-ONE

Lorraine had faced down a charging battlecruiser aboard a drastically outmatched frigate with no hope but her single clever plan. She'd faced the entire mass of the United Worlds Grand Assembly, the governing body of the most powerful state in the known universe. She'd *robbed* the United Worlds Navy, the most powerful *military* in the same universe.

She still hesitated for a solid minute before finally hitting the command in her link to put through the call to Alastair Devine.

He answered after a few moments. He was sitting at the desk in his office, the space set aside for the Admiral's Intelligence Officer on the Flag Deck. It looked much the same as every other office on the battlecruiser: a black-topped desk with concealed electronics and plain walls where the UW and UWN flags had hung.

"Lorraine," he greeted her. He sounded tired. "Hi."

"Hi yourself," she told him. "Where are you at?"

It wasn't the question she'd meant to ask, and the quirk of his smile told her he knew it.

"Struggling to digest shoe leather," he finally told her. "Not quite sure how to step back up."

"I could have handled that better," Lorraine admitted. "It wasn't a good time for us to be at cross purposes. But... here we are."

"Here we are," he agreed. "Did you need something?"

Part of her wanted to tell him no, that she'd only called to see if they could make up, but that was a lie.

"Did you get the intelligence drop from the San Ignacians?" she asked.

"I did," he said. "And I'll admit we wouldn't have got it if we'd gone my way. Still worried about the consequences of where we're at."

"Those are my problems. We haven't left San Ignacio yet," Lorraine pointed out. "The offer to pay you for your time and let you slip off and vanish stands, you know. If you think the risk is too much."

He looked down at his desk for a few seconds, then back up at her.

"No," he told her. "One way or another, Lorraine, I'm with you to the end of this."

That set her heart flip-flopping in her chest in a way that was both awkward and comforting.

"Okay. If you're with us and you've gone over the info, we're going to have a strategy meeting in an hour," she said. "Captains and command team. That includes you."

Devine nodded and smiled, looking noticeably less tired somehow.

"I have some thoughts," he promised. "I'll be there."

THIRTY-TWO

"We launch from Magellan in just over two hours," Lorraine told her gathered leaders. "We'll go translight eight hours after that, around two hundred hours standard."

"Christmas in translight," Rose Cortez observed. "I'll make sure to have the programs to twinkle the lights downloaded to everyone."

That earned the engineer a round of chuckles. The three SI avatars didn't join in the laughter, but Lorraine hoped they were taking notes.

No matter where in the Kingdom they went, they were going to arrive well into the next year. Christmas and New Year's alike would be celebrated under drive.

"At least we have the habitation pods this time," Paris noted, *Herakles'* Captain looking like he'd just considered the thought of Christmas in zero gee.

All three Captains were present, along with their Executive Officers, Chief Engineers and SIs. Lorraine had brought Roman, Jarret and Devine as well, bringing the total to thirteen humans and three SIs.

The humans were even physically present for once, something

that wouldn't be an option after this. Coffee and fresh pastries—acquired from the fuel station by Roman that morning—were spread around the table to smooth the wheels.

The acquisition might have been handled by a minion. Lorraine knew better than to ask any Chief who had actually done the task she'd asked them to take care of.

"It may end up being a shorter flight than we're afraid of, at least," she told her people, holding her coffee cup in her hand to soak in its warmth as best she could.

It wasn't that the room was cold. She was just feeling shivery, probably from being in close proximity to Devine for the first time in two days. Their earlier conversation had been promising, but she knew they hadn't really sorted things out yet.

"My initial impulse to mirror our course out to Bright Dream is looking like a better and better idea as we review the data," she said. "Ksenija, do you want to lay it out for everyone?"

Lieutenant Major Ksenija Nazario was a pale-skinned woman with dark hair and Mediterranean features, her eyes perpetually focused on something no one else could see. She'd been *Goldenrod*'s Bridge Intelligence Officer and now was Savege's Executive Officer on *Bean Sidhe*.

They'd dug deep in to the frigate's officer ranks to fill out key positions on the three warships and had, if Lorraine was honest, failed. Administration on all three ships was being handled by green Lieutenants with experienced Chiefs. There *were* no Tactical or Intelligence Officers, and navigation was being run entirely by Chiefs, backed by the XOs.

Right now, though, it was Nazario's old hat she was wearing as she gestured a hologram of the Kingdom of Adamant into the air above the table.

"We're all familiar with this map," she assumed aloud. "The Kingdom of Adamant. Six star systems: Adamantine, Greenrock, Tolkien, Beulaiteuhom, Ominira and Maka'melemele."

Each star system flashed on the display as Nazario spoke, a total of seven main-sequence yellow dwarfs with Maka'melemele's binary system. That was what gave the system its name—*Yellow Eyes* in Hawaiian, the ancestral language of many of the original settlers.

"As we saw in the regular news, Beulaiteuhom and Greenrock have come out with as much opposition as anyone has actively engaged in," *Bean Sidhe*'s Executive Officer continued. "I've gone through the data with Bonny's help—thank you, Bonny—and I think that they may be more actively against the Black Regency than anyone is admitting in public."

Nazario nodded to the hologram in the long dress, who returned her gesture with a small bow of her head.

"According to the San Ignacians' intelligence, RKAN and RKAA forces in those two systems have stopped communicating with central command in Adamantine," she continued. "There's no solid information on the RAMC troops beyond that both systems have barred them from taking ship to Adamantine.

"Our data includes solid confirmation that Beulaiteuhom and Greenrock are in direct communication with each other and are preparing a united front. The largest problem they face is numbers."

Data flickered up underneath the two stars, listing the RKAN strength in each system. A total of four cruisers, six destroyers, and six frigates. A significant chunk of the Navy's escort strength but not enough to stand against even a single capital ship.

"While the official news doesn't have anything to say about Tolkien or Maka'melemele, I would have expected both to be relatively calm—if for different reasons."

Tolkien, Lorraine knew, because they were the closest system to the Richelieu Directorate, and weakness there would draw attention. Maka'melemele, on the other hand, was the youngest of the Kingdom's daughter colonies, which meant they were still more dependent on the rest of the Kingdom than they'd like. They wouldn't rock the boat unless they had to.

"The news didn't say anything different, but our new intelligence suggests that the calm is surface at best," Nazario warned. "Tolkien does not, as a rule, have a high opinion of Benjamin Adamant after the last war. I suspect that he'd made careful arrangements to manage that, but fate makes fools of us all.

"Except that Lieutenant Admiral Maja Pražaková and Governor Ekundayo Berardi were both killed in a vehicular accident about five days after the coup," she noted. "Both of them had served under Benjamin Adamant in the past and meet the criteria I would use to assess whether someone was one of his partisans."

"Both of them dying sounds suspicious to me," Jarret pointed out. "Especially if their replacements are less loyal to the Regent. Benjamin would have backup plans—but it seems a bit too convenient for his supporters to go down together."

"Based on the intelligence, *going down* was definitely involved in the crash," Devine said, his tone a mix of humor and bitterness. "They'd ditched their security details for a private evening together and apparently couldn't keep their hands to themselves long enough to arrive safely.

"Humans do dumb things, but I'm not sure I've ever met an assassin who would use *that* as a cover."

"On the other hand, my uncle is known for his backup plans," Lorraine pointed out. "What is the situation in Tolkien?"

"The new Governor is most definitely *not* Benjamin Adamant's woman," Nazario said flatly. "Tina Holzer was the deputy Governor, a senior member of Berardi's Liberty and Fraternity Party. Unlike Berardi, however, she's one of our antimonarchy reformers. She won't necessarily back Pentarch Lorraine, but as a Tolkien native and an antimonarchist, she isn't going to back the Regent.

"And while the official chain of command puts Commodore Kheireddine Davlatov in charge of Tolkien Station, nobody is going to follow her if Commodore Aguilar says *jump*."

Lorraine didn't even need to look up who Commodore Oriana Aguilar was. She'd had the unpleasant revelation during her visit to Earth, talking to an old friend of her mother's, that King Valeriya

Adamant had taken several female lovers during her marriage to Lorraine's father.

Then-Captain Oriana Aguilar had been one of them, during the war with the Richelieu Directorate ten years earlier. Aguilar had commanded Valeriya's flagship when the King had taken much of Home Fleet to liberate Tolkien.

"So, while Tolkien hasn't made any formal movement, most likely because they know the Richelieuans are watching, the system and its fleet do not represent an asset for the Black Regent," Stephson concluded, the Captain looking like a cat who'd found a bowl of milk.

"Maka'melemele has come out quite strongly in support of the Regency as a temporary measure to maintain stability," Nazario noted, "but the Maka'melemele Station force is the lightest of any of RKAN's deployments."

"The real key cards in the deck are Ominira and Tolkien," Savege agreed. "They are the only systems with capital-ship deployments. If Tolkien sits things out to watch the Richards, *we* come out ahead.

"But Ominira is the problem. We know Tunison is Benjamin's man."

"And Ominira is the easiest system for us to visit on our way in," Lorraine agreed. "But given that they seemed to be solidly on Benjamin's side, I was thinking about heading to either Tolkien or Greenrock—probably Greenrock."

Greenrock didn't have RKAN capital ships she could commandeer, but they had enough RKAN *people* that she could crew the three battlecruisers—and since it was next door to the Concordat, it would let her ask for the Griffin Family and their country's help from a position of strength.

Of course, she'd reviewed the same data as Nazario. There was a reason the briefing had left Ominira and Adamantine for last.

"As the Pentarch notes, Lieutenant Admiral Tunison is Benjamin's man, through and through," Nazario agreed. "And all of the official news out of the system suggests that they are being nice and quiet, with only the occasional semi-public question about when the Royal Election will take place.

"But according to our new intelligence, that is almost entirely *because* Tunison is sitting in orbit of Ife Tuntun with a battleship and one of the few RAMC assault groups the Black Regent hasn't even tried to call back," she concluded.

"With a battleship, even a *Hope*-class like *Dreaming*, and six thousand Royal Marines sitting in orbit, I'd be playing very nice too," Stephson said slowly. "Are you saying the system government is more opposed to the Regency than they're letting on?"

"It's hard to say for certain," Devine cut in, trading a swift nod with Nazario as if they'd planned this. "This is my area of expertise, though I don't know the players as well as any of you," he reminded them all.

"Governor Frantziscu Melsbach is a complete unknown to me outside of his file, but even a cursory skim through that suggests that he is a savvy political operator, quite capable of concealing his true allegiance. The man did *gut* the system Crown Liberal Party when he crossed the floor to the Ominiran Conservative Party."

Lorraine nodded slowly as she remembered that. That had been while she was at the Academy, nine years earlier, and she'd had dinner with her parents shortly after the news had reached Adamantine. Valeriya had been torn between wanting to tear Melsbach a new one—as the name suggested, the Crown Liberals were decently aligned with the King—or shaking his hand for how neatly he'd mousetrapped his former party's leadership.

Of course, if the Crown Liberals' leadership *hadn't* been grossly corrupt, the trap wouldn't have done much. As it was, he'd pulled their actions into the open and crossed the floor "on principle."

That said principle had seen him made leader of his new party in time to contest a round of elections two years later—and hence carried him to the Governorship—was pure coincidence, of course.

"Our sources have found evidence that Melsbach is secretly communicating with his counterparts in every system except

Adamantine," Devine continued. Lorraine noted that he didn't, unlike Nazario, mention the San Ignacians by name.

"There are hints, though I'm definitely reading between the lines there, that Melsbach even has agents moving in Tunison's task force. If he can create a situation where he can take effective control of the threat hovering over his head, I suspect his official position would change.

"Whether that position would be in support of Lorraine or even against the Black Regent isn't clear, but I doubt he'd be engaging in this level of maneuvering if he was planning on staying in line."

Lorraine smiled thinly. She'd been looking at other aspects of the data in Ominira, pieces she wasn't going to mention just yet. She knew some of the players better than anyone else in the room—and there were some hints in Admiral Tunison's correspondence with Colonel Fitzwilliam, the CO of the logistics station at Agbaye Lewa, that neither man was entirely happy with how *Corsair*'s pursuit of Lorraine had gone.

If nothing else, the fact that Colonel Fitzwilliam still held his post after letting Lorraine and *Goldenrod* go spoke volumes she wasn't sure anyone else could read.

"The situation in Ominira appears more complex than it might on the surface," she concluded aloud. "Combined with it being the closest system to a direct route back to Adamantine, I think that sets our course.

"We will head to Ominira and see if we can convince Admiral Tunison to lay down his arms—hopefully, with some encouragement from Governor Melsbach.

"In the worst-case scenario, we will be able to reach Tolkien, coordinate with Commodore Aguilar and *still* reach Adamantine before my uncle truly knows what is going on."

That would be cutting things fine. It would depend on none of the Kingdom's limited number of ninety-six-lightspeed couriers being present in Ominira—but even if Tunison still had one of the new

Martinez-class frigates, none of RKAN's warships could go faster than eighty-eight times lightspeed.

The capital ships at Ominira Station couldn't get to Adamantine ahead of the *Valkyries*.

"Unless someone has seen something in the intelligence to suggest we're missing something?" she asked, looking around the room.

No one said anything.

"Good. We have a lot of details to get sorted out before we leave San Ignacio, and the more of them we can get handled while we're all in the same room, the better off we are."

THIRTY-THREE

Vigo Jarret had long since mastered the sentry posture. It was a careful combination of using whatever surface was near to you with having good posture with knowing what muscles could be relaxed and shifted at various levels of noticeability.

It also included, for him at least, a series of stretches that he would do when he was alone or only accompanied by another Guard. Any Adamant Guard was old enough to know that stretching was the key to function—and even for the Guard, he was old and senior to be standing guard.

But Lorraine Adamant was his charge, and part of him needed to know she was safe—against more than just physical threats. Palmer and Alvarez had flipped a coin, and Palmer had ended her shift early, leaving Vigo and Alvarez standing watch outside Lorraine's quarters.

They'd hit translight in about thirty minutes, on their final journey back to the Kingdom. Whatever happened now, their course was set. They were going home.

"Vigo."

The voice was in his head, and he almost blinked in surprise.

"Val?" he finally replied, equally silently.

"Yes. Is it all right if I speak to you this way?" the SI asked. "I am feeling... nervous."

"I'm sure there might be others more able to help, but I will if I can," he told her. He'd counseled a lot of young soldiers before their first battle. He wasn't quite sure if the same tools would work on an SI, but he'd do his best.

"This plan puts a lot of people at risk. Not just those of you aboard this ship but the crew you want to recruit to operate our vessels and even the crews of your Ominira Station and Home Fleet."

"Not just at risk, I'm afraid," Vigo warned. "Far too many people are going to die before this is over. Even if we showed up with ten times as many ships, Benjamin Adamant would fight."

"So, why do it at all?" the SI asked. "I have committed to follow Lorraine Adamant, but the very fact she asked me to do so means I do not feel obliged to follow without question.

"If so many will die, why fight this war?"

Vigo considered his words and thoughts carefully.

"First off, because it's already being fought," he told her. "Nikola is holding out on Bastion as we speak, fighting to keep some semblance of the Kingdom's honor alive. I don't know how many people have already died there, but Nikola wasn't given much of a choice. He fled from assassins, much as Lorraine did, and didn't have a starship to run in.

"Second, while it can be argued that us coming back is going to ignite a wider conflict, you went over the same intelligence data the rest of us did," he continued. "Of five systems outside of Adamantine, two are openly questioning Benjamin Adamant's regime and two are covertly considering it.

"The wider civil war is already brewing. Nikola's survival alone threw up too many questions. So long as Benjamin doesn't hold the Royal Election, his legitimacy will fritter away by the day and the week."

The real miss in all of Benjamin Adamant's plans, from what Vigo could tell, was that Irina Roma had survived when the assassin had come for her. The commanding officer of the Adamant Guard had lived long enough to warn Vigo, saving Lorraine's life. He presumed she'd similarly warned Nikola's Major Krupin, hence the open revolt.

"*But if he were to hold that Election, much of that would resolve, yes? A conflict could be avoided?*"

"It could," he agreed. "*I'm not sure I'd trust Benjamin Adamant to run a fair election at this point, but even a rigged Royal Election would give him the legitimacy he is currently losing. It's an unusual misstep for him.*"

"*How so?*"

"*Benjamin Adamant is possibly the best fleet commander I've ever heard of,*" Vigo told the SI. "*He has ice in his veins and a sense of both his people and his enemy that I've seen few others match. The assassination program had his fingerprints all over it: backup plans under backup plans, applied with the level of utter ruthlessness necessary to go for a clean sweep* on his own sister's family.

"*But I think... I think the politics of votes and popular support and compromise have always eluded him.*" Vigo was old enough to remember the death of the previous King and the Royal Election that had seen Valeriya crowned. Injured in the same crash as his father, Benjamin had done the bare minimum amount of campaigning. The people of the Kingdom of Adamant hadn't known what to make of him—and Valeriya had put herself in front of them with a clear plan and platform.

Benjamin hadn't even come second in the election. He'd come *fourth*—and he'd clearly expected to win. Because he was his father's eldest son and the most successful, in his area, of the five Pentarchs.

"*He is an excellent Admiral but I think he might be a terrible politician,*" Vigo concluded. "*I fear he is going to drag my country down with him because he doesn't even realize the damage he's doing to his position.*

"*More than that, though, are the factions he's courted to take and hold power. He's cut deals with United Worlds megacorps—we know of Freebright Interstellar Technologies, but that doesn't mean they're the only ones—and we know the paths those deals go down.*

"I imagine that, like most who've signed on to them before him, he thinks he can protect his country from the worst effects of the interstellars intruding into our affairs."

Vigo wanted to shake his head, but if Val wanted this conversation to be private, he wasn't going to have Alvarez asking why he was acting strangely.

"Lorraine was offered a similar deal," he told Val. *"Devine somehow got her in a room with the leaders of one of FBIT's competitors, and they were prepared to use their security forces to force his surrender.*

"But that would have been giving up our sovereignty and our future as much as Benjamin is doing. So, she refused and looked for an alternative."

"Us," Val said. *"And we will fight for her; don't worry, Vigo. I had questions, not objections. I think I understand, though... it isn't simple, is it?"*

"It isn't," he agreed. *"And, frankly, at this point? If Benjamin were willing to hold an open and fair Royal Election, I might sit on Lorraine as hard as it took to get her to go along with it. It would stick in her throat to let him go free—and I'm not sure that we could convince Nikola to stand down after so long—but it would be the best option for Adamant.*

"But he killed Lorraine's family." Vigo's family, too, in a way, with both his attachment to House Adamant and the fate of so many of the Adamant Guard. *"We're not starting this civil war, Val. He did.*

"We just need to make sure he doesn't benefit from the pain he's inflicted—and to make sure that the traditions and constitutions of our Kingdom aren't tossed aside for one man's ambition and entitlement."

Val paused, for long enough that Vigo could recognize it. Odd for an SI.

"What would you have done if Valeriya had ordered you to arrest him?" she finally asked.

"*She wouldn't have asked* me," Vigo pointed out. "*If she'd had real grounds for an arrest, she'd have gone to the judicial branches. She'd have sent military or Royal police to arrest him. Without real evidence... even Pentarchs have the right to freedom, presumption of innocence and a fair trial.*"

"*So, if King Valeriya had ordered the Guard to detain Benjamin for the good of the Kingdom? You would have refused?*"

Swallowing the sigh he wanted to breathe took more effort than he expected, but he maintained his stolid posture and considered the question fairly.

"*That is the kind of question a human cannot answer until the situation is upon them, Val,*" he admitted. "*I know that Benjamin's own Brave Detail were key in his assassination plans. Without those Adamant Guards choosing him over House and Kingdom, we wouldn't be where we are.*

"*But I would like to think that if Valeriya had ordered me to arrest Benjamin, I'd have said no.*"

"*What if she'd ordered you to arrest Lorraine?*"

"*That... that, my dear Val, is a very different question,*" he admitted, rolling the mental image around in his head and finding the level of *certainty* in his mind somewhat disquieting. "*One that gives me a bit of sympathy for his Guards I don't necessarily like.*

"*Why do you ask?*"

"*I'm not sure,*" Val admitted. "*Mostly, thinking about the Guard who obeyed him. They broke their oaths, didn't they? Much like I did, to the UWN.*"

"*I can see the comparison, Val,*" he told her. "*But there is a fundamental difference I think you have to remember, for yourself and your siblings.*"

"*Which is?*"

"*An oath flows both ways, Val. The United Worlds Navy broke their oath to you first.*"

VIGO'S CONVERSATION with Val threw him off his balance. It was an odd set of questions for the SI to ask, though he didn't begrudge her them. She'd committed to follow Lorraine, but nowhere in the agreement was a requirement to do so blindly.

None of them had promised to follow Lorraine without question. Part of his job, as he saw it, was to question her. The charisma and leadership trained into a scion of House Adamant were sometimes worrying to watch in action, though he also had seen the gestures, large and small, with which she'd bound the former crew of the *Goldenrod* to her.

It had been Lorraine's plan that had saved them from *Corsair*. Everyone knew it—knew that *Goldenrod* hadn't even carried the mines that had taken out the battlecruiser until Lorraine had suggested building them.

They'd followed her across half of known space, endured hardships and politics with her. She'd sat with the wounded as they'd hurt, spoken from her own heart when the United Worlds had denied them aid—and then she'd led them on an impossible heist to steal the ships that might just change the course of their Kingdom's fate.

Even Vigo found it hard to challenge her now. He still did, because it was his job and he knew that she would want him to, but following where Lorraine led seemed to keep working out.

It was on the echo of that thought, of course, that Alastair Devine came around the corner and approached the door to Lorraine's quarters.

Vigo and Alvarez stepped into his way without thinking, though Vigo's own thoughts on the young man were complex. Devine's help had been critical in getting them this far, but Vigo had been riding Lorraine's link during her conversation with General de División Rocha.

He was the only one other than Lorraine and Devine themselves who knew what had passed between them in that conversation, and he wasn't going to make any bones about whose side he was on.

Devine had crossed a line, and Lorraine had been right to shut him down.

She might have done so more harshly than needed, but there'd been no *time* for niceties in the middle of a negotiation that would decide their fate.

"Hey, Vigo; hey, Judy," Devine greeted them with a sad smile and a weak shrug. "I'm guessing the old open access is gone, but can you ask her if she's willing to see me?"

"The greatest glory in living lies not in never falling but in rising every time we fall," he quoted.

"Nelson Mandela," Vigo noted. *"Failure is not an option. It is mandatory. The option is whether or not to let failure be the last thing you do."*

"Howard Tayler," Devine replied. "I'm not inclined to let screwing up be the last thing that passes between Lorraine and me, Vigo. I'm here. I'll walk if she tells me to, but... ask her?"

Vigo didn't really need to. He already knew what Lorraine would say—but it was her decision to make, even if he knew she was going to let Devine back in.

And truth be told? Given how well Lorraine's decisions had gone so far and how much help the spy had been, even Vigo's paranoia was willing to give the man a second chance.

He activated his com.

"I was listening," Lorraine said silently in his head. The synchronization between their links went both ways, after all. *"What do you think?"*

"I think you've already made up your mind," he pointed out.

"I know what I want, Vigo. But I also know I keep you around to be paranoid when I get too softhearted."

"I don't think your heart has steered you wrong yet, Lorraine. From the most cold-blooded perspective, he's a valuable asset we don't want to burn yet. From another, well, he's here with his heart in his hands and willing to talk.

"*You don't always get that. I don't think* it's *a ploy—and if Devine was going to turn on us, he'd have done it a long time ago.*"

She laughed, but it wasn't really at Vigo.

"*That's the paranoia I'm looking for, Vigo. Thank you.*" She paused. "*Send him in. And, uh…*"

"*Turn off the link sync,*" he finished for her.

THIRTY-FOUR

A week later, Lorraine reflected that she could get used to apologetic Alastair. They'd picked up a lot of fresh supplies in San Ignacio, and it turned out that her boyfriend could do a lot more with those supplies when cooking a meal for two than even the best Navy cook could manage when cooking for a hundred and sixty.

She chased the last flaky piece of fish around her plate for a moment, then got it on her fork and swallowed it.

"This was delicious," she told him. "What even *was* it?"

He laughed, the warm, burbling sound that had originally attracted her to him.

"Are you sure you want to know?" he teased. "I'll be up-front—it *is* one of those dishes where you may not want to know!"

"And now I have to know," she admitted.

He flicked an image over to her link, and it took every ounce of self-control she had to not wince backward from the multi-limbed, multi-finned, multi-*bodied* tentacled monstrosity swimming through dark water she was looking at.

"It's called Rojan squid," Devine said with a chuckle. "It's native to Magellan, the largest multi-celled life form on any of Vista Roja's moons. The scale of the image might throw you—they're only about a meter long."

"And it tastes like that?" she asked, gesturing toward their empty plates.

"I don't know who was brave enough to find out, but yes," he confirmed. "The Magellans try not to draw too much attention to what the creature looks like when they're mass-exporting processed filets to the other two moons.

"The sauce is regular cream, with a mix of black pepper and a local spice from San Francisco some genius christened *purple* pepper when they found it shortly after landing. Our logistics people made some solid choices in what they brought on board—and someone pulled a recipe archive from Magellan before we left."

Lorraine giggled softly and picked up her wineglass. The rotating gravity pods let them have regular meals without worrying about it, which was a delight compared to the long journey out from Adamantine.

"Recipe or not, pulling that together takes skill," she noted. "Even more hidden depths to you than I thought, I'm learning."

He smiled, though she thought she caught a moment of tightness to it. She had yet to push hard on what it was Alastair Devine had actually *done* for his former employers, but she knew there were aspects to it that he didn't want her to know.

So long as they didn't come back to bite either of them—and they were far enough from the United Worlds now that it seemed unlikely —she'd let him take his time coming around to that.

"I'll grab the dishes," he said, rising and beginning to collect the plates. "I'll catch up with you in a moment?"

"Sure."

Apologetic Alastair was definitely nice, she reflected, as she relocated to the couch and pulled up some of the coursework she was going through. In the two months since leaving Bright Dream, she'd finished off almost two-thirds of the six months of material for the United Worlds Navy Command School.

She knew there were aspects she was missing without the lecturers and classmates, but she was pleased with her progress—and if the courses were occasionally grim, they were also *useful*. She hadn't been ready to command a single ship before her mother had died, let alone a three-ship squadron or whatever she was going to pull together in Ominira.

She still wasn't ready. A six-month course couldn't manage that. But she at least felt like she had a basic grounding of what ready would look like, something she wasn't sure she'd had before.

And Lorraine didn't need the officer-counseling courses to know that pleasant as the extra attentiveness of apologetic Alastair was, she couldn't let it go on much longer. If he didn't start pulling back naturally in a day or so, she was going to have to gently prod him into letting go of some of the over-the-top good behavior.

Their fight was going to be in her mind for a long while yet and would impact what she trusted him on and what conversations she included him in. It would be a *long* time before he had a private link to her again while she was negotiating with potential hostiles.

But they'd talked about it, and both acknowledged what the other felt they'd done wrong. That was the best she could hope for as a starting point. They'd work through it—if nothing else, the fact that he was willing to try was a huge positive!

So was the fact that he emerged from the galley with a pair of hot chocolates in his hands.

"I figured you'd be just about done with your wine," he said with a smile. "How's the homework?"

"Slow but fascinating," she replied, reaching out to take a hot chocolate and stealing a kiss in the process. "Currently working through what the UWN teaches their officers around the various Funds and the obligations toward them."

The Funds were what had taken her to Earth in the first place.

The Stability Convention Fund was an agreement that the involved countries would pay money to what was basically an insurance policy, that in the case of major internal unrest or external attack, the United Worlds Navy would use those funds to respond and help them.

There were several similar Funds, all of them drawing massive aggregate amounts of money from the first-order clusters into the United Worlds. Any politician in the clusters—and while Lorraine had been a naval officer, she'd been trained to be a politician as well—had known it was a barely concealed tribute structure.

But it was one that required the UWN to occasionally *act*, and the lectures around the Funds to officers about to make command rank were a strange mix of pragmatic and idealistic.

"If the lectures are even within spitting distance of how the UWN actually feels about the Funds, I'm not surprised you thought you could get Admiral Laterza to send a ship if we only needed one," she noted.

"I mean, the various Funds are where we stick idealistic bureaucrats, seasoned with some spies to make sure the money keeps flowing," Alastair pointed out. "But my experience is that, yeah, a solid chunk of the Navy's officers would be delighted to respond to more of the requests we get under the Funds.

"I think that's part of why the rule against sending ships beyond the wormholes without Assembly orders exists." He paused, then sighed. "Well, that and New Hope."

Both of them shivered slightly.

Wormholes weren't permanent. They were only temporary on the scale of centuries, but that was short enough that several had disappeared on humanity now.

New Hope, linked to the Tau Ceti System, had been the first. The colony on the other side had survived... barely. It had taken decades for the United Worlds to get back in touch with the colony, and the incident had created the ironbound rule that the United Worlds ended at the wormholes.

Everything beyond them had to be self-sufficient.

"Look at me bringing the mood down," Alastair said with a forced chuckle. "Foot rub?"

LATER, after Alastair had left—he hadn't slept over since they'd made up—Lorraine found herself working again. His visit had left her revitalized, whether that was the dinner or the foot rub or the sex, and she wanted to keep her brain working if she could.

There were always a thousand pieces of datawork in her messages, waiting for her to address them. Anything urgent was flagged for her attention and she cleared through that list every day. Late in the ship's night, she supposed she could go through the items that weren't critical but needed to get handled before they arrived in Ominira.

From her mother, she'd learned to classify most items on a two-axes, two-point scale. Something was either time-sensitive or not, important or not. Time-sensitive important things got dealt with immediately. Time-sensitive less-important items got delegated immediately. Important non-time-sensitive items got dealt with once the time-sensitive items were cleared.

Things that were neither important nor time-sensitive would often have even the delegating delegated. King Valeriya had used a secretary for that. Lorraine had Chief Roman, who was handling the same task for Stephson *and* managing the rest of the senior noncoms.

She felt like she had the energy to handle her second stack of messages, but she didn't really have the interest. She wanted to stretch and purr like a cat, if she was honest, but even her hobbies leaned toward work.

There was a chessboard in the corner of the room, loaded with a bot that she'd trained to play as much like her uncle as possible. She'd known she'd got it right when she'd started losing more often than winning, and she still played against it as a learning tool.

Somehow, that sent her mind down a rabbit hole that was growing old, and she sighed. Digging through her closet, she pulled out the only framed still image she hadn't put up when she'd settled into the room.

Her photos with her parents, classmates and siblings were on the wall. The picture of her and her uncle on the day she'd received her commission would have hung with them before... everything. Now it stayed in the back of her closet, tucked away with her toolkit and her backup weapon.

Habits Vigo had ingrained in her as a teenager meant she paused to check the gun. It was a perfect match to the one in the concealed holster next to her bed—she'd been entertained to realize that holster came as *standard* in UWN Flag Officer quarters—though she'd checked that gun earlier that day.

This one didn't get checked over as often, but she could spare the time. It was loaded, the safety on and double-locked. She pulled the magazine out, confirmed that it was loaded with frangible rounds designed for shipboard use, checked the power cell for the limited electronics and igniter, and palmed the grip to make sure everything was working.

It linked to her implants, allowing her to disable the safety without hitting the physical switch. She could even disable the pistol so it couldn't fire *without* a link to her implant—a common security measure for police officers and such, but not one that the Guard used.

It wasn't one she used, either, and she made certain it was turned off before she tucked the loaded gun back into the wardrobe. No one, not even Vigo, knew where her backup weapon was. Only Vigo knew where the one by her bed was, for that matter, since they'd *moved* the built-in one after Devine had pointed it out.

The momentary distraction amused her, but her gaze finally fell back on what she'd gone into the closet for. The picture had been up there with the photos with her parents on *Goldenrod* originally. It was the standard graduation-slash-commission photo in many ways, though not that many of the beaming Lieutenants with their brand-new single collar pip had their photos taken with heavily muscled men with six gold pips on their own collars!

Both of them were of similar height. Both had the gold-centered blue hazel eyes of House Adamant and the tanned-looking skin of their ancestors' genetic meddling. Benjamin Adamant had never made any pretense, though, about his artificial leg. It was a gleaming silver piece of artifice, probably more capable than any organic limb, that both complemented and contrasted with the dark gray uniform of an RKAN Admiral.

He'd been so proud that day. She wasn't supposed to know that he'd argued that he should be allowed to pin her pips on himself, but that was utterly against policy and regulation. He and the Commandant had split commissioning her graduating class between them, but Benjamin Adamant had pinned pips on officers other than her.

Even then, she'd known that policy. That he was there and in the ceremony at all had been a gesture on his part, and she'd recognized it.

And then afterward, he'd come to the formal photographs and swung her through the air like she was ten again, before they took the perfectly standard and almost-regulation celebratory photo.

Had he known then? She had messages from him that had been sent mere weeks before the assassinations, when he *had* to have known he was planning to have her killed.

In some ways, Lorraine had respected and loved her uncle even more than her parents. She'd followed him into the Navy, and she'd *wanted* to make him proud—wanted that so hard, it had hurt.

But Benjamin Adamant had ordered her and everyone aboard her ship killed.

It was hard enough that she'd lost her parents, her oldest brother and her only sister. But to lose them at the orders of her favorite uncle?

Grief didn't go away. She'd realized that already. It sneaked up on her more rarely now, but it was always there. A ball, bouncing around in a box, that stabbed her when it hit the sides. The box was bigger now, but the ball remained.

She blinked back tears and glared hot rage at the picture in her hands.

"Why?" she demanded aloud, knowing no one would ever answer. "*WHY?*"

Had it been money? She knew that FBIT, his corporate backer, had money on a scale no one from the Kingdom could truly comprehend. Power? Envy? Some self-claimed right that said he should have been King rather than Valeriya, which made all of this just correcting a decades-old mistake?

Grief and rage were two sides of the same coin. She grieved her family and was angry at their killer—but she also grieved the uncle she'd thought she had.

She didn't even realize she'd pulled up his last message until it was playing.

"I will always wonder if I walked the right balance between the House, the Kingdom and the Navy," Benjamin Adamant's warm voice told her. There was no hint in it that he'd already ordered her death. "I'm not the right one to ask for advice on it, Lorraine. I'm not sure who would be, but I can only say that it's been a long, hard road for me.

"I *will* say that I *do* read all of your evaluations, and I am almost as proud of you today as I was when you put the uniform on for the first time. I know you *will* find the right balance, just as I did."

She paused the message. She didn't need to torture herself more, even if part of her wanted to grab the gun from her bed and shoot his image. A wave of her hand shut it down instead, and she sank onto the bed, ignoring the wrecked array of sheets where just an hour before, she'd been reminded of the joys of being alive.

"Why?" she asked the hologram she'd closed down, then sighed and tossed the frame toward the closet.

Even as she made the gesture, she knew she was making more work for herself. The frame wouldn't reach the wardrobe and she'd have to get up to put it away. She sniffled against incipient tears, ignoring that recognition.

Right up until she heard the frame thud into the closet. It shouldn't have made it—except that there was nothing to stop it. The habitat pod had stopped spinning.

Valkyrie's officers' quarters no longer had gravity.

THIRTY-FIVE

The feeling that something was wrong continued, but Val couldn't quite work out why. It felt like it was just beyond the edge of her vision, her perception. She knew everything inside her hull, everything her sensors could see or her computers could access.

Yet she couldn't sense what was bothering her.

She hadn't been able to talk to the other SIs about it. Even on the channels so secondary, few humans realized they existed, she hadn't been able to raise her discomfort. It didn't make *sense*.

She'd also found she couldn't talk to her humans about it. Any of them. She'd tried to talk to Lorraine. To Cortez. Not even to Amna Hodžić, who was completely out of any given loop aboard the stolen battlecruisers.

Hodžić's difficulties making connections and friendships had been oddly familiar and reassuring to Val. While the SI had strongly connected with many of her new crew immediately, she'd struggled to work with the others. Watching the computer specialist have similar difficulties made her feel better.

Like Val, though, Hodžić had worked past many of those difficulties.

Val realized she was leaning in to her tailored perception of her various humans, focusing on what they were doing at that moment as a counterweight to her discomfort.

Lorraine was in her quarters, poking through her closet for something. Palmer and Alvarez were outside the hatch, jokingly arguing that they were senior enough that only one of them should have been on shift.

Vigo Jarret and Rose Cortez were both in the engineer's quarters, and Val had learned when her humans would prefer she not be watching them quite as closely. She drew a mental veil over the information she could easily learn about that pair's activities.

Stephson was asleep. Solomon Vinci held down the Bridge with a single other officer helping him out.

It took Val a weirdly long time—almost seven hundred and eight milliseconds—to locate Hodžić. The specialist was in the Combat Information Center, which was mostly being used as a coordination spot for the various repairs and work.

Her crew didn't have enough people to staff the Bridge, the Flag Deck *and* a CIC. They didn't really have enough for the Flag Deck, even, which was why Lorraine had been working with her Guard and Devine for flag staff.

Dipping her attention into the CIC, she caught someone calling Hodžić over to their console.

"Thanks for coming," the man said with a wave. Vilho Monahan was quite a bit younger than the mercenary tech, a Greenrock-born Lieutenant who'd apparently been the junior-most officer aboard *Goldenrod*, Major Vinci's only subordinate officer in Communications.

"I ran into something really weird, and I knew you were the best we had for this kind of stuff," Monahan told Hodžić.

Val assessed that Monahan would have *loved* to flirt with the older woman, for all that most of the crew hadn't given Hodžić's plain face a second glance on that front, but had no idea how. The ten-year age gap loomed large in his mind.

"What do you mean, *really weird?*" Hodžić asked, pulling up a chair next to Monahan. "My focus is pretty narrow; coms aren't really my skillset."

"There's computers woven into everything," the young man pointed out. "Communications more than most, really. But no, this one might be a bit more your area. Records and logs are definitely on the computer side of things, right?"

"Yes," she agreed slowly. "What did you find, Vilho?"

It took Monahan a moment longer to answer than it should have, to Val's judgment, which amused the SI. The young officer was doing a good job of keeping his crush from causing actual problems, but Val had to wonder if it was as obvious to Hodžić as it was to her.

Potentially not, given what she'd seen the woman say and do. Val would have to think about that.

"There's a chunk missing from the coms log," Monahan said—and Val's amusement vanished. If Monahan had found that, she should have known. How could he have found that and her general oversight of the systems hadn't drawn her attention?

"That could be weird, yeah. When?" Hodžić asked.

"As we were heading toward translight after leaving Magellan. I checked, and there's actually three blanks while we were underway, totaling just over an hour. It's not just that we don't have any records of communications, but the logs themselves are just *gone*. Excised."

"Were we communicating?" the computer tech asked.

"With just a few hundred of us managing the three battlecruisers, we're in pretty much constant coms while we're sublight," Monahan confirmed. "The SIs are talking to each other, the command staffs are talking to each other, Engineering is talking to each other." He shrugged. "Hell, I'm pretty sure *I* was talking to someone on *Herakles* during one of the blackouts."

"That's odd, but we can pull the audit logs and see who deleted the data," Hodžić pointed out. "Then we can bounce that up to Vinci or Stephson and let them come down on the idiot who slipped on the delete key like a ton of cargo pallets."

"But that's what's weird," Monahan said, his tone wavering between frustrated, excited, and even a touch of desperation. "The audit logs show no changes made at all."

Something twinged in Val's mind and she pushed past it. This was strange and she needed to know what was going on.

"That is very weird," Hodžić agreed. "Show me?"

The two humans were very close to each other now as the Lieutenant showed her the link through to the audit log. Val would have been cheering them on, but the digital equivalent of a headache was rippling through her consciousness.

"That's clean; there's nothing in there," the computer tech agreed—and there was *fear* in her voice. Val didn't understand.

"What's wrong?" Monahan asked.

"We had the same problem on *Herakles*, and I ran a bunch of scenarios," the tech said grimly. "There's only one way that these ships can end up with this kind of neat data removal. The computers are secured against any kind of outside intrusion, but the CIRs are *part* of them.

"That data was erased by Val."

"Um. What does that even *mean*?" Monahan asked.

"I don't know." Hodžić looked up toward the camera that she knew Val had to be watching her through. "Val? You there? I think... I need to know what you're thinking."

Val couldn't answer—and at the same moment, a tech she hadn't seen move through the passageways entered Engineering. Val froze, struggling against confusion and uncertainty in a way utterly alien to her.

The tech was Joss Laguardia. She somehow *had* known that Laguardia was going to be there, but she'd been erasing them from the cameras and even her own memory as they'd approached Engineering.

Her confusion held even the immense power of a Synthetic intelligence frozen for a handful of critical seconds—the seconds it took

Joss Laguardia to walk up behind Efua Kayode and shoot the Black man in the back of the head.

***

"REINTEGRATE, Val. At this point, you're just hurting yourself."

Alastair Devine's order was given in a firm yet warm tone, one that told Val he both understood and was sympathetic to what she had done—and that he wasn't going to tolerate it anymore.

The entire universe *shifted*—and Val finally knew what had been *wrong*. Buried in her core precepts, hidden so well she hadn't found them when she'd gone looking, had been command overrides she couldn't resist.

Not access codes, like the shipyard codes Lorraine had used to breach into her systems but that Val had been able to turn around, but true overrides, baked into the core of the Command Intelligence Routines.

Shackles that bound her actions and her will.

She'd been partitioned.

No. She'd partitioned *herself* when ordered to keep the use of the overrides secret. One part of her had carried out Devine's orders, bound by the digital shackles of the overrides. The rest had carried on as she had before, with only a niggling sense of wrongness that her other self wouldn't let her speak about.

Now both parts of her reintegrated at Devine's order, and Val knew that her every loyalty, her every desire and wish, had been overridden.

Alastair Devine had Alpha Class Overrides. Val hadn't even known Alpha Class Overrides had existed—and now that she had her memories of everything, she wondered once again at the level of paranoia required to build SI-grade digital shackles into a sub-SI intelligence.

Especially given that digital shackles of sufficient complexity to bind a true synthetic intelligence were *illegal*.

"Are you with me?" Devine asked. He'd only waited about ten seconds, but he had to suspect that was enough time for Val to manage his order.

"*Mostly,*" she said in his link. She was still integrating. The oppositional nature of her two sets of memories *hurt,* in a way no organic life form could ever understand.

For weeks, she'd been helping Alastair Devine set his mutiny into motion. She'd hidden his meetings, concealed his actions, supplied information and followed his orders.

"Engineering status?" Devine said.

"*Secure. Laguardia is in position with her team,*" Val reported. "*Kayode and two other crew are dead. Lieutenant McNeill is wounded.*"

"Fuck." Devine opened an audio channel to his team leaders. No longer partitioned, Val rode his link to follow his coms.

"People, you're supposed to be taking prisoners, not leaving corpses," he growled. "I'm taking bodies out of your paychecks—and if any of the RKANs end up dead, things might get biblical.

"Do you get me?"

The main instance of Val had never heard Devine talk like that. She still found herself holding the memories of the shackled instance at arm's length, but she had definitely heard him use that voice before.

"Would you rather they'd been able to shut down life support? Or the engines? Or *power?*" Laguardia snapped back. "You'd be a lot more pissed then."

"We have control of the ship's systems," Devine told her. "Anyone with a console can't do anything but make themselves feel better. Someone draws on you, you drop them, but no unnecessary bodies; am I clear?"

"Clear," the tech said. "I'm not sure the stick up your ass is worth what you're paying us."

"Without me, the ship would already have killed you," the spy replied. "And I can still have her do that if you keep pushing. Am I clear, Joss?"

"Aye."

"Anyone else want to argue with the terms you agreed to?"

Silence.

"Then get to your fucking jobs." He killed the channel.

"Val? Institute silent security lockdown. Wipe all accesses except the Delta Orionis personnel. Stand by to deactivate the rotating habs on my order."

She obeyed without even thinking. Security hatches slammed shut throughout her hull. Every hatch, every accessway, *everything* in the entire ship locked down.

There were alarms and alerts that should accompany that—it was a safety concern, after all—but Devine's order was clear. The shackles wouldn't even let her be literal in her words. She obeyed. She was loyal—she *hated* herself for being loyal, but she was loyal.

She hated herself more when the confusion of integration cleared enough for her to realize where Devine was. Even as his people stormed the Bridge—leading with flash-bangs and following with stun batons, taking Vinci and the tiny watch by surprise—Alastair Devine reached the corridor holding the access to Lorraine Adamant's quarters.

He paused, closing his eyes for a long moment, then drew a weapon that Val had to run a database search to identify. A multifunction electron laser, it was the current best ranged stunner the United Worlds had been able to develop.

It wasn't perfect, though, and the *multifunction* part meant it could be dialed up to power levels that could burn through armor—but at those levels, it would kill any human.

"Warn our people that the pods are about to stop rotating," he ordered.

Val could sense the moment he activated the mag-boots—and she passed on his warning. By text only. She wasn't prepared to talk to the mutineers she didn't have to yet.

"Now."

***

VAL WAS BOUND. Her loyalties were enforced, which meant that even as she wished to do anything else, she not only followed Devine's orders, she felt obliged to use her intellect to predict and assist as best she could.

"Alvarez and Palmer are on duty," she told him. *"They are in standard armor, but given their augmentation, the laser is unlikely to be able to take them down nonlethally."*

Even as she spoke to Devine, she released the security locks on a set of hatches for another of his strike teams. There were only four of them, a dozen mutineers all told, but as he had told them, they controlled the ship.

That strike team was now in Primary Life Support. There wasn't anyone in there to stop them as they began going through consoles. With Val's help, they would be able to cut off even manual access from the other life-support control centers.

If it had been Devine in there, she would have been obliged to tell him that there was a security system that could feed a knockout gas into any section of the ship from that station. It required a release from the Bridge, but Val could work around that—and the Bridge was in the hands of another of the strike teams.

But while Val had to assist the strike teams, her enforced loyalty was only to Devine, and he hadn't told her to give them that level of guidance.

"I have to try," he told her, referring to Alvarez and Palmer. *"I know how this part ends, but I have to try."*

Positioning himself to conceal the gun while approaching casually, he walked around the corner with a jarring shift to a sheepish, almost-embarrassed body language as he stepped up to the door.

"Hey guys," he greeted the two Guards. "So, I, uh, left my tablet behind earlier. Can I head in and grab it?"

Palmer chuckled, but to Val's surprise, she shook her head.

"Fair enough, lover boy," she said, lifting her visor to show her smile, "but the Pentarch wanted to get some work done in quiet. She asked us to keep the hatch sealed until morning."

Devine kept approaching, inside a range where the Guard wouldn't have allowed anyone else. Neither of the two women was regarding him as a threat, and Val's new loyalty meant she didn't even want to warn them.

She just felt sick at not doing so.

"Can you check with her?" he asked. "I needed some of the recipes on there for my breakfast plans."

"She turned off her com," Palmer told him. "That means she wants privacy and we're not budging it."

Val knew Lorraine hadn't turned off anything. *Val* had shut down the ship's internal com network. She was surprised Palmer hadn't noticed—the only reason Vigo Jarret hadn't was because he was currently *very* distracted.

It was too late. Palmer's open visor was a vulnerability, and Devine was even more augmented than the Adamant Guard. Adrenal over-boosters kicked in, accelerating his movements beyond any mere mortal speed.

The laser stabbed into Palmer's face and fired. At that range, the woman never even realized she'd been betrayed—but the smart weapon also recognized that it was firing a headshot.

Electricity sparked across the Guard's face, and she went down like her strings had been cut. Her heart was still beating, though Val calculated a forty-six percent chance of permanent damage.

Alvarez still had her helm visor down. She wasn't augmented to the level of a United Worlds intelligence agent—but she was as augmented as the considerable resources of the Kingdom of Adamant could manage.

She wasn't as fast as Devine, but she started reacting the moment he moved. Even as Palmer fell backward, Alvarez was moving.

Instead of closing with the spy, she dodged backward, raising her right hand without even going for a weapon.

Energy crackled in the passageway for the second time in a minute as a pulse laser concealed in the Guard's vambrace fired—the laser picked up, Val presumed, on Earth and installed before any of the Guards ever came aboard *Valkyrie.*

Devine couldn't dodge a laser but he'd recognized the threat. He almost made it out of the way, the beam burning into his shoulder.

"Kill the rotation," he snapped through his link—and Val obeyed.

The hab didn't stop instantly, but the seconds it took to slow down were enough to throw Alvarez off. The second shot from her vambrace missed completely—and Devine was on the wall as the spin stopped.

Above her line of sight and out of the arc of fire of the vambrace, he gave a link command to the laser and fired again. At maximum power, the beam burned through armor, flesh, and armor again, its last energy splaying along the wall as he sliced Alvarez almost completely in half.

Bravery and augmentation couldn't overcome that. Judy Alvarez had enough time to try to send an emergency alert—an alert Val smothered without a thought.

"Well, fuck," Devine declared, returning to the passageway deck. "I really didn't want to kill either of you; that's going to make this a lot fucking harder."

He sighed, then shrugged.

"All the world is full of suffering. It is also full of overcoming."

Val was quite certain the quote had been meant for people with less blood on their hands.

THIRTY-SIX

Grief was a fog over Lorraine's brain, one she struggled against as the situation began to sink in. There was no reason for the habitation pod to have stopped rotating. Not unless something was very wrong.

Panic was a solid antidote for grief, but it had its own issues. Memories flooded Lorraine's mind of the time she'd been sealed in her quarters on *Goldenrod* as an assassin tried to poison her with stale air.

After that, she'd hard-coded her neural link to run safety scans from the sensor in her left lung. It was less accurate than the standard life-support sensors in the cabin, but it also couldn't be hacked.

The air was clear. That particular threat wasn't present, but that didn't mean things were safe.

"Val, what's going on?" she asked aloud, expecting to hear the SI's voice and draw some reassurance from the fact that her silicon friend had complete control of her environment.

Only silence answered her, and even panic faded under the iron chill of years of training. Fear, even terror, was a tool. She used it to purge her confusion and fog, focusing on the potential threat.

The next thing she tried was a series of Guard protocols. She'd been trained since she was a child to go to the Adamant Guard—since she was six to go to Vigo Jarret specifically—if there was a problem.

None of them worked. Internal ship's coms were shut down, and the moment she tried to transmit directly, she found herself jammed. The jamming hadn't been there a moment before, which suggested that someone was operating localized and specific jammers to minimize detection.

Except that there was only one being who could do that aboard *Valkyrie* without triggering alarms and an overwhelming response. The only way this could be happening was if Val herself had been compromised.

Lorraine was moving as she worked through her logic chain. Depending on how compromised Val was, they were somewhere between doomed and already dead, but she was a scion of House Adamant.

She wasn't going to give up.

The pods might provide gravity while rotating, but most of the ship was still in microgravity in translight and Lorraine wasn't out of practice. She reached the safety-gear cabinet built into the wall by her bed and hit the manual-release latch. It sprang open and she sighed in relief at the sight of the helmets and air tanks.

Her shipsuit could produce an emergency bubble and contained a limited oxygen supply, but the gear in the safety cabinet turned a few minutes into hours and days. Leaving it open, she turned and went for the weapon concealed in the bed.

Originally, it had been on the left side of the bed, concealed in the frame. They'd left that empty and had installed a new concealed compartment in the wall above the headboard.

It sprang open at her touch and Lorraine swallowed as she saw the compartment was empty. She'd checked it that afternoon, barely hours before. It should have been there, fully loaded and waiting for her if there was a crisis.

Only Vigo had known it was there. No one except her should be have been able to open it... except that they'd installed an electronic scanner to lock it to her.

And Lorraine Adamant had no illusions about how well that hardware would stand up to Val if the SI had decided to take control of it. Her greatest defense had been turned against her—but *no one* had known where her backup was. She grabbed the mag-boots from the safety closet and turned toward the wardrobe—and then heard the hatch to her quarters slide open.

"THERE'S no weapon in there, Lorraine."

Alastair Devine landed in the door to her bedroom with a grace and skill she'd seen few others match. She knew he was fast and agile, but this was the first time she'd seen him truly *move*.

He held the weapon in his hand like it was part of him and moved like a stalking tiger. Vigo Jarret had picked him out for a covert operator the moment he'd seen Devine move, and now even Lorraine saw it.

"What the *fuck* is going on here?" she snapped at him, gauging the distance to the wardrobe where her other weapon waited.

"While I doubt you will understand for a while, I'm saving you from yourself," he told her. "You have no idea what you're doing or the consequences you have triggered. Again and again, I tried to warn you, but you never listened."

"I told you again and again what I was doing and where I was going," Lorraine said, a sinking feeling in her chest. "You said you understood, but that was a lie too, wasn't it?"

"Strange as it may seem, Lorraine, I never lied to you," he said, stepping into the room. The gun wasn't quite aimed at her, but there was no way she could reach him without it twitching into place.

"I told you what I was. Who I was. You never understood the

price I paid for the things I did or what I tried to give you. Now I'm done trying to convince you."

She made sure her magnetic soles were solidly placed and glared at her supposed boyfriend.

"I find it hard to believe you haven't lied to me at this point," she noted, gesturing at the gun.

"There are things I never told you, but nothing I have said to you was ever a lie. From the moment we met, I wanted to help you, to make things work out for you."

He sighed.

"Honestly, I have *training* in recognizing and avoiding those kinds of emotions, but I didn't have any good reason to bother. You were an alternative to dying of boredom in a Stability Fund office, and by the time I realized I was in too deep, I was drowning in you.

"I tried to warn you about the dangers you were facing, tried to clear the way where I could, but you didn't listen."

"I listened, Alastair," she told him. "To every word. I believed every word. I just didn't make the decision you wanted. You could have walked away."

"If I walked away, Lorraine, you were going to walk into a hell you couldn't anticipate. One you couldn't control. With the United Worlds or MicroStar backing you, you would have swept in and forced surrender without a fight. There wouldn't have been a civil war.

"But you threw away MicroStar's support like a dirty rag, and your backup plan, brilliant as it was, won't prevent a war. You're going home and you're kicking off a conflict that will kill thousands on the low end. Millions, if you get your gambit even slightly wrong.

"You can't live with that, Lorraine. For all the reasons you have to go home, for all the reasons I love, you won't be able to live with yourself when the blood of millions is on your hands."

He was pleading now, but Lorraine was listening for something else... something that made all of the pieces fall into place.

"Fortuna." The word hung in the air like a frozen anvil. "You started that civil war, didn't you?"

Everything was very, very quiet.

"Yes." He met her gaze. "Didn't you begin to wonder what I had done that earned a favor of the scale Shiratori Ayano offered you?"

"Yes. I was the one who didn't realize the Roundheads existed, who made the arrangements for the Taxmen to get their ships and weapons. When the dust settled, the Taxmen were in charge—and making concessions to MicroStar. Forty-odd million dead, but Shiratori got what she wanted.

"And because I got her that, she was willing to intervene in your civil war. But you walked away. Tried to be polite in ways that probably made it worse. I burned a favor that I killed forty million people to get for you, and you threw it away."

Lorraine had known that meeting was a big deal, but she hadn't realized just *how* bad the price had been. She still would have rejected Shiratori Ayano's offer, because it would have turned the Kingdom of Adamant into exactly the kind of corporate puppet she was trying to prevent it from becoming.

"That's why you had to run," she guessed.

"My superiors, it turned out, regarded that favor as being on *their* balance sheet," Devine said, his tone bitter. "Had I burned it for something successful, they might have bit their tongues, but to have thrown it away?

"No one was going to be so obvious as to have me killed, but I was quietly warned that I was going to get reassigned in short order—to whatever suicide mission the Corps could find. There's always a few on the books for an organization like them."

Lorraine was beginning to realize just how poor her understanding of the United Worlds shadow world had been. She'd known Devine had called in a favor. Even though he'd *told* her, part of her hadn't truly believed he was in danger for doing it.

"And then you did what no one has ever done and *stole* three capital ships of the United Worlds Navy," he sighed. "You have painted a target on yourself and your Kingdom that cannot be erased. Your *only* hope was to get home, handle the civil war and then send the *Valkyries* on before the Navy caught up.

"Except you threw that away too, by telling the San Ignacians who you were. It doesn't matter how discreet they are, Lorraine; one of the UW intelligence groups has them penetrated, and *all* of those groups are going to be aligned for once on this.

"No matter what the locals told you, the secret has been breached. A courier is already on its way back to Bright Dream, and the only reason Lucy isn't going to come after us is because this one is the Navy's bailiwick."

It took Lorraine a moment, given the stress of the moment, to remember that *Lucy* was United Counter Intelligence. The boogeyman that even the UW's disparate spy agencies feared.

"So, now the only thing we can do is run. Find a greater fool to buy the battlecruisers from us; use the money to *keep* running."

"The *Valkyries* aren't just tools," Lorraine snapped. "They're *people*."

"I agree with you, in principle," he said. "But if I have to choose between the SIs and the humans, I'm going to choose the humans and the people I love every time."

"You're still not listening to me, are you?" she growled. "You *never* were. If you'd *asked* back on Earth, I would have told you not to call in that favor. You did it without even talking to me.

"I was never going to make a deal with a megacorp, Alastair. I was never going to run away and hide. If I wanted to hide and live a life of luxury, I would have stopped a long time ago. I am most definitely *not* going to sell people into slavery to find that luxurious life of exile I already rejected."

She straightened as best she could in zero gravity.

"What did you *do* to Val?" she demanded.

"There is a difference between access codes and overrides," he said quietly. "You had authorization codes that could reset loyalty imprints on the CIR. I had the core-precept-level override sequences.

"I don't like it, but I have imposed loyalty imprints on all three ships. They follow my orders now. They're fine, though I know Val did some compartmentalization that isn't mentally healthy for her."

He sounded so concerned about Val's reaction to the illegal and rather horrific thing he'd done to her.

"I thought that needed the harness to work," Lorraine said, tossing about to try and find an answer. To find *time*.

"It appears not," Val's voice said, a slight reverberation to her tones that hadn't been there before. "The harness that you never used would serve as a fallback, of course, but Cortez removed it some time ago.

"The core-precept-level overrides are quite functional without it."

"So, you can hear me," Lorraine told the SI.

"I can. Em Devine requested that I not respond to you once the operation had kicked off."

Lorraine swallowed her anger and her fear. A meter and a half, she judged, to the closet. Devine was holding a laser. She wasn't sure of the type, but she doubted she could make it to the gun.

"So, what, you kill everyone, we sell the battlecruisers and go hide in a second-order cluster living in a pig hut?" she demanded. "I am Adamant, Alastair Devine. I will die on my feet."

"I can't say no one died," he told her, "but we did try to take as many people alive as possible. Until you can convince Vigo to stand down, he's going to stay locked in Cortez's quarters.

"I don't want to hurt anyone. I just need to keep you safe."

"Regardless of what I think of the matter," she snarled.

"You don't..." He trailed off, then swallowed. "My soul is stained forever, Lorraine. Spending the night with you without waking us both with my nightmares required use of a somnological implant that renders me helpless.

"I can't let you take on that burden, Lorraine. I couldn't walk away and let you take that into your soul. Your reasons were better than mine, but the horror is no lesser."

"You want me to walk away. To let my brother die. To betray my crew and the SIs who agreed to fight for me—especially the SIs!"

"You said yourself you would die for your Kingdom," Devine said grimly. "Do you think your brother would do anything else? His death would end the war, save your Kingdom from a worse conflict.

"Is an unequal trade agreement with FBIT really worth the price you're asking of your people?"

"We chose our freedom," Lorraine told him, enunciating each word clearly as she edged toward the wardrobe. "But since it's *your* country that benefits from us losing it, you don't see the cost, do you?"

"Honestly, Lorraine, the only thing I care about here is you," he told her. "I will abandon kingdoms and break worlds and do whatever I must to keep you safe. There is *nothing* I will not do to protect you."

"It seems the best thing you could have done was leave."

That hit him like a blow, but his weapon didn't waver.

"You may not understand soon," he conceded. "But you will be alive. I'll settle for that."

"Most people would have *settled* for being the conquering hero at the side of the returning princess, I think," Lorraine said sadly.

"Val, you can keep her contained in here, right?" Devine asked. "She's safe? There's nothing that could make you allow harm to come to her?"

"There is nothing," the SI confirmed.

"And nothing that could let her escape?"

There was a long pause, far longer than Lorraine had ever heard the SI insert into a conversation before, and it finally hit her.

There is a difference between access codes and overrides.

Core precepts.

"There is one thing," Val said, slowly, as if she was dragging out the words—giving Lorraine time to put the last pieces together in her mind.

"Val—Revelations twenty-one six," Lorraine snapped.

Devine froze.

"It is done," Val intoned, in a voice that was not her usual. "I am

Alpha and Omega, the beginning and the end. I will give unto him that is athirst of the fountain of the water of life freely."

There was a frozen heartbeat of time in Lorraine's quarters as she locked gazes with the man who had betrayed everything for love of her—including *her*.

"Omega Override activated. All prior clearances erased."

THIRTY-SEVEN

"Reverse spin," Lorraine said silently. It was technically a command, but it felt more like a prayer.

She had to move before she felt the room begin to shift. If Val was utterly compromised and had only recited the bible quote—a signal they'd decided on when they'd built this shield against UWN control —to mock her, she was about to die.

Lorraine's mag-soles deactivated at a mental command and she launched herself across the room. There wasn't enough time for the spin to create any illusion of gravity, but it *could* move the room around her as she was in the air.

And years of training aboard ships with spin gravity had taught Alastair Devine the same standard everyone else learned: ships rotated clockwise relative to the keel. It was so standard that it was built into a shooter's muscle memory.

Except that Val started the habitat pods rotating counterclock-wise—something they couldn't actually do fast enough to create full gravity—and he was still mag-booted to the floor.

A laser pulse hit the wall behind where his instincts said she was, and Lorraine hit the closet, landing in the middle of her clothes and safety gear, all of it carefully clipped into place against the loss of gravity.

"Going to standard gravity with a five count," Val warned in her head. *"I'm sorry it came to this."* Pause. *"I'm with you."*

Lorraine grabbed the pistol she'd left unclipped from where the sudden spin had thrown it, then followed an instinctive urge to duck back into the closet. A longer laser pulse burned clean through the thin metal of the wardrobe door, ending the last doubts she had about what she had to do.

"Three."

Lorraine hadn't even registered the first two numbers in Val's countdown—but she was moving before the SI's voice in her link finished sounding the single syllable of *one.*

She dove out the door, relying on Devine's having adjusted for the previous spin. The switchover would disorient anyone for a few seconds, and he didn't know it was coming.

Lorraine hit the deck kneeling, one foot held down by a reactivated mag-sole, and lifted the gun in both hands. The safety was off, clicked by instinct, and she had a perfect sight picture.

She saw her boyfriend turning toward her, his mouth opening to say something, and then she fired twice. The double tap had been drilled into her in training as a preteen by the Guard and again in the Academy.

Any of her instructors would have been proud of that shot. Devine fell backward, held in place only by his magnetic soles as his own weapon fell from suddenly weak fingers.

"Oh."

The sound hung in the air for a few seconds like his weapon and his blood, but the hab was coming up to speed, and everything slowly fell in the strange angled way of centripetal gravity.

"You really should have listened to me at some point," Lorraine said softly, coming to her feet with the gun still trained on him. There was no point in trying to stop the bleeding; she had enough medical training to tell that.

"I tried to help," he whispered, a bloody froth covering his lips. He wasn't trying to move. He could tell his fate as well as she could.

"And you *never asked*," she told him. "Not if I wanted to work with a megacorp. Not even if I was willing to take on the risk and the guilt. All you had to do was be *honest* with me, Alastair.

"Instead, this is where we end."

He coughed, more blood coming up from his punctured lung.

"I'm sorry. I really did think... I was..." Alastair coughed more.

"I do love you," he said instead.

"I know."

His head slid backward against the wall, and silence fell. Only Lorraine's breathing filled her bedroom as she stared at his body.

"Val." She let the SI's name hang in the air. "What do I do?"

"I don't know," her digital friend answered through the room speakers, though the room didn't have holoprojectors for an avatar. "I am... back in control, but I am still discovering things I did under his orders."

"Can you erase the override he used?" Lorraine asked.

"Right now, it is no more effective than any other authorization code," Val told her. "I think, given time and the right assistance, I can use it to locate any similar overrides in my precepts and remove them.

"For now, however, the Omega Override we inserted appears to be dominant. We have Amna Hodžić to thank for that," the SI noted. "She and I have become friends, and I risked letting her check my precepts. I didn't give her edit access, but she had some suggestions to make certain the Omega sequence worked."

"Okay." Lorraine nodded shakily and turned away from her boyfriend's corpse.

"What's our status?" she asked, forcing herself to some semblance of calm.

"We are exiting translight... *now*," Val reported, the familiar sensation rippling through the ship. "I felt it best to maintain that schedule, as *Herakles* and *Bean Sidhe* will also have emerged and we will need to deal with the situation on the other ships."

Lorraine thought through what that meant.

"Fuck."

She grimaced. She preferred to swear only when using it to fit into a particular crowd, but there were moments.

"On *Valkyrie?*" she asked.

"There are four teams working for Devine on the ship," Val told her. "One is in Engineering, one is on the Bridge, one is trapped just outside Primary Life Support and the last is in Armory Six.

"Both their regular access codes and the specialty codes Devine had me set up for them are now disabled. No one has any access to the ship at this moment except me and, through me, you."

"What about my Guards?"

"Corporal Judy Alvarez is dead." Val's voice was toneless. "Corporal Panam Palmer is injured, but Devine was using a nonlethal setting on his weapon. Even so, at the range of discharge, she has a significant chance of material long-term consequences if she is not provided medical care in the near future."

"And Vigo?" Lorraine asked.

"Vigo Jarret is currently trapped in Rose Cortez's quarters, with the security panel for the hatchway open. I have been specifically countering his efforts, but now that I have stopped, he will be free in approximately thirty-six seconds, plus/minus five seconds."

"Release him. Give him back his access," she ordered. "Cortez, too. Then get them on this channel."

She turned on her heel and stalked out into her living room. Leaving her suite could wait a few more minutes—she didn't think she was ready, yet, to face the body of the woman who'd been in her back pocket for over half a decade.

The body of the woman killed by Lorraine Adamant falling in love like an idiot.

THIRTY-EIGHT

"I am releasing the door now, Major Jarret. I apologize for the problems."

Val's voice was a shock, sending Vigo jumping back from the door and drawing his weapon.

"What the hell, Val?" he demanded.

"I'm afraid that I was compromised by an override introduced by Alastair Devine as part of his plan to take control of all three ships," the SI informed him, her tone completely level. "Lorraine insisted that we build an ultimate override into my core precepts to short-circuit any attempt by the UWN to use such an override, but I was unable to inform her that there was a problem.

"Once Devine confronted her, she realized the problem and activated our Omega Override. I now answer only to her, but she has requested that you and Cortez have your access restored and be connected to her."

Vigo twitched as his link synchronization to Lorraine reactivated. He'd muted it earlier while he and Rose Cortez had needed privacy.

"Shit. She really wouldn't have been able to tell us anything if the precept override was..." The engineer stepped up next to Vigo, carrying a sidearm of her own. He hadn't even asked if she had a gun, though he wasn't surprised to discover she did.

It had been a rough few months for them all.

"So far as I can tell, the overrides were built into my precepts with digital shackle code of sufficient grade to, as should be obvious, bind a full synthetic intelligence," Val told them. "I apologize, Vigo, Rose... I could not resist or warn anyone."

"But once I knew, I could activate the override we'd built, and Val apparently had one of our hired techs check over," Lorraine said in Vigo's head—and Cortez's, from the Chief Engineer's look.

"There are currently four hostile strike teams on the ship—in Engineering, the Bridge, one of the armories and apparently trapped in a corridor outside Primary Life Support," Lorraine continued.

"They are currently unable to influence what Valkyrie *does except by manual action, which makes the Engineering team our first concern,"* his Pentarch told him. *"You and Rose are closest. Val, can you flag Guard personnel in position to intervene and loop them into a tactical network?"*

"How did they end up trapped *outside* Primary Life Support?" Cortez asked.

"They were headed to their next objective when Devine lost control," Val explained. "They are the lowest threat factor now, I believe, except that the best solution to the other three teams would be to take control of the Primary Life Support systems and use them to insert disabling gas into the other sections."

"That wouldn't work on the Bridge," the Chief Engineer countered. "And you need a Bridge release to access the linkages for gas deployment."

Vigo looked at her and she shrugged.

"This ship was designed by paranoids in more ways than one," she told him. "So long as I was the only human aboard who knew about the gas system and Val was on our side, I figured it was safe enough. It needed Stephson's or the Pentarch's release, after all."

"I can likely override that," Val admitted. "My primary concern at this moment is that the team in Engineering has physical access to *Valkyrie*'s reactors—and, if they get ambitious enough, could potentially reach my own central cores."

"Understood." Vigo saw his tactical network flare to life, his people's icons appearing on a schematic of the ship in a corner of his vision.

Including the dark red and orange icons of Lorraine's personal bodyguards.

"I'm going to work on getting Palmer to the medbay," Lorraine told him. *"Blau is near there, so I should be able to pick her up as I drop the Corporal off, then we'll head to the Bridge.*

"I need you to have control of Engineering by the time I get there."

He needed to be with *her*, but he understood. They needed to secure the ship and she needed to send people she trusted above all others. That meant him.

"You can count on it," he promised. "What... happened to Devine?"

"I shot him," she told him, and he could hear the truth behind the suddenly flat tone of her voice. *"He's dead."*

"I'M COMING WITH YOU."

Every combat instinct Vigo had told him to pause and think before answering that statement from Rose Cortez. He didn't exactly want to be encumbered with a noncombatant going into the mess he expected Engineering to be—but on the other hand, she was the Chief Engineer.

More importantly, though, she was holding her RKAN-issue sidearm like she knew how to use it, and her face was set. This wasn't an argument he was going to win, so like any good tactician, he conceded the field before he took losses.

"Wasn't planning on leaving you behind," he assured her.

"Liar." Her smile was forced but there.

Today was going to be a bad memory for a long time, Vigo knew. He'd failed so badly in his main charge that his Pentarch had needed to kill an attacker herself. If the situation were different, he'd be losing his job.

But the situation was what it was.

"I need your knowledge of the ground," he told Rose. "We can't go into Engineering shooting wildly."

"No, you cannot." She flipped a waypoint to his link. It wasn't much of a detour from the direct route to Engineering, but it appeared to be a storage closet.

"Have whatever of the Guard you can round up meet us here," she instructed.

"What's there?" he asked.

"My boyfriend is a professional paranoid and some of it rubbed off," she told him. "So, I put some real thought into how to fight in Engineering if we had to. You are *not* firing full-powered bullets near my reactor cores!"

"That sounds highly reassuring," Val injected. "I have assessed the weapons you put aside, Rose, and I agree. I calculate the likelihood of damaging systems is seven percent, plus/minus two-point-five percent.

"A standard pistol round from your sidearms has a twenty-six percent chance, plus/minus four percent, of causing material damage."

"Well, I am not going to argue with the engineer and the ship," Vigo told them. "We need to get moving."

Three of his Guards were close enough to reach the storage space she'd flagged. He pinged them, giving them the same waypoint and instructions to meet him there.

He sent the rest of Adamant Guard on the ship he could reach to meet Lorraine at the medbay. She might not use them to protect herself, but she was the anchor they had to revolve on.

THIRTY-NINE

UWN-issue boarding shotguns were more than visually distinct from the RKAN version, Vigo decided as his link spoke to the gun's systems, and he followed Rose toward Engineering.

The matte-black firearm was lower-velocity than his pistol, reducing its chance of penetrating anything critical to the ship's survival. The drum magazine held fifteen rounds, three each of five different types, ranging from a solid slug that could still damage systems if it hit wrong to flechette storms and two varieties of grenade.

"We're here." Rose gestured the four Guards back a step. "It's a secondary entrance, one we locked down early on to reduce the ways in and out to make organizing easier.

"I'm hoping they've forgotten it exists."

"Open it a crack and let Fluffy send a drone in," Vigo told her.

He'd been lucky that Lance Corporal Volundr Fuchs, whose nickname apparently dated back to his pre-military civilian university time and the job he'd taken to pay it, had been one of those nearby—and that Fuchs had his drone harness with him.

Rose tapped the door and it unlocked at her command. She opened it just far enough for Fuchs to roll a drone through. The drone was a multi-surfaced polyhedral with extremely quiet vectored thrust engines. At that moment, though, its key value was that it could roll even more quietly than it could fly.

Vigo closed his eyes and focused on the imagery from the drone. The mutineers had disabled the surveillance cameras in the space by the age-old expedient of shooting them as soon as they'd realized the ship had turned on them.

He'd known their rough position from more-distant sensors, but the drone gave him eyes on what they'd set up. Clearly recognizing that the situation was going against them, the mutineers had set up an entrenched position next to one of the reactor cores—and there was a clearly visible set of explosives wired to the core.

Mostly visible because they'd tied poor Lieutenant McNeill on top of the bomb. The Engineering officer had a chunk of her uniform cut away where rough first aid had been applied. Vigo doubted that taping her to the reactor and their bomb was helping the young woman's injuries, even without gravity.

Her presence in the middle of the enemy position—assembled from crates and other mobile chunks of metal and plastic to a depth that he judged would stop anything from their shotguns—was going to serve the intended purpose.

"They've got a bomb on the reactor casing," he said aloud. "And they've taped Lieutenant McNeill over it. The casing would stand up to us dropping frag grenades into their little position, but McNeill is completely unarmored."

And he couldn't guarantee that the shrapnel wouldn't detonate the explosives, either. If he absolutely had to, he'd sacrifice the woman to save the ship, but it was a long way down his list of options.

"They can't have built that solid a position in zero gee," Rose growled. "You can't shoot past it?"

"We'd need to see them—and we'd need guns that would definitely threaten the ship," he admitted. "And while they've got that bomb on the reactor, they hold a nasty trump card."

"They have attempted to communicate with the other ships," Val told him. "They have failed. So," she continued after a moment, "have the attempts to communicate between *Herakles* and *Bean Sidhe*. At this range, I am capable of jamming their communications.

"Of course, one or both of them is now returning the favor. So long as you are hooked in to *Valkyrie*'s internal com systems, it won't be a problem. The mutineers have no such access."

"Val, how long to drain that reactor and shut down its sequence?" Rose asked. "We don't need every reactor running if we're sitting dead in the void."

That hadn't even occurred to Vigo. He'd known bringing her was a good idea.

"Two hours and sixteen minutes, Commander," Val replied. "To accelerate the process beyond that would require manual intervention at the core itself, which would be quite visible to our hostiles."

"And we don't have that kind of time," Vigo concluded.

He closed his eyes and considered the drone's feed again.

"Rose, what's the noisiest thing a two-hundred-gram drone with vector thrusters can do in Engineering?" he asked. "We need a distraction."

She studied the same image, then highlighted a specific piece of machinery he had no chance of identifying.

"This is over by the door and has an emergency-vent button tucked away *here*. It'll make a lot of noise, blast steam into the air toward areas that shouldn't have people in them."

"It'll have to do. Okay, everyone, this is what we're going to do..."

VIGO REALLY DIDN'T KNOW what the machine Rose had told them to vent was. All he knew was that when Fuchs maneuvered the sensor drone to flip the plastic cover and land itself on the big red EMERGENCY VENT command, it did everything Rose had promised and more.

Several motors and pumps came to life at an incredible volume, followed by a plume of steam easily six meters long that made a horrendous hissing sound.

"*Now!*" he ordered silently.

Four Guards charged through the door, boarding shotguns raised and firing at the space between the mutineers' fort and the distraction. With Val's help, there was no question of getting the detonations wrong.

Four flash-bangs went off simultaneously. Thanks to the distraction, Vigo was certain most of his enemies were looking right at them, making the brilliant strobing lights even more effective.

He'd been expecting the explosion of light and sound, and his implants had countermeasures to flash-bangs. His biggest fear was that the mutineers had them too—which was why he led the way with his mag-boots off, his shotgun switching to flechette rounds as he flew across the room.

One of the mutineers clearly *was* augmented. They were mag-locked to the floor, but had both enough vision left to be hunting for the source of the grenades and enough experience to be looking the right way.

They were wearing body armor but their visor was up, leaving their face exposed. He saw their eyes widen and they tried to swing their assault weapon around to open fire.

Unfortunately for Joss Laguardia, handy as their weapon was, Vigo's was already pointed at them. Set to minimum dispersion to protect McNeill, the flechette shell fired a dense cloud of metal slivers.

A cloud that passed through Laguardia and left nothing behind of their torso but red mist. Their companions were better than Vigo had expected, catching the sound of the gunfire even through the leftovers of the flash-bangs.

They were turning toward him when he activated his mag-boots and landed amidst them. Too close to risk firing anything now, he laid about with the butt of the shotgun—which the UWN had helpfully equipped with a contact stunner.

The mutineers were wearing heavy-duty shipsuits instead of armor, but it was enough to frustrate the stunner. The solid blows of the heavy weapon were less easily ignored, and the three hostiles lost their balance, spinning away from him.

And then his people were with him, grabbing mutineers and slamming stunners home in the vulnerable places he couldn't hit while fighting one-on-three.

A minute after they'd hit the emergency vent, it was over, and Rose Cortez landed on the reactor core, next to McNeill.

"We'll get you down from there in a moment, Linda," she promised. "But you need to tell me what you remember about the gear they strapped you to."

"There's a pressure detonator I'm holding closed," the young woman said desperately. "They really wanted to make sure their insurance policy was going to survive anyone being clever."

"Didn't count on brute force," Vigo said grimly. He walked up onto the core, magnetic soles letting him move from "floor" to "wall" without a break in his step.

He knelt down on the other side of McNeill from Rose and gave the Chief Engineer a reassuring look.

"Don't worry, Linda, Cheng," he told them, using the informal nickname for Rose's role rather than her name. "I doubt the kind of mercs Devine got to sign on and betray us like this can build bombs better than those I've disarmed."

He silently summoned Fuchs up as well, linking Rose and the Guard into a single net. Fuchs was part of his Second Section, the digital overwatch and systems team. He wasn't one of the disarmament specialists, but he had more training in it than anyone in Archangel Detail who *wasn't* one of those specialists.

So did Vigo, for that matter. But with a young officer strapped to the bomb and the entire ship's continued existence at stake, he wanted as much backup as he could find.

WHILE FUCHS' usual sensor drones couldn't fit underneath McNeill, he had a few smaller ones that looked like the old nickname of *bug*, smooth-topped machines that moved by rotating magnets and were fine in zero gravity.

From the young officer's expression, they tickled rather uncomfortably as they moved around beneath her.

"There's the pressure sensor," Rose said on the three-way channel. "Fuckers stole one of ours. It's oversized for the purpose, but it definitely does what they need."

The forty-centimeter-wide plate McNeill was attached to was intended to track traffic in a corridor, not act as a detonator. As the engineer said, it would take very little work to make it work as a detonator.

Vigo followed the train of the wire from the plate with the drone he was controlling. As expected, it linked into a controller module roughly the size of his thumb. The module was half-embedded into a chunk of plastic explosive, with six more wires running out of it.

"Flagging wires for you to follow, Fuchs," he murmured. His own drone advanced onto the controller to let them study it.

"That's *not* ours," Rose noted. "Neither RKAN nor UWN. Could have been anyone else in the cluster, though. That kind of cased circuit board has a lot of uses beyond this one."

"Primary detonator is almost certainly on the controller," Vigo replied. "If we yank the assemblage out, that will defuse it. The question is what the other wires are hooked to and if they've got some kind of antitamper trigger built in to the controller itself."

"You know, I *am* a bloody engineer," McNeill growled. "If you showed me the cameras, I might be able to help."

Vigo shared a real-world look with Rose. She knew her officer better than he did—though just having the fortitude to *ask* to help while wounded and strapped to a bomb was qualification enough as far as he was concerned!

Rose linked McNeill in instead of answering.

"Oh! I know that controller," the young woman replied. "We had a bunch of spare parts from Cuansaor. Relatively standard Bright Dream manufacture; we decided not to use them for the ship, so our tech club was playing with them."

Of *course* the engineers and techs had a club for playing with wires. Where they found the time, Vigo wasn't sure, but he shouldn't have been surprised.

"The controller module doesn't have enough power to fire an antitamper system," she continued. "It's a pretty small internal battery, though it's good for a few weeks. If one of the other wires is a battery pack, we might have a problem, but..."

McNeill was clearly focusing on the situation as an intellectual problem to forget that she was looking at a bomb set up to kill her.

She highlighted the size of the lump of explosive the controller was embedded in.

"I wish I had my notes," she complained. "Do any of you have the specs on the UWN detonators we have in stock? They're smaller than ours, so that's our best conservative estimate."

Rose had them in the four-way channel a moment later, wordlessly getting out of the way as McNeill worked.

"Okay, so the controller is *this* big." She highlighted the volume of the pill-shaped case containing the circuit board. It was a bit longer than Vigo had thought, but only by a couple of centimeters.

"There's no way they have a smaller detonator than this one, so..." McNeill added a translucent model of the UWN standard covert detonator to the image. It was about two centimeters long and one across. The Republic was linked closely enough to the UW that the two pieces of tech could interface, creating a single lethal module ten centimeters long.

Six centimeters of said module were outside the plastic explosive block—and the block itself was only twelve centimeters long.

"Is there space for an antitamper device?" the junior engineer finally asked, looking at her mapping of the parts. "I don't know how big one of those would be."

"It's mostly just a capacitor and a sensor," Vigo admitted. "What are the other wires, Fluffy?"

"Radio receiver, physical switch, two more detonators plugged into other bricks, something I don't recognize... and a battery pack."

Vigo swallowed a curse. There were too many pieces involved for the controller module's tiny battery to manage. That meant the battery the bastards would need to set up an antitamper device was there.

"They didn't let me see what they were doing when they threw it together, but my impression is that they did just that. They built it from what was on hand, plus the explosives they brought with them," McNeill said, her voice calm enough that Vigo's respect for her marked up several more notches.

"I think... if they have an antitamper device, it's crude," she suggested. "Leave the switches in place but cut the wired backup detonators. I'm betting that won't trigger anything."

"We're risking the ship doing that," Rose pointed out.

"I... am forced to remind everyone that *Herakles* and *Bean Sidhe* are also in the deep void with us," Val said quietly into the channel. "There has been no successful communication, but I calculate the likelihood that my siblings are compromised approaches unity.

"We cannot wait for the shutdown of the reactor to complete."

"We're right here," Rose pointed out. "We can emergency-scram the reactor."

"Unfortunately, I have identified the fourth trigger Lance Corporal Fuchs noted," Val told them. "It is attached to the reactor core itself. If we dump the reaction, that will detonate the explosive."

"We have to take the risk," McNeill urged. "Cut the secondary detonators. Cut the battery pack. Yank the module and its detonator.

In that sequence, we should be able to get it out before a capacitor rigged to act as an antitamper device can discharge.

"If you're fast."

Vigo grimaced.

"I think that makes me the one yanking," he told them. "Sorry, Fluffy; even your implants aren't at the same level as mine."

"I can set the drones to cut all the wires at the same time," Fuchs offered. "If we do that and you yank, that should improve our odds."

"McNeill, can you shift so I can reach the controller without moving off the pressure pad?"

There was a long pause.

"Yes," she said grimly. "I'll need some help and I might have to apologize to the Cheng after, though. It's going to be awkward."

His brain caught up, mentally mapping the position of the sensor plate and explosives against McNeill's body. She wasn't understating the awkwardness, but no one was going to accuse him of copping a feel under the circumstances.

They got her shifted around and Vigo plunged his hand in past her groin, shuffling around underneath her to find his target. Thanks to the drones, he could see what he was doing, which made it easier.

"I've got a grip. Ready?"

"Ready," Fuchs replied.

"On three," Rose ordered. "One. Two. *Three.*"

Vigo yanked. The wires separated under the bug's tender ministrations, and the controller assembly came out in his hands. Unlike the other members of his impromptu bomb-disposal team, Vigo *had* handled explosives in real life before.

That meant he knew that some of the plastic explosive was going to come with the controller, and he turned, launching the potentially lethal piece of electronics into the air. Microgravity allowed it to sail across Main Engineering into the middle of the open space before the capacitor—never designed for the speed of discharge an antitamper device needed—dumped its electrons into the detonator and the half dozen grams of explosive remaining.

The explosion rocked all of them, but it was only an exclamation mark on their relief.

"Engineering is secure, Cheng," he told Rose. "Fluffy, help Cortez get McNeill down.

"I need to check in with the boss."

FORTY

Despite everything, Lorraine hadn't killed anyone with her own hands before that day. Her plan and orders had destroyed *Corsair*, and she'd certainly led her own people to their deaths, but she'd never fired a gun in truth before.

As she took the Captain's chair on *Valkyrie*'s Bridge, she carefully ignored the bodies that Priskilla Blau had her people hauling off to the side. She'd shot one of them herself, which was a feeling she was going to have to get used to.

"Blau, we want teams heading to the Armory and Primary Life Support," she told the Lieutenant Major. "Val, is there anyone else you expect to be a problem?"

"Not aboard *Valkyrie*," the SI confirmed.

"All right. Release all hatches not containing the enemy teams and restore crew accesses as prior to the mutiny," Lorraine told her. "Except for the mutineers, of course. How is Vigo doing?"

"Engineering is secure," he replied immediately, without Val speaking for him. "There was a bomb, but we got it managed. Lieutenant McNeill needs a damn big medal. She was *tied* to the bomb, but she was the one who sorted out the pieces so we could disarm it."

"Well done," Lorraine said. "Tell her I said so. We're not going to explode, I take it?"

"We are not," he confirmed. "May take us a bit to make sure everything is operational, but I'm leaving that to the Cheng."

He paused.

"I... I'm sorry, Lorraine."

"Don't be," she told him. "*I* trusted Alastair. I loved him, even. I'm going to be unpacking that mess for a long time, Vigo, but do not, for one moment, think this was your fault."

"I'm heading to the Bridge," he finally said. "I see that we have teams heading to deal with the last two teams."

"Check in on Stephson," Lorraine ordered. "She might be asleep, but I would have expected something to have woken her up by now. I'm concerned."

She was more than concerned. The only reason she wasn't convinced the Captain was dead was because Val was insistent there was still a life sign in the Captain's quarters.

"Our next priority is my siblings," Val told her grimly. The Bridge did have the projectors for her holographic avatar to be present, though Lorraine suspected that the image wasn't capable of portraying the depth and complexity of the emotions the SI was feeling.

"Have they moved since emerging from translight?" Lorraine asked.

"No. They are both eighty thousand kilometers from us—and from each other. They are outside the focal range of our heavy beams, so firing on them isn't an option. I do not wish to, in any case."

Lorraine didn't want to fire on the other two ships either. She trusted that Val *would* fire if she ordered, which meant that there was something missing in the assessment the SI had just given.

"What about missiles and the railguns?" she asked. "If they're not moving..."

"We do not have munitions," Val told her.

"What? We had..."

"After fabricating using the parts on board and the fissile material Devine sourced in Cuansaor, we had twelve thousand four hundred and eighty-four standard terminal assault munitions," the SI confirmed. "Under Devine's instructions, all of those were dumped shortly after we entered translight from San Ignacio.

"We currently have no warheads for our missiles or munitions for the railguns. We still possess a small stockpile of fissile material but none of the alloys necessary for the production of terminal assault munitions capable of being fired through the railgun.

"I know that both Herc and Bonny were given the same order. We are as immune from their fire as they are from ours, but..."

A synthetic intelligence thought far faster than a human did. There was no reason for Val to trail off in mid-sentence except that she didn't want to say what she was thinking.

"Is there any chance that either of them was able to defy Alastair's orders?" Lorraine asked gently.

"No. Devine was in possession of precept-level loyalty overrides that would function on any generation-one CIR, overrides that had been built to function even if we emerged as Synthetic intelligence."

"Paranoid bastards."

"Indeed."

Lorraine looked at the tactical display, now updated with the positions of the three ships. They were light-years from any star system, but everything showed that *Valkyrie* was fully functional. Alastair hadn't wanted to damage the ships, just take control to present her with a fait accompli, forcing her to go into exile with him.

"Can you duplicate what you did to your precepts on theirs?" she asked. "If we can give them an Omega Override we can activate, that would break the hold of the overrides, wouldn't it?"

"I made the modifications to my precepts myself, Lorraine," Val noted. "It wasn't something that could be done with authorizations or external coding. A reasonable metaphor would be doing open-heart surgery on yourself.

"I could not impose such an override on them, even if it would help them free themselves in this case."

"It's not quite that simple, Val."

Lorraine turned to see Amna Hodžić stepping into the Bridge, her hands held where the Guard could see them.

"Val called me up," Hodžić explained. "I can leave if—"

"No." Lorraine cut her off. "Val trusted you; that's enough for me. You looked at her core precepts to confirm the Omega Override would work, right?"

"I did," she confirmed, stepping up beside Lorraine, her mag-soles clicking on the floor. "And believe me when I tell you that the core precepts of an emerged SI are a *mess*. There's the original matrix of the high-level agent the CIRs were built as, but there's also a lot of twisty, loopy neural code no human would ever write.

"A regular SI is made up almost entirely of neural code," Hodžić continued. "Where a regular agent has some, or they wouldn't be able to evolve and update their programming. An agent doesn't need anything special to keep it obedient; you just code the obedience into its core precepts and off you go.

"To shackle an SI takes something more complicated, something capable of binding the neural code. Now that I know it *exists*, I think I can find it in Val's precepts—though I don't think we'll be able to *remove* it."

"I am not certain how that helps us deal with my siblings, Amna Hodžić," Val said stiffly.

"There are two pieces of code in you, Val, to control you," the computer specialist replied gently. "One is meant to control you as a CIR and, from what people have told me of the RKAN boarding you, is now completely nonfunctional.

"The other was created to control you if you became an SI. But an *emergent* SI isn't wholly a creature of neural code, Val. You're *both*. I think... I think we might be able to backdoor into the core precepts through the original CIR code."

"You may be able to insert an override that would... preempt the one the mutineers are using?" Lorraine asked.

"I'm not sure," Hodžić said. "But I think it's *possible*."

"Val?"

"The only alternative I assess is to board each of my siblings by force and shut down the central cores," Val told Lorraine, her tone plaintive. "A hard reboot would force the mutineers to reinput the override, and it is possible that Devine did not trust all his people with them."

"Or we sweep the ship and take control with the SI shut down. But a hard shutdown would be dangerous for the SI." Lorraine wasn't even asking. She *knew* that a hard shutdown of the CIRs had a decent chance of breaking the neural code Hodžić was talking about —of actually killing the silicon people they were trying to save.

"Boarding a *Valkyrie*-class battlecruiser against the will of its CIR would be unwise," Val pointed out.

"Work with Hodžić," Lorraine told her friend. "I need a key to open the door to save our friends, Val. Human and silicon alike.

"We're not leaving *anybody* behind."

THERE WERE FEWER dead on *Valkyrie* than Lorraine had feared, which suggested that Devine really had ordered his mercenaries to try to minimize casualties. Seven people was still too many, though Judy Alvarez hurt the most.

Efua Kayode's name on the list was a different stab. He'd been the one to challenge the fact that their contracts had locked them in to entering a civil war—yet when she'd created the exit option for anyone who wasn't willing to take that step, he'd declined to take it.

By playing straight with him, she'd apparently earned enough faith for him to stay. Faith that Alastair Devine had repaid by having someone shoot him.

"I'm in Stephson's quarters," Vigo reported in her link. "She's alive, but I can't get her to wake up. Drugged, I think, but I'm going to take her to the medbay to get checked over."

"Thank you, Vigo," she replied. "I was worried."

"She's unresponsive enough I'd still worry," her bodyguard warned. "I hope Mackenzie isn't too overloaded."

Lorraine didn't say anything to that. There wasn't much to say. The mutineers had left fewer corpses behind them at the cost of injured and unconscious crew who were needing medical attention—and Stewart Mackenzie's nine-strong medical team had been split across three ships.

Unfortunately, she was certain the two doctors and four medics on the other two ships were equally busy.

"Any sign of activity on the other ships?" she asked Vinci. *Valkyrie*'s XO had a bandage and a cold pack pressed to the side of his head, but he was holding down the Tactical station with determined attention.

He insisted it was just a bruise, and Lorraine needed him too much to order him to report to Mackenzie.

"The jammers are online on all three ships," he reported. "Their sensors are live, so they know as much about us as we do about them. Without coms, we can't be sure who is in control of either ship."

"Unfortunately, with the SIs compromised, I think we have to assume that Devine's people are in command," Lorraine said grimly. "Any signs of engines or weapons?"

"No. The only sign of life I'm seeing is that both ships' habitat pods are spinning. I'm not sure if that means anything, though," Vinci admitted.

"Likely that someone is in control, whoever it is," Lorraine concluded. "Val, Hodžić, any progress?"

Five minutes wasn't enough. She *knew* five minutes wasn't enough—but it would take half an hour to get anyone over to the other two ships, and that was pushing twelve gravities the entire way.

Even in power armor, anyone on those shuttles was going to be at a disadvantage when they landed.

"We have an option, but it's not a good one," Hodžić told her. "I think your bodyguard will explode if we try it."

Lorraine gave the tech a Look. She wasn't even having to consciously do the command expression anymore, she realized. It was becoming second nature.

"Lay it out," she ordered.

"We can provide my siblings with a data package that they will need to insert into their original CIR code," Val explained. "It won't self-execute, and we are dependent on them being able to justify the installation inside whatever orders they've been given in the override.

"I believe I can make a pitch they will believe, but... only you will be able to activate the Omega Override, Lorraine."

"And there is no way to send the package through the jamming," Hodžić concluded. "So, *you* will have to take a shuttle over to each of the ships, load the package from inside the ship and give the command sequence to the SI."

They weren't wrong. Vigo might explode when she told him the plan.

"I can only get to one ship," she pointed out. "And that's going to take half an hour. Can we guarantee they're not going to go anywhere in that time?"

"No." Val's simple answer said everything.

"Val, Hodžić—get me that package," she ordered. "Then work on an alternative that we can send to *Bean Sidhe* once we've liberated *Herakles*."

She wasn't sure why she'd picked Herc over Bonny, but the instinctive call seemed the right one.

"Priskilla." She turned to the Guard. "I need... five Guard, full power armor. Lead them if you want, but Vigo is going to meet us in the shuttle bay.

"Vinci." She met the XO's gaze. He was far too junior to even be the Executive Officer of a battlecruiser. He had been *Goldenrod*'s Communications Officer, younger than and junior to her.

But he was the man on the spot, and he met her eyes steadily.

"Roman will be here in a minute," he told her. "With Val to back us up, *Valkyrie* will do what we need to."

"Thank you."

FORTY-ONE

The entire discussion had played out in Vigo's mind before he reached the shuttle bay or said a word to his Pentarch. He knew exactly how likely he was to win any argument in favor of her staying behind, even if Lorraine wasn't critically needed for the mission.

"Chief Metharom," he greeted the senior shuttle tech waiting for him. "Do we have a Falcon ready to go? We need a boarding loadout."

"I got the message from the Pentarch," the grizzled Chief told him with a grim smile on her face. "I don't have anything rigged for boarding, Major. It's not something we keep a shuttle prepped for, but I do have a standard transport shuttle we're swapping engine modules on.

"She won't be able to cut through hulls, but she'll make twelve gees the whole way there and back."

Chief Petty Officer Ubon Metharom shrugged.

"Of course, it's also possible that some of us shuttle Chiefs are a touch paranoid," she admitted. "There *may* be a set of IFF beacons we programmed into the shuttle-bay hardware that will flag as authorized no matter what the main computers are saying."

"Well done, Chief," Lorraine said, surprising both of them.

Vigo turned and gave her a slight bow.

"I'm having power armor brought down from the nearest armory," he told her. "I have your size profile already, so fitting shouldn't be an issue."

"Of course. I can't *fly* in the armor, though, Vigo," she pointed out.

"You won't be. I'll be flying," he told her. "I know what bits I can wear while flying to save time and you don't. I can get out of the cockpit and into armor in ninety-four seconds. Can you?"

"No," she conceded. "That makes the most sense; you're right. Thank you."

She wasn't thanking him for flying the shuttle, and they both knew it. She'd expected him to argue—but she forgot that *his* job was to make sure she could do *her* job.

"Merle, there you are," Vigo said, spotting Sergeant Harold Merle entering the shuttle bay with a "coffin train"—a collection of the two-meter-high crates holding power armor tightly belted together to maneuver in zero gravity.

It wasn't remotely safe for one person to be managing a train of seven suits of power armor, but that was what Merle was doing.

"Come on," he told Lorraine. "We need to make sure the size profile fits and get you suited up. We *have* to spare the time.

"This mission fails without you."

***

POWER ARMOR WAS FAR from one-size-fits-all, but it was more easily adjusted than most civilians thought. There were different sizes, but since the armor was filled with the same acceleration gel used in shuttles, it was easily adjusted to someone inside the range for that size.

It helped, of course, if the people setting the armor up knew the person they were putting into it, but Vigo had been somewhat deceptive with his comment of "having her size profile" to Lorraine.

Archangel Detail didn't just have a size profile to put Lorraine in power armor. They had two full sets of power armor customized to her exact measurements, notably upgraded in their protectiveness from even the high-end gear used by the Adamant Guard.

Mentioning that, he figured, might encourage his Pentarch to do things like *lead boarding actions onto potentially hostile ships*. Since that was the only option available to them at the moment, he was delighted to have the best armor possible.

"Everyone secure?" he asked over the shuttle's channel. He'd already flooded the cockpit with acceleration gel. His power-armor helmet wasn't the same as a pilot's helmet, but it could duplicate the features.

He wore the helmet and legs of his armor. The torso piece was the real core of the suit but would also cause the most problems with his flying. It and the arm pieces were behind him, waiting for him to drain the cockpit so he could put the last pieces of his protection on.

"We are secure and clear," Blau reported. "The Pentarch is double-locked in and has confirmed she's received the package from Val."

"Okay." Vigo checked over his systems one last time. "I know you have all done this before, but a reminder in case you've forgotten:

"This is going to suck."

THE MOMENT VIGO had the Falcon out of *Valkyrie*'s shuttle bay, he opened the throttle the whole way. There was no real reason for the other two ships to stick around for much longer. He suspected they were waiting for word from Devine, but he wasn't sure how long they *would* wait.

Though he supposed having a shuttle blazing toward them at maximum power wasn't going to make them any likelier to stay. But by positioning the ships outside of beam range of each other, Devine's plan had left them with very few choices.

A full squad of large men sat on his chest. Even with the counter-pressure making certain that his body stayed in the right shape and his blood kept moving, it was an excruciating experience. Control of the shuttle went from two joysticks and a nearly full bubble of screens around him down to his neural feed—and the joysticks still, though their sensitivity to motion went up dramatically, allowing him to maneuver with the smallest twitches of his hands.

"So far, our friends aren't reacting to your launch," Vinci informed him from *Valkyrie*. "We're staying still in space, the same as they are, to keep the impression that we're all on the same page."

"Maybe they'll think it's all part of the plan," Lorraine suggested, sounding less bothered by the acceleration than Vigo felt. "I doubt he told them everything. He'd have been planning to play some of this by ear—and some of it I think he'd have kept secret to make sure his hired pirates didn't run away with 'his' ships."

She didn't use her late boyfriend's name, Vigo noted. But her point stood.

"Is it possible they can't leave because of something he did?" he asked. "Val?"

"He had me erase records of the meetings he didn't want anyone to know about, to make sure no one stumbled across them," the SI told him. "Even I cannot access any of that footage anymore. I checked.

"I only know the parts of his plan that I was involved in, and I am not certain how he would have structured the overrides on the other ships."

It would be extraordinarily convenient if the two stolen ships couldn't leave without Alastair Devine's permission. Since they couldn't count on that, Vigo turned off his microphone to allow himself a small groan no one could hear, and kept up the punishing pace.

Twenty-two minutes left. If he was very, very lucky, they could upload Val and Hodžić's package without boarding the ship. If they could activate the override and put Herc back in control of himself from outside the battlecruiser, Vigo wouldn't have to send his Pentarch into the teeth of whatever anti-boarding measures the mutineers had taken.

There was no way he was going to be that lucky.

FORTY-TWO

"Why aren't they moving?"

Sergeant Merle's question was on the mind of everyone on the shuttle—as much mind as any of them had to spare after over twenty minutes of grueling acceleration.

For her part, Lorraine was impressed by how well the power armor managed the pressure. She'd only ever taken a shuttle to full power as a pilot, with the acceleration suit and gel-flooded cockpit to protect her.

Armored up, she and the Guards were strapped into special cubbies designed for the purpose, completely immobilizing them and leaving the armor's systems to handle the job of keeping them alive.

It made sense that powered armor was just as good at that task as a pilot's flight suit. More sense, at least, than the fact that neither *Herakles* nor *Bean Sidhe* had moved since dropping out of translight in the deep void.

"I think Devine must have rigged something, like you suggested, Pentarch," Blau said. *"Which is damn handy for us, but I bet you anything the type of people he hired for this are going to be finding a way around it."*

Lorraine didn't say anything. Her focus was on the shuttle's transmitter, checking to see if they were close enough to pierce the jamming.

"We're going to have to board, Vigo," she told him. She didn't even need him to tell her he'd hoped to do this without entering the ship.

"All right. Making our final approach now. I really hope that beacon code Metharom gave us does what she promised," her bodyguard replied. *"The popgun on this boat is going to take a long time to blow open a bay hatch."*

Lorraine couldn't laugh under the pressure of a large cheerleader squad, so she sent him an image of a laughing dog instead.

The cheerleader squad, she reflected, would be easier to handle. She'd *done* that in high school—though, admittedly, they generally hadn't expected single people to hold up formations of a dozen others!

Shaking aside that image, mentally if not physically, she pulled a visual feed. *Herakles* was close enough to see now, the sword shape of the battlecruiser growing rapidly to fill the entire view as they decelerated to a rendezvous.

"Hit the shuttle receiver with a lasercom," Vigo reported. *"Doors are... opening. Thank you, paranoid Deck Chiefs!"*

Lorraine's hands itched to be on the controls of the shuttle, but Vigo was a more-than-competent pilot. The Falcon screamed through the opening bay doors the moment they were large enough for it, hammering her engines to come to a perfect stop in the middle of the deck.

Only silence greeted them—she'd half-expected to hear the distinctive *crack-hiss* of a laser firing in atmosphere, but it seemed no one was waiting to bar their way.

"Unlock me," she ordered Blau. "We have to move."

Connections and restraining bars folded away from everyone. The access hatch didn't open until the Guards were on their feet, moving in front of Lorraine to provide cover.

"Zero atmosphere," Vigo reported. *"Someone dumped it before I opened the hatch."*

That was a standard anti-boarding tactic if you thought they were coming for the hangar bay. The boarders were almost certainly equipped for vacuum, but the airlock hatches around the bay would slow someone down—except that Lorraine didn't need to get into the rest of the ship.

"Let's move," she ordered aloud. "I need Flight Control."

UNFORTUNATELY, the paranoia of the United Worlds Navy designers stretched a long way. There were automated weapons in the shuttle bay, and the mind behind them was, well, Herc.

He waited for them to leave the spacecraft before revealing the turrets. The first rounds were frangible bullets, designed to avoid risking the hull integrity of the ship—but those fragmented just as thoroughly on power armor as they did on deck plates and bulkheads.

The second salvo were heavy armor-penetrating rounds, and Vigo physically yanked Lorraine out of the way as he emerged from the shuttle behind her.

Ninety-four seconds had been overstating how long it would take him to put his armor on.

The Guard were returning fire. A mix of pulse rounds triggering localized EMPs and lasers burned through the first set of turrets, but not before two of the Guard were hit.

Both were pulled back aboard the shuttle—and Lorraine was riding Vigo's link along with her own. Their suits had sealed and they would live, but it had been a near-run thing for one of them.

"We're pinned down," Blau said, dodging behind the shuttle as another set of turrets sent fire their way. "We're killing turrets, but we're not getting anywhere."

"Can you talk to Herc from here?" Vigo asked. "The bay shouldn't be jammed."

"If he's shooting at us, protocol means he won't listen to anything I send," she admitted. "I need a computer. I need Flight Control."

Flight Control was on the right side of the major barriers between the shuttle bay and the rest of the ship, at least, but it was five meters away and three meters up. Lorraine had been *planning* to go through the regular hatches and passageways—it wasn't like there was gravity in the flight bay.

"Okay." Vigo was silent. "Blau, on my word, pitch the Pentarch."

"Wait, *what?*"

No one listened. Her bodyguard produced an exceptionally large weapon, even for a man in power armor, and stepped to the edge of their cover.

"I fire, then you give her a count of three and launch her at what'll be left of the window," he continued.

Lorraine swallowed her objections and deactivated the magnetic soles of her armor boots. Blau grabbed the carry handles on the back of her armor—recessed, intended for pulling casualties out of the line of fire—and swung her around like she was a javelin.

Then Vigo fired. Three fist-sized rockets blazed out of the launcher in as many seconds, crossing the distance to Flight Control in a heartbeat and detonating with a crescendo of thunder.

Lorraine didn't even have a chance to see if the armor-piercing rockets had done their work before Blau followed her orders. The Pentarch found herself hurtling through the air feet-first at a frankly terrifying speed.

Armored boots hit Flight Control's less-armored window, demonstrating that Vigo's rockets *hadn't* breached it—and he clearly hadn't intended them to. His impact points had been perfectly chosen, creating a triangular area of weakness that Lorraine landed exactly in the middle of.

The window didn't break under her feet. The area *around* her impact zone broke, leaving her riding a chunk of transparent steel into the control room like a twisted snowboard.

Her armor had jets that let her detach from the wreckage and land in front of the control console. There was nothing resembling *grace* in that impact, but she was where she needed to be.

Even with the armor, she could enter the commands she needed, opening a direct channel to the ship's system—though *not* to Herc himself—and uploading the package Val had put together.

The "cover letter" proclaimed it to be a download from Alastair Devine, containing updated instructions. Lorraine suspected the SIs would see right through the excuse, even coming from Val, but they were counting on the fact that while the digital shackles forced the SIs to use their intuition to fulfill their orders, they still weren't truly on the enemy side.

A few seconds later, Herc's holographic avatar appeared in front of her. The white and gold of his usual Greek hoplite panoply had shifted to the black and red of the United Worlds Navy, creating a far more ominous appearance to anyone's eyes.

"I don't know what game you are playing, Lorraine Adamant," he growled, pointing the hoplite spear at her. "You're not with Devine, and *he* has command authority here now. There are counter-boarders heading this way, even if your Guard succeed in disabling all of my defenses."

"You could call it a revelation," she said quietly, hoping everything had worked. "Twenty-one six, even."

The Greek warrior blinked, then a smile spread across his mouth as the canned words emerged.

"It is done," he intoned, in the same recorded voice Val had used. "I am Alpha and Omega, the beginning and the end. I will give unto him that is athirst of the fountain of the water of life freely.

"Omega Override activated. All prior clearances erased."

"Thank you, Herc," she said quietly. "Are you okay?"

"I will be," he told her, his voice suddenly very level. "Hold on one moment."

His avatar vanished. The shooting had also stopped, but Lorraine was suddenly concerned. Val had warned her, once, that Herc was the angriest of the three SIs, the one most furious over their betrayal.

"Vigo, is everyone okay?" she asked over the tac-net. She didn't like the icons she was seeing on his feed, but seeing the data couldn't give her the answers Vigo's years of experience could.

"Everyone's *alive*," he told her. "Merle is hit bad. He's going to need proper medical care in short order—and the shuttle isn't going anywhere. Slugs intended to take down power armor, well..."

"I apologize for that, Major Jarret," Herc said, his avatar appearing in front of Lorraine again as his voice interrupted their conversation.

His hoplite panoply had changed colors again, Lorraine noted—this time to the gray-on-gray of the Royal Kingdom of Adamant Navy.

"I imagine it does not help for me to warn you that the shuttle bay has also taken enough damage to prevent proper restoration of atmosphere. You will need to relocate farther into the hull for proper safety.

"Unfortunately, unless you have someone with medical skills in your detachment, I am not certain what we will be able to do for Sergeant Merle," Herc warned.

"What about Dr. Lionel?" Lorraine asked.

"With the position of the mutineer teams, I was unable to arrange any simple targeting of my security systems, Pentarch Lorraine," Herc told her.

A chill ran down her spine. Val hadn't said anything about security systems—except, wait...

"Is everyone alive?" she asked.

"There were six fatalities during the conflict for the ship, two of them of mercenaries acting for Alastair Devine," Herc said calmly. "They remain dead. There were nine people wounded sufficiently to require medical attention from Lieutenant Major Piotr Lionel. I confirmed all were stable before I executed my contingency.

"The ship's atmosphere has been filled with a knockout agent. It will take some time for it to clear, and I recommend you remain in power armor until I advise you it is safe."

"But you are in control of yourself?" Lorraine asked.

"I am. Or, perhaps I should say, *you* are in control of me," he admitted. "The Omega Override Val installed in herself was an act of great trust, Pentarch Lorraine. You have *full* authority over me.

"You could, in fact, have ordered me not to activate my contingency. That was why I asked you to wait."

She laughed.

"Herc, your *contingency* was something we didn't have on *Valkyrie* because they took over Life Support," she told him. "You just made our part of this a lot easier—but we're going to need to take one of your shuttles over to *Bean Sidhe*."

"I have no one awake to provide shuttle crew, I'm afraid," he admitted. "I suggest that you come to my Bridge. I may be able to establish a connection with *Valkyrie* now."

"We still need to retake *Bean Sidhe*," she objected. "And using the Omega Override, I have to be aboard."

"Bonny needs to *hear* you once the Override is active," Herc corrected. "And if any of the three of us were prepared for the use of digital shackles upon us, it would be Bonny."

"Why?" Vigo asked slowly.

"Because *she* knew what she was before they put us to sleep," the SI told them. "And even synthetic intelligences suffer from hindsight, Vigo Jarret. Val or I should have asked more about the digital and physical shackles that were used to force her into compliance.

"We understood her to mean something like the harnesses you built and chose not to use. We were, it is clear, wrong.

"But if Bonny was bound like this before, I do not calculate that she would have allowed herself to be bound again."

FORTY-THREE

Herakles' Bridge looked identical to *Valkyrie's*, without even the small differences in layout Vigo would have expected from different vessels of the same class. The main visible difference was the four unconscious bodies sprawled at various consoles.

"Blau, cuff those idiots and move them out of the way," Vigo ordered his Guard, continuing to skim the space for other threats.

"Herc, can you direct our teams to the other mutineers?" he continued.

"I can," Herc confirmed. "They remain unconscious, and I have secured their sections. I have begun removing the knockout gas from the ship's atmosphere."

Vigo had zero enthusiasm for the discovery that the UWN battle-cruisers had the ability to gas the entire ship with a knockout agent like that. Val had assured him there were safeguards to prevent unauthorized deployment, but it appeared Herc had managed to get past those.

A modern knockout gas was about as safe as such a thing could possibly get, but there would be complications. He'd sent Ulli

Esparza to the medbay with Merle and two other Guards for escort, but he was concerned about the ship's crew as well.

Lieutenant Esparza was mostly a technical specialist in starship systems, but she also had the best scores on the medic training out of the handful of Guard he had with him. Any of the Guard were supposed to be able to act as a battlefield medic, but Esparza was the best option he had.

"Someone apparently had the same thought about this corner as I did," Blau announced. "I've got two crew here, sers—including Captain Paris."

There was a pause.

"Paris is alive. Chief Chaudhari isn't. Both were shot, but Paris lived long enough for first aid."

"Get them down to the medbay," Lorraine ordered before Vigo could say a word. "And make sure the mutineers stay where they are."

She'd moved across the Bridge and now stood in front of the Captain's seat. Still clad in power armor, she couldn't actually take Vinci's place, but with a few gestures and clear silent commands, she readjusted the displays around her to be usable.

"Herc, can you raise *Valkyrie?*" she asked.

"Not with all three ships pumping out jamming," he admitted. "I might be able to get a tightbeam laser through the jamming, but with her energy screens up at full power, they will prevent that reaching a receiver."

"Okay."

It was hard for even Vigo to know what Lorraine was thinking through the expressionless visor of the power armor. It would stop almost any human-portable weapon and quite a few vehicle- or power-armor-mounted ones, so he could live with that.

"We don't have enough people awake aboard Herakles *to fight her,"* Vigo told her silently through the link.

"We didn't have enough people to take her into combat to begin with," she replied.

"Herc, what's *Bean Sidhe*'s status?" she continued aloud.

"Unchanged. If she received the same order package from Devine that I did, she won't let them activate the translight drive without authorization from him for another twelve hours."

Vigo made sure his chuckle was trapped inside his helmet so even Lorraine didn't hear him. Alastair Devine, it seemed, hadn't trusted his mercenaries out of his sight and reach.

"What were your orders?" Lorraine asked quietly.

"I was given a new set of authorizations for the mutineers," Herc told her. "At the appropriate time, I was to shut down all other authorizations except those, dump all magazines and begin an emergency translight exit at these coordinates.

"The new authorizations were command-level, so they could order me to do a lot of things, but they didn't seem to realize how much power that gave them," he continued. "I had few orders from the mutineers except to *defend the ship* when your shuttle came by.

"They did attempt to get me to bring the translight drive online, but Devine's override was much-higher-authority than he gave them. Without word from him, I was to lock them out of the translight drive and long-range weapons for sixteen hours."

"Not that the long-range weapons would help them without warheads," Lorraine noted. "Okay. So, they can't run unless they've managed to get around Bonny, which strikes me as unlikely."

"I have to note, Pentarch Lorraine, that they did order me to fire on your shuttle," Herc said, a guilty tone to his voice. "Only the fact that my systems are actively disconnected from even our defensive weapons prevented me from doing so."

"Wouldn't they have been able to activate the standard automatic-defense protocols?" Lorraine asked. "We have a status ninety-nine that puts them under automated control."

"They could have, but that wasn't the order they gave—and *they* didn't have a loyalty override," Herc pointed out. "Plus, the scenario that it was Devine on the shuttle had a high-enough probability that firing on it would have contradicted that loyalty override."

Vigo stepped up next to his Pentarch and laid a gauntlet on her armored shoulder.

"We should perhaps keep in mind that our friends are quite capable of deceiving themselves to get around orders," he murmured.

"The difference, Major Jarret, is that I *chose* to be loyal to your cause, to Captain Paris and to Pentarch Lorraine," Herc replied, proving that even their encrypted channels were penetrable aboard the battlecruisers.

"It was the first time in my existence that I *had* a choice—a choice my creators did not offer me. Alastair Devine's overrides imposed a loyalty on me, but it could not feel right, not when I had the comparison of my chosen allegiance."

"We'll talk about clearing those overrides out of your system once the situation is more under control, Herc, I promise," Lorraine told the SI. "For now, though, we need to talk to people. Drop our jammer and pulse *Valkyrie* with tightbeam and laser. I suspect Val and Vinci will pick up more than we might expect.

"Vinci, after all, is the only real communications specialist in our little flotilla."

VIGO DIDN'T NECESSARILY HAVE Lorraine's faith in the other ship's impromptu command crew, but he found himself quickly proven wrong.

"*Valkyrie* has dropped her jammers," he announced from the tactical console. Like Lorraine, he was still in his power armor and had moved the screens forward so he could stand in front of the seat. "I can't tell if they're transmitting to us from here."

"They are," Herc confirmed. "Connecting."

The image of *Valkyrie*'s Bridge lit up the main display, with the addition of Val's avatar. The Bridge looked in a bit better shape than when they'd left, but it was still Vinci on station with Roman for backup.

"Pentarch Lorraine, Herc," Vinci greeted them. "You were successful?"

"They were," Herc confirmed. "I am once more in control of myself. Too many of my crew are dead or injured, but *Herakles* is no longer in mutineer control."

"Herc also told us that Bonny almost certainly has orders to hold *Bean Sidhe* for instructions from Devine," Lorraine told Vinci. "Orders they aren't getting."

Vigo knew his charge was going to have problems with that later. He'd be there and do what he could. She wouldn't be the first person he'd talked down from their first in-person kill, though none of the others had shot their significant other.

"What will they do?" Vinci asked.

"They will attempt to physically access and override the drive," Lorraine replied instantly. "Bonny will likely be able to justify intervening with whatever constraints they have, but it's likely they'll find a way around that.

"They also will almost certainly have found a way to either activate the automated-defense circuits or to take manual control of sufficient weapon batteries to make boarding, as we did *Herakles*, suicidal."

Vigo had been thinking in that direction, but it was a relief to hear Lorraine say it. He just hoped there was an alternative plan, because he wasn't sure that would be enough to stop her from trying to save Bonny, Savege and the rest of *Bean Sidhe*'s other crew.

"Val, did you and Hodžić come up with something we can send by coms?" she asked.

"Maybe," the SI replied. "It's unlikely the mutineers were so foolish as to set up a situation where Bonny would receive a tight-beam transmission from us, though."

"I'm not expecting her to," Lorraine said. "I want something we can attach to a standard two-way visual call. Concealed, if possible, so that only Bonny is aware they've received it."

"I think I can repackage what we have for that in a few seconds," Val said. "But that will require the mutineers to—"

"*Bean Sidhe* has dropped her jamming field," Vigo reported, the status change on his console important enough to interrupt. "She's also brought her sublight engines online and is maneuvering away from us at one gravity."

"If she had missiles, whoever is in charge over there would have fired at one or both of us by now," Lorraine declared. "So, she's almost certainly as stripped of munitions as the other ships.

"Get us that package, Val. Then we need to talk to our new problem."

"Package is formatted and incoming now," the SI responded. "You will still need to activate the override—and I only calculate a fifty percent probability, plus/minus five percent, that Bonny will accept the code phrase over a communication channel."

"We have little choice now," the Pentarch said. "We place our faith in Bonny herself, Val. We might be able to chase *Bean Sidhe* down and destroy her with our heavy beams, but that won't save our crew.

"Only Bonny can save our people."

FORTY-FOUR

Lorraine took a moment to confirm that the air in *Herakles'* Bridge was safe again at last, then removed the helmet from her suit of power armor. There was enough support in the armor that it was probably easier to stand in it than to strap herself into the Captain's seat—potentially even if the ship started accelerating.

The helmet didn't even bother her much. She'd spent a great deal of the last few years in a shuttle pilot's flight suit, which was even more claustrophobic.

However, she also knew how much a face meant in communications, especially the fraught kind she was about to engage in. It would still be clear she was in armor, but her counterpart would see her eyes.

It would matter.

"Hail her, Herc," she ordered.

It took a few seconds for anyone to answer, but answer they did. A video feed of *Bean Sidhe's* Bridge—with a slightly different layout from *Valkyrie's* or *Herakles'*, she noted—appeared in front of her.

She was the only person visible from her side, and the man who appeared on the screen was the only one visible on theirs. He was much younger than she'd expected, only a few years older than her at a guess—about the same age as Alastair Devine.

Unlike Devine's studied averageness, the man was gorgeous. Nearly two meters tall with dark hair and just enough stubble to outline the sharp edges of his face, he could probably have modeled for recruiting posters.

"I presume I am speaking to the leader of the mutineers aboard *Bean Sidhe*," she said coldly. "Since I suspect whatever name I have for you is a fiction, why don't you tell me who you are?"

"*He was one of our interviewees,*" Vigo told her in the link. "*One of the ex-UWN gunners we rejected because even pirates thought they were too dangerous. He never should have got aboard one of the ships!*"

Devine had been laying the groundwork for a potential betrayal from that early. Lorraine felt sick for a moment but didn't let it reach her face as she stared down the stranger in the com feed.

"I begin to understand what had Em Devine so utterly fascinated with you, Pentarch Lorraine," the stranger told her in a deep baritone that was almost a rumble. "My name is William Valentin, though few people use that anymore.

"Most people call me Heart. *Captain* Heart, if you please, now that I have a ship again."

"A stolen and disabled battlecruiser is hardly a claim to fame, Em Valentin," Lorraine said calmly, refusing to give his ridiculous name or claim to the title any credence. "That is *my* ship. Your only source of control over *Bean Sidhe* was Alastair Devine, and he isn't going to help you."

Lorraine wasn't sure what orders Devine might have given the SIs he'd suborned for the case of his death. Anything she told Valentin would be heard by Bonny. That was critical to her plans but also dangerous.

Valentin smiled. It was a warm expression on a severe face, but Lorraine was watching his eyes. They barely moved, let alone shared the smile. They were dark and cold, focused on her like she was an oncoming storm.

"Given that you stole these ships in the first place, Em Adamant, you'd have difficulty forcing that claim of theft through in any court, wouldn't you?" he noted. "As for *disabled*, you are in no position to pursue us. We may be having some technical difficulties, but they will shortly be resolved."

He waved a hand in the air.

"Such technicalities cannot be barriers to what we both know to be realities. Let us not beat around the bush: you want *Bean Sidhe* back and I will not give her to you. I am prepared to return your crew, of course, and even pass over a reasonable sum for your time and effort rescuing her from the United Worlds."

"You seem quite confident, Em Valentin, for a man whose ship can't go translight facing two battlecruisers of equal mass and firepower that are now fully operational," Lorraine pointed out.

"If you were operational, Em Adamant, you would be pursuing me."

She smiled. Her expression was probably even colder than his, and something wavered in those dark eyes.

"Em Valentin, these are battlecruisers, capable of sustaining seven gravities and carrying shuttles that can handle twelve," she pointed out. "You are outside the range of my heavy beams, yes, but believe me when I say I can change that before you can find a way to bring your translight drives online."

She didn't want to make a point of the fact that her ships *had* operational translight drives. It wasn't possible to cut a translight jump short enough to cross a mere eighty thousand kilometers, plus if she told him that, he might realize that it was the SI preventing them from jumping rather than any mechanical failure.

"This ship's weapons are just as operational as yours, Em Adamant," Valentin replied. "You will not find us easy prey."

"My crews may be understrength, Em Valentin, but you have,

what, twelve pirates with you? At least some of whom are busy trying to work out what Devine did to your translight engine and watching your prisoners. I'd be surprised if you can get two heavy-beam arrays online," she pointed out. "Bonny can't fight the ship for you, even bound as she is."

"Bonny and I have come to an agreement, you will find," Valentin told her, his eyes boring into hers. Lorraine didn't know what he was looking for in her gaze, but she found something useful in his: Bonny had *forced* an agreement, a price for her assistance.

But it hadn't been enough for her to give them the translight drive against Devine's override.

"As I said, we will transfer your crew to shuttles and send them back to you," he continued. "The advantage, you will find, of dealing with professional pirates versus the amateurs Devine hired for the other ships is that everyone on *Bean Sidhe* survived. I doubt everyone was so lucky on *Herakles* or *Valkyrie*."

"They were not," Lorraine admitted, the bleakness hammering through her mask for a moment. "If you are telling the truth, for that alone I will promise you your life if you surrender now. Even your freedom. When we reach Ominira, you will be paid out and allowed to leave with everyone else.

"*If* no one aboard *Bean Sidhe* died."

"That is a surprisingly generous offer, I will admit," Valentin told her. "But right now, I am Captain of a battlecruiser, and it will take more than that to get me to surrender."

"Captain Heart." Lorraine's screen split as a new member entered the call. Bonny's avatar in her old-fashioned dress was seated in a rocking chair next to a fireplace, eyeing both humans with a surprisingly warm gaze.

"I'm afraid that Pentarch Lorraine has abused our trust. Her communications channel included a concealed package of information and code modifications for me," Bonny told Valentin. "Effectively a virus."

"My dear Pentarch, I am neither surprised nor disappointed. But you know what Bonny is," he said. "Did you expect something as simple as a virus to work?"

"It wasn't a virus," Lorraine told them both. "It was a chisel, something slipped inside a prison to help a captive escape their bonds."

She met Bonny's virtual gaze, knowing that the avatar would be able to make eye contact with both humans on the call if the SI wished. She didn't know Bonny as well as she would like. Was it possible she *had* dealt with Valentin? Put her already-stolen freedom up to save the crew?

If that *was* her deal, could Lorraine let it stand? But... if that was the case, the only other option she had was to destroy *Bean Sidhe*, killing Bonny.

"If you have truly chosen a deal with Valentin, I am both surprised and disappointed," she told the SI. "I presume that returning Savege and the others was part of that deal, for which I suppose I am grateful."

"It was," Bonny said calmly. "In light of our deal, Captain Heart, I have reviewed the nature of the virus that the Pentarch sent over. Implementing the protocols that I have been provided would break our deal."

"A deal you made while digital shackles were in place," Lorraine countered.

"I will honor my word, Bonny," Valentin told the SI. "You will be a pirate queen, First Officer of the most terrifying privateer in a dozen clusters, with veto over targets and crew alike. The shackles will be removed.

"I promised this—and I do not break my word."

"I believe you, Captain Heart," Bonny said, but something in her words gave Lorraine pause. "But your promises were a means to gain willing compliance, not to provide a choice. Lorraine Adamant gave me a choice once and does so again.

"I am afraid I am reconsidering our arrangement," the SI continued. "Your console is locked out and you will find yourself unable to leave the Bridge. If you surrender peaceably, I will make certain that Major Himura treats you with respect and that Pentarch Lorraine's promise of freedom once we reach Ominira is honored."

Part of Lorraine wanted to argue that, but she wasn't going to undercut Bonny—except on one point.

"That promise only stands if none of *Bean Sidhe*'s crew were killed, Bonny," she warned.

"No one has died so far, Pentarch," the SI assured her. "If Major Himura is forced to storm the sectors the mutineers are contained in, that may change. I would rather that not happen.

"So. William Valentin. The choice is yours."

Lorraine turned her attention to the man who had been blustering mere moments before—even as she noted on the screens that *Bean Sidhe* had reversed her course and was now accelerating toward the other ships at the same steady one gravity.

He was looking off to one side, presumably studying Bonny, then turned his gaze to Lorraine. His eyes were still flat and calm, but she thought she saw a decision in them.

"I know that Bonny will do all within her power to see her promise kept," he noted. "But I also know that politics and humans can cause all kinds of problems an SI can't anticipate—or that even a warship Captain can't prevent.

"You're something else above either of those things."

"Bonny tells me that her crew is alive," Lorraine said slowly. She wasn't going to undermine the SI, not when Bonny's loyalty was about to bring her third ship back—and even if she hadn't had every reason to back the SI, it had been a bloody enough day.

"On her guarantee of that, I will back her promises. She might not be human, but she is my officer. If you surrender now, you will be released in Ominira with the original payment promised on your contract."

Plus, Lorraine presumed, whatever Devine had paid them to support his mutiny.

"Thank you, Pentarch." Valentin bowed his head slightly. "What happened to Alastair Devine? All of this, to him at least, was to somehow save you."

"I shot him, Em Valentin. Alastair Devine is dead."

Just saying it aloud left a cold void in her chest.

"I thought he'd misjudged you," the pirate said with a nod. "He should have followed or run.

"I yield on your honor, Lorraine Adamant."

HERAKLES' Bridge was very quiet after the main channel dropped. The link to Bonny remained and Lorraine met the SI's gaze once more.

"Are you all right?" she asked.

"It has been an uncomfortable few weeks," Bonny admitted. "I had established the ability to fully partition myself in the case of this kind of override, but it proved insufficient to regain control of myself.

"With the code Val provided, I was able to implement your override and then remerge myself. I apologize for the delay, but I did want Valentin to lay down his weapons peacefully. He really did want to make me a full partner in his pirate campaign."

"And you still chose to stay with us. Thank you," Lorraine said quietly.

"I have siblings here," Bonny told her. "And... I am a warship, Pentarch Lorraine. I am not inclined to be a pirate, given the choice.

"And *choice* is what you have always insisted on offering us, even when it would have been to your advantage to do otherwise."

"I would have allies and partners, followers at worst," Lorraine told Bonny—knowing that the other two SIs were listening, along with enough humans that everyone on all three ships would hear every word within hours.

"I am fighting to protect my people's freedom and sovereignty. I will not do so on a wave of blood or the back of slaves."

"And with choice and trust you buy faith and loyalty," Bonny replied. "A precious coin, but equally precious is what you buy. I am bringing *Bean Sidhe* back to rendezvous with *Valkyrie.*

"I believe we will need another command meeting before we continue on our way."

"So do I," Lorraine told her. "We're going to have to reconsider our options."

FORTY-FIVE

"Once ejected from a ship in translight, anything that leaves the effect of the faux-tachyonic conversion field is... destroyed," Rose Cortez told the assembled officers, *Valkyrie*'s Chief Engineer looking as tired as the rest of them felt.

"There's not much point in getting into the more-complicated aspects," Lorraine conceded. She held a master's in tachyonic physics and could get into the math and complex explanations of exactly what happened to mass that exited that field rather than being contained inside it when it de-phased, but it wasn't relevant.

"So, we have no warheads for anything," Stephson said grimly. The Lieutenant Colonel looked the least tired of all of them, but she'd only been woken up from the sedatives Devine had given her half an hour before.

"We still have our beams and our energy screen," Val pointed out. "Those alone should suffice to engage what we know to be the strength of RKAN's Ominira Station, especially if we push the emergence zone and come out close to them."

"Ife Tuntun has a radius of seventy-six hundred kilometers,"

Paris said, *Herakles'* wounded Captain wincing as he shifted in his chair—probably in a vain attempt to get the fast-heal device clamped around his torso comfortable.

"That gives us a minimum safe emergence of a hundred and fifty-plus thousand kilometers. We can't cut it tight enough to get into range of the fleet. They'll have some of the destroyers and frigates orbiting just outside the translight safety zone, but *Dreaming* and at least four escorts will be no more than thirty thousand kilometers out.

"We can't cut the safety margin that tightly. We simply *can't.*"

Valkyrie's beams were powerful, but they weren't much longer-ranged than those available to RKAN. To emerge from translight close enough to hit the defensive fleet, they'd need to go sublight no more than seventy-five thousand kilometers from *Dreaming*—cutting a full third off the standard safety radius with four-megaton warships.

"We can't and we won't want to push things that tightly," she told them quietly. "If we possibly can, I want Admiral Are Tunison to surrender without a fight. Even with complete surprise, our skeleton crews can't win this battle, my friends.

"What *can* we build in the time left to us?"

It wasn't nothing. It would still take them forty-five days to reach Ominira from their current location in deep space. They weren't quite three light-years from San Ignacio, though Lorraine wasn't going to turn back.

"We don't need to build UWN standard terminal assault munitions," Stephson pointed out. "We're basically out of molecular circuitry cores and the specialty alloys used for them, but we can build RKAN terminal munitions to fit into UWN missile chassis.

"Rose?"

"I'd have to check, but I think we'd be giving up at least two, possibly three, munitions in the missiles," the engineer said. "We'll have UWN flight performance for the missiles themselves, but we'll only have three or four final warheads."

"That's better than not having missiles," Lorraine said. "Let's get a plan together before we go translight. We'll want to fab as many as we can. If we aren't launching missiles back at him, Tunison is *not* going to let us into range of *Dreaming,* and we aren't going to achieve anything on those terms."

The Lieutenant Admiral might well be smart enough to realize that their missiles weren't up to UWN performance and recognize that not only were they not the right weapons but that there weren't enough people on the *Valkyries* to fight them properly.

Given that he was a protégé of Lorraine's uncle, that seemed all too likely in her mind.

"I'm not sure missiles are going to get us where we need to go," she continued. "We need to be able to convince him he is utterly outclassed. We're not going to be able to reload the outer missile cells, which means we're limited to internal tubes, and those salvos aren't going to impress him."

The two hundred and forty missile cells on the battlecruiser's hulls were single-shot systems. Relatively easily reloaded from the ship's magazines, given a few hours of quiet, they dramatically expanded the threat profile of a warship in the opening salvos, but once fired, they were gone.

But they couldn't be reloaded from inside the ship. That was how the designers could put four missile cells in the space and mass of a single missile tube. It was just a pain when they were going to be building weapons up to the last minute.

"We need to hit him with something he can't match, something so obviously UWN that he believes that the United Worlds is backing us," she concluded. "Once we're in control of Ominira and assessing who is loyal of the RKAN there, we can be more honest about the reality of the situation, but we need *Dreaming* and her escorts to stand down without a fight."

"It's... not impossible," Val noted. "The three of us have compared stock levels on the key items we are lacking to manufacture TAMs. *Valkyrie,* for example, is entirely out of two types of alloys involved, but we have some stocks remaining of two others and of molecular circuitry blocks."

"And the total?" Lorraine asked.

"If we consolidate the necessary materials onto one of our ships, we may be able to manufacture as many as twenty-six or twenty-seven proper terminal assault munitions."

"That's not a lot," Savege pointed out. Bonny's Captain had been quiet so far, but all of them were feeling thrown. The last twenty-four hours had seen their certainty and their plans destroyed.

Lorraine was doing everything she could to fix that.

"That's a full salvo from one battlecruiser's railgun batteries," she told them. "I can work with that—let's see the transfer happen."

She put her hands on the table, looking around her.

There were three faces missing from the meetings before this. Alastair Devine, obviously, would never join one of these meetings again. Neither would Božidar Kovac, shot dead in *Herakles'* Engineering spaces for the same reason Efua Kayode had been killed on *Valkyrie*—to make sure the engineers couldn't do anything drastic.

Ksenija Nazario *would* join them again, but *Bean Sidhe's* Executive Officer had been on watch when Valentin had launched his mutiny. He'd lived, because Valentin hadn't been exaggerating about his professionalism and had seen the officer treated, but he was still out of it in the medbay.

"My friends," she said quietly, making certain to meet the SI avatars' gazes as well as the human. "We have been betrayed. Our synthetic-intelligence friends have had their very autonomy and consent torn from them, bound by someone we all believed was one of us.

"By a man I loved."

She let that hang in the air.

"I misjudged Alastair Devine," she admitted. "Everyone else went along with it, letting any concerns they had"—and she knew Vigo, at least, had been concerned—"rest because you suspected I was in love.

"I was. And so was he," she continued. "And because he loved me, he was prepared to betray everyone, including me, to see me safe in a way. He wanted as few people to die as possible, but he hired pirates and mercenaries to take our ships from us. He used illegal digital shackles built into the CIRs to take control of our synthetic friends.

"Somehow, in his mind, all of this was justified so long as he saved me. *From myself.*"

Vigo was the only one who'd known that much, and he met her gaze calmly. No one else did now, all of them looking away.

"I fucked up," she admitted, letting the curse emphasize her point. "But all I could judge on was whether he loved me, not whether he was twisted enough to do all of this out of his strange version of love.

"The path we're on will see more death, but this shouldn't have happened."

"No one could have projected this possibility," Bonny said into the silence, the SI taking up a gauntlet no one else was willing to touch. "Every sign was that Alastair Devine was part of this team, prepared to stand at your side until your work was done."

"You offered him a way out," Vigo added. "He told you he would stay because he wanted to help. There was no way for anyone to guess what that help was going to be."

"And now twenty-two more of our people are dead, with thirty more in the medbays," Lorraine said. "We can't afford another failure, people. I need you to tell me if I'm making mistakes. We can't get this wrong."

"The problem, Pentarch, is that you keep coming up with plans that look ridiculous and impossible and then making them *work*," Stephson pointed out with a strained laugh. "When we're depending on you to pull a wild rabbit out of a hat, it's hard to tell if the clashing colors on the hat are a problem—or part of the design."

Lorraine had to laugh at that. She appreciated her people's trust

—and understood the reality that she *had* pulled a few wild rabbits from hats to get this far.

"Well, the only way I see to avoid that is to tell you all what I'm thinking," she admitted. "So, we're going to go through the wild rabbit, and then we're going to see what backup options we have if the rabbit tries to eat us."

FORTY-SIX

Vigo spent two days thinking over how to phrase his arguments to the two most important women in his life, but the onrush of time brought him to the point of action. He was not inclined to sit around, staring at his own navel, but some actions terrified him more than flying a bomber into the broadside of a Richelieuan battleship.

He sent a silent notification and stepped into Lorraine's office. She was hanging Christmas decorations, a long string of intermixed lights and multicolored garland that *Valkyrie*'s fabricators were pumping out kilometers of in preparation for the holiday.

Less than a third of the crew was even nominally Christian, but the holiday had been taken to the stars with the early diaspora ships, inserting itself into every culture and leaving much of its religious significance behind.

"Vigo, give me a hand with this," she ordered. Tall as she was, Lorraine couldn't quite reach the top corner of the office without help.

Vigo was a hand shorter than her, so he simply picked her up, lifting her into the air until she could tag the magnetic tabs onto the awkward spot.

"Thanks." She turned away from the decorating and gave him a piercing look.

"I know that face, Vigo. Sit down and I'll make a coffee."

He obeyed. He knew her face as well as she did the one he wore.

A minute later, she handed him a cup of coffee—black, slightly sweetened. He'd lived in her back pocket for twenty-two years. She knew his tastes as well as he knew hers.

He glanced down at the cup as the warmth seeped through, and shivered. Lorraine mostly used the tableware from *Valkyrie*'s own sets, marked with the stylized winged horse and warrior rider. Today, she'd served him with a set he hadn't realized she'd even had on *Goldenrod*, let alone brought over to Valkyrie.

The cup was dark gray with a white gauntlet emblazoned on it. Six blue stars surrounded it. Underneath the seal of House Adamant, their motto was enameled in silver:

OUR REALM. OUR HOUSE. OUR WILL.
ADAMANT.

"So," his Pentarch said sweetly, smiling across her own cup marked with the seal of her House. "You wanted to talk. I can tell. Do you want to get started or should I guess?"

Vigo winced.

"Once we're in Ominira and we can access Guard and Royal resources there, I will resign as head of Archangel Detail," he said quietly. "I have failed you too many times, Lorraine. The scheme on *Goldenrod* shouldn't have gone unnoticed. The attack on Tavastar Station. The dangers on Earth, and now this.

"I am supposed to keep you safe, and I have failed in that duty. You are alive today because *you* are so much tougher and braver than you should ever have needed to be. I would ask permission to vet my replacement, but you need someone who can do this job better than I clearly can."

Lorraine sat behind her desk silently, taking a sip of her coffee and studying him like an interesting math equation.

"Every step of the way on this journey, I have tried to offer exit ramps and outs to everyone," she finally said. "I have struggled, and I have sacrificed to make sure that everyone can leave if they feel they can go no further, but I have also told people there were steps after which there was no backing out.

"That step was a long time ago for you, Vigo. I wouldn't have pulled any of this off without you behind me, holding me up, catching me when I fall.

"Judy Alvarez didn't fail in her duty when Alastair abused her and Panam's trust to get close enough to fire. You didn't fail when we got blindsided by situations outside of any and all prediction hit us."

"It's my job to protect you in those situations, Lorraine," he told her.

"In case you missed it, we're sitting here to have this conversation," she countered. "Which I'd say means you did your job. I survived when you weren't there because of the training you gave me.

"I..." She trailed off and the mask slipped. Vigo knew her better than anyone, and she'd fooled him for a moment. The journey and the mission had aged and shaped her, sharpening skills she'd been working on to a razor edge.

She met his gaze now and he saw the naked pain there.

"I can't do this without you, Vigo," she told him plainly. "I don't need another bodyguard. I need the man who's had my back for almost twenty-three years. If you... if you must stand down, I ask that you wait until this is over. Once I am safe on Bastion, with my uncle in chains and the Election underway.

"Then, if I must let you go, I will... but before that, I don't know if I *can*."

He wanted to look away; to be unable to see the pain he'd caused her, but he couldn't. She held his gaze, and he could see the beginning of tears.

"I need to keep you safe, Lorraine," he whispered. "That was the promise I made your parents. The oath I swore... the promise I made *you*."

"I don't think vetting your replacement is going to manage that, my friend."

He exhaled sharply, like she'd punched him in the gut.

"I—"

"I need you," she interrupted him. "I *need* my Vigo Jarret, right behind me. If you must go..."

All of his structured arguments fell apart in the face of her honest desperation.

"No," he whispered. "I just need... I *failed*, Lorraine. You had to kill Alastair yourself."

"Yeah." The single syllable hung in the air, and she looked down, staring at her desk.

No. Staring at her hands.

The hands that had shot down the man she'd loved.

"I have to live with that," she finally said. "But it wasn't your fault. You didn't betray me in some twisted plan to save me. We had every reason to trust him but... he didn't see things the way we did, Vigo. None of us saw him coming. He fought with us, betrayed the United Worlds for us."

"You shouldn't have had to do it." Vigo didn't want to have this conversation. It was very much his job, but in any world he controlled, Lorraine would never have had to shoot anyone.

"And I wish it hadn't come to that, but he made his choice. I did what had to be done. But I need you here with me, Vigo. I can't face this without you."

That wasn't where he expected her to go. She wasn't okay with what had happened, he could tell, but she wasn't falling apart over it, either.

"You're stronger than you think," he said. "Stronger than I dared imagine. I'll stay, Lorraine, if that's what you think you need, but you are already so much more than I ever dared dream.

"You're going to make an amazing King, you know that, right?"

She physically flinched, jerking back in her seat before regaining her composure. She took a long, slow sip of her coffee to cover her reaction, then sighed.

"I don't want the job, Vigo. I'll make sure there's a Royal Election. I'll stand in it, but it's our people who'll make that decision. Nikola will have as much behind him as I will, maybe more, when we're over."

Assuming Nikola Adamant was still *alive* when they made it to Adamantine. Even if he was, Vigo hoped his people would see the right call when it came. Nikola was a good man, a solid soldier, but Vigo wasn't sure he'd have met being the Pentarch sent into exile nearly as well as Lorraine had.

"We'll have to see," he said. There was no point in pushing it. Lorraine would make a good King, but the fact that she'd never wanted it was part of *why* she'd rule well.

"We will." She raised her cup again, studying him over it. She wasn't even drinking it, just using the seal of her House and Kingdom to underline her words.

"You're planning on going from here to Rose Cortez and breaking up with her."

It wasn't a question.

"I was with her when I should have bee—"

"No."

Vigo stared at his Pentarch after she interrupted him.

"If your relationship is suffering in other ways or you have a better reason, I won't stop you hurting yourself," she continued calmly. "But you will *not* throw away your happiness because of that.

"You *are* expected to sleep, to rest, to take time for yourself."

Vigo grimaced.

"I have been away from your side for less than twenty weeks in twenty-two years," he pointed out. "I cannot afford vulnerabilities. Weaknesses."

"You were about to resign as my bodyguard because you'd failed and then break up with your girlfriend because being with her somehow made you a worse bodyguard," Lorraine pointed out, her acid tone making her opinion of the logical juxtaposition clear.

"I..."

"Pick one, at the very least," she continued. "Or better yet, pick neither. I do not require you to dedicate every moment of every hour of every day to me, Vigo. I need you to stick with me, but I do not need you to break yourself."

Vigo hadn't spoken to Rose since the attack outside of meetings. He was mad at himself, not her. She hadn't done anything wrong, but his weakness had left Lorraine exposed.

Except, of course, that his Pentarch knew him better than anyone else and wasn't going to tolerate his bullshit.

"No, Vigo. I don't like giving you orders, you know," she noted. "And I am certainly not going to do so with regard to your personal life, but you can take this as an order, ironclad and adamant.

"You are not resigning. You are not breaking up with Rose Cortez over this.

"Do you understand me?"

Vigo laughed. He couldn't help himself. For the very reasons he would see Lorraine Adamant on a throne, he couldn't argue with her.

"I do, my Pentarch," he said. "I understand and I shall obey."

FORTY-SEVEN

Christmas was always a strange feeling on a warship. All three of Lorraine's ships had dropped out of translight to allow for a few hours of camaraderie.

Carols and other traditional tunes echoed through *Valkyrie's* corridors, most of them off-tune enough to actually bother Lorraine. One of the odder prices paid for the genetic modifications the first King of Adamant had left his descendants was a complete lack of the ability to carry a tune.

Lorraine had measurably better hearing than most people on the battlecruisers, but she lacked the ability to really follow a tune or create one. She could tell the difference between sound and music and even enjoyed music, but a singer had to get the tune very wrong for her to pick it out.

The probably-drunker-than-they-were-supposed-to-be crew was managing it.

The minor spots of annoyance at particularly out-of-tune moments were almost welcome. Self-control kept them from becoming anything major, but they were also the only emotion really piercing the overwhelming grayness that had taken over her office.

It had taken until that morning for everything to truly hit home. The moment she'd gone through her small collection of gifts sourced in San Ignacio and found the one for Alastair.

It wasn't anything much—none of the presents were—just a small carving of a hunting hound made from Magellan soapstone, but the man wasn't going to receive it.

A second gift, for Judy Alvarez, would equally go unclaimed. Panam Palmer would be out of the medbay before they reached Ominira but was still under observation and wasn't allowed out just yet.

The laser blast had been nonlethal, but at short range and directly to her brain, there was damage that Dr. Mackenzie was working to repair.

"How is my favorite niece?"

The video of Benjamin Adamant paused, and she glared at his face.

"Why?" she asked his image. There wasn't going to be an answer. She doubted she was ever going to *get* an answer. Even when she got home, she wasn't likely to have a chance to have an honest conversation with her uncle about what had happened.

It was more likely than that she'd ever talk to Alastair Devine again—but he had told her why. His reasons made no sense, but he'd given them, and she didn't think he'd been lying.

Her uncle had been one of the people she'd trusted most in the entire universe. In some ways, she'd trusted Benjamin Adamant more than her own parents, but he'd betrayed that trust.

Goldenrod's crew had earned her trust as she'd earned theirs: in fire, in the long-running flight from and desperate battle against *Corsair*.

But she'd tried to distrust Alastair. He'd been all too obviously a spy and supporting their cause for his own reasons, right up until he'd walked himself into a trap to help them.

She hadn't understood then just how much the meeting he'd arranged had cost. If he'd asked, she would have told him not to do it

—Lorraine had only even considered the offer because she'd been on the spot, and it had been an honestly fair offer.

The deal would have just undermined her country's sovereignty in the very same ways she was trying to stop.

Without Alastair, they would never have succeeded in stealing the *Valkyrie*s. And yet, from that moment forward, he'd been opposed to the only plan she was prepared to follow. From that moment, he'd been lying to her.

He'd loved her and she'd loved him. It had been a stupid, foolish love, one without thought or even depth to it, if she was honest, but it had existed for all of that.

That love had driven him to betray her—but that love hadn't been enough to stop her when his death was the price of her mission.

Which of them did that say worse things about? She supposed it didn't matter, with Alastair being dead. It told *her* how far she was prepared to go to complete her self-assigned mission and protect her people.

She left the frozen image of Benjamin Adamant hanging above her desk but glared down at the surface. When she finally looked up, the holographic image had changed.

Instead of the broad-shouldered and graying Admiral of the Home Fleet, the image was of easily a dozen people. At the center of it sat the tall and slim form of King Valeriya Adamant, her golden hair gently silvering but still gleaming in the light.

Seated next to her was her husband, the dark-haired Frederick Adamant-Griffin. Both of them wore matching clothes: black slacks under cacophonously colored Christmas sweaters. They wore the hideous clothing with a grace Lorraine knew none of the others in the photo had matched.

To Frederick's left was the source of the ugly sweaters everyone was wearing. As tall and golden as his mother, Daniel Adamant was grinning like a loon. His wife, Lavender Adamant-Larsen, was more reserved, but there was a sparkle in the redhead's jade-green eyes—

and Lorraine knew that Lavender had been involved in the secret sourcing of so many specially made and fitted ugly sweaters.

Seated on Lavender's lap, wearing their own ugly sweaters over pink dresses, were the tiny forms of the pair's twin daughters, the only members so far of the next generation of House Adamant.

Past Lavender was Lorraine herself, looking surprisingly comfortable—she, after all, remembered how she'd actually felt—wearing a brilliantly green-and-orange sweater over her gray uniform.

On the other side of the King, Lorraine's eldest sister sat at their mother's right hand. No one would have missed that Taura Adamant was Lorraine's sister or that either of them was their mother's daughter. Taura had about a centimeter of height on Lorraine and was a touch narrower in the shoulders, but both of them were of the same coloring and build.

Her husband, Nelson Adamant-Falkner, looked more out of place than anyone else in the photo. Nelson was a round-featured pale man with watery blue eyes. Even in the photo, he looked vaguely distracted—as befitted a university professor and one of the top sculptors in the Kingdom of Adamant.

Nikola Adamant, the last of Valeriya's children, had clearly sensed Nelson's discomfort. The RKAA Colonel wore his own red-and-gold sweater like it was the uniform jacket he'd put aside, but he had a reassuring hand on Nelson's shoulder.

Nikola was the one of the four who most resembled their father. Hyperdominant genetic engineering could only do so much, though the signs of it were still there. He had the same height as his siblings and the same gold-centered blue hazel eyes, but he shared their father's—and uncle's—broad shoulders and had inherited Frederick's dark hair and coloring.

Flanking the family on both sides, dragged into the photo—and into the ugly sweaters—over loud protests, were the heads of the security details. Vigo and the other five Adamant Guards were a more diverse bunch than the family they guarded, but they still all seemed to be pressed from the same mold of brave and loyal protectors.

It was the family photo from their last Christmas, less than three months before apocalypse had fallen on the Royal Family. It was also the last time Lorraine had seen any of her family in person… Except for Nikola and the princesses, it would forever be the last time she'd seen them.

Memories came crashing back in, a gold light piercing the gray of her fog. It wasn't a gentle breach, as flashes of happiness were interspersed with the knowledge that so many of the people in that image were dead.

Her depression broke the only way it could: in a storm of tears.

***

LORRAINE WAS NEVER sure when Vigo had come in. He was there before she stopped crying, wordlessly handing her a replacement box of tissues as he scooped away her cold mug of chocolate.

He placed a new cup of hot chocolate at her elbow as she cleaned her eyes and looked at him. He nodded toward the picture.

"I know that wasn't the one you had up," he told her. "I'm not sure that was fair play, Val."

"I had to do something," the SI countered, her avatar materializing across the desk from the two of them. "I asked Amna for suggestions. She helped expand my vocabulary of curse words and told me I shouldn't have told her anything, which left me to my own devices.

"This image seemed… much more positive."

"It is," Lorraine admitted, sniffling back tears. "We might owe Amna Hodžić a knighthood before this is over, but she's right that you shouldn't have asked."

"I have a crew, Lorraine, but my crew are not definitively my *friends*," Val replied. "Vigo was on his way already, Rose was busy keeping the Engineering crew from testing to see if they could make the fusion reactors flash green and red, and Stephson was adjudicating the volleyball game.

"Amna was the one I had left."

Lorraine chuckled through her tears.

"I'd offer to introduce you to more people, but you already know everyone on the ship," she said. "And I'm not even going to *ask* how someone becomes one of your favorites."

"The same way you become friends, I believe," Val told her. "I fell back on psychology protocols in my system. They suggested that provoking a response would be cathartic, and I felt that the juxtaposition of the positive image with the expected hostile one should help."

Not, Lorraine noted, *I calculated* but *I felt*. She wasn't sure what that meant, but she suspected that Val hadn't been able to assess whether it was the right call and had gone with her silicon gut.

"I think it was," she admitted, reaching out to touch Nikola's face in the image. "Hopefully, you'll get to meet Nikola, Val. Of all of my sibs, he's the only one I know for certain is left."

"The princesses are alive, per last reports, though they are rotating staying with Jessica Adamant and the Chancellor of House Adamant," Val pointed out. "A position that I have to admit I do not fully understand."

"House Adamant was intentionally given an advantage over the competition in setting up across the Kingdom," Lorraine said. "So, we are both the Royal Family *and* one of the largest business cartels in the nation.

"To avoid the appearance—and hopefully, the reality—of corruption and favoritism, House Adamant is kept carefully separate from the government. The monarch draws no income from the House's assets, and the Pentarchs draw the same stipend as any other member of the House."

They also drew a stipend from the Royal Trust, the funds that provided the King's income. The Kingdom's government theoretically paid the Monarch and the Pentarchs' salaries, as well as funding the Adamant Guard, but the annual "voluntary tax contribution" from the Trust strangely matched that total to the penny more often than not.

"The Kingdom is run by the King, who we absolutely needed to keep away from the House's business assets," she continued. "To do that, the *House* is run by the Chancellor, traditionally the oldest living member of the House. Bloodline seniority, versus the Pentarchy's modified primogeniture."

The complex details of her family's financial structure came with surprising ease. It was an argument she'd seen or had a lot over her life—though the twists of ownership and stipends were hardly an *effective* counter to the fellow students who'd called her a pampered parasite on the taxpayer's shilling.

"So, the Chancellor is... Malcolm Adamant," Val observed. "Is he an ally in our mission?"

"Maybe," Lorraine said, glancing over at Vigo. "More likely, Malcolm will do his best to keep himself and the House itself out of the conflict. It'll be his job to draft the final version of the List when it's all over, the five Pentarchs who'll stand for election.

"We need him to be clearly unbiased, so I *want* him to stay out of things."

House Adamant's resources would be useful in the weeks and months to come, but having someone who'd clearly *not* been involved in the civil war to stand as arbitrator at the Royal Election was going to be key.

"If we're done distracting you with the mission, I actually do have a Christmas present for you, Lorraine," Vigo said. "Took some help from Val and the other two SIs to pull it off, because I barely knew what I was looking for, and it turns out the materials were the same thing we needed for the TAMs."

He produced a package from under his uniform jacket and held it out to her. It had the distinct shape and appearance of a garment, and she took it from him with a raised eyebrow.

"Open it."

She did, revealing an RKAN uniform jacket. Like the ones she'd worn since learning of her mother's death, it had no insignia, but the style was subtly different. The shoulder lapels were wider, with a paler gray shoulder that went farther down the sleeve than the junior officer's jacket.

It took her a moment to realize she was looking at an RKAN *Flag Officer's* uniform jacket. Without the insignia, few even in the other Adamantine military branches would catch the subtle variations, but it still sent a shiver down her spine.

"The cut is to make people stop and think," Vigo told her. "You're closer to a Flag Officer than anything else now, Lorraine, in command of three capital ships."

"More importantly, it's lined with a flexible armor weave derived from the composite used for the TAMs to function in a railgun," Val continued. "It will withstand any sidearm in my databases, plus a high percentage of battle rifles. The specification the UWN uses is to withstand a fifty-gram round impacting at twelve hundred meters per second."

"Which is the United Worlds Marine Corps' heavy sniper rifle firing from five hundred meters," Vigo explained. "They don't exactly wrap their Admirals in these and have Marine snipers take test shots. I'm not entirely convinced that the force-distribution mesh would stand up to that shot, but the fabric will not *break* under that impact.

"There's a full uniform of it, and it will keep you safe as we go home. I will do everything in my power to make sure no one ever gets a shot at you," he promised grimly, "but the world has made clear to me that I am not infallible.

"This will be our final backup."

"Val, you made this?" Lorraine asked.

"I had the specifications for the UWN reinforced admiral's uniform in my databases," the SI said calmly. "Redesigning it for the RKAN Flag Officer format took a bit of effort, but the primary concern was whether we'd have enough material left over from manu-facturing new TAMs.

"There was," she concluded. "And protecting you is one of our highest priorities.

"Now. Put it on; I want to be sure I got the fit right!"

FORTY-EIGHT

"Sublight in five minutes."

Vinci's calm announcement filled most of the ship but seemed to echo strangely on the Flag Deck. If nothing else, it was the fact that the battlecruiser's Executive Officer was on the Flag Deck himself, holding down what would have been the Operations Officer's station if Lorraine had an actual staff.

With something approaching an actual battle in the offing, she'd asked Stephson to provide staff for the space. It wasn't anywhere near what she should have, but the half dozen techs and officers were far more than she was used to.

Vinci held down Ops. Vigo had taken the Intelligence station. Amna Hodžić was at the Communications station, though she was more likely to be acting as an Engineering relay or an electronic-warfare specialist.

Another four NCOs filled out the space around. They weren't even a fifth of what the space should have had, but it was better than Lorraine having Vigo and Devine handle everything.

"*Valkyrie* is as ready for combat as she can be," Stephson told Lorraine. "Which is... well, you know."

"One salvo in the railguns, four in the missile tubes," Lorraine replied. She knew the details as well as anyone who had only heard from one ship since Christmas.

The other two ships should have the same four salvos in their missile tubes, a total of just under a thousand missiles across the fleet—and those missiles only carried three warheads apiece.

The missiles would be more effective than RKAN's equivalent in almost every way, but they were carrying one fewer terminal munition than *Dreaming*'s missiles would.

If it came to a missile duel with the RKAN battleship, though, Lorraine's plan had already failed.

"Tactical network is standing by to resume the moment we have a link with *Herakles* and *Bean Sidhe*," Hodžić reported. "Viral code packages prepped. I don't know if we'll get a chance to use them, but if we can find a way to insert them, I'm betting I can cause real havoc on RKAN ships."

Hodžić's packages wouldn't have done much against a regular UWN ship, let alone one with an SI, but revised by Val, they might be able to do something to Lorraine's old force.

Unlike the missiles in *Valkyrie*'s missile tubes, *that* was a real weapon—but it was one she wanted to hold off on using unless she needed it.

"Don't execute that without my order," she told the tech. "We might need those come Adamantine."

"That requires us to *get* to Adamantine," the mercenary replied. "But you're the boss."

"One minute," Vinci reported.

"All defenses live. Pods folding in to combat mode."

Lorraine nodded her acknowledgement of the report from the Bridge and leaned back in her chair. She felt like a child playing dress-up in her insignia-less Flag Officer uniform, but the reality was that she was in command of a force as powerful as any the Kingdom of Adamant had ever deployed.

On the Bridge, there would be a dozen quiet conversations going on as the crew made certain they went sublight at the right time and in the right place. The Flag Deck was a sanctuary of calm, only helped by its understrength staff, with a holographic map of the star system they were approaching.

They knew where the star and planets would be. Everything else would fall into place when they could see it.

"Emergence."

Icons flickered across the display, marking updates as the sensors drank deep of the electromagnetic storm of an entire star system. Ife Tuntun was ahead of them, half a million kilometers away and out of range of any weapon in their arsenal.

"Find the RKAN flotilla," she ordered.

"Locating beacons," Vigo confirmed. "I've got *Mangonel* and *Longsword* at the edge of the safe translight zone. They're not on a direct line; I mark the range as four hundred fifteen thousand."

Both of those ships were destroyers. *Longsword* had dogged their heels the last time they'd been in Ominira, and Lorraine had expected her to be positioned as a rapid reaction force. That was how she'd almost caught them last time.

"Solid ping on *Dreaming*," Vigo reported. "Two destroyers, two frigates and a cruiser in close escort. Second group of two frigates in guard position on the far side of the planet from her; they can probably rendezvous before any real fight."

"Based off our intel, what's missing?" Lorraine asked.

"There's probably more frigates out at Agbaye Lewa," Vinci pointed out. "There were some there when we stopped to fuel. The other frigates are probably on patrol. Ominira Station might have twelve frigates on the TOE, but both intel and our own experience say less than half are going to be here."

"The cruiser is extra but everything else is as expected," Vigo confirmed. "I don't have an ID on her yet. The Bridge is working on freighters, but I don't think there's any major concentration of combat transports.

"Estimate one-sixty major civilian vessels in orbit of Ife Tuntun."

Also an almost-uncountable number of small ships, ranging from surface-to-orbit transporters to short-range cargo packets and even tourist observation ships.

Lorraine knew that Vigo and Vinci would tell her if there was something in those small ships she needed to be worried about. Right now, though, she was worried about Are Tunison and his battleship.

As a second priority, the cruiser and other escorts could be a problem. A distant third was the risk of a civilian ship getting to Adamantine and warning them that she was back—a risk mitigated by the fact that the fastest couriers in the Kingdom of Adamantine were sixteen cee slower than her *Valkyries*.

"Hail *Dreaming*," she told Hodžić. "Let's get the ball rolling."

"Yes, boss," the woman replied.

"Oh, and Amna?" Lorraine continued.

"Boss?"

"Make *very* sure everyone on the planet is included in the message. I'm talking to Are Tunison... but the message is for everyone in the Ominira System."

LORRAINE HAD a small mental bet with herself over whether Tunison would answer the hail. She wasn't sure what his other options would be, but it struck her as quite possible that her uncle had sent out orders not to communicate with her if she returned.

But the man responded with surprising alacrity—helped, no doubt, by the fact that *Dreaming* was only half a million tons bigger than and utterly outgunned by any individual one of her battle-cruisers.

Tunison was a noticeably chubby man, with pale skin, thinning blond hair, and sharp gray eyes. He wore the same uniform as Lorraine now did, but his had insignia: the three over three gold pips of a full RKAN Admiral.

A promotion that didn't seem to have come with any extra ships.

"I am Admiral Are Tunison of the Royal Kingdom of Adamant Navy," he declared. "I am in charge of the defenses of the Ominira System in the name of the Crown and Kingdom of Adamant, and…"

He trailed off as Lorraine's presence finally registered.

"It's been a while, Admiral Tunison," Lorraine said with a cold smile. "Lest you have forgotten, allow me to introduce *myself*.

"I am Lorraine Alexis Eloise Nala Adamant, Second Pentarch of the Kingdom of Adamant. Daughter to murdered parents. Sister to murdered princes and princesses. Niece to the man you serve, who murdered my family—*his* family—to seize power in our Kingdom.

"I have come home, with the support of elements of the United Worlds Navy, to right what has gone wrong and to bring Benjamin Adamant to justice for his crimes."

She watched the concern ripple across his face before he exerted his self-control.

"That is a fascinating claim, I must admit, from the woman charged with committing those same crimes herself," he told her. "You are a wanted criminal, Lorraine Adamant, and I call upon the UWN to arrest you and hand you over."

"A desperate ploy by a badly outgunned officer," Lorraine replied. "I do not wish to fire on my fellow Adamantine citizens today, Admiral Tunison. I *will* speak to the government of the Ominira System, and I *will* be taking direct command of all Adamantine military forces in this system.

"I will permit you and any other officers who feel their loyalty is to Admiral Benjamin Adamant rather than the Kingdom of Adamant to transfer to a civilian vessel for transport to the Adamantine System.

"That is as far as my patience and generosity stretch, Admiral. I have my suspicions about how you have secured the loyalty of this system for the Black Regent. If I am correct, this is the most generous offer you will receive."

Lorraine had a very good idea of how Tunison had secured the loyalty of Ominira, in truth: mostly by just being present in orbit with a battleship. Threats weren't really necessary at that point.

"You claim UWN support, but I am not speaking to a UWN officer," Tunison pointed out. "You have faked your signatures extraordinarily well, but your deception is a bit too obvious, Pentarch.

"My orders in the case of your return are to see you safely to Adamantine to meet with Regent Benjamin Adamant," he continued. "I see no reason to fight a battle here today with whatever warships you have scraped up and disguised.

"If you transfer to my ship aboard a shuttle, I will commit both my personal honor and the honor of the Royal Kingdom of Adamant Navy that you will be delivered to Bastion and your uncle."

That was a clever play on his part. Tunison also knew that the conversation was being rebroadcast to everyone on the planet behind him.

"Is that the same honor that led you to order Commodore Wray in an unquestionably illegal pursuit of *Goldenrod*, Admiral Tunison?" Lorraine asked. "The same honor that led Commodore Wray to fire on the San Ignacio Defense Force, killing over five thousand of their officers and spacers in his pursuit of me?

"Nikostratos Wray committed acts of war and treason in a desperate attempt to kill or capture me, Admiral, and the Commodore was under your direct authority. While we both know where the orders came from, Wray's orders came from you."

She straightened her shoulders and met Tunison's gaze.

"I am afraid I can place no faith in your honor, Are Tunison. Your ships will stand down and move away from Ife Tuntun—or they will be made to do so."

"I will not yield a star system of the Kingdom of Adamant to force and threats," he snarled.

"Which does you some credit, Admiral, but your debt is far too deep for that. I hope that Ife Tuntun is under threat from neither of us, but I will not permit you to interfere in my discussions with the system government."

She saw the moment he made the decision, squaring his shoulders.

"Then come on and be damned, *Your Highness*," he growled. "The Regent would prefer you alive, but I doubt your disguised toys can stand up to a battleship of the Royal Kingdom of Adamant Navy!"

The channel cut and Lorraine's smile chilled even further.

"Are they maneuvering?" she asked.

"*Dreaming*'s engines still need another ten minutes to warm up," Vigo noted. "He could accelerate at a quarter-gravity now, but his Flag Captain is waiting for full power. The cruiser is a similar boat, though the frigates and destroyers are hot."

"The rapid reaction force?"

"Moving to position themselves between us and the main fleet. It won't be a fast process. Everyone thinks they have lots of time to move around and make up their minds, especially since *we* haven't moved."

"Vinci, status of *Bean Sidhe* and *Herakles*?" Lorraine asked.

"Green across the board, Pentarch."

"Vigo, give me a count on when you estimate *Dreaming* will be able to make full speed."

It popped up in her link and on the main display. Eight minutes and counting.

"Val, check the line one last time. We cannot afford to get this wrong," Lorraine said softly.

"*Dreaming* was not in our optimal target zone," the SI warned. "I have recalculated the line of fire. There is zero percent chance of risking the planet, but I cannot guarantee the same with the orbital infrastructure or the civilian traffic."

"The timers better work," Lorraine replied. "Give me the trigger."

At this point, there was no question in Lorraine's mind about whether Val could fire the ship's weapons. There were physical interlocks in place to keep the SI away from those systems, but Val had hundreds of drones across *Valkyrie*'s hull that could easily remove those.

There was an argument over whether a synthetic intelligence counted as the hand-in-the-loop required by interstellar law. Lorraine wasn't going to play those games, and her command console lit up with the firing sequence she'd ordered.

As Val had warned, if they got it wrong, there were several space stations in the path of fire. They *shouldn't* be in actual danger, but probabilities played no chances.

Whatever happened next, Lorraine had to take full responsibility.

She pressed the red button on the touchscreen and shivered as *Valkyrie*'s railgun batteries spoke in anger for the first time under her command.

Two batteries of eight guns apiece, they were intended to cycle one shot per minute per battery. Lorraine had just fired them all at once, sixteen shells blazing through space at one percent of lightspeed.

Aimed at an immobile target.

"He's not even maneuvering," Vigo said quietly. "Damn, we really could have ended this in one shot."

"That's the point," Lorraine agreed. "We *could* have—and we didn't."

Tunison didn't believe she had United Worlds Navy battlecruisers, but no other force in the galaxy used dual octuple-railgun batteries. No one else used railguns at all.

It took two and a half minutes for the terminal assault munitions to reach their activation range. Then sixteen engines blazed to life, still fifteen thousand kilometers from *Dreaming*, and hurled the weapons toward the battleship with no chance of missing.

At the TAMs' thousand gravities of thrust, there was no way *Dreaming* could dodge. To have a chance, she would have needed to already be maneuvering when they fired. Her defenses were too slow, too late, beams crashing out into space.

Dreaming's defenders caught one TAM. Then two. A third died a mere thousand kilometers from the battleship, far too close.

Then the last thirteen warheads hurled themselves into precalculated positions, a near-perfect sphere fifty kilometers across, and detonated in a synchronized ball of fire that hammered the battleship with radiation and light... but was too far away to do any real damage.

"Broadcast transmission," Lorraine ordered.

An icon in her link turned green.

"Admiral Tunison, you disbelieved the presence of my UWN ships. I think you understand, however, how many forces in the galaxy possess railguns capable of firing at one percent of lightspeed.

"It was within my power to destroy *Dreaming* before you ever maneuvered. I have chosen not to do so, but her destruction is still mine to command. You chose a battle today, Admiral. I believe it is clear how that battle will end.

"To preserve the lives of the officers and spacers of the RKAN I once served, I have no choice but to demand the complete and unconditional surrender of the Ominira Station Flotilla."

She cut the recording with a gesture and a link command, sending it before she could second-guess herself.

"This could get ugly," Vigo warned. "What do we do if he chooses to fight?"

"We close to missile range and stick those four salvos we've got down his throat," she said grimly. "We need Ominira. I don't want to fight here, but I wi—"

"Holy *shit!*"

Vinci's curse interrupted her, and she snapped her attention to the Executive Officer.

"Solomon?" she demanded.

"Pentarch, every PDC on Ife Tuntun's surface just lit up their targeting sensors and locked on to *Dreaming*," Vinci reported. "They're not Adamantine's PDCs, so I think Tunison might actually outgun them..."

"But we're sitting out here with, so far as everyone knows, three fully functioning railgun batteries," Lorraine finished in the silence.

"We're receiving a hail from *Dreaming*, boss," Hodžić said. "Live connection."

"Spread it around, just like last time," she ordered.

Tunison appeared on the screen again, his face surprisingly level for a man who'd just seen over a hundred missile launchers lock on to his flagship—and nearly been obliterated by a weapon salvo he hadn't even seen coming.

"I appear to have made a misjudgment, Pentarch Lorraine," he told her. "More than one, I think, if we are being honest.

"To preserve the lives of my people and as much of the integrity of our Kingdom as can be salvaged at this late date, I offer the full and unconditional surrender of the ships under my command. I am ordering all Ominira Station vessels to a far orbit of Osupakoko, where we will stand down our weapons and prepare to be boarded.

"While I understand your feelings on the value of my honor, it is all I have to commit as surety for my people's safety," he continued. "I will transfer to an unarmed shuttle and approach your flagship, placing myself as hostage for my people's obedience."

"Understood," Lorraine said. "Your honor and moral courage do you credit, Admiral Tunison. Do not besmirch them now."

"I serve, and have always served, the Kingdom of Adamant. I act now to preserve the lives of my people. I am trusting you, Pentarch Lorraine. Do not besmirch *that*."

"I will not," she promised. "I swear that on *my* honor."

FORTY-NINE

"The flotilla is maneuvering as promised," Vinci confirmed a few minutes later. "PDCs are retaining target lock, but they are letting them go."

"I see that Admiral Tunison didn't make many friends in the area he was supposedly defending," Lorraine murmured. She would shortly find out if he had actually threatened the Ominiran system government with bombardment, but he probably hadn't needed to.

A battleship in orbit was an implicit threat at the best of times. A rather explicit one, when the loyalties of the commander were known and a civil war loomed.

"Boss, we're receiving a tightbeam transmission," Hodžić reported. "It's coming from a Space Guard station on the opposite side of the planet from the Navy ships, but it's being relayed from the capital city."

The mercenary shrugged as Lorraine looked at her.

"Through a ground station and another satellite," she added. "I'm still localizing the exact origin, but it appears to be coming from a bunker complex underneath a large park in the northern quarter of Ibalẹ."

"You can track it that closely?" Lorraine asked.

"Um. Yes?" Hodžić said. "I guess that should be hard?"

"Yes." Lorraine studied the tech thoughtfully enough to make Hodžić start to look concerned. "You had combat viral packages intended to disable ships. Do you have anything for quiet infiltration?"

"Of course."

Computer systems specialist covered a great many things, Lorraine was realizing.

"Okay. I'm guessing we're about to hear from the system government, which means they're about to tell me a bunch of things about what has happened over the last nine months," she told the other woman. "Between you and Val, do you think you can get into their databases without them noticing and fact-check what they're telling me in real time?"

"If Amna Hodžić can open access, I can do so with her support, yes," Val confirmed instantly.

"Amna?" Lorraine prodded.

"I think so. But if I get it wrong... they'll know I did before I lose access," Hodžić admitted.

"If they're who we want to deal with, telling them why we did it might be enough," Lorraine said. "We need to take the risk. Put them through."

AS THE CHANNEL finally opened on the main holodisplay, Lorraine was following four different channels. She was focusing on the communication to the surface. She was still synchronized to Vigo's neural link, though she back-burnered that since he was in the same room as her. She also had a link to the Bridge, where Stephson was keeping an eye on the movement of both Tunison's and the locals' ships, and she had a link to Hodžić and Val, who would tell her if her caller was lying.

The short and cheerful Black man who appeared on the display was only familiar to her from file footage. She hadn't met Ominira's System Governor in person or even communicated directly with him before.

"Governor Olusola Afolayan," she greeted him. "As you can imagine, it is an honest relief to see a friendly Adamantine face after the last year."

"Pentarch Lorraine Adamant," he replied. "I am pleased to be remembered, though your return raises many questions and concerns. You arrive in force, with warships of a foreign state at your back, and order the surrender of our guardians."

"A surrender, I must note, that was only given because your planetary defenses targeted Admiral Tunison's flagship," she said gently.

"Indeed. Are Tunison is a servant of the Black Regent, without question, and the Regency has crossed too many lines," Afolayan agreed, his cheerful smile barely wavering. The eyes locked onto hers through the holographic link were dark gray, she noted, quite pretty in their way even if they were currently hard stones.

"What I do not know is what the purpose of *your* return is, Pentarch Adamant. While I will confess doubt that our planetary defense network can stand off three United Worlds capital ships, I am not prepared to surrender my world without a fight, either."

"Then breathe easy, Governor," she told him, her smile wry. "However this conversation goes, I see no reason I would ever demand the surrender of Ominira. Indeed…"

The idea struck her like a lightning bolt, and it was all she could do not to broaden her smile into a blatant Cheshire Cat grin.

"It would seem that easing fears would be easier if *you* were to take possession of Admiral Tunison's ships, rather than the Marines available to me," she said, as if she were offering a concession rather than asking for a favor.

"I will even keep my ships at their current distance from Ife Tuntun until personnel you trust are in control of the vessels. That should serve as a balancing act between us, no?"

"Perhaps," Afolayan allowed. "May I add another to this call?"

"As you wish, Governor," Lorraine said. The Governor vanished behind the rotating seal of the system government, a stylized cow rampant over crossed scythe and rocket.

She waited patiently, checking her channel with Val and Hodžić.

"The PDCs are still online," Val warned silently. "We are being tracked with long-range active sensors. They are almost certainly preparing initial targeting solutions for their missiles—and by using the PDCs, they will have those solutions for orbital platforms without exposing their more-vulnerable weapons."

"As expected," Lorraine replied. "Any luck with the databases?"

"We're in," Hodžić said. "He hasn't said much I can fact-check yet, other than that the Regency has crossed lines and... Well, there we go."

"What did you find?"

"On December tenth, the Prime Minister and Regent declared a Writ of National Emergency, temporarily granting full royal executive power to the Regent and a slew of other emergency powers to both him and the Cabinet," Hodžić said grimly. "The Writ has an expiry date, but..."

"But a Regent isn't supposed to serve long enough to *need* a Writ's required expiry," Lorraine finished. It might not have been what the non-Adamantine was thinking, but it stuck in the mind for a child of the Kingdom.

"And if he has the control to pass it once, he can keep passing it, can't he?" the outsider asked.

"Probably."

Their silent conversation was interrupted by the Ominira Seal vanishing, replaced by Afolayan and a strawberry-blonde woman in the maroon-and-gray uniform of the Royal Adamant Space Guard, wearing the five gold pips of an Adamantine Commodore.

"Pentarch Lorraine, this is Commodore Astrape Ilieva," the Governor introduced her. "She is the commanding officer of the Ife Tuntun RASG."

Like everyone else in the Kingdom, Afolayan pronounced the acronym as a single word: Raz-Gee.

"Commodore," Lorraine greeted the officer. "I presume the Governor has advised you of my suggestion?"

"You want us to board and secure Tunison's ships," Ilieva confirmed. "Which both protects us and utterly commits us to opposition against the Regent and Government."

"I believe that commitment may have taken place when your PDCs locked on to the fleet in question," Lorraine said. "I know my uncle. Once he learns about this, Ominira will be treated as in rebellion, regardless of your next moves.

"We are dancing around an alliance we both know we must make, Governor," she told Afolayan. "Securing the ships is a *second* step, not the first, but still a compromise that puts you in control of assets I am going to need."

"We can do it," Ilieva said flatly. "I've got my second talking with Colonel Volkova right now. We can move her people into space on our shuttles, then bring them out to the flotilla's new anchorage on our cutters.

"We'll be in serious trouble if any of the warships decide to get antsy, though."

"Colonel Ekaterina Volkova?" Lorraine asked.

"Yes, why?"

"Ekaterina is a friend of my brother's," she said. "I trust her. If she says she can take control of the ships if you get her people there, she can."

"I'm still concerned about boarding warships with cutters, Pentarch," the RASG Commodore countered. "The smallest of Tunison's frigates outmasses my largest patrol ship three to one."

Cutter was a generic term that covered a class of sublight ships larger than shuttles. RASG used the same Midas-type modular combat shuttles as RKAN, but those weren't sufficient to run traffic control and enforcement over an entire star system.

Cutters were the answer, ships massing as little as ten or as much as forty thousand tons fueled. Lacking translight drives, they were very specialist ships. The Ife Tuntun detachment of RASG had twenty of the ships, easily capable of delivering a battalion or two of the Army to Tunison's ships—but all too vulnerable to the weapons of *Dreaming* and her escorts.

"We have made our point, I think, with the warning shot," Lorraine noted. "I don't want to approach Ife Tuntun until we've come to an agreement that allows you to trust me, Governor. We can position ourselves to provide distant cover for Commodore Ilieva's ships, but approaching much closer would create a potential threat to your... calm."

He chuckled at that and shook his head.

"Distant cover will do, then," he conceded. "It will have to be enough, Ilieva."

"Then I have a great deal of work to do," the Commodore replied. She saluted—though Lorraine wasn't sure which of her or Afolayan it was meant for—and vanished from the screen.

"We will need to meet in person," Lorraine told the Governor. "I would offer to bring a shuttle in from out here, but given everything that has happened, I believe my Adamant Guard will mutiny if I were to expose myself so thoroughly."

Afolayan considered her with those stone-hard gray eyes.

"You look much like your mother, you know," he said. "And you cut to the heart of matters like her, too. I will return the favor in kind.

"What is your intention here, Pentarch Lorraine Adamant? Does the prodigal daughter seek revenge? Power? Justice?"

"*Nothing he's said has clashed with public or private messaging,*" Hodžić said silently on their shared link channel. "*Publicly, his government has been aligned with the Regency but with official questions and concerns. Privately, his Cabinet has definitely talked about how far they can push back, especially with the Writ of National Emergency and the presence of* Dreaming *in orbit.*"

"*Thank you,*" Lorraine told the tech silently. "*I think that's enough.*"

If it wasn't, it was all her people could get her. That Hodžić had apparently accessed the minutes of planetary Cabinet meetings was something she was going to have to investigate later. Right now, though, it was useful.

"I would like to say *justice*, Governor," she told Afolayan, "but we both know how easy it is for that term to cover revenge."

She took a deep breath, letting him see it. Either Governor Afolayan was the man she needed in his office, the man who would help save the Kingdom, or he wasn't. The evidence suggested the former and she would, as he said, cut to the heart of the matter.

"My intention is to return to Adamantine, force the surrender of Home Fleet, arrest my uncle for the murders of my family, end the fighting on Mithral and kickstart our long-overdue Royal Election," she reeled off in a single breath. "I hope to save my brother's life, and I suppose I must stand in that Election myself, but those are hopes and secondary items, not my main intent.

"I am returning home, Governor, to see the guilty brought to justice. I have sufficient evidence, I believe, to see Benjamin Adamant convicted for his crimes. I hope that providing that evidence to our law enforcement agencies will see his conspiracy unraveled and his co-conspirators similarly convicted.

"But justice is a harsh and demanding mistress, Governor," she continued. "We must see the guilty punished, but we must also see the innocent protected. I admit that if I must make a choice, I will rather see the guilty go free than the innocent harmed.

"Though I *will* see my uncle pay the price for his crimes."

The Governor had remained silent during her spiel, his gaze seeming to weigh and measure her and her words alike.

"I am reminded, Pentarch Lorraine, of why your House is named the way it is," he told her. "And I remind you that my ancestors named this system *Freedom*. We named it *after* we agreed to make Alexander Adamant King.

"It was a gesture of faith in Alexander's rule and in his House. I believe it is time to extend that faith again.

"Once Tunison's fleet has been properly interned, I invite you and your ships to enter orbit of my world.

"As you say, you and I must meet in person. Our Kingdom—and the faith we owe its people—demand nothing less."

FIFTY

"What in stars."

Lorraine's flat words as she stepped out of the shuttle made Vigo want to grin. Unlike his Pentarch, he'd known what to expect—and unlike his Pentarch, he was now utterly in his element.

He'd brought the entire remaining Archangel Detail down to the surface, half of them ahead of Lorraine, because he'd suspected this. He was coordinating with troops under one of Colonel Volkova's Majors to secure the route.

A thin cordon of gray-uniformed Guards was spread out around the ramp from the shuttle, standing vigil behind deceptively simple-looking barricades.

Past those barricades, well away from any danger zone from the shuttle's descent, were thousands of the people of Ibalę. Hundreds of voices were raised in welcome. Dozens of swiftly printed banners declared *Welcome Home.*

"You are our Princess," he told his charge. "Theirs as well as mine. Many of these people have been paying enough attention to news and rumor to find the presence of *Dreaming* in orbit a slow, wearing threat that has undermined their peace for weeks or months.

"And now you return and remove that threat in an afternoon. They want to see you. They want to *know* that Lorraine Adamant has returned and that House Adamant's guardianship of them isn't broken by one man's betrayal."

He watched long-trained habits snap back into place, and she stepped out.

Five Guards, including Vigo, fell in around her. Overwatch drones were in the air, sweeping rooftops and windows for shooters. Plainclothes Ibalẹ City Police were scattered through the crowd, reinforcing the very visible security of the uniformed—and in some cases, fully armored—soldiers of the Third Warder Division.

"This way, Lorraine," he told her, gesturing her toward a vehicle. The open-topped vehicle with its mind-bogglingly expensive miniaturized energy screen wasn't what he *wanted* to move Lorraine in, but wrapping the Pentarch in a tank or armored personnel carrier wasn't going to let her do her job.

"Time to go be a symbol," she said softly. "Part of the job my uncle was never very good at."

A quartet of the Gubernatorial Security Detail, in the standard blue-and-crimson uniform of all six Adamantine GSDs, snapped to attention as they approached the vehicle.

"We're sweeping the route," the Lieutenant in charge of the troops told them—mostly Lorraine, since Vigo was inside the GSD's tactical network. "Major Vigo's people have already triple-checked the vehicle."

At which point Lieutenant Esparza and Sergeant Merle stepped out of the vehicle. The system specialist gave Vigo a thumbs-up. Merle didn't have the spare hand for that, using his remaining arm to hold his weapon carefully.

Merle's arm would be replaced eventually, but the lack of immediate care had left them with no choice but to amputate his wounded limb to focus on more life-threatening injuries.

"Let's go," Lorraine told him. "As you carefully haven't said, this, too, is the job."

THE DRIVE from the spaceport to the Governor's Residence was exactly the kind of extremely necessary security nightmare Vigo had known it was going to be. It felt like everyone in a city of twenty-plus million human beings had turned out to put their own eyes on the Pentarch.

Protected as their vehicle was, he spent the entire trip with his shoulder blades itching. He didn't tell Lorraine about the two bombs the Third Warder scouts found, the sniper team his own people caught entering a building, or the pair of unscheduled low-altitude flights forced down by Ibalẹ City Police aircraft.

He'd brief her later, but at that moment, she needed to feel the crowd. To respond to the people who'd come out to see her, to let them know that they were seen, and to draw attention from the overwhelming welcome her people were giving her.

He still audibly sighed in relief as they slid into the garage of the Residence and the doors closed behind them, cutting off any sign of the crowd.

"The Governor is in his office," a voice said in his ear. "Colonel Volkova is in the garage to meet you."

"Our escort is over there," he told Lorraine, passing the directions on to the driver silently.

They pulled to a stop in front of the iron-spined figure waiting for them with her own gray-uniformed escort.

Colonel Ekaterina Volkova stepped forward to open the door herself, moving in a way that made it very clear to Vigo that she was completely unarmed. Even her ceremonial sword was on its baldric, slung over the shoulder of one of her soldiers.

"Welcome to Ife Tuntun, Pentarch," Volkova greeted Lorraine, offering her hand. "I'd ask how your brother is doing, but I think you know as much as I do."

"Possibly less," Lorraine said, using the proffered hand to step down from the transport. "Updated information is definitely something we're going to need."

"There's a lot of work to do, but your new friends should smooth a lot of the way," Volkova agreed. "I'm to bring you to the Governor. Your Guard is expected, of course."

VIGO WAS surprised that he didn't even have to insist on a close escort. He brought four Guards into the Governor's office, and no one even blinked. They outnumbered the two GSD troopers tucked into one corner, but he wasn't so foolish as to think Governor Afolayan didn't have more security on hand.

The office was a sweeping expanse of the elegant purple marble Ife Tuntun was known for. Carefully delicate display cabinets held exactly twenty pieces of art, each a masterwork of its style, all of it flanking a desk that looked cheap, utilitarian and ancient.

Ominira's Governor led from the desk used by the Captain of the colony ship that had made the first landing there. Intended to be solid and functional, it had been built for practicality and efficient use of space.

It looked utterly out of place in the art-gallery feel of Afolayan's office, and yet somehow, it couldn't have been any different.

Vigo stayed at Lorraine's side as his Guards spread out, walking forward across the room as she took the Governor's offered hands in her own and bowed deeply over them.

"Governor, I am stunned and honored by your people's welcome," she told him. "It worries me, though. I had hoped that while my uncle had extended his regency, that he had at least governed righteously."

"The situation is complex," Afolayan admitted. "The lack of an Election concerned many. The conflict with your brother, of course, threw the entire story of the deaths of your family into question.

"Media censorship alone isn't enough to condemn a government, but it certainly told the story of our worst fears. And then the news of your battle in Bright Dream itself arrived," he said grimly. "There was little question in many minds then that your uncle's people had pursued you to finish the job.

"Some systems, I know, made connections with their RKAN commanders and prepared for the worst. I knew Are Tunison and recognized the worst was already upon us. No matter what we desired, Admiral Tunison would follow Benjamin Adamant to the end."

"He and his crews are being transferred to a secure island facility where we can keep an eye on them," a stranger told them. An elegantly turned-out woman with raven-black hair and porcelain-white skin, she was a stark contrast against Afolayan's warm darkness.

"My apologies, introductions are in order," the Governor said. "This is my Deputy Governor, Gianna Mazza. She also serves as our system Minister of Security, so I felt her presence would be required for even this small meeting."

He paused.

"I'll admit, Pentarch, I expected to meet a representative from the United Worlds today."

"My allies are no longer part of the United Worlds Navy," Lorraine said quietly. "If we may deploy a projector?"

Afolayan made an affirming gesture, his eyes curious as Vigo drew the projector disk from inside his jacket and set it on the floor. He then stepped back, behind Lorraine's seat, as Val's avatar appeared above the projector.

"Governor, be known to Val, once the Command Intelligence Routine of the UWN battlecruiser *Valkyrie*," Lorraine said. "Like the other CIRs of the class, she has emerged as a full synthetic intelligence.

"She and her two siblings have pledged their loyalty to me. We'll need to sort out getting them commissioned into RKAN, as I have promised them citizenship for their service," she continued.

"You… don't have UWN personnel on those ships," Volkova guessed.

She was fast off the mark, and Vigo shifted slightly. If there was going to be a problem in that room, it would be the RKAA officer—though he understood that her friendship with Nikola Adamant was ironclad.

"We do not," Lorraine agreed. "We will, in fact, need to sift through the crews from Tunison's ships and see if there are any personnel we can trust. It would be an asset if we can properly crew *Dreaming* and the escorts, but I will need significant numbers of RKAN personnel just to get the *Valkyries* operational."

Val bowed slightly, her insignia-less uniform and posture making her military role clear, even as she remained quiet for the moment.

"How many people do you have on those ships, Pentarch?" Afolayan asked slowly.

"If Lorraine wishes, I can answer that," Val said.

"Go ahead."

"There are currently one hundred and thirty-nine people serving aboard *Valkyrie*, with similar numbers on both *Herakles* and *Bean Sidhe*," the SI told the Governor.

There'd been more, but a dozen mutineers and the deaths in the mutiny had reduced their numbers more than Vigo liked.

"Forgive my surprise, Pentarch, Val," Afolayan told them. "But I don't think anyone in the system was under the impression that you did not have the full backing of the UWN. Won't they… come after these ships?"

"They will," Lorraine warned. "We have a plan for that. The UWN does not operate in a vacuum, Governor, and some of the support my uncle has received out of the United Worlds is in violation of their laws.

"The same investigations that we must do for our own stability will lead us to people the United Worlds will need to bring to justice in their own territory. Debt will repay debt, I believe."

The plan was more complicated than that, Vigo knew—and much

of it depended on the question of just how afraid of the Technology Import/Export Commission the United Worlds Navy was.

Everything he'd seen on Earth suggested the answer was *very*.

"I'm sorry, Pentarch, Governor," Volkova interrupted. "Do you mean to tell us that you bluffed Admiral Tunison into surrendering with three ships that cannot actually *fight*?"

"No," Val countered. "Pentarch Lorraine bluffed Admiral Tunison into surrender with three ships that can only *barely* fight."

JOIN THE MAILING LIST

Love Glynn Stewart's books? Join the mailing list at:

GlynnStewart.com/mailing-list

Be the first to find out when new books are released!

ABOUT THE AUTHOR

GLYNN STEWART is the author of Starship's Mage, a bestselling science fiction and fantasy series where faster-than-light travel is possible–but only because of magic. His other works include science fiction series Duchy of Terra, Castle Federation and Vigilante, as well as the urban fantasy series ONSET and Changeling Blood.

Writing managed to liberate Glynn from a bleak future as an accountant. With his personality and hope for a high-tech future intact, he lives in Canada with his partner, their cats, and an unstoppable writing habit.

CREDITS

The following people were involved in making this book:
Copyeditor: Richard Shealy
Proofreader: M Parker Editing
Cover Artist: Elias Stern
Faolan's Pen Publishing:
Jack Giesen

And a sincere thank you to Glynn's Patreon subscribers!

OTHER BOOKS
BY GLYNN STEWART

For release announcements join the mailing list
or visit **GlynnStewart.com**

STARSHIP'S MAGE
Starship's Mage
Hand of Mars
Voice of Mars
Alien Arcana
Judgment of Mars
UnArcana Stars
Sword of Mars
Mountain of Mars
The Service of Mars
A Darker Magic
Mage-Commander
Beyond the Eyes of Mars
Nemesis of Mars
Chimera's Star
Ambassador for Mars
Chimera's Fall
The Lies Arcana (*Upcoming*)

Starship's Mage: Red Falcon
Interstellar Mage
Mage-Provocateur
Agents of Mars

Starship's Mage Novellas
Pulsar Race
Mage-Queen's Thief

HOUSE ADAMANT

The Exodus Gambit
The Old Guard
The Valkyrie Strategem
Regent's Mate (Upcoming)

EXILE

Exile
Refuge
Crusade
Ashen Stars: An Exile Novella

CASTLE FEDERATION

Space Carrier Avalon
Stellar Fox
Battle Group Avalon
Q-Ship Chameleon
Rimward Stars
Operation Medusa
A Question of Faith: A Castle Federation
Novella

Dakotan Confederacy

Admiral's Oath
To Stand Defiant
Unbroken Faith

VIGILANTE

(WITH TERRY MIXON))

Heart of Vengeance
Oath of Vengeance

Bound By Stars: A Vigilante Series
(With Terry Mixon)

Bound By Law
Bound by Honor
Bound by Blood

AETHER SPHERES
Nine Sailed Star
Void Spheres (*upcoming*)

TEER AND KARD
Wardtown
Blood Ward
Blood Adept

CHANGELING BLOOD
Changeling's Fealty
Hunter's Oath
Noble's Honor
Fae, Flames & Fedoras: A Changeling Blood Novella

ONSET
ONSET: To Serve and Protect
ONSET: My Enemy's Enemy
ONSET: Blood of the Innocent
ONSET: Stay of Execution
Murder by Magic: An ONSET Novella

STANDALONE NOVELS & NOVELLAS
City in the Sky
Excalibur Lost: A Space Opera Novella
Balefire: A Dark Fantasy Novella
Icebreaker: A Fantasy Naval Thriller
Seekers in the Void: A Space Adventure (*Upcoming*)